MORE PRAISE FOR
THE B[...]

A C[...]

"Everyone's favor[...] [...]ight, is back in *A Cook[...]* [...]isty tale, it features foo[...] [...]and a mysterious antique cookbook that binds them all. Kate Carlisle's most delectable installment yet. Don't miss it!"

— Julie Hyzy, *New York Times* bestselling author of the White House Chef mystery series and the Manor House mystery series

"Well plotted.... Carlisle keeps the suspense high as Brooklyn sleuths her way through a host of chefs and other suspects to the satisfying resolution."

— *Publishers Weekly*

"A true whodunit, *A Cookbook Conspiracy* highlights Carlisle's story line skills, her love for books, and her always-endearing heroine. It's the latest example of the author's recipe for success."

— *Richmond Times-Dispatch*

"*A Cookbook Conspiracy* is another superb entry—and this one is succulent as well—in Kate Carlisle's witty, wacky, and wonderful Bibliophile series. Quirky characters and an intriguing cookbook with a fabulous history add to the fun. Highly entertaining."

— Carolyn Hart, author of the Death on Demand mystery series

"This is an entertaining cozy mystery that weaves the professional cooking process (and Brooklyn's amateur attempts) into a good old-fashioned whodunit."

— Once Upon a Romance

"Another outstanding mystery in this series."

— Lesa's Book Critiques

continued ...

"Carlisle cooks up a great whodunit in the latest Bibliophile mystery.... With a wealth of entertaining characters and fascinating facts on bookbinding thrown in, it's a winner!"   —RT Book Reviews

Peril in Paperback

"Kate Carlisle never fails to make me laugh, even as she has me turning the pages to see what's going to happen next. If you like suspenseful, intelligent mysteries with a sense of humor, *Peril in Paperback* is your passport to hours of entertainment."
—Miranda James, *New York Times* bestselling author of the Cat in the Stacks mystery series

One Book in the Grave

"Engaging.... Delivers the same mix of sharply humorous writing, fascinating details about the world of rare books, and a romance-infused mystery."
—Reader to Reader Reviews

Murder Under Cover

"A terrific read for those who are interested in the book arts and enjoy a counterculture foray and ensemble casts. Great fun all around!"
—*Library Journal* (starred review)

"With interesting characters, inviting locale, exceptional dialogue, and great visualization of bookbinding techniques, this is the best one yet in this fantastic and brilliant series."   —The Cozy Chicks

The Lies That Bind

"Kate Carlisle weaves an intriguing tale with a fascinating peek into the behind-the-scenes world of rare books. Great fun, and educational too."   —*Suspense Magazine*

"I highly recommend this series to any book conservator ... who enjoys encountering a cast of quirky characters and a heroine who just can't keep herself out of trouble."
—The Bonefolder

If Books Could Kill

"If you're headed to the Edinburgh Book Fair this month, you should pack comfortable shoes, a raincoat with a hood, and a copy of Kate Carlisle's bonnie little mystery."
— *Fine Books Collections*

"Carlisle's story is captivating, and she peoples it with a cast of eccentrics. Books seldom kill, of course, but this one could murder an early bedtime."
— *Richmond Times-Dispatch*

Homicide in Hardcover

"Saucy, sassy, and smart—a fun read with a great sense of humor and a soupçon of suspense. Enjoy!"
— Nancy Atherton, *New York Times* bestselling author of the Aunt Dimity mystery series

"A cursed book, a dead mentor, and a snarky rival send book restorer Brooklyn Wainwright on a chase for clues—and fine food and wine—in Kate Carlisle's fun and funny delightful debut."
— Lorna Barrett, *New York Times* bestselling author of the Booktown mystery series

"A fun, fast-paced mystery that is laugh-out-loud funny. Even better, it keeps you guessing to the very end. Sure to be one of the very best books of the year! Welcome Kate Carlisle, a fabulous new voice in the mystery market."
— *New York Times* bestselling author Susan Mallery

"Who'd have thought book restoration could be so exciting? . . . *Homicide in Hardcover* is good reading in any binding."
— Parnell Hall, author of the Puzzle Lady mystery series

OTHER BIBLIOPHILE MYSTERIES

A COOKBOOK
CONSPIRACY

A Bibliophile Mystery

Kate Carlisle

AN OBSIDIAN MYSTERY

OBSIDIAN
Published by the Penguin Group
Penguin Group (USA) LLC, 375 Hudson Street,
New York, New York 10014

USA | Canada | UK | Ireland | Australia | New Zealand | India | South Africa | China
penguin.com
A Penguin Random House Company

Published by Obsidian, an imprint of New American Library, a division of Penguin Group (USA) LLC. Previously published in an Obsidian hardcover edition.

First Obsidian Mass Market Printing, May 2014

ISBN 978-0-451-41597-4

Printed in the United States of America

For Christopher, with love.

Acknowledgments

I want to thank the "real" Kevin Moore of the Anaheim Public Library Foundation for her amazing generosity and support. Thank you, Kevin!

As always, I am grateful to my perceptive editor, Ellen Edwards, for keeping me and my wild ideas on track, and to my agent, Christina Hogrebe, for her unwavering support and good cheer. Thanks, as well, to the wonderful people at Penguin Group (USA) and New American Library who work so hard to keep the Bibliophile Mysteries rolling on. A special thanks to illustrator Dan Craig, who creates the beautiful covers that give us all such a lovely glimpse into Brooklyn's world.

To Jenel Looney, whose ingenuity is truly awesome and inspired, thank you a million times for all you do.

Many thanks to Hannah Dennison, who kindly shared her memories of Gipping-on-Plym with me.

Finally, I'm grateful to my family, who not only put up with my erratic schedules and scary deadlines but also live in fear—and rightly so—that anything they say or do will one day be used in a book. Thank you. I love you all.

Chapter 1

These be words I truly wrote from my own experience and in my own style, not borrowed from another nor glossed over with fancy words I cannot abide.
—The Cookbook of Obedience Green

I don't mind admitting I'm a little obsessed with food. A childhood spent competing with five brothers and sisters at the dinner table will do that to you. I grew up loving good food as much as I love old books, which is saying a lot since I'm a bookbinder and old books are my life's blood.

My current food fixation is cheeseburgers, but I'm not picky—I love everything. Last month I was hooked on doughnuts. Before that, it was tamales. Chocolate is a constant, of course. I get happy chills when I see a new building going up in my neighborhood because it means that food trucks will start showing up every morning to feed the construction crew. And me. I love food trucks.

So given my deep admiration for all things foodie, it seems a cruel joke that the universe declined to endow me with even the teensiest smidgen of cooking talent. Damn you, universe! You can be a real bully sometimes.

And never was your cosmic cruelty more evident than the day my oddball sister Savannah received her Grand Diplôme from Le Cordon Bleu in Paris, France. Savannah a chef? It wasn't fair!

Let's break it down. There are two kinds of people in the world: the ones who claim they "forgot to eat lunch" and the ones (like me) who have never missed a meal. Savannah has been forgetting to eat lunch throughout her life. How she wound up in the Wainwright family is a question for the ages. Equally perplexing is how she ended up in charge of a world-class gourmet kitchen. The girl forgets to eat!

Don't get me wrong; I love Savannah. I love all of my siblings. My peacenik parents always encouraged us kids to treat each other with infinite kindness and unconditional love, even while we were pulling each other's hair and stealing Barbie dolls and Legos.

So last year when Savannah returned to Dharma, our hometown in the Sonoma wine country, and opened Arugula, a high-end vegetarian restaurant, I was thrilled for her. I marveled at her innovative menus and wine pairings. I cheered her fabulous reviews. I was in awe of her divine ability to create a chanterelle glaze that could so perfectly complement a heavenly pillow of delicate, hand-shaped ravioli, thus providing the perfect juxtaposition of taste and texture on the tongue.

But come on, universe! What about me? You couldn't even give me a heads-up on how long to boil macaroni? Because I'm telling you, those instructions on the box are always wrong.

"This shouldn't be so difficult," I muttered, tossing the empty cardboard pasta box into the trash. I stood alone in my kitchen and stared in disgust at the mushy pasta draining in the colander. I'd been so careful this time, followed the directions to the letter, but once again the universe was out to get me.

I grabbed my wineglass and took a fortifying sip before reaching for yet another test noodle, biting into it, and sighing in dismay. Yup, this one was just as soggy as the others. I turned the colander over and tossed the entire batch of pasta down the garbage disposal.

"What a waste." I was debating whether to torture another package of pasta or just call for a pizza when my doorbell rang. I dried my hands on a dish towel, then jogged around the kitchen bar, down the hall, and into my workshop, where my front door was located.

Months of strange comings and goings in my building had me checking the peephole before unlocking the door and throwing it open.

"Speak of the devil," I said by way of greeting Savannah.

"Me? The devil?"

As she entered my home, she pushed her raincoat hood back and I blinked. It was still startling to see her smooth, shaved head instead of her usual mop of curly hair, but I had to admit that the bald look worked for her. Her facial features were petite and refined and she seemed to radiate healthy living. And if you were going to go eccentric, why not go bald?

"Yes, you." I took her damp coat and hung it on the back of a tall workshop chair. "I was just thinking of you as I threw another batch of disgusting overdone pasta down the drain."

She wiped away an imaginary tear. "That's so sweet. I think of you that way, too."

"Sorry, but I'm frustrated." I led the way back to the kitchen. "It's just not fair that I am completely incapable of boiling water, and then there's you. I don't get it."

"Ah." She smiled. "Well, look on the bright side. I destroy books."

"True." My sisters and I had always been voracious readers, but none of us would read a book after Savannah was finished with it. Not only did she scribble in the margins, but she would mark where she'd left off by dog-earing the page. It was barbaric. She liked to sadistically crack the spine to keep a book splayed open. If you valued a book, you never lent it to Savannah.

As a professional lover of books, I felt my stomach clench whenever I had to see her slapdash bookshelves.

Without bothering to ask, I reached into my cupboard for another wineglass and poured her some of the 2009 Pinot Noir I'd been sampling.

"This is good," she said after taking a sip. "Light yet jammy with earthy undertones."

I smirked. "Much like yourself."

She nodded. "Thank you."

"What are you doing here? I mean, I'm happy to see you, but I can't remember the last time you visited."

"I know it's been a while." She perched her butt on one of the barstools at my kitchen counter. "I came into town for a meeting this afternoon and decided to take a chance that you'd be home."

I sat down across from her. "Do you want to stay for dinner?"

She barely resisted a sneer. "Only if you're having takeout."

"Definitely."

"Will Derek be here?"

"He should be home any minute."

She grinned. "Okay, I'll stay."

That was an easy decision. I reached for the phone. "Let me call in the order and then we can talk."

After ordering enough pizza and salad for a family of eight, I hung up and poured us both more wine. My cell phone buzzed and I checked the text message. "Derek says he'll be here in twenty minutes."

"Good. That gives me just enough time to ask a favor."

I watched her dig into her oversized tote bag and retrieve a small, colorful bundle. I was pretty sure I recognized the wrapping. "Is that a Pucci?"

Her eyes lit up. "Yes. Do you remember when I bought these for everyone?"

"Of course. I still have mine." The Christmas she'd spent in Paris while attending Le Cordon Bleu, she had sent each of us girls a wildly vibrant French silk scarf.

We'd all thought she'd been terribly extravagant until I visited her and discovered that they sold the scarves on every street corner in Paris.

She handed me the bundle. "Can you fix this? It's pretty old, but maybe you could clean it up and stick a new cover on it or something? I want to give it as a gift."

I slowly unwrapped the silky material and found a book inside. Casting a quick frown at Savannah, I bent to study the book more carefully.

It wasn't just *old*; it was really, really, *really* old. Its faded red cover was made of a thin, supple French morocco leather, the type that had been used for centuries to make personal Bibles and religious missals. The binding style was known as *limp binding*, which made it sound sort of sad and saggy, but in reality, the slim, flexible construction allowed the book to be left open flat for easy reading without someone having to hold it.

I examined the spine and found it rippled in some spots and thinning in others. The gilding, while faded, was still readable. *Obedience Green*, it said.

"Obedience Green?" I rubbed my fingertip over the pale golden letters. Was that the title of the book or the name of its author? Maybe it was the name of the bindery that had produced it. I opened the book, taking note of the dappled endpapers before I turned to the title page—and gasped. "It's handwritten. In ink."

"Yeah," she said, swirling the liquid in her wineglass. "It's kind of hard to read in places, but it's cool, isn't it?"

I stared at the book's impressive title. *The Cookbook of Obedience Green: Containing Three Hundred Curious and Uncommon Receipts and Including Miscellaneous Articles of Useful Domestic Information and a Brief History of My Life, by Obedience Green, many years Cook and Housekeeper to the Eminent War General Robt. Blakeslee.*

Curious and Uncommon Receipts? I had no idea what that meant, but if Obedience had been a housekeeper, perhaps she'd recorded her household grocery receipts or something. I turned a few more pages to read an introduction in the same fancy handwritten script as the title page. It was slow going, especially since every *s* looked like an *f*.

I had no idea what the author meant when she promised to *offer the most modern receipts presented in the most elegant manner.* It wasn't until I reached the Table of Contents page that I realized what she meant by *receipts.* My clue was at the top of the page, where she had written *Herein a bountiful listing of receipts and a practical bill of fare for every season, every month of the year.*

"Recipes!" I looked at Savannah. "Because it's a cookbook."

"Duh," Savannah said, her eyes rolling dramatically as only a sister's could. "Can you fix it up or not?"

"Of course I can fix it, but I'm not sure I should."

"What's that supposed to mean?"

"The book might be too important."

"Oh, for goodness' sake." Clearly annoyed, she stood and folded her arms across her chest. "It's just an old cookbook, Brooklyn."

"It's not just *old*, Savannah." I returned to the title page and searched for a date. I finally found it scrawled at the end of a long, run-on sentence that listed various contributors' names. *MDCCLXXXII.* I dug back into my grammar school brain and did a quick translation of the Roman numerals. *M* was one thousand, *D* was five hundred, and *C* was one hundred. So, one thousand five hundred, six hundred, seven hundred. Seventeen hundred. *L* was the Roman numeral for fifty. *X* was ten, so three *X*'s after the *L* made it eighty. Plus two *I*'s.

1782. Yikes.

I took a few fortifying breaths until I could finally scowl sufficiently at her. "It's *over two hundred and thirty years old*." I showed her the date, then clutched the book to my breast. "That makes it extremely valuable just on its surface, never mind its historical or cultural value.

And it's written by hand! It's beyond rare. Where did you find it? What are you going to do with it?"

Her shoulders slumped and I felt mine sinking, too. My sister could be so clueless sometimes. And right then, it was obvious that she thought the same of me. "What does it matter to you? Why do you always have to ask so many questions? Can't you just do as I ask? Just—" She fluttered her hand at me. "You know, do that thing you do. Dust it off and put a pretty cover on it."

I glared at her. "Do I tell you how to make a soufflé?"

She laughed a little as she held up her hands in surrender. "Okay, okay. But if you could . . . I don't know. Just fix it. I'll pay you whatever it costs if that's what you're worried about."

"You know I don't care about the money," I muttered, still too fascinated by the book to get completely riled up at her. I was used to people undervaluing books, especially these days when you could download a classic novel onto your phone for free. But it was frustrating to know that my own sister couldn't recognize the book's value. Savannah was many things: chef extraordinaire, bald as a baby, free spirit, vegetarian. But book lover? Nope, not Savannah. Not in this lifetime.

Ignoring her, I inspected the book's Table of Contents and couldn't help smiling at some of the old-fashioned terms used for the various chapters:

> *Mutton Flesh: A Primer*
> *Drying and Salting of Flesh and Fyshes*
> *Tongues and Udders*
> *Collaring, Potting and Pickling*
> *Fricassees*
> *Syllabubs and Jellies.*

I thumbed carefully through the pages, but stopped abruptly when I saw the words *I delivered a baby today. My first experience and possibly the only time I'll ever do such a thing, for it was frightening and messy.*

"Hey, looks like part of the book is a journal." I paged to the beginning of the section.

> *8 March 1774. In high spirits. Today we set sail for America. Through the good graces of Miss Ashford at Budding House, I have obtained an apprenticeship with Mrs. Branford, cook and housekeeper to His Lordship General Robert Blakeslee, lately appointed Royal Governor of Massachusetts. Mrs. Branford has vouchsafed to instruct me in the art and science of food preparation, of which I confess to know little.*

> *11 March 1774. Today Mrs. Branford scolded Cletus, the ship's cook, for adding garlic to the dishes. While happily employed by the French, she advised, garlic is nonetheless better suited to the medicine chest than to the kitchen.*

> *17 March 1774. Storm coming. Ship rocking violently and I am unable to eat.*

> *18 March 1774. Overcome with grief. Mrs. Branford has been swept overboard in a savage gale.*

"Oh, no!" I closed the book reluctantly. "This is amazing." Skimming my hand across the aged leather cover, I felt a sense of the author's trepidation. She didn't know how to cook! I could relate to that, but not to the fear and awe she must have experienced traveling across the ocean to live and work in a strange land in the middle of a revolution. I couldn't wait to read more.

And I wondered again how Savannah had come into possession of this odd, intriguing cookbook. On the spot, I decided I would swing by the Covington Library tomorrow and show the book to Ian McCullough, my old friend and the Covington's chief curator. I so enjoyed making him drool with envy.

"Earth to Brooklyn."

"What? Oh, sorry." I set the book on top of the Pucci scarf. "Okay, look, I'll clean and repair it and I'll tighten these joints and hinges that have come loose, but I won't give it a pretty new cover." I held up my hand to stop her from saying something more snotty than she already had. "It wouldn't be ethical. This book is bound to be historically significant, which makes it extremely valuable in its present state."

She made a pouty face, but it was mostly for my benefit. "I suppose you're right."

I patted my heart. "Hearing those words? It never gets old."

"Nobody likes a smart-ass."

"Look, why don't I make a pretty leather storage box for it? I can design a matching suede or leather pouch, too, for extra protection. It'll be cool."

"Really?" The storm clouds disappeared from her eyes and she relaxed a little. "Okay. Good. But can you make it sort of manly-looking? Nothing frilly."

"Sure. I've got a fabulous piece of dark red leather I can use, and Derek brought me back some amazing endpapers from Brussels. They're beautiful."

"How romantic of him."

"Hey, he knows me."

She gave me a warm smile. "That's nice. Really it is."

"So when do you need it done?" I asked.

"Two weeks from tomorrow."

I wrapped the book in the scarf and tied the ends protectively. "Who are you giving it to?"

"Do you remember Baxter Cromwell?"

"Of course." I frowned. "Wait. There's no way you're giving this book to Baxter. Why in the world would you do that?"

"Why not?"

It was my turn to roll my eyes. "Because he's a scumbag jerk?"

Baxter Cromwell was an old friend of Savannah's from her time in Paris. They had attended Le Cordon

Bleu together and they'd dated for a few months. I knew that because I had visited Savannah while she was living in Paris, in a flat with three other students, one of whom was Baxter.

I had begged for a place to stay for two weeks and Savannah had offered to let me sleep on her floor. I had seized the opportunity because even though I would be sleeping on the floor, at least I would be sleeping on the floor *in Paris*. With the money I saved on a hotel room, I could buy more baguettes, croissants, cheese, wine, and chocolate. It was a no-brainer.

But one night while there, I awoke to find someone crawling into my sleeping bag. He already had his hands on me by the time I started screaming. It was my sister's so-called boyfriend, Baxter Cromwell. What a pig!

Despite my outrage, Savannah didn't take Baxter's betrayal very hard. Oh, there were a few rough days, but she finally brushed it off, admitting that she should've expected it. "That's what I get for hooking up with a charming scoundrel," she'd said. And yet she had remained a loyal friend to him? It was a mystery to me.

After graduating, Baxter had taken his Le Cordon Bleu education and charmed a few money people into backing him so he could open a small café in London. He parlayed that into a chain of upscale restaurants around the city, quickly gaining a reputation as a raging jackass. No big surprise. But instead of ruining his career, his outlandish personality helped turn him into a reality show star. A female producer for one of the food networks met him and declared his food better than Gordon Ramsay's—and Baxter was so much cuter! Not a particularly high bar to surpass, according to my best friend, Robin, who was an unabashed reality show junkie.

Over the next few years, in addition to the television shows, Baxter worked relentlessly to expand his restaurant empire, opening new bistros and grand food palaces all over the world. Now the aforementioned scumbag was a household name. It wasn't fair.

I looked at Savannah curiously. "Are you traveling to London to see him?"

"No, he's coming here. He's opening up a place in the Mission District."

"Really?" I shouldn't have been surprised. The Mission was the latest San Francisco neighborhood to be dragged into gentrification. Don't get me wrong; much of the area was still seedy and it wasn't giving up its gritty underbelly without a fight. I always held on to my purse when I went walking around there.

But lots of cool new restaurants and hip boutiques were sprouting up daily along Eighteenth Street and up and down Mission and Valencia, all the way over to picturesque Dolores Park and several blocks farther in all directions.

I tried not to make a face, but I was dismayed to know that I would soon be sharing my beloved city with the likes of Baxter. There was nothing I could do about it, though. Savannah seemed happy and I had to admit that the trendy but rough-around-the-edges Mission District was an ideal location for an opportunistic slug like Baxter Cromwell to make a killing.

"He's got a fantastic two-week opening planned," Savannah explained, excited and clearly ignoring my strong feelings against Baxter. "It's going to be huge, the foodie event of the century."

"Of the century?"

"Maybe bigger," she said, ignoring my sarcasm. "He's featuring a different visiting chef every night. Some of our old friends from Le Cordon Bleu are coming to cook."

"Is Kevin coming?" I asked. Kevin Moore had been Savannah's roommate and best friend in Paris. Despite her boyish name, Kevin was all female and beautiful to boot. She'd been so nice to me while I was staying there. I couldn't wait to see her again.

"Kevin and Peter will both be here," Savannah said.

My heart gave a little tug on hearing Peter's name. I'd developed something of a crush on him while I was visiting Paris. "Are they still together?"

"No," Savannah said, and made a sad face. "They broke up a year or so after I left Paris, but Kevin insists they're still friends. It's too bad. They always seemed to be so much in love."

"I thought so, too. I'm sorry they broke up." But it would be cool to see them again, anyway. "Who else is coming?"

"Raoul and Margot and some others you might know. Baxter's giving each of us a night to highlight our own styles of cooking."

"That sounds like fun." And the thought of seeing Savannah's fine-looking friend Raoul again sounded equally fun.

"It will be," she said. "And it's very generous of Baxter, so be nice to him."

I curled my lip. "If he's nice to me. Anyway, I'm excited for you. Will you get us reservations for your night?"

"Of course. I'll call tomorrow. It's going to be a sell-out."

I could believe it. It was a clever idea and would surely receive lots of media coverage. If only Baxter hadn't been the one to come up with the concept.

"So you're giving him this book as a . . . what? A thank-you?" I tried to keep the tone of incredulity out of my voice, but it was impossible. It was such a waste of a beautiful, rare book. Couldn't she just buy Baxter a box of chocolates or something?

"Jeez, Brooklyn. Lighten up about the book." She poured herself more wine. "If it's any of your business, I'm giving it to Baxter because it originally belonged to him. He gave it to me while we were dating in Paris. And to tell you the truth, I'd forgotten all about it until he called out of the blue to ask me to cook at his new place.

When I remembered that I still had it, I thought it would be fun to give it back to him as a surprise."

"Oh." I didn't know which detail shocked me more. The fact that my sister had literally forgotten that she possessed such an exquisite old book or the fact that the book had originally belonged to Baxter, who didn't seem the type to appreciate such a fine piece of art and history.

I capitulated with a nod. "Okay, I get it now. So, was it handed down through his family?"

"I don't know exactly." She sipped her wine as she considered for a moment. "I realize you think it's special, but Baxter didn't. I remember him brushing it off as some tacky English village version of a ladies' church society cookbook. He thought I would be amused by some of the horrible old recipes. We laughed about them, and then he told me to tuck the book away and forget I ever had it. He seemed sort of embarrassed about it, which I thought was terribly endearing at the time."

"Oh, please. The man is as endearing as a badger."

"I know." She laughed lightly. "I was an idiot."

"No, Bugs," I said fiercely, using her childhood nickname for emphasis. (Savannah had been given the middle name of Dragonfly, so naturally we kids had always called her Bugs.) "Baxter was the idiot, not you."

She set her wineglass down and hugged me. "Thank you. But you can see why the book isn't as valuable as you seem to think it is. If it was, then why would he ever have given it to me? I wasn't important to him, so why would he give me something so rare? It's not like he considered me anything more than a fling."

"True, and that's his loss."

"Well, thank you again."

"You're welcome." I let her sip her wine in silence for a moment, then added, "So I don't suppose you'd reconsider giving him the book."

She chuckled. "Nice try."

"Worth a shot," I said with a shrug.

Her expression turned somber. "The thing is, Brooklyn, I want the book out of my life."

"Then give it to me," I said instantly. "I'll give it to the Covington Library and you won't ever have to deal with it again."

"But I would still feel a connection to it."

I started to argue but noticed her eyes were bright with tears. "What do you mean?"

She swirled her wine a little self-consciously. "I found the book with a bunch of other stuff I've been holding on to for years. Silly things that I haven't been able to let go of all this time. It's taken me years to figure out what my life's all about, and I think those stupid little mementos have been weighing me down psychologically. I figure it's time for me to shed some of that baggage and fly free. Starting with this book."

Coming from someone else, her insightful words might've caused me to contemplate my own psychological baggage. But in truth, she sounded so much like our wacky, astral-traveling mother that I just had to smile. "Okay, little birdbrain. I'll clean up your book and help you find your wings."

We laughed together, but inwardly I was sighing. It was too bad that the delicate old cookbook would be returned to Baxter. Did he know how valuable the book was? Apparently not, if he'd given it away in the first place. That made it even more irritating that my sister intended to hand the precious book back to him.

On the bright side, though, the book was mine to enjoy for the next two weeks and I was already making plans for it. First I would photocopy the fragile pages and read them for fun. And in my head, I was already sketching out the design for a unique, masculine case in which to house the book. At some point during the week, I wanted to run over to the Covington Library to let Ian check out the cookbook.

Curious, I unwrapped the book once more and carefully paged through the recipes. I was tempted to try out some of those old-fashioned recipes on Derek. He was English, after all. Wouldn't he enjoy some original down-home English cooking? Perhaps something pickled? Or fricasseed? Maybe a lovely syllabub? There were only a few ingredients in a syllabub, and the directions made it sound easy. Did I dare? Why not? I was sure I could whip one up for Derek, as soon as I figured out exactly what in the world a syllabub was.

Chapter 2

As Savannah regaled me with the latest gossip from Dharma, I felt a subtle vibration radiate up from the floor, causing my feet to tingle. "Derek's home."

"He is?" Savannah looked around.

"Can't you feel the building shake?"

"No." She paused. "Oh, wait. I can feel something, like, it's kind of . . . shivering."

"That's it."

"That's Derek?" Her eyes widened. "He makes the building shiver?"

"No, nutball," I said, laughing. "It's the elevator. Whenever it starts moving, it shakes the building a little."

She smirked. "Nice selling point."

"I think so." I liked the shaking because it meant that nobody could sneak up on me in my own home. "I'm pretty sure Derek's on the elevator."

My six-story loft building had begun life as a corset factory back in the 1900s. When it was converted into modern, loft-style condominiums a few years ago, the developers updated everything except some of the more charming vintage features. Those included the old freight elevator with its worn, thick wood plank floor and collapsible iron gate that expanded or folded up to let passengers in and out. It was indeed a selling point.

Whenever the heavy lift began its ascent from the garage, everyone living here could feel it. While it had alarmed some of my neighbors initially, I found the advance warning comforting after a number of unwelcome strangers had tried to invade my home over the last year.

Savannah opened the pantry and grabbed a box of crackers to munch on. "Glad to know Derek's not so superhuman that he causes an entire building to tremble."

"Shows you what you know," I murmured, then snickered when she smacked my arm.

"Stop bragging," she whined. "I've become a sex-starved spinster in my old age."

"You just work too hard," I said. "Besides, we're practically the same age, so let's shut up about being old." I went still as I heard the click of my front door lock. Even knowing it had to be Derek, I found the sound was momentarily disconcerting.

"It's me, darling," he called out immediately, knowing I still worried about someone breaking into my place. Which made him totally superhuman in my book.

"'Darling,'" Savannah whispered on a sigh. "Isn't he romantic? Especially with that accent."

"We're in the kitchen," I said loudly, then walked around the bar and into the dining area to greet him.

If my breath happened to catch a little whenever I saw him, I could live with that. Today he wore an elegant black business suit, and his dark, close-cropped hair and military bearing were a perfect counterpoint to his glittering blue eyes and knowing smile.

My sister might mock me later, but I didn't care. Derek was just so hot. Tall. Self-confident. *Mine.*

Even without the help of the ancient elevator, Derek

could make me tremble. But I wouldn't be so cruel as to mention that to Savannah anytime soon.

He tossed his jacket over a dining room chair and pulled me close for a hug and a kiss. I held on to him for an extra moment, savoring his closeness and his subtle scent of forest and spice.

He spotted my sister over my shoulder and eased back. "Savannah, what a delightful surprise. Are you staying for dinner?"

"Yes, she is," I said. The doorbell rang and I twirled my hands in the air as if I'd just made magic happen. "And there's dinner now. I'll go buzz the guy into the building."

"Weren't you going to make pasta this evening?" Derek asked as he poured himself a glass of wine.

"I don't want to talk about it." I rummaged through my purse to find cash, then headed for the front door.

"You know she's a hopeless mess in the kitchen, right?" Savannah said.

"I heard that," I shouted.

Savannah snorted. "With ears like a desert fox."

I met the delivery guy at the top of the stairs, paid him for the take-out food, then watched him trot downstairs and waited to hear the sound of the ground-floor security door shut behind him. I hurried back inside, locked and dead-bolted my door—I had become a real security freak—and jogged to the kitchen. After shoving the pizza, box and all, into the warm oven, I found space in the refrigerator for the large chopped salad. Grabbing napkins and utensils, I set the dining room table while Derek pulled plates from the cupboard and added them to each place setting.

Savannah set the wine bottle on the table and kept us entertained with her latest adventures in the restaurant biz. Somehow she worked her way back around to my dismal cooking skills.

As I pulled the pizza box out of the oven, I admitted, "I'm getting better at chicken, but I still can't make pasta to save my life."

Derek stepped forward, brushing my hair back as he lifted my face and kissed me lightly on my temple. "Not to worry, love. You're good at so many other things."

"Aww, sweet," I said, and kissed him on the cheek. "Thank you."

"Break it up, you guys," Savannah groused. "I'm a lonesome, bitter woman and the sickening picture of you two nuzzling and cooing is now imprinted on my brain forever."

I smiled up at Derek. "Our work here is done."

"Excellent," he said, winking at Savannah. "Let's eat."

I offered Savannah the use of our guest room for the night, but she was eager to get back to her restaurant in Dharma to refresh her stockpot.

Ooh, a stockpot was waiting for her. My sister led such a fascinating life. No wonder she'd been whining earlier.

We walked her down to her car and as soon as she drove away, I turned to Derek and pounced on something I'd noticed during dinner. "How do you know Baxter Cromwell?"

"I never said I knew him," he demurred as we walked back to the elevator.

"I saw your reaction when Savannah mentioned him and his new restaurant. You didn't look happy."

"Aren't you the attentive one?"

"Don't change the subject," I said, although I tended to become easily distracted whenever Derek slipped his arm around my shoulder.

"I've never met the man personally," he finally admitted, "but I've done business with him. Several years ago, he hired my company after being threatened by a competitor."

Derek's company, Stone Security, provided investigative services and security to wealthy individuals and organizations all over the world. His personal expertise was arts and antiquities.

"I'm not surprised to hear he was threatened," I said. "He's so unpleasant."

The elevator came to a shuddering stop on our floor, and Derek led the way back to our apartment. "Cromwell was one of those idiotic clients who demanded the highest level of protection, then never followed a single bit of advice, thereby putting my entire crew in danger."

"He was actually receiving death threats?"

"That's what he claimed, but we never saw any proof. After a few weeks, we canceled the job. It was much ado about nothing."

"He probably did it for publicity."

"He also reneged on the bill," Derek added casually. "So I'll be interested to see how much money he's poured into this new restaurant."

"Wow. Along with everything else, he's a con artist."

"He is exactly that." He poured the last of the wine into our glasses and handed me mine. "I'm concerned about Savannah's friendship with him."

"I am, too." I took a sip. "Still can't believe she's giving him back this priceless book. He doesn't deserve it. But she doesn't see it that way."

Briefly, I filled him in on Savannah's Le Cordon Bleu years in Paris, including my visit and my run-in with Baxter.

Derek was not amused. "For you to work on this book just so Savannah can give it back to him seems a supreme waste of your talents."

"I don't mind doing the work, but the thought of her giving it back to Baxter is so annoying, I can barely stand it."

"You never know," he said, as he rinsed our empty wineglasses and put them in the dishwasher. "Perhaps something will occur that will change Savannah's mind."

"Or maybe Baxter Cromwell will refuse to take it from her." With a sigh, I switched off the lights and we headed for the bedroom. "If only."

*   *   *

The enticing scent of coffee pulled me out of a deep sleep. I'd had the strangest dream, so I remained under the covers, very still, while I verified that I was in my own house and not in a nightmare high school. I hated nightmare high school dreams. They always ended the same way: naked test taking and teachers turning into giant lizards. Why?

Shaking off the dream, I threw back the covers and hopped out of bed. After washing my face and brushing my teeth, I raced out to the kitchen, hoping Derek hadn't left for work yet. I found him at the stove, where he was flipping several pieces of bacon.

"Oh, thank you, God," I whispered.

He turned. "Call me Derek."

"Ha ha. But since you made bacon, I'll call you anything you want me to." I wrapped my arms around his waist and just held on to him for a moment. *Right here*, I thought. *Everything is right here.*

"You were dead to the world when I got up," he said. "I thought you might sleep a while longer."

"Then you shouldn't have made coffee. It woke me up."

"Ah, my mistake." He rubbed my back, moving his hands slowly up and down my spine. Then he patted my butt. "Get yourself a cup, then, and go sit down. Breakfast will be ready in five minutes."

But he didn't let go and it was good to know he seemed to need the connection as much as I did. It was sort of like breathing. For a moment we simply existed together, drawing strength and sustenance from the contact. Soft light filtered in through the kitchen window as time drifted by.

He kissed the top of my head. "Go sit now or we'll have burned bacon."

"Can't have that," I murmured, but succumbed to one more heated kiss. And now my thoughts were so scattered that I had to take a minute to remember what it was I should be doing. As Derek moved over to the stove, I glanced around the room. Ah, plates. Plates would be useful. I reached into the cupboard for two of them and placed them on either side of the bar where napkins and utensils were already set.

After pouring myself a cup of coffee, I sat on the one stool inside the kitchen and watched Derek work.

"This is a treat," I remarked. "You're usually long gone by the time I'm up and drinking coffee."

"I felt like spending a few extra minutes at home having breakfast with you." He cracked four eggs into a bowl and whisked them into a froth.

"I'm glad." I wrapped both hands around my heavy mug and took a slow sip as Derek popped two pieces of bread into the toaster. "So when do you think the construction crew will start tearing the house apart?"

He turned. "Thank you for reminding me. I didn't want to bring up the subject last night while your sister was here, but we need to talk about that."

Two months ago, Derek had broached the subject of our living arrangement. I had taken it to mean that he was planning to move out, because that's how I roll sometimes. But he'd actually been thinking of buying my next-door neighbor's loft. If I was amenable to it, he'd said. We would tear down some walls and design a much larger place that would be big enough for both of us and our two careers.

"Is there a glitch?" I asked.

"Not exactly, but we now seem to have another choice of plans."

I swallowed my coffee. "What is it?"

He pointed toward the back of the house. "Our original plan was to break through the back bedroom and make it the master, expand the hallway, enlarge the living space and add two more bedrooms."

"Right."

"But now the space directly beneath yours has come onto the market. It's considerably smaller than this one. One bedroom, one bath, and an office alcove. We could join them by building a wide staircase and balcony along the east wall to create a mezzanine effect. It would add quite a bit of drama, but we wouldn't be able to expand the size of any of our existing rooms. In fact, it would decrease the square footage of the living room." He shrugged. "But we'd have an entire suite of rooms to use as guest rooms and office space."

"You don't sound thrilled with that idea."

"I'm not." He spooned fluffy scrambled eggs onto each of the plates and added the strips of bacon. "But it's your decision to make. This is your home, after all. I want to give you all the available options before I forge ahead with plans that'll surely disrupt your life for several months at least." He turned to butter the toast, adding, "As if my presence hasn't already disrupted things for you."

I stared at his muscular shoulders and well-toned back. I should've been mesmerized by the sight—and I was. But I was also surprised. Was that *apprehension* I'd just heard in his voice?

Derek? Showing fear?

I suppose it wasn't out of the question, at least when it came to our relationship. Recently, he and I had spent several long weeks apart. At one point, he had been off on assignment in Europe while I had traveled to Lake Tahoe to attend a weeklong house party with my neighbors, Vinnie and Suzie.

There had been a misunderstanding. A certain woman had answered Derek's cell phone when I called him. I knew Derek would never cheat on me or betray me, but the incident had caused me to question our relationship. Again.

The thing was, the two of us had almost nothing in common. Derek went off on these top secret assignments regularly. His life was filled with danger and excitement. My life wasn't quite the same. I mean, it wasn't like I was some kind of country bumpkin bookbinder (although I did tend to wear my comfy old Birkenstocks while working). No, my life was full and complicated and, yes, interesting, I thought. But exciting? Dangerous? Not exactly.

On the other hand, I could be sparkling and sophisticated, having been raised in the heart of Northern California's wine country and now living in an artsy area of San Francisco. If you were willing to overlook the aforementioned Birkenstocks issue, I was one classy babe.

But then there was my strange proclivity for finding dead bodies. And tracking down murderers. And being threatened with death on more than one occasion.

So maybe my life could be considered sort of exciting and dangerous, although I had never purposely sought out danger and adventure.

Derek, on the other hand, made his living that way.

So those were some of the thoughts I'd been pondering while away in Lake Tahoe. Frankly, I'd worried that we might not survive together in the long run.

So imagine my shock when I learned that Derek had experienced some of those same worries and concerns. He'd admitted as much to me and had come home determined to show how much he loved me and wanted to build a life together.

So the note of worry in his voice cut straight through me. Did he still harbor doubts about my feelings for him? If so, they were baseless.

"I love you," I said, staring at his back. "You can disrupt my life anytime you want."

He turned and crossed the kitchen in two steps, lifted me up from the barstool, and drew me into his arms. Covering my lips with his, he held on to me as tightly as I'd ever been held. Then he buried his face in my hair.

"I love you, Brooklyn."

"Good," I said. "That's a good thing." I stroked his back, smoothed his hair, comforted him. He seemed to need it. And that was nice to know.

After a long, quiet moment, I leaned back and looked at him. "To answer your question, I'd like to follow our original construction plan and keep everything on this floor. We'll have lots more room, more open space, and easier access to all the bedrooms."

"Good," he said, breaking into a smile. "I agree."

"Besides," I reasoned, "all that running up and down the stairs all the time would get old. No, your first plan is better and I can't wait to get started on it." I paused a beat, then added, "So how's that toast doing?"

He chuckled. "It's ready. Are you?"

"Starving."

We sat and while we ate we talked over the construction plans and the timetable.

Derek took a last sip of coffee. "My only real concern is the noise you'll have to endure once the demolition begins."

"I'm not worried about the noise," I insisted, taking another bite of toast.

"You say that now."

He was right. The noise would be awful at times. But the thought of all those strangers tramping through my home disconcerted me more than any noise they would make. I wasn't going to bring that up right now, though.

He glanced at his watch. "I must get going."

"I've got to get to work, too. Leave the plates. I'll clean up."

"Thank you, love." He slipped his suit jacket on and used the dining room mirror to straighten his tie. I didn't know a whole lot about men's fashions, but I was fairly certain his gold-striped tie cost more than most of the outfits in my closet. Good thing I worked at home. In my Birkenstocks. And my pretty pink-and-green-striped socks.

"Are you starting work on Savannah's cookbook today?" he asked as we walked to the front door together.

"I'll start on it tomorrow. Today I think I'll take the book over to show Ian, and then go have copies made of the pages."

"You don't usually copy the pages, do you?"

"Not usually, but I thought I might try out some of the recipes."

Despite years of professional training in security and

intelligence, Derek couldn't disguise that look of apprehension fast enough. "Ah. Hmm. That sounds nice."

"That's what I figured you'd say, since they're old English favorites."

"English food. Are you sure that's what you want to try?"

"Absolutely," I said, watching him. "I was thinking of learning how to fricassee something."

I actually saw him shudder.

"Oh, come on," I said with a laugh. "I'm not that bad a cook, am I?"

He coughed to clear his throat. "There really isn't a safe answer to that, is there?"

"Not really."

"Well, then." He touched my cheek. "You're simply perfect just as you are."

"And you're a very good liar."

He laughed, kissed me good-bye, and walked out the door.

"So I suck as a cook," I muttered as I shut the door behind him. "But I'll improve with practice."

Determined now, I opened Obedience Green's old cookbook and looked up desserts. I didn't find that listing, but remembered that the British often referred to dessert as *pudding*. There were several dozen pudding recipes and I quickly read the first one. It contained cornmeal and salt, and Obedience's directions included this: *To steam your Pudding, spoon ingredients into a cotton bag and suspend from a hook above the pot of stew.*

"Not the sort of pudding I had in mind, girlfriend." I flipped a few more pages until I found the desserts and focused on one she called *A Sweet Syllabub Made from the Cow*.

By *cow*, I figured Obedience meant that milk was one of the ingredients. But in fact, her directions included milking one's cow so that the milk squirted right into a quart bowl of hard cider, nutmeg, and sugar.

"Oo-kay, I'll pass on that one."

Among the puddings were several recipes for syllabubs, all of which seemed to feature copious amounts of alcohol. In fact, alcohol seemed to be the only basic difference between a pudding and a syllabub. Not surprisingly, I opted to make a syllabub. And I found a recipe that didn't require buying a cow. Obedience called it *An Exceptional Syllabub To Serve a Traveling Dignitary*.

Pulling out a pad and pencil, I made my shopping list. I could do this, damn it. I would become a good cook if it killed me.

Chapter 3

It is to be noted that in all meals consisting of only two dishes, one should be boiled.

—*The Cookbook of Obedience Green*

If I'd thought my cooking would improve over time, I was sadly mistaken. I had attempted a different syllabub recipe three nights running, and each time the gluey mess ended up being dumped in the garbage can before Derek got home from work. I tried not to hold it against Obedience, whose book was a pleasure to read, if not to cook by.

I had learned within the first few pages of Obedience's diary that she had been only eighteen years old when she boarded that ship for America. And she was an orphan. One of the ladies who volunteered at the orphanage had been the one who'd arranged her apprenticeship with Mrs. Branford, the cook who was swept away in the storm.

Obedience spent two months crossing the Atlantic. Several days after the storm that took the cook, Lord Blakeslee called Obedience into his stateroom and promoted her to the job of head cook, thinking she knew what she was doing. But she didn't! And she was petrified at the thought of being banished from his service once they reached America. So she worked up the nerve to ask Cletus, the ship's cook, for advice and recipes.

I was impressed with her bravery and persistence and decided that if she could sail to a wild new land all by herself, I could manage to whip up a stupid dessert, couldn't I?

Apparently I couldn't.

The following night, instead of dessert, Derek and I took our wineglasses into the living room and I read him passages from the cookbook.

"So in lieu of actually eating dessert," he said, "we'll read about it."

"Yes, and you should thank me for it," I said, thinking of the curdled mess I'd tossed out earlier. I cozied up next to him, opened the book to a random page, and showed it to him. "Can you believe she wrote this entire book in longhand? Isn't it cool?"

He studied the page, then handed it back to me. "It's remarkable. What are you going to read me?"

I flipped to the next page. "This is one of her medicinal recipes. 'A Cure for Convulsions.'"

"Never know when you'll need that."

I read the first line and started to laugh. "Ew, I hope not. She says, 'Collect a half dozen live mole rats; tap them with a knife in the throat until they are dead. Open and remove the entrails. Arrange these in a large flat pan and dry in the oven for three or four days until they have turned to soft stone. Place them in a cloth bag and pound them to powder. Sift through a sieve. Mix powder with ginger water and feed by droplets thrice an hour throughout the night.'"

"Sounds more likely to *cause* convulsions than *cure* them," Derek said.

As I read a few more medicinal cures and laughed with Derek, I mentally forgave Obedience for causing me to throw out yet another dessert. And I grew more and more resistant to the thought of giving the book back to Baxter.

But it wasn't my choice to make. My only job was to refurbish the book and build a storage box for it. That was what I did best, unlike cooking.

The next day, I began work on Obedience's fragile cookbook. I was hoping that once I tightened the joints and resewed the pages, the book would have new life and be able to hold itself together for another few hundred years. I also wanted to regild the spine to make Obedience's name shine. I considered it a small thank-you for giving me hours of reading enjoyment, even if some of her recipes were downright scary.

I grabbed another cup of coffee and my trusty bag of malted milk balls and headed for my studio. At my worktable, I laid the book out on the clean surface and took care of the preliminaries. I measured it, recording the figures in a notebook, and then I snapped a bunch of photographs of the book from all sorts of angles. With a book like this, it was important to make sure everything I did was cataloged. Even if Baxter shoved it into a drawer, the cookbook itself was still historically significant and deserved some attention to detail.

I brushed it clean of any dirt particles, then slowly, carefully, removed the leather cover from the text block and began the process of snipping and picking out the old threads, restacking the pages as I went before sewing them back together.

After the leather cover was reaffixed, I debated on what sort of dressing to apply to clean and revitalize the faded red leather. The one I chose was a mixture recommended by conservationists, basically a blend of neat's-foot oil, lanolin, and odorless kerosene. The oils were animal-based natural lubricants. The kerosene helped the leather absorb the oils and would evaporate over several days. I'd created my own concoctions back in school, but nowadays I simply ordered them through an online bookbinding supply company and had them delivered in handy jars.

Before applying the oil, I wrapped the text block in heavy butcher paper to protect it. Then I rubbed the dressing into the leather and watched the discolored surface soak it up. After waiting an hour or so, I buffed it until it was a rich dark red. I was certain Obedience would've been happy with the results. I certainly was. The book cover was lustrous and supple again and would hold on to its beauty, thanks to the book box I planned to design.

The following week, Derek and I walked into BAX for our eight o'clock reservation. As Derek gave the maître d' our names, I glanced around. Most of the tables for the second seating were filling up quickly. The spacious room pulsated with energy and laughter. And as much as I hated to admit it, Baxter Cromwell's new restaurant was flat-out gorgeous.

His designers had brought the lush, vibrant Hispanic influence of San Francisco's Mission District into the large, open space. The decor was wildly colorful, with massive flower arrangements and exotic, lively murals on three walls.

But it was the fourth wall that drew my gaze.

"Now that's different," I said, staring at the long wall, which was covered completely in rough slabs of brown and black slate. Thin streams of water trickled and bubbled from the ceiling down the jagged slate surface, finally collecting in a narrow, shiny copper pool that ran the length of the wall. It was so cool and unique, I was mesmerized. I had to force myself to look away in order to follow the hostess to our table.

Despite the many visual distractions, Baxter's main room was elegant and sophisticated with its coffered ceiling and soft lighting.

"Brooklyn! You made it!"

I thought it might be Savannah calling to me, but when I turned, I saw a familiar dark-haired beauty speed-walking around the tangle of tables in order to greet me.

Did you ever meet someone and instantly want to be their friend? That's how it was for me when I first met Kevin Moore in Paris. She was smart and funny and self-deprecating and so warm and generous I wanted to move to Paris just to hang out with her. That never happened, of course. She had visited Savannah a few times over the years, so I'd seen her every so often. But she owned a restaurant in London now, so unless I was willing to relocate, we would never be as close as I'd once hoped.

"Oh, Kevin," I said, as I was pulled into her enthusiastic embrace. "It's great to see you."

She held me at arm's length. "Good lord, how long has it been? You look freaking fantastic. I hate you for that. What happened to your hair? I love it."

I fluffed my hair. "Same as it always was."

"No, no, it used to be short and feathery. Now it's longer and—oh, never mind. You blondes just piss me off."

She laughed and gave me another exuberant hug before I could say one more word. Her voice was exactly as I remembered: posh British accent dripping with dry wit. But in other ways she'd changed dramatically. She'd been little more than a gangly teenager in Paris, a string bean, all legs and arms. Now she was lovely and lithe and all grown-up.

"You look beautiful," I said, and meant it.

"Don't be ridiculous," she said. "I'm stained and sweaty."

Her white chef's coat was indeed a mélange of nasty splotches and mysterious smears.

I gave her an innocent smile. "But it looks great on you."

"And you're full of it," she said with a grin.

I'd once asked Kevin how she got her boyish name

and she told me her parents had met while waiting at the same bus stop on Kevin Street in Dublin. It wasn't far from the National Archives, where her father had been giving a lecture. They fell in love at first sight and vowed to name their first child Kevin.

"They were probably counting on a boy," Kevin had quipped.

If she'd had my wacky parents, who'd named all of us kids after the city in which we were conceived or born, poor Kevin would've ended up with the name Dublin. I liked Kevin better. It had a poetic charm that suited her.

Savannah had told me later that Kevin's father had been a famous English writer who'd given up his worldly goods to become a missionary in Africa.

Kevin's dark ponytail swished back and forth as she scanned her stained jacket. "This is all Baxter's fault. Your sister is supposed to be in charge tonight, but he's the one ruling the roost. He's run me ragged and we've only just started the second seating. I'm cooking tomorrow night, so I'm concerned, but I'm hoping he'll back off once he sees that we all know what we're doing."

"I hope so, too." I tugged Derek forward and introduced him to Kevin.

"He's a Brit? You hooked a Brit?" Kevin stared at me. "How in the world did you manage it from all the way over here in the States?"

"I have no idea," I said, speaking the truth. "Just lucky, I guess."

Derek grabbed my hand and kissed it. "I'm the lucky one. Can't believe I snagged her."

"Aw, that's sweet, isn't it?" She narrowed her eyes as she looked at Derek. "Let me guess. Sussex?"

"Oxford."

"Damn!" she said. "Not even close."

Derek studied her. "And you? Cornwall?"

"Closer guess than mine, but no cigar. Devon." Kevin laughed and glanced at me. "Sorry, Brooklyn. All Brits seem to play this game when they meet on neutral territory. We try to guess where we're from based on our accents."

"Oh, we Yanks do that, too," I said. "I'm tough to figure out since I have no discernible accent."

The two Brits exchanged glances, and Kevin burst into laughter. "Right. You just keep on believing that." She patted Derek on the shoulder, then turned to me. "I'll let you get to your table. Promise me we'll catch up later? I'll be in town for two whole weeks."

She rushed off without waiting for a response, and our attentive yet discreet hostess continued to lead us to our table as though we hadn't stopped to talk.

Once we were seated, she handed us our menus and an extensive wine list and said, "Chef Baxter has listed a few of his own specials, but he hopes you'll choose to enjoy the offerings of his featured chef tonight, the wonderfully talented Savannah Wainwright, whose expertise is haute vegetarian cuisine."

"We will," Derek murmured.

I nodded. "Thank you."

The hostess smiled and walked away.

"Everything is perfect," I said, admiring the gold-rimmed white chargers and Riedel stemware. "Positively haute."

Derek's lips twisted sardonically. "It's intolerable, isn't it?"

"Yes, damn it." I didn't want to like the place. I tried to scowl, but my heart wasn't in it.

He reached for the wine list while I glanced at my menu. But I couldn't concentrate. How in the heck had Baxter managed something so swank? So fabulous? Toads like him shouldn't be this talented. "I guess I'm happy everything looks beautiful and of course I'm happy that Savannah's cooking tonight. But part of me wishes Baxter wasn't so popular and didn't have such excellent taste in everything."

Derek scanned the room and admitted, "It really is a phenomenal space."

"I know," I muttered. "That waterfall is amazing. And his staff seems competent and friendly, so I suppose he's trained them well."

"Bastard."

I chuckled. Why did swearwords sound so refined when spoken by Derek?

"I guess it's silly not to enjoy the evening," I said.

"Yes," Derek said, nodding. "We'll order champagne to improve our mood—what do you say?"

Once the bottle was opened and our glasses were filled, we raised them in a toast to new experiences. As I sipped, I noticed the place was filled to capacity and a number of guests had begun table-hopping. Most of the people here seemed to know someone else in the room.

It made sense that many of the first week's guests would be friends or business acquaintances of Baxter's or the other chefs. Either that or serious foodies. I hoped that indicated that everyone would be extra appreciative of the food, for Savannah's sake. I knew from firsthand experience that if they gave her strictly vegetarian menu a chance, they would fall in love with it.

It probably didn't hurt that Savannah had been receiving rave reviews from every food critic in the Bay Area since she first opened Arugula. Some of these customers had to be here because of her, right? Not just because Baxter Cromwell had opened a new hot spot.

As I lifted my champagne glass for another sip, I saw another white-jacketed chef crossing the room and heading directly for me. I recognized him instantly and cried, "Peter!"

"Hello, you," he said, spreading his arms to greet me.

Scooting out from the booth, I hugged him hard. "It's so good to see you. How are you?"

"I'm marvelous," he said. His Devonshire accent was as distinctive as I remembered and he was even more adorable, if that was possible. "Kevin said you were out here, so I had to come see for myself." He hugged me again and then twirled me around before setting me back on my feet. "This night can't get any better."

Over Peter's shoulder I could see Derek's eyebrows shooting up. I wondered if his reaction was due to his hearing yet another British accent or to the way Peter continued to cling to me.

I eased back from Peter, eager to introduce him to Derek. As they shook hands, I said to Derek, "Peter attended Le Cordon Bleu with Savannah and Kevin. And Baxter, of course."

"Of course," Peter said dryly. "Can't forget Baxter now, can we?"

"Apparently not," Derek muttered.

"Peter and Kevin shared a flat with Baxter and Savannah," I explained. "They let me invade their living room for two long weeks that summer. I was such a pain."

"You were sweet," Peter said, nudging me gently. "We all got to be great friends."

"Well, most of us did," I said, reminded of the ugly sleeping bag incident with Baxter.

Peter apparently remembered, too, and glowered. "You should've let me kill him, Brooks."

"I know. Silly of me."

"And now you've gone and found yourself another Brit. Just to make me jealous, no doubt." He tsked, then winked to make sure Derek understood it was all in fun. "Where do you hail from, mate?"

I smiled. Just as Kevin had done a few minutes ago, Peter was playing the British guessing game. His approach was more direct, though.

"A bit northwest of London," Derek said cryptically. "And you?"

"Gipping-on-Plym, one of the tiniest villages in Devon." Peter's expression softened. "Smaller than your elbow but pretty as a picture. Forty miles northwest of Exeter, if you know the area. Middle of nowhere, but we boast a film festival, a rather interesting church museum, and a champion tar barrel racing team."

"Both Kevin and Baxter grew up there, too," I explained to Derek.

"And all three of you became chefs?"

"Yes," Peter said. "Odd, isn't it? But Kevin and I were always talking about food and cooking, so we finally decided to give it a go. Baxter just . . . well, he's not exactly known for his original ideas."

"You must have been good chums," Derek remarked, ignoring the note of bitterness in Peter's voice.

His eyes clouded reflectively. "At one time we were."

Just then, I noticed yet another chef, a gorgeous blond woman whose chef jacket was still pristine white, greeting acquaintances at a nearby table. "Peter, who is that?"

Peter whipped around. "Ah. That's Colette. Didn't you meet her in Paris?"

"I don't think so. I don't remember her."

"She's married to Raoul. He's here, too."

"Ah, Raoul." I definitely remembered Raoul. At the time, I thought Raoul Luna was one of the most stunning men I'd ever seen. Picture a cross between Jimmy Smits and Antonio Banderas, with Paul Newman's blue eyes. Tall, dark, and dreamy. Or as the French would say, *Tout simplement magnifique.* (That was years before I met Derek, of course, who is far and away the most handsome—and dangerous—man in the world.)

"Lucky Colette," I said, still watching her. She was glancing around the room now as though she wasn't sure what to do next. She reached for the necklace she wore around her neck and twiddled with whatever stone was hanging on it for a minute. Not seeing anyone else to talk to, she turned and walked back to the kitchen.

"I suppose," Peter said. "They own their own restaurant in Florida and have a couple of kids." With a hint of disdain he added, "Raoul is Colette's pastry chef."

"Nothing wrong with pastry," I mused, envisioning Raoul doing . . . something . . . with a bowl of whipped cream frosting. I quickly shook away the image.

"No," Peter said, "but there's something wrong when

a chef with his talent gives it all up to play with sugar and dough. Raoul was a true master chef, while Colette barely graduated." He wiggled his eyebrows and added, "I'm guessing she made him an offer he couldn't refuse."

"Maybe," I said. Peter clearly considered Raoul's current position as pastry chef a subservient one, but I didn't see anything wrong with it. Desserts were a vital part of a restaurant's menu. To me, at least.

"I'm afraid I must return to the kitchen before Baxter beats me with an egg whisk." Peter gave a quick nod to Derek. "But we'll visit later."

"Sounds good."

He gave me a resounding kiss on the lips, then moved on to greet friends at another table. I was about to slide back into the booth when I heard a high-pitched "Yoo-hooo!"

I turned in time to see Montgomery Larue dashing toward me. Another chef I'd met in Paris. This place was crawling with them.

"My sweet petunia blossom!" he cried, then wrapped his big arms around me and lifted me off the floor in a powerful hug. When he put me down, I was weaving a little. The man had strong arms.

"It's been forever," he said. "And don't you look fabulous!"

"Thanks, Monty," I said. "I've missed you."

It was true. Monty had been one of Savannah's dearest friends from the first day they met at Le Cordon Bleu, and he still visited her at least once a year. Monty had been born and raised in the wilds of Louisiana and couldn't escape from there fast enough. As he had once explained in that sweet-as-syrup Southern accent of his, "Honey, a large gay man with a penchant for drama and a taste for haute cuisine will not survive for long in the bayou."

Monty had relocated to Boston and owned two popular restaurants there. I introduced him to Derek and they shook hands firmly. Then Monty patted his chest to get his heart pumping again. "Dear lord, girl, it's a good thing I didn't see him first."

Derek looked mildly alarmed and I giggled. Montgomery always could bring out the giggles in me.

"Now, I would love to stay and chitter-chat with y'all." He glanced warily over his shoulder. "But I've gotta run before Cromwell comes after me with a switch."

"It's not that bad, is it?" I asked.

"You have no idea," he said darkly, as he wiped his slightly damp forehead with a handkerchief. "I'm telling you, he is on a reign of terror." He turned and stuck out his tongue in the general direction of the kitchen.

"I'll protect you," I said in a teasing tone.

"Sweet girl," he said, and shoved his handkerchief into his back pocket. "We'll catch up later, won't we?"

"I can't wait."

He blew me a kiss, then walked off rapidly toward the kitchen.

I slid back into the booth, almost exhausted by the exchange. "That was Montgomery. He's wonderful."

"Yes," Derek said, and took my hand. "But, darling, you must've left out a few key bits of history when you recounted your summer in Paris."

"Oh, you mean about Peter?" Apparently, Montgomery hadn't been wonderful enough to distract Derek from my tête-à-tête with Peter a moment ago.

"Yes. Peter."

I bit my lip and stared at the ceiling. "Did I leave something out?"

"I believe so." He squeezed my hand. "You can fill me in on the rest of the sordid details over dinner."

Our waiter arrived and both of us chose Savannah's prix fixe selections. Five courses, each with wine pairings. I was tingling with excitement. I did love a good wine pairing.

While I dined on a salad of lightly grilled asparagus with lemon pistachio *gremolata* and fresh goat cheese (paired with a crisp Central Coast Viognier), Derek savored his Bengali potato croquettes with coconut, chiles, and cilantro served with some sort of spicy dipping sauce and mint chutney. They were accompanied by a manly Spanish Rioja that managed to perfectly complement the multitude of strong flavors on the plate.

As we dined, I told Derek the whole silly story of my Paris adventure. He'd already heard about Baxter trying to invade my sleeping bag, so I continued from there. At first, Savannah had blamed me for luring Baxter to my bed. I was appalled! We had a big fight and I was so mad at her and her beastly boyfriend that I almost left Paris.

Derek and I were interrupted by the waiter, who brought us tender cannellini beans in a mild tomato stew, served with orecchiette pasta, sautéed spinach, and garlic.

My main course was wild mushroom raviolis in an amazing green garlic butter sauce and dusted with *Grana Padano*. Our thoughtful waiter, whom I had begun to refer to as the Enabler, brought me an extra serving of the aged cheese and explained that it was less salty and more delicate than Parmigiano-Reggiano. Good to know when one was bulking up on cheese, right?

My new best friend, the Enabler, also snuck me a second glass of the Russian River Valley Pinot Noir that had been paired with the ravioli. A good thing, because besides its well-known medicinal qualities, the wine helped soak up all that extra cheese.

In between bites, I related how Kevin and Peter had convinced me to stay in Paris. Baxter had made himself scarce, so I finally agreed. Peter and Kevin took me under their wing and gave me their own private chefs' tour. It was a whirlwind of tastes and sensations and flavors. When we weren't dining in some hole-in-the-wall bistro in the Marais or stopping to try the French version of a hot dog and French fries at an outdoor counter in the Latin Quarter, we would eat at home with one of the fledgling chefs whipping up their latest creation. They were my new best friends forever.

By the end of that first week, Savannah had come out of her snit and admitted that her now ex-boyfriend was a loathsome bloodsucker. The four of us celebrated her return to sanity by hopping a train to the Champagne region for a weekend of overindulgent fun. I was in heaven. While playing tourist, staring up at the dazzling Chagall windows in the cathedral in Reims, I fell a little bit in love with Peter.

After watching me moon over Peter all weekend, Kevin was sweet enough to pull me aside and quietly inform me that she and Peter were a couple. They'd been so discreet that I hadn't even realized it! Of course, I'd been too self-involved in my own problems to notice. Kevin was so kind to me despite my lame attempt to steal her boyfriend. Honestly, I was so utterly dim-witted; it still made me cringe to think of it.

After relishing my last bite of buttery ravioli, I shook my head. "The consensus after that was that the Wainwright women weren't exactly reliable when it came to picking appropriate men."

"But then you met me," Derek said easily.

"And you accused me of murder."

He smiled wolfishly. "Got your attention, didn't I?"

"Oh, definitely," I said, laughing.

For dessert, Derek and I had both chosen the *bignolès*, an Italian version of the French profiterole, those small round pastry puffs that were deep fried and usually stuffed with ice cream and dipped in chocolate sauce. But Savannah had filled her *bignolès* with an ultra-fluffy custard, then drizzled them liberally with warm, salted caramel sauce.

I almost passed out. "Oh, my God. I love my sister." Maybe it was the caramel sauce talking, but damn, this stuff was orgasmic. I wondered if it would be too tacky to lick the bowl.

It was after eleven o'clock when the kitchen finally stopped production. Baxter and Savannah came out to take their bows to our enthusiastic applause.

"Isn't she marvelous?" Baxter gushed. He grabbed Savannah's hand and thrust it into the air as though they were two politicians onstage. I saw Savannah's eyes widen as he pulled her arm up higher than she could comfortably reach.

The six other chefs stood behind the two of them and all of them applauded politely. Since several of them had complained to me earlier about Baxter, I knew their approval was forced.

Baxter introduced them all with a brief but animated explanation of their cuisine styles and which night of the week they would be cooking. There were Peter and Kevin, of course, and Raoul (looking as dashing as I remembered), Colette, Margot, and Montgomery.

Margot maneuvered her way past the cluster of chefs and slipped her arm through Baxter's, and I suddenly remembered my first impression of her in Paris. We'd all gone to a party and she was there. You couldn't miss her. She was tall, thin, redheaded, and wild. She wore a bright pink minidress, with boots that stretched halfway up her thighs. She had seemed fun and snarky at first, but as I got to know her, I found her to be calculating and manipulative. I noticed she would look around the room and find the person or group who could do her the most good, then migrate over to them. She always said the most clever things, but they didn't seem natural. It was as though she'd been practicing her lines for days in anticipation of the moment.

Baxter didn't seem to mind her attentions and pulled her closer. Were they involved with each other? I couldn't help but speculate.

"I'd advise you all to make reservations every single night for the next two weeks," Baxter said jovially. "You won't want to miss any of these stellar evenings."

I wondered how Derek would feel if I made those reservations.

"Tonight I expect you've all become vegetarian," Baxter continued. "I know I have, thanks to Savannah. She is a gift from the gods."

There was more applause, even though he sounded completely phony to me. Because of it, I clapped louder than anyone. I was proud of Savannah and I couldn't have cared less what Baxter thought of her cooking.

"Thank you all so much," Savannah said, rubbing her shoulder. It was probably sore from Baxter's yanking her arm up, but she looked happy anyway. Exhausted but happy. The bright red beret she always wore when cooking was perched jauntily on her bald head and her white jacket was pristine. I had a feeling she might have slipped on a clean one before entering the dining room to take her bows.

Savannah turned to Baxter. "And thank you for this lovely opportunity, Baxter. It was great to be back in the kitchen with you."

He winked at the crowd. "I can think of another room I'd rather be in with you."

Ugh, what a toad. Savannah was a professional chef and Baxter was a chauvinist jackass. But the crowd laughed and hooted nevertheless. Meanwhile, Baxter was still as big a jerk as he'd been in Paris. Still keeping it classy. *Not.*

Savannah held up her hand to silence the crowd. "I'd like to take a moment to present Baxter with a little something as a way of saying thank you."

"Something for me?" he said, his smirk turning lascivious. "Listen, sweetheart, if you really want to thank me ..."

Savannah smacked his arm lightly, then signaled me to bring her the package.

As I grabbed the gift and slid from the booth, I thought of the hours I'd spent on the book box, creating a tasteful outer design with a spare line of gold tooling and raised bands on the spine to resemble the book within. I mourned the care I took to fashion the plush inner cushion that fit

the restored cookbook like a soft glove. I'd used the endpapers Derek brought back from Brussels to line the
box's interior, and the swirls of dark red and gold gave it
a luxurious, masculine feel along with the slightest touch
of whimsy I thought Obedience would enjoy.

With little enthusiasm, I walked over to Savannah and
whispered, "Are you sure?"

"Give it to me," Savannah hissed.

I sighed and passed her the book box, which I'd
wrapped in shiny silver paper and ribbon. She turned
and handed it to Baxter. "This is for you."

I returned to the booth in time to watch Baxter, wearing a greedy grin, rip the paper off to reveal the lush red
leather cushion-inlaid box. A beautiful design, if I did
say so myself.

He turned it every which way and then shook it.
"Okay, yeah, it's a box."

I wanted to run over and slap him, but Derek clutched
my arm. He knew me too well.

"Open it," Savannah urged.

He rolled his eyes at the crowd, then set it down on
the nearest guest table, unlatched the cover, and lifted it.
Pulled out the suede-and-leather-lined pouch and stared
at it. "What the hell is this?"

I struggled to pull away from Derek, but he held on to
me. Didn't he understand that Baxter Cromwell needed
to be beaten with a bat? If only I'd had one in my bag.

"You'll see," Savannah said gaily, her voice rising with
anticipation. "Look inside the pouch."

"This is ridiculous." He gritted his teeth. Was he angry? Why? Was it because the crowd's attention was focused more on the gift than on him? Probably.

He loosened the ties, held out his hand, and turned the
pouch upside down. The venerable cookbook slid out
onto his palm. He bobbled it before catching and holding
it with both hands.

He stared at the book. His hands began to shake and
his lips thinned. In fear? Or fury? Or what?

I thought for a second that he would lash out at Savannah, but he quickly recovered. Smiling too brightly, he shoved the book back into the pouch, grabbed the box, and tucked everything under his arm.

I wanted to run over and rescue poor Obedience and her cookbook, but my attention was abruptly diverted by Kevin's expression. She stared at Baxter in outrage, her face turning redder by the second. She looked angry enough to slay someone, preferably Baxter.

Then all of a sudden, she spun around and glared at Savannah with so much raw anger that I flinched.

Holy crap. What was that all about?

"What is it?" somebody called from the audience.

"Never mind, folks," Baxter said with a calculated chuckle. "Just an old inside joke. Eh, Savannah?"

It wasn't my imagination; Baxter was visibly shaken by the gift. And so was Kevin. The other diners didn't seem concerned as they chattered and drank the last of their beverages.

I traded glances with Derek and could tell he was as worried about Savannah as I was. But she was flush with happiness and didn't seem to notice, while Baxter did everything he could to ignore her and the old book.

He waved and tried to be jovial, but his nerves were still showing. Finally he shouted, "G'night, folks," turned, and rushed back to the kitchen. A few of the chefs followed him out.

Savannah was all smiles as she shook hands with some of the customers. After a moment, she started to follow the other chefs, but stopped to pick up the wrapping paper Baxter had abandoned on the table.

I was about to jump up and help her when Peter moved over to assist. He handed the crumpled paper to one of the busboys, then wound his arm around her shoulder and walked her out of the room.

I was stymied by everyone's reactions, but Kevin's troubled me the most. I thought her head was going to explode when she saw that cookbook. Why? Had Baxter promised to give it to her instead? Or maybe it had nothing to do with the cookbook. Maybe it was all about Baxter and Savannah. Was she jealous?

Thinking perhaps I'd imagined or exaggerated the whole thing, I turned to Derek for confirmation. "Did you catch Kevin's expression?"

"Yes, I saw it," he said, his jaw tight. "That was not the same sweet girl you introduced me to earlier this evening."

"No. She looked ready to kill someone."

"Not someone," he said. "Baxter. I wouldn't have been surprised to see her smash a bottle of wine over his head."

"She didn't look too happy with Savannah, either."

But why? Was Kevin resentful of Savannah? Was she in love with Baxter? That was impossible. She had to know he was a complete cheat when it came to relationships. Of course she knew. She'd been there in Paris when he cheated on Savannah. She had felt the same way we all did. Hadn't she?

I had too many questions and no answers.

The tables began to empty as customers paid their bills and left for the evening. We were sliding out of our booth when Savannah returned to chat with us.

"Everything was delicious," Derek said, giving her a kiss on the cheek.

"Thanks." She was beaming and I could tell she was on cloud nine. Except for those last few moments, the evening had been a big success.

I hugged her. "The *bignolès* are to die for."

"They're my favorites, too," she said.

Since she was planning to stay overnight with us, I asked, "Are you ready to leave now?"

"No. Do you mind? I'm so wired, and some of us are going to stay and have a drink together. We want to catch up with each other, and Baxter needs to discuss the schedule. I can catch a cab back to your place or have one of them give me a ride."

"We weren't sure what you wanted to do," I said, "but we were planning to stay in the Mission for a while anyway. Derek's partner recommended that we check out a Brazilian band over at the Elbo Room."

"That sounds like fun," she said.

"It should be. So we can swing by after that and see if you still need a ride. And by then I'll be ready to grab an ice cream cone around the corner at Bi-Rite." I looked at Derek. "Best ice cream in the city."

"Ice cream?" Savannah glared at me. "You're still hungry?"

"No, but I will be. That's a whole hour from now." Did I really need to explain this to her?

She threw up her hands. "Stupid question. You're like a bottomless pit."

It was hard being misunderstood by my own sister. "We are talking about ice cream."

She sighed, then chuckled. "I know. Go. Get out of here."

"Dinner was fantastic," I said. "You're awesome."

Derek touched her shoulder. "We'll be by in an hour or so and see if you're still here and need a ride. If not, we'll see you at home."

I pulled my key out of my purse and handed it to her. "Just in case you get there first."

"Thanks," she said. "I'll probably hitch a ride from one of these guys." She gave me another quick hug. "The book box is gorgeous. I think Baxter was blown away."

In more ways than one, I thought. "He looked a little shell-shocked."

"I know," she said, beaming.

I hated to bum her out, but I had to tell her what I'd seen. "Kevin didn't look too happy about it."

"What do you mean?"

I hooked her arm in mine and leaned closer. "Trust me, if looks could kill, you and Baxter would be dead on the floor right now."

Savannah shook her head. "You must've misread her. Kevin's been in a great mood all evening."

"Maybe so, but the minute Baxter held the cookbook in his hand, her whole attitude changed. She looked furious."

"Brooklyn, you can't be serious." Savannah looked around furtively, not wishing to be overheard. "She was probably reacting to something else, or she's just tired. We're all exhausted. You must be mistaken."

"I don't know. Derek saw the same thing I did. And I'm sorry, but I have to admit that Baxter didn't look happy, either. Is there something about this cookbook you're not telling me?"

She was taken aback, but that turned quickly to annoyance. "For the hundredth time, it's just a damn book. Get over it. Seriously, you're imagining things."

She started to walk away, but I pulled her back. "Fine. I'm sorry I said anything. But just in case, please be careful, especially with Kevin. She really didn't look happy. In fact, why don't you just come home with us now?"

"You're being silly," she whispered heatedly. "Kevin is one of my dearest friends. She's never been mad at me in her life. Ever. So just back off."

She whirled around and stomped off toward the kitchen. I stared at her back until she disappeared around the corner. Then I sagged against the plush booth. Maybe she was right. Maybe Kevin's infuriated reaction had nothing to do with the cookbook.

But I didn't believe that, did I? The instant that cookbook came out of its pouch, Kevin's demeanor had changed. I was just surprised that her laser focus on Baxter and Savannah hadn't drilled holes into the two of them. It had put the fear of God in me from all the way across the room.

"Now I'm afraid to leave her here," I said to Derek. "Am I crazy? Did I imagine that whole thing?"

"No, you didn't, but I think she'll be fine with all the

chefs here. And while we're gone, perhaps she'll have a chance to talk things over with Kevin."

"I hope so."

"Don't worry so, love," he said. "Savannah's surrounded by friends and we'll only be gone for an hour."

It sounded reasonable. I took one last look toward the kitchen. "I guess."

"Come on, then." He took my hand and I leaned my head against his shoulder as we walked toward the door.

"I'm going to need ice cream for sure."

"Of course," he said. "And after that I'm going to teach you how to samba."

Chapter 4

Who knew Derek was such a wild man on the dance floor? And who didn't love a guy who continued to surprise you?

The Brazilian band performing at the Elbo Room was indeed hot. We had trekked a few blocks east to the venerable San Francisco nightclub to catch the last half of the show and managed to snag two seats at the crowded bar upstairs. On the wall above our heads was a stuffed marlin. Really. Who hung marlins on the wall anymore? It made a forceful decor statement.

We drank mojitos. It seemed to fit with the moment and the music and the marlin.

We danced. Derek and I had never danced together before and certainly had never danced the samba. Wow, was all I could say.

The band, Los Whackos del Poblano, was not just hot—they were on fire. The lead singer played electric accordion and the horn section took up half the stage.

They were a jivin' group, and damn loud. I hadn't been inside a nightclub in more than a year, so I'd forgotten how completely fried my ears could get from spending time in a small room filled with hard-core musicians and blasting amplifiers.

As we walked out onto the sidewalk after the show, I shook my head and tried to clear my brain. "Are your ears working yet?"

"Beg pardon, love?" Derek said, stopping to peer at me. "I see your lips moving but I can't hear you."

"I think I've gone deaf."

He put his arm around my shoulders as we walked up Valencia toward Eighteenth Street. "I trust it's a temporary condition."

"Ah, so you can hear me. I can sort of hear you now. You sound as though you're in a tunnel."

"I'm encouraged. I think we'll survive."

"Thank goodness." I stopped, stretched my neck sideways and back, then stared up at the sky. "Oh, dear, I've turned into an old fogey, complaining about the noise. That's just sad."

"It is." He smiled at me. "But did you have a good time, old thing?"

"I did. It was fun. And who knew you could samba like that?"

"Blame my mother for forcing us into cotillion at an early age."

"Good for her," I said. "You were a maniac out there. I never knew you had so many hidden talents."

"Ah, darling," he said, gazing down at me, "I have depths you've not yet plumbed."

I shook my head again. "I can't believe you can say something so ridiculous and manage to sound so sexy."

His eyebrows lifted. "I know there's a compliment in there somewhere."

"There is, I promise." As we walked, I checked my wristwatch. "Uh-oh. We've been gone almost an hour and a half. I hope Savannah got a ride home."

"We'll just stop by the restaurant to make sure."

We reached Eighteenth Street and waited for the light to turn green. I tossed my hair back, grateful for the cool night air after sweating on the dance floor for the last hour. When the light changed, we crossed the street and headed west toward Dolores Park, where we'd left the car. Baxter's restaurant was on the way.

Once past Guerrero, the street grew darker. We stopped talking and Derek urged me to walk a little faster. A few minutes later, we reached the corner where Baxter's restaurant stood.

"Closed," I said.

Derek nodded. "Definitely closed."

I cupped my eyes to get a better look through the glass-fronted door. "There's a light on in the back. She might still be in the kitchen."

Without much thought, I reached for the doorknob. To my surprise, it opened, so I walked in.

Derek grabbed the back of my jacket. "Where are you going?"

"Just checking to see if Savannah's here."

"Brooklyn, stop," he said sharply. "You don't know who's in there."

"It's probably some of the chefs," I whispered. "And if not, you'll protect me, right? It'll only take a second to check."

He scowled but followed me inside.

The door eased shut behind him and the first thing that hit me was the complete silence. There were no bustling waiters, no trickling waterfall, no cheerful chatter or clinking of glasses or tapping of silverware against plates. Not that I expected to hear any of that in a closed restaurant, but the sounds of the waterfall would have been nice.

With the next step, I felt a chill. The darkness of the room gave me pause. It was silly to be afraid with Derek right here, I thought. Giving my eyes a few seconds to adjust, I ventured forward, first tiptoeing past the front podium, then stepping down into the dining room.

I barely avoided plowing into a table, thanks to a passing car's headlights bouncing off the coffered ceiling and casting odd shadows on the walls. Liquor bottles lining the bar caught the light, too, creating multicolored crystal shards that shimmered across the high-gloss oak floor.

I made it to the far end of the room and turned down the short hall that led toward the kitchen. A pale glow of light shining through the porthole on the swinging double doors guided me the rest of the way.

As I pushed the door open, a horrific scream erupted.

Derek tried to yank me backward, but my forward momentum caused me to stumble into the room instead. That's when I saw my sister Savannah kneeling on the tiled floor, a huge triangular bloodstained knife clutched in her raised hand.

She whipped around and the sudden movement caused her scarlet beret to slip off her head. Her eyes were wide and her cheeks were stained with tears. She was still screaming, so I took one more step toward her. That's when I saw someone lying on the floor beside her.

It was Baxter Cromwell. His eyes bulged open and his white chef's coat was torn and spattered with blood. He lay unmoving on the cold, hard tile, as dead as he could be.

I'm no chicken, but the sight of all that blood splashed on his coat, along with the bloodstained knife, was enough to make my knees wobble. My vision blurred and things began to spin. I couldn't breathe.

"No, you don't," Derek scolded as he grabbed me.

"Y-yes, I do," I mumbled, and sagged into his arms.

Ten minutes later, after Derek had smacked my cheeks a little too eagerly and muttered, "Snap out of it" a few dozen times, I was back on my feet and pacing the length of the bar while we waited for the police to arrive. I was still breathing a little heavily, but I was fine. Alive, anyway.

Savannah sat on one of the barstools, looking dazed and confused. Thanks to Derek's quick thinking, she now wore thin rubber gloves over her bloodied hands. He'd seen the box of disposable gloves on a shelf by the industrial dishwashing machine and had urged her to put them on to protect any blood evidence on her hands.

I forced a glass of water into Savannah's glove-sheathed hand and told her to keep sipping it.

"I didn't kill him," she whispered.

"I know, sweetie."

She rubbed her forehead with the back of her hand and strained to look at me. "How do you know?"

"Because you're a vegetarian."

"Really?"

"No, you twit," I said softly. "It's because I know you. You don't step on spiders. You wouldn't hurt a bug to save your own life. And you wouldn't stick a knife in someone's gut and kill them in cold blood, no matter how big a jerk he was. So I know you didn't do it, but I just wish you'd seen who did."

"Me, too." Her shoulders sagged and she looked exhausted enough to slide off her seat. I eased her stool closer to the bar so she could lean her elbows on the shiny surface.

I just didn't want her to fall asleep. We had turned every light on full blast, so the room was illuminated as brightly as if the sun were blazing down on us. Derek had locked the front door in case any passersby got the idea that we were open for business.

I decided to try and keep Savannah talking. Maybe something would click and she would remember a detail that might help.

"Did you see anyone run out the back door?" I asked. The kitchen door leading to the back alley had been wide open when we arrived. The killer must've run out that door and disappeared down the alley. At least that was my best guess. If it was true, we might've missed him by only a few seconds. Maybe we'd even passed him on the sidewalk earlier. The thought gave me goose bumps.

"I don't think so," Savannah said for maybe the umpteenth time. Her tone was dull and her eyes were unfocused. I'd never seen her like this before, and while I understood that she was freaked-out, I didn't have time for it.

"That answer's not going to work for the police, Savannah," I said quietly. "You either saw someone or you didn't. I know you're tired, but you need to remember everything that happened after we left you earlier tonight. You should talk it out. I can help you. We can go over it all before the police get here."

She nodded but said nothing.

Derek stepped close, pressed his lips to my ear, and murmured, "She's in shock, love. Let her be for now."

"But the cops are going to drag her off to jail. I can't let that happen."

He touched my hair lightly, smoothed one thick strand off my cheek. "We'll make sure it doesn't."

Staring up at Derek's face, I absently counted the few fine lines that branched out from the corners of his intelligent blue eyes. I knew he'd worked some dangerous jobs, been in a number of harrowing situations. Even if he hadn't told me about them, his eyes would have given him away. They were constantly assessing, occasionally challenging, always compelling. I wondered which of his adventures had earned him the most wrinkles—not that he had many. Just enough to make him interesting. Some of them were from laughter, I knew, but most were hard-won. And all of them had gone into building the character of the man who stood by me tonight.

My heart swelled. What outstanding deed had I done to deserve his loyalty and love? It was stunning to know that he occasionally wondered the same thing about me.

"I'm so scared," I whispered.

"I know." He wrapped his arms around me and held me for a long moment.

I sniffled. "I'm going to lose all my friends."

I heard him chuckle. "Probably."

"Oh, thanks." He was kidding, but it was a deep, dark worry of mine. Discovering murder victims was both aggravating and frightening, so much so that I'd finally gone to my parents' spiritual advisor, Guru Bob, for advice and counsel. He had suggested that the gods may have decided that I was the Chosen One, so to speak, who'd been designated to obtain justice for these victims.

The Chosen One. Really? That's what I got for seeking the advice of a guru.

Wasn't it the job of law enforcement to obtain justice for crime victims? Of course it was. But it was also true that the police I'd dealt with could always use some extra guidance. So if tonight was any indication, it seemed I might be stuck with this role for a while. Because sure enough, here I was again, staring at another suspicious death.

It wasn't fair. I had a day job. I didn't want to be involved in another murder.

But this was no time to whine about it. Poor Baxter lay dead on the cold floor a few feet away, and I was making it all about me. Yes, Baxter had been an odious pest, but that didn't mean he'd deserved to be murdered in cold blood in his own restaurant, for heaven's sake.

"I didn't kill him," Savannah blurted. "Why should I go to jail?"

Derek and I turned and stared at her. The dullness was gone. She appeared irritated now. It was a much better look on her.

"You shouldn't," I said, moving toward her. "But they'll want to talk to you because you were the one holding the knife that killed Baxter."

"But I didn't kill him," she said again.

"I know. But how did you end up holding the knife?"

"It was sticking out of his . . . ugh." She grimaced.

"Out of his stomach," I coaxed.

She rubbed her own stomach. "I'm going to be sick."

"No, you're not." I jumped closer and gripped her arms, holding her upright. "Come on. Deep breaths. Don't lose it now."

She took a couple of fast, deep breaths, then her head wobbled. "I feel faint."

"No!" I looked at Derek in dismay and the muscles of his jaw tightened in response.

All he needed was another weak-kneed Wainwright woman on his hands. But what could I say? I couldn't stand the sight of blood and, admittedly, had fainted on more than one occasion. Savannah had even more right to faint, but that didn't mean I would let her.

Frankly, the stronger reason why I'd felt woozy was because for a minute there, seeing Savannah kneeling on the floor in front of the bloodied body of Baxter Cromwell, I'd experienced an alarming case of déjà vu.

I'd flashed back to the night I found my old book-binding mentor, Abraham Karastovsky, dying in a pool of his own blood. Kneeling next to him, I'd discovered he was barely alive and had tried to revive him, but failed. With his last breath, he had whispered the clue that ultimately helped me solve his murder.

Derek had found me kneeling there with Abraham's blood on my hands. I'd taken one look at those red smears on my palms and blacked out completely.

I shook the memory away.

"I'm fine," Savannah muttered finally. "It's just . . . all that blood. And Baxter. I can't believe he's dead."

"Can you tell us what happened?" I asked again, as gently as I could.

She swallowed some more water and I took the glass from her to refill it.

"I—I went to the ladies' room while everyone was saying good night. It took me a while to wash up. I was exhausted, but I wanted to clean myself up a little. You know how it is after a long night of cooking. I felt like food was jammed into every one of my pores."

"Mm, nice image," I said, being careful not to mention that I had no idea how it was after a long night of cooking. I didn't cook, remember?

She granted me a wan smile. "My food is healthier and I use less fat, but I still need to wash my face at the end of the night. Anyway, there's a small couch in the ladies' room, so I sat down and closed my eyes for a minute."

"Did you fall asleep?"

"I didn't think I did." She squeezed her eyes shut, then opened them. "Maybe I did fall asleep for a few minutes. I must've, because when I came out here, all the lights in the place were off."

"When you left to go to the ladies' room, who was still here?"

She thought for a moment. "Peter, Kevin, Baxter, Margot, and Monty."

"That's almost everyone, isn't it?"

"Is it? Wait." She thought for a moment. "Colette was still here, but she was just leaving. Raoul had left an hour earlier. He wasn't feeling well, so he took a cab back to the hotel. Colette had their rental car and I was thinking of asking her for a ride back to your place, but she'd been so cranky all day that I didn't want to spend another minute with her."

"Why was she cranky?"

Savannah lifted her shoulder. "Can't say for sure, but those two weren't getting along very well."

"Raoul and Colette? Are you kidding? Who doesn't get along with Raoul?"

"His wife, apparently." She met my gaze and almost smirked. "I know, right? Raoul is such a doll. She must be nuts."

I noticed Derek's sideways glance at us.

"We're going off topic," I said. "Let's see. Was anyone else still around? Any waiters or kitchen staff?"

She stared at the ceiling and tried to think. "One of the bartenders stayed to serve us drinks, but after a while he cleaned up and left. A few of the kitchen staff were still here, prepping for tomorrow. But we stood around talking for so long that they all left, too. It was getting really late. By the time I took off to the ladies' room, everyone but the chefs had left."

"Okay, and how long do you think you were in there?"

"Maybe eight or ten minutes?"

"And you came out and the lights were off. What did you do?"

"It was a little creepy," she said. "I called out 'Hello,' but nobody answered. Then I saw the kitchen light was on, so I went in there."

"And Baxter was on the floor?"

She swallowed with difficulty. I'd forgotten to get her more water, so Derek went behind the bar, found a full bottle of water in the refrigerator, and handed it to her.

"Thanks." She twisted off the cap and took a big gulp. "Yes, he was on the floor."

"Was he dead?"

"No." Her shoulders shook and she rubbed her arms to stave off the chills. "He was still gasping for air, so I didn't think, I just grabbed the knife and pulled it out."

"And that's when we walked in?"

"Well, a few seconds later." She took another drink of water. "He gasped and choked first, then, yeah. He died."

"I'm sorry." I reached over and took her hand.

She seemed lost in her own world for a minute, then said, "That fish knife was his pride and joy. He told us how he found it in Singapore."

I'd seen the knife. It was massive, bigger than any kitchen knife I'd ever seen. The blade was about twelve inches long and eight inches wide, curving dramatically along the razor-sharp edge.

"He bought it from one of the roughneck Asian fisher-men who sell their catch right on the dock next to their boats. He'd never seen another one like it."

"Why is it curved like that?" I asked.

"It makes carving up the largest types of fish a lot easier. You slide the blade under the gills and just start slicing."

"Interesting," I said, frowning.

"He said he paid six dollars for it."

"Sounds like a bargain."

"I'll say. It would cost several hundred dollars at Williams-Sonoma." She tried to snicker, but her face crumpled and she began to sob.

"Oh, honey." I grabbed her and held her. My eyes got watery, too, since I was constitutionally incapable of letting her cry alone.

After a minute or two, her shoulders stopped shaking. She hiccupped once or twice, then took some deep breaths. "I'm okay. It's just . . . wow. Horrible."

"I know. I'm so sorry you have to go through this."

"Yeah. Me, too. Thanks."

I glanced over at Derek, who was walking the perimeter of the dining room, making sure the windows were locked and secured, studying the street traffic. He couldn't help himself, I guess.

His face was a study in composure. He would be the perfect buffer between Savannah and the police detectives. It helped that he had an impressive law enforcement background after working with British intelligence for many years. The detectives we had worked with in the past called him by his title: Commander. It suited him.

Savannah, truly exhausted now, folded her arms on the bar and rested her head on them. I left her and met Derek halfway across the room.

"How's she doing?" he asked.

"She's beat. I don't know how she'll deal with the police."

"She'll be fine," he said, taking hold of my hand. "She'll rally. She's your mother's daughter."

"Aw," I said, smiling. "That was the exact right thing to say."

He shrugged. "It's true."

We continued walking along the waterfall wall. "You know, Derek, this could've been a simple robbery gone wrong. The back door was wide-open when we walked in and this isn't the safest of neighborhoods."

"It's possible, of course," he said. "The police will have to interview the kitchen staff to find out if anything has gone missing."

I stopped dead. "Oh, hell. The cookbook." I didn't give him a chance to respond as I raced across the room to Savannah.

"Wake up, Bugs," I said, rubbing her back to get her attention.

"Are the police here?" she asked, her voice groggy.

"Not yet. Savannah, the cookbook. Where is it?"

Baffled, she glanced around, then frowned at me. "We don't use cookbooks, Brooklyn. Baxter's got a notebook of recipes and—"

"No, no," I said in a rush. "The old cookbook you gave back to Baxter, with the leather box I made. Where is it?"

"Oh, for God's sake," she said wearily. "It figures you'd only care about that stupid cookbook." She waved her hand, dismissing me.

"I don't only . . . Never mind." I couldn't get too miffed at her in her present condition, but I *did* care about that book. And I wasn't about to let it get damaged or destroyed by some overzealous fingerprint cop during a police search.

Or worse. What if it was bloodstained? What if Baxter had been holding the book when he died? It could be ruined beyond repair.

Save the book. The phrase and the policy had been drilled into my brain at an early age. With that one thought in mind, I rushed back to the kitchen to search for Baxter's cookbook. But as I reached out to push the door open, I stopped.

Really? Was I seriously going to strut into the very room where the bloody corpse of Baxter Cromwell lay sprawled on the floor?

"That would be a big *N-O*," I muttered, shivering at the thought, and trudged back to the bar. "Okay, it's probably on a shelf in the kitchen, safe and sound. I'll get it later. After, you know, they take him away."

"You're nuts," Savannah muttered.

Derek was more sympathetic. "Do you want me to find the book for you?"

"Would you mind?"

"Of course not. We should get it out of there before it winds up in police custody."

I breathed a sigh of relief. Derek understood what could happen to the book if we didn't take charge of it immediately. "Thank you."

But just as he turned toward the kitchen, a deafening cacophony of police sirens blared out, followed by the screeching of multiple brakes, ending directly outside the front door of the restaurant.

There was no time to search for the book.

The police had arrived.

Chapter 5

To bake a pleasing chicken pie, have on hand a chicken recently killed and plucked thoroughly.
— The Cookbook of Obedience Green

"Jeezo, Wainwright, I thought we were friends. Why you do me like this?"

That was SFPD detective inspector Janice Lee's smart-ass greeting to me as she strolled across the expansive restaurant dining room. She was followed by her partner, Nathan Jaglom, and two men carrying thick steel briefcases. The two guys were dressed more casually than the detectives, and I figured that with those fancy cases, they had to be the crime scene investigators.

Four uniformed cops had walked in a minute earlier and had already scoped out the kitchen and Baxter's body. Now they were securing the doors inside and out with yellow crime scene tape. Derek, Savannah, and I were corralled into the bar area and told to stay put.

"I'm sorry, Inspector Lee," I said, and meant it. After all, it was one o'clock in the morning. No wonder she looked less than thrilled to be here. "It's all my fault. I

begged the dispatcher to call you guys because I know
you're the best."

I didn't mention that she'd be less likely to think I was
the killer if I actually asked for her.

Lee paused to consider my words, then nodded. "True.
We are the best. I admire your perceptiveness. But I can't
forgive you for interrupting the awesome *NCIS* mara-
thon I was in the middle of."

"Sorry about that," I said. "I can tell you how season
two ends."

"But then I'd have to kill you."

"Inspector Lee, lovely to see you again," Derek said
as he approached and shook her hand.

"Hello, Commander Stone," Janice Lee said, her voice
suddenly half an octave higher. Derek had that effect on
all women, no matter how kick-ass tough they were.

Derek turned to her partner. "Inspector Jaglom, how
are you?"

"Hey, there, Commander." Inspector Jaglom lifted his
chin in greeting. "Ms. Wainwright. How're you doing?"

"I've been better." I shook his hand. "But it's good to
see you, Inspector."

"Yeah, you too." Jaglom nodded absently as he took
out his notepad and began to make notes. He rubbed his
sleepy eyes with one hand and I felt another twinge of
guilt. He wore a rumpled shirt under his sports coat and
he looked like he'd been dragged out of bed, forced to
cut short a good night's sleep. Which was, no doubt, exactly what had happened, given the time of night.

Because I paid attention to such things, I noticed that
Inspector Lee had added a few more pounds since the last
time I'd seen her. She was a beautiful woman, but she'd
been painfully thin when we first met. Since then, she'd
given up cigarettes and had begun to gain weight. She probably hated the weight gain, but she was tall enough to handle a few extra pounds. I thought she looked happier and
even prettier than before. So much so that I wondered
whether she might have a new boyfriend.

She probably wouldn't take kindly to me asking her if that was the case. Maybe I'd bring it up later.

She looked around the room, taking in the coffered ceiling, the murals, the slate water wall, the glass-backed bar. Untying her fabulous Burberry trench coat, she draped it over the back of a barstool. "Nice place."

"Nice, yeah. Except for the pesky dead body that's bleeding out on the kitchen floor," I said gruffly.

She cocked her head. "That's sarcasm, right?"

I sighed. "I suppose it is. Sorry."

"Don't be. You almost sounded like a cop there for a minute." She sniffled and patted her chest dramatically. "You make me so darn proud."

I shook my head. "You're a strange woman, Inspector Lee."

She bared her teeth in a grin. "You betcha."

Homicide inspector Janice Lee had been a part of my world ever since the Abraham Karastovsky murder. She'd also been assigned to investigate the Layla Fontaine murder last year at the Bay Area Book Arts center, where I'd been teaching a bookbinding class. And then there was the grisly Alex Pavlenko murder a few months ago, which took place in the bedroom of my best friend, Robin. Robin had been devastated and vulnerable, so I wasn't about to let her face the cops alone. I was right there when the detectives showed up.

Most recently, Inspectors Lee and Jaglom had worked on the murder case of Joseph Taylor, a Richmond District bookstore owner I'd known for years.

I had discovered poor Joe's dead body in his shop, surrounded by his beloved rare and expensive books. Someone very evil had sliced his neck open with a paper-cutting knife.

Who said the book biz wasn't cutthroat?

So I couldn't blame Inspector Lee too much for her snippy remarks; the fact was, we did tend to meet under gruesome circumstances. But I liked her, and I was sure that underneath her prickly surface, she liked me, too.

We had similar tastes in Szechuan food and good wine. I coveted her trench coat and most of the shoes I'd seen her wear. We should've been great friends, had even planned to meet for a glass of wine sometime, but murder kept getting in the way.

While Derek and Inspector Jaglom spoke in quiet tones over by the row of booths along the wall, Inspector Lee pulled out her notepad and focused on me. "I'll just get some of the preliminaries out of the way so we can move on to the main event." Flipping through the pad, she came to a clean page and began to scribble something on it. "So, tell me about the dead body in the kitchen. Male or female?"

"Male. Baxter Cromwell. He's the owner of this restaurant."

She gasped. "The bad boy chef? He's dead?"

"Yes."

"Crap," she muttered. "That's gonna bring out the bloodsucking paparazzi."

I was surprised she'd ever heard of Baxter, let alone expressed distress over his demise. But I supposed even cops watched the Cooking Channel. *Bad Boy Chef* was the lame title they'd chosen for Baxter's cooking show, but it suited him and it had made him famous.

I hadn't even considered the fact that Baxter was a celebrity and the news of his murder would be broadcast around the world. Part of me wanted to begrudge Baxter his fame because he'd been such a louse to both me and Savannah, but then I thought of him lying dead in the kitchen and my resentment faded. Slightly.

"Please don't tell me you liked him," I said.

Lee thought about it. "It was a good show and he was entertaining enough. But he thrived on creating confusion and distrust among his contestants. I could see how someone might learn to hate him enough to kill him. Did you know him?"

"Yes. And he was as big an ass as you can imagine."

Lee stared up at me through narrowed eyes. "So did you kill him?"

"Of course not," I said, scowling. "Why would you even ask that?"

She shrugged. "I'm a homicide cop and a murder has just happened, so I ask. That's why I'm here, right? Because there's been a murder. What I can't figure out is, why are *you* here? Is this how it's always going to be, Wainwright? Murder happens and you show up?"

"No!" And there went my blood pressure. "I stayed because my sister found the victim lying in—"

"Get off her back, Jan," Jaglom said, elbowing his partner's arm. "Let's get down to business."

"That's what I'm doing, Nate," she said mildly, and craned her neck to get a better look at Savannah for the first time. "Your sister, Wainwright?"

I frowned at her sudden interest, but it was my own fault for mentioning Savannah. "Yes, my sister. And she didn't kill Baxter, either."

Lee raised an eyebrow at my snarling tone, but it was too darn bad if she took offense. I wasn't about to let her browbeat Savannah to tears.

"Savannah," I said briskly, since she'd zoned out again and I needed to get her undivided attention. "This is Detective Inspector Lee, the homicide detective I was telling you about."

Savannah's eyelids fluttered as she brought the world back into focus. She blinked at the cop and quickly hopped off the barstool. Holding out her hand to shake the inspector's, she said, "I'm so happy to meet you. Brooklyn has said so many nice things about you, and I'm as confident as she is that you'll find Baxter's killer and bring him to justice."

Inspector Lee was clearly bemused by Savannah's enthusiastic greeting. My sister shook her hand firmly and energetically, and I could see a tiny portion of Lee's cynical outer coating melt in the face of Savannah's positive vitality.

Lee finally pulled her hand away and tried to regain her command over the situation. "Ms. Wainwright, I'd like to ask you a few questions about your relationship with the deceased."

"Of course, yes, please ask me anything," Savannah said. "I'll do anything I can to help you."

"Inspector," I interjected quickly, "you don't know my sister yet, but believe me, she didn't have anything to do with Baxter's death. Really, she doesn't have enough killer instinct to swat down a fly."

"Flies have just as much right to life and happiness as we do," Savannah said.

Ugh. No they don't, I thought.

Lee's eyebrows popped up, and then her eyes narrowed skeptically as she turned and looked at me.

I just smiled and nodded. "Yeah, she's for real." After all, we were talking about the girl who had once become a fruitarian to protest the senseless killing of vegetables.

"Carrots have feelings, too," had been Savannah's battle cry back in the day.

Now as a chef, she was willing to slaughter baby carrots and squash and onions left and right. And yet, there was still no way she would ever hurt another human being. It wasn't in her fiber. But Lee would have to ask the questions, anyway. I had faith that she would come to the same conclusion soon enough.

"Are you going to interrogate me at police headquarters?" Savannah asked the inspector.

"That probably won't be necessary, not right away," Lee said, equivocating. "We'll need to examine the crime scene first, so I'm going to ask you to sit tight here in the bar area for a little while."

"Okay. Oh, but wait." Savannah held up her gloved hands. "Can I take these off?"

Lee shot me another glare, so I rushed to explain that while waiting for the police to arrive, Derek had come up with the brilliant idea to glove her hands to protect any evidence she might've picked up along with Baxter's blood.

Inspector Lee couldn't argue with Derek's logic, but

she wasn't happy with one part of my explanation. Turning to Savannah, she said, "You touched Mr. Cromwell's body?"

"No, I just touched that bloody knife," Savannah said. "It was sticking out of his stomach and I thought it would help if I got it out of him, but it didn't help. He died anyway."

"Aw, jeez." Lee looked at me and shook her head. "I'm having déjà vu all over again."

"Tell me about it," I muttered, and my stomach took another dip. As I'd realized earlier, Savannah's scenario with Baxter was alarmingly similar to my own experience the night of Abraham's murder. I'd managed to get plenty of his blood on my hands, too.

Inspector Lee turned to one of the CSI guys standing nearby. "Claypool, you got your kit with you?"

He gripped his heavy briefcase. "Never leave home without it."

"We'll need a couple of swabs and some evidence bags over here."

Claypool rushed over and set his silver case on an empty barstool. After carefully removing Savannah's gloves, he stuck them in separate bags and labeled the bags with a black marker. Then he pulled out a long cotton swab and a small vial of liquid. He rubbed the cotton tip over Savannah's bloody right palm, then added a few drops on the swab and watched it turn a different color. He dropped the swab into a straw-sized plastic container and snapped it shut, then repeated the procedure with her blood-smeared left hand.

"Better take her shoes and jacket while you're at it," Lee added. So Savannah slipped out of her chef's coat and her shoes and handed everything over to CSI Claypool, who packed it all into large evidence bags.

"That was fascinating. Thank you," Savannah said. "May I wash my hands now?"

"Yeah, hold on." Lee glanced around and spied the one female officer standing near the hostess podium, going over the surface with her flashlight beam. "Hey, Fleischman, can you accompany Ms. Wainwright here to the ladies' room?"

"You bet," Fleischman said, and jogged across the room to meet Savannah.

Jaglom approached with Derek. "Jan, the commander here tells me there were half a dozen other chefs here tonight, all old friends of the victim. They're all staying at Campton Place over in Union Square and Cromwell provided rental cars or limo service for all of them. I'm thinking we ought to have one of the uniforms round them up and get them over here for preliminary questioning."

Lee grimaced. "Tonight?"

"We have to," he said. With a shrug, he added, "If one of them is our guy, we could lose trace evidence if we wait till morning."

"Good thing I've got DVR," she muttered, then soldiered up. "Okay, let's do it. You want to bring 'em here or meet 'em down at HQ?"

"Might as well do it here," Jaglom said, glancing around the room. "Saves time and they can each walk us through it one by one."

Lee considered, then nodded. "Sounds like fun."

"Be right back." Jaglom motioned to the nearest uniformed officer and met him halfway. They talked for a minute, then the inspector wrote something on his notepad, tore the page out, and handed it to the cop, who nodded as he read it.

"We're going to be here all night," I muttered, and decided to kick my shoes off.

Derek said nothing, just nodded and put his arm around my shoulder.

Jaglom turned back to his partner. "I've asked Commander Stone to check out the kitchen with us. He was first on the scene and I want him to verify that nothing's been disturbed."

"Good plan," Lee said. "Let's get this done."

Derek and Jaglom led the way, followed by Inspector Lee and the two CSI guys.

I glanced around. My sister was still in the ladies' room with her police escort. One cop was on the phone and the other was still searching the front part of the restaurant. I decided to stick with Derek and the detectives and followed a safe distance behind them.

We turned down the hall and saw the fourth uniformed officer standing guard at the kitchen door.

"Marston." Jaglom nodded to the cop as he snapped on a pair of thin rubber gloves.

"Evening, Inspector," Officer Marston said.

Lee slipped her hands into gloves also, and then noticed me following her. "You're not going in there."

"I won't touch anything."

"That's right, because you're not going in there."

"But I need to make sure something wasn't stolen."

She didn't bother to hide her irritation. "What?"

I gave her the quick version. "Savannah gave Baxter a red leather book box I made. There's an old book inside. I didn't see it when we came in earlier and I'm worried it might've been stolen."

"A book," she said derisively.

I speared her with a look. "An extremely rare, very fragile, two-hundred-thirty-year-old book. It could provide a motive for the murder."

"I'll check on it," she said brusquely, and marched off to join her partner and Derek, already in the kitchen.

I lingered a few yards behind until Inspector Lee disappeared into the kitchen. Then I gave a little wave to Officer Marston, who nodded and pushed the door open for me.

"Thanks," I said, and slipped inside. Apparently, he hadn't gotten Inspector Lee's directive to keep me out. I wasn't about to give him a heads-up on that.

I pretended to be invisible as I hovered near the door. Peering around for the book box, I deliberately shielded my eyes from the sight of Baxter's body in the middle of the room. Unfortunately, I didn't have to see the body to know it was there. I could smell the blood. Had my ability to detect that acrid odor grown more acute because of the many crime scenes I'd come upon recently? Another weird question to ponder.

I ignored the police activity and focused on the walls and counters and shelves between the cooking and service areas. But I didn't see the book box or the cookbook itself anywhere.

Derek stood beside the back door leading to the alley. It was closed now. "This door was ajar when we arrived. I would wager that the killer exited here, ran down the alley, and disappeared."

"Who closed it?" Lee wondered aloud.

"I pushed it closed," Derek admitted, then explained, "I was careful. Didn't touch the handle, just shoved the wood panel with my shoulder. I didn't want to take the chance that someone would wander in."

"Probably a good idea." Jaglom crouched to study the lock and the door handle. "I tend to agree on general principle that whoever did it left this way. I can't imagine he'd go skipping through the restaurant and out the front door. He'd be sure to be seen that way."

"He or *she*," Lee added.

"The killer could also be a stranger who snuck into the kitchen through that open door," I said, busting myself. Now Lee would probably toss me out of the kitchen, but I had to say something to divert her from honing in on Savannah as her main suspect. "It could've started out as a crime of opportunity. The door was open. Baxter was the only one left in the kitchen and the thief might've thought he was easy pickings. But Baxter fought back and the guy grabbed the first weapon he could get his hands on. The fish knife."

They all stared at me and I shrugged self-consciously. "It's just a theory."

"Not a bad one," Jaglom said as he used his gloved hand to pull the door open cautiously. Stepping out into the back alley, he took a look around, staring to his right and left for several long moments. He pulled a small flashlight from his pocket and angled it in both directions, then walked out of sight. After a minute, he returned to the kitchen. "It's black as pitch out there at this time of night. And it's not an alley, just a passageway between buildings, maybe three feet wide, with a gate leading to the sidewalk. The gate's open, so I'm guessing that was the escape route. We'll need to get a search started ASAP."

"Too late to canvass the neighbors," Inspector Lee mused as she took a cursory look outside. "We'll get a team to go out first thing in the morning. Somebody might've seen or heard something."

Mrrooowww.

We all turned at the sound coming from the open door and watched a cat poke its head inside.

"Hey, kitty," Inspector Lee said, crouching down to lure the cat closer. When it rubbed its fat, furry body against her leg, Lee gently scratched its neck. "Where'd you come from? I'll bet you saw something bad going on here earlier. You want to talk about it?"

I stared at her in disbelief. Once again, Inspector Lee had managed to surprise me. "You're a cat lover?"

She stood and glared at me. "Wainwright, I thought I told you to stay out of here."

But I was paying attention to the cat. "Is it hungry?"

"I doubt it," Jaglom said. "That's the fattest cat I've seen in a long while."

"I suspect it's been well fed," Derek said dryly, picking up the big cat before the creature could wander farther into the kitchen. After holding it in his arms for a moment, he began to laugh. "Good lord, this animal is hugely pregnant."

"Aw, it's a mom cat," Lee said, giving it a quick scratch behind its ear.

"Kittens," I said eagerly, before I could stop myself. What was I thinking? This was an alley cat, probably feral. Except there wasn't an alley outside the door, just another building. Fine, she wasn't an alley cat, but still, I didn't need a kitten, for God's sake.

But the cat was friendly, with very pretty, attentive blue eyes. And Derek wouldn't have picked her up if she hadn't been clean. Her fur was mostly white, but her face was black and she had a few black spots scattered across her back and on all four paws. She looked like she was wearing four little black boots. I mentally named her Bootsie.

"She's well fed and cared for," Derek said, holding her up for a cursory examination. "But there's no collar. I wonder if she has a place to go home to."

"I hope she's not homeless," I said.

"We're working here, people," Lee groused.

But she'd already revealed her soft marshmallow center, so I just smiled and kept my mouth shut. She and Inspector Jaglom got back to the business of examining the body and the surrounding area for possible clues.

Derek reluctantly set the cat down outside and closed the heavy door to keep it out.

Bon chance, Bootsie, I thought, feeling a little sad that I wouldn't get a chance to see the pretty mom cat's kittens.

Derek noticed my look and gave me a sympathetic smile. There he went, reading my mind again.

"That knife is ridiculous," Inspector Lee said as she knelt near the body. "It's huge." She gingerly clamped the tips of her fingers around the end of the knife handle while the CSI guy leaned over and held a large evidence bag open for her.

"It's heavy, too," she added as she slid it into the bag.

Jaglom snorted. "I think that blade was bigger than my head."

Lee glanced over at her partner. "And that's saying a lot because we all know you've got a big head."

Jaglom pushed a thick strand of curling gray hair off his forehead. "My wife says a big head is a sign of wisdom."

"Your wife should be a stand-up comedian."

He chuckled. "She keeps me laughing."

For the next ten minutes, I stuck close to my unobtrusive spot near the swinging door, watching the detectives work when I wasn't scrutinizing every visible inch of the room in search of some spot where Baxter might have shoved the cookbook. There were cupboards and shelves everywhere, but they all seemed to be taken up by equipment or utensils or dishware.

With Inspector Lee occupied, I tiptoed along the back wall and carefully began opening the sliding cabinets. A stack of large stainless-steel bowls took up one entire shelf. I checked inside the bowls, but there was no book box hiding there. The other side held three extra food processors. The next cabinet revealed more large white plates on the bottom shelf, salad plates on the top.

I was growing discouraged. It was possible that the book was in here somewhere, but I remembered Baxter's reaction to receiving Savannah's gift earlier that night. It was beyond dismissive. Baxter had been downright contemptuous of the book and couldn't seem to get it out of his hands fast enough. Considering that response, why would he take the time to find a protective hidey-hole for a book he didn't want in the first place?

I wouldn't be surprised to find out he had flung the book across the room or tossed it on a wet counter.

So where was it? Had the killer taken it as a token or a prize? Had one of the other chefs casually lifted it with plans to keep it? Or did one of them have an even stronger reason for wanting the cookbook?

Did the book contain something valuable? I considered the recipes I'd read so far and rejected that idea.

But what about the intrinsic value of the book itself? Rare, unique, wonderful. How could anyone leave it behind? But not everyone loved books for their own sake. Maybe the killer had grabbed it to sell for quick cash.

I thought of Kevin's visible reaction to seeing the book. She'd certainly had her eye on it. Had she stolen it? I hoped not. Because right now, I was fairly certain that whoever had taken the cookbook was also the person who had killed Baxter.

I finally left the detectives to their business and wandered out to the bar to keep Savannah company. She had fallen asleep again with her head resting on her arms, so I whispered her name a few times.

She opened one eye and saw me. "I'm so exhausted."

"I know, Bugs." I sat on the barstool next to her. "Bad enough that you've been on your feet all day, but then you had to go through the trauma of finding Baxter dead. I blame myself for not forcing you to come home with us earlier."

"It's not your fault," she said.

Wasn't it? I wondered. It seemed to be my karma to come across dead bodies lately. And I wasn't even sure I believed in karma. Wasn't it like payback for something I'd done in a previous life? Whatever it was, finding dead bodies was getting to be a habit with me. And more and more frequently, the people I loved became collateral damage.

After another ten minutes, Lee and Jaglom walked back into the bar. Inspector Jaglom apologized to Savannah for keeping her waiting.

"That's all right," she said. "I know you're busy taking care of Baxter."

"Thanks for your understanding. Would you mind coming with me now to answer some questions?"

"Are we going to the police station?" she asked again. She was so tired, she sounded like a naive young girl.

"No, no. Let's just find a quiet table on the other side of the room."

"Okay." As she slid off her stool, I noticed her shivering, so I grabbed my coat and handed it to her. "Here, put this on."

"Oh, thanks, Brooks." She tossed it over her shoulders, pulled it tight around her, closed her eyes and sighed. "So much better."

My crazy bald sister could be outspoken, judgmental, and crabby as hell. But right now she looked so vulnerable, it almost broke my heart.

"May I sit with her?" I asked Jaglom. "I promise I'll be quiet."

He thought about it for a moment. "Sure."

I took her hand, and we followed the good-hearted inspector to the far corner of the room. He picked out a table for four and sat down across from us with his notepad open in front of him.

"So you're a chef," Jaglom began. "That must be an interesting way to make a living."

"I love it," she said. "My specialty is vegetarian cuisine."

"Ah. Now, I know that's a healthy way to eat," he said, patting his round stomach, "but I'm more of a burgers-and-fries man myself. Probably obvious, right?"

Savannah smiled and I wanted to hug him.

"Now, Savannah, can you tell me what happened tonight? After the restaurant closed, who else was here besides you and Mr. Cromwell? Just start wherever you want and I'll interrupt you if I have a question."

Savannah recounted everything she'd told me and Derek earlier. Jaglom stopped her often to ask her to repeat something or to clarify something else. She named all the chefs and brought up what Baxter had said about the fish knife. She remembered some details she'd left out of her explanation to me and Derek.

Suddenly the front door was shoved open, causing us both to jolt.

"What the hell?" Inspector Jaglom muttered, then relaxed as two techs wheeled a gurney into the restaurant. "It's just the team from the medical examiner's office."

"Hear we've got a pickup," one of the guys said, and the other one snickered. I could tell they were a regular laugh riot around the morgue. A serious-looking woman walked in behind them and waved to Inspector Jaglom. I figured she must be an assistant medical examiner.

Savannah looked stricken by the lackadaisical attitude of the techs.

"It's okay," I murmured, slipping my arm around her. I could feel her shaking.

"But they'll take him away," she whispered.

"Right. And they'll find out exactly how he died and maybe figure out who did it. That's a good thing. So just relax, okay?"

Easy for me to say. I'd forgotten all about Baxter being taken off to be autopsied. I shuddered at the thought.

Fleischman, the female cop, jogged over to lead the gurney guys to the kitchen. Within seconds they all disappeared around the corner.

Savannah stared at the front door for a full minute before Jaglom coughed tactfully. "Can we continue?"

"Yes," I said firmly.

Savannah nodded, took a deep breath, and began again. It took her a while to get back up to speed, but as she spoke about Baxter and her chef friends, she grew more animated and began to sound like her regular self.

The inspector took lots of notes and asked questions intermittently. He made Savannah repeat a few more things, assuring her that he just wanted to write the words down exactly as she related them.

He seemed to believe her. If that wasn't true, then he was definitely better at playing the good cop than his partner was. And as soon as that thought crossed my mind, I worried that Inspector Lee might show up suddenly to play the bad cop. I glanced across the room to check up on her and saw her deeply involved in an intense conversation with Derek. Good. I hoped he would keep her busy until it was time to go.

Some time passed before the assistant ME and her tech guys reappeared with their gurney. This time, though, they had a passenger, Baxter, zipped up inside a black body bag. The guys negotiated the tables and chairs expertly and rolled out the door as quickly as they had come in.

As silence fell, Derek approached the table. "I hope I'm not interrupting."

"Nope." Jaglom closed his notepad and shoved it back into his pocket. "I think that's it for now."

Savannah seemed surprised. "Are you sure?"

He pursed his lips. "I won't beat around the bush, Ms. Wainwright. You're a person of interest in this investigation, so I'll advise you not to leave town for the time being."

Savannah looked alarmed. "But I don't live in town. I live in Sonoma."

"She owns a restaurant in Dharma," Derek explained. "We always know where to find her."

I flashed him a grateful smile.

"I'm there all the time," Savannah added.

Jaglom glanced at all three of us before he nodded, then took his notepad out again and jotted down the name of the restaurant and several phone numbers.

"Please call me there anytime. I want to help." Savannah looked at me. "Can we go home now?"

"If it's okay with the inspector." I glanced at Jaglom.

He nodded. "You're both free to go for now."

"Then let's go." I shook hands with Inspector Jaglom. "Thank you so much."

He seemed to recognize that I was thanking him for being considerate to my sister, and he returned a gentlemanly salute. I just prayed that his amiability stemmed from his belief that Savannah was truly innocent.

Chapter 6

The female in almost every instance is preferable to the male, and peculiarly so in the Peacock, which, while superbly plumaged, is tough and stringy when chewed.
—*The Cookbook of Obedience Green*

Just as we were gathering our belongings to leave for the night, Savannah's chef friends trudged into the restaurant, herded by two cops. Every one of the chefs looked like the walking dead. They'd obviously been roused out of a sound sleep.

I would have had more sympathy for them if I hadn't been stuck here for the past few hours myself.

Colette saw Savannah first and ran to hug her. "I can't believe he's dead." She sobbed quietly on Savannah's shoulder.

"I know," Savannah said, sniffling. "It's horrible."

Kevin, looking stunned and bleary-eyed, plodded over and clutched them both. "We saw him less than two hours ago. It can't be true."

The group hug grew larger as the other chefs joined them. There were more sniffles and moans, and I had to walk away because I was starting to well up again. My eyes wouldn't survive the night if I kept crying. I didn't even like Baxter Cromwell, but I still couldn't keep the tears from falling as I watched and listened to his friends mourn him.

My gaze focused in on Margot, who stood on the sidelines watching and waiting, just as I'd seen her do before. After a moment, she approached Savannah and gave her what looked like a warm, meaningful hug.

"You poor thing," Margot murmured. "Have you been here the whole time?"

"Yes. I was so exhausted, so I went to rest in the ladies' room while I waited for my sister to pick me up, and then I walked into the kitchen and—"

"Savannah!" I cried.

"What?" She whipped around. "What's wrong?"

"I need your help with something."

"Okay, okay," she muttered, then looked at Margot. "I'll be right back."

I grabbed her arm and dragged her into the ladies' room.

"What are you doing?" she said irately. "What happened?"

I checked under the doors of the two stalls to make sure we were alone, then locked the door. "You can't discuss the details about what happened tonight with any of your friends. Especially about you finding Baxter and pulling the knife out of his gut."

"Why not?"

"Because from now on, this is a criminal investigation. If you discuss the details, you could be giving the killer a way to frame you for murder."

She groaned with impatience. "That's ridiculous."

But I could tell I'd frightened her, and I gripped her shoulders for emphasis. "Just please don't say anything to anyone except the police. Or me and Derek."

"I don't see what the big deal is," she whined. "My friends would never do anything to hurt me."

"Oh, really?"

"Yes, of course."

"I wish you were right, but unfortunately one of your friends could be Baxter's killer."

"Brooklyn, that's—"

I held up my hand to stop her. "Let's play a little game. Say I'm the killer."

"Oh, come on."

"Humor me. So you and I are talking and you confide in me that you're the one who found Baxter. And I'm fascinated! I want more particulars because, you know, we're friends. And you can't help but go into all the gory details about pulling that big, bloody knife out of him."

She made a face, but I could tell she was catching my drift.

"So when it's my turn to talk to the cops," I continued, "I let it slip that all those years ago in Paris, Baxter treated you so badly and cheated on you and finally dumped you. He hurt you really badly. I might elaborate on some of the fights you two used to have."

"You're getting silly."

I ignored her. "And when I'm asked to tell the nice detective what happened earlier, I'll tell him that I came back to the kitchen to get something I forgot, and I saw you and Baxter in the middle of a terrible argument. You were so angry with him, I was afraid to interfere, so I just left quietly."

Savannah frowned. "But we weren't arguing."

I rolled my eyes. She could be so obtuse sometimes. "I know you weren't. But I'm a desperate killer and I'm willing to do anything to escape being caught. So I have to make up lies, get it? Okay, so I also remember seeing that big, sharp fish knife right there on the counter next to you while you were arguing with Baxter. So I mention that to the cops."

"Why would you do that?"

"Because I don't want to go to jail!"

"Oh, right."

My sister was brilliant, but she was tired. I knew she understood what I was saying; it was just taking her some time to catch up.

"So as I talk to the cops," I continued, "I'm planting seeds, making stuff up, laying the groundwork to make *you* look like the guilty one. Because, after all, you were seen with the bloody knife in your hand. You told me all about it."

Savannah opened her mouth, then closed it.

"Do you get what I'm saying?" I asked, because I could never be sure she was paying attention.

"Yes, yes," she said crossly. "I get it. I still don't believe one of my friends could've killed Baxter, but I understand what you're saying."

"And you won't say a word about anything to anyone?" I reiterated.

"I said yes."

"Okay. We can go back out there now."

"Sheesh."

Fine, I was a pain in the neck, but at least my sister wouldn't go to jail. Not if I had anything to say about it.

Once the two detectives had everyone's names and basic information, they split up the interrogation duties. Lee took over the private dining room located off another hallway behind the bar, and Jaglom settled at the table at the far corner of the front room where he had interviewed Savannah earlier.

I wasn't sure if they had planned it that way or not, but Inspector Lee ended up interviewing all the men, while Jaglom spoke to all the women.

The cops had given Derek and me the okay to go home, but Savannah didn't want to leave her friends. She was worried that the police might cart one of them off to jail, so she wanted to be here to lend her support. She insisted she wouldn't be able to sleep, anyway.

I was about to protest when Derek murmured, "You know you want to stay, too."

It was true, damn it. So did that make me a crime

scene junkie? Or a homicide detective groupie? More
questions with no answers.

Since I was staying, I wanted to pay close attention to
what was going on. From my seat at the end of the bar, I
watched the interplay between Inspector Jaglom and
each of the chefs he interviewed. Occasionally I could
snatch a snippet of conversation—because I did indeed
have ears like a desert fox, as Savannah had claimed recently.

Then I overheard Kevin say the word *cookbook*. I
watched her carefully and saw her grit her teeth as she
rocked in her chair, holding her stomach as though she
was in pain. It was subtle, but I saw it on her face.

Was she talking about the cookbook Savannah had
given Baxter? She seemed agitated, but just as anxious
to hide her reactions from the inspector. Unfortunately
I couldn't hear the words she was saying.

I had to get closer, but discretion was key. I stood and
stretched and yawned, then said in a clear voice, "You
know, I think I'll be more comfortable waiting in one of
those padded booths."

Yeah, discretion was my middle name.

Halfway across the room, I slid casually into a booth,
got myself settled, and folded my arms on the table. Resting my head on my arms, I pretended to doze off. My hair
fell in a curtain over my face, giving me the perfect shield
for sneaking peeks at Kevin. I could hear her better, but
it was a little tough to see her through all my hair.

It gave me a new level of respect for Cousin Itt from
The Addams Family.

Kevin was still speaking so quietly that I could catch
only every other word or so. What I did hear, while intriguing, seemed to have nothing to do with the subject
of murder or bodies or bloody knives. Or even cook-
books.

But then one word she said jumped out at me. "Blackmail."

Blackmail? Was Baxter being blackmailed? He didn't

seem like the type of person who'd willingly pay off a blackmailer, even to keep an embarrassing or incriminating secret hidden. No, Baxter was the type who would expose the blackmailer to the world and reap the commercial benefits. But maybe not. I suppose we all had deep, dark secrets to hide.

Could Kevin have been blackmailed? She didn't seem overwrought as she discussed the subject with Inspector Jaglom, but again, I couldn't hear every word.

My eyes popped open. What if *Savannah* was the one being blackmailed? But wait. There was no way Savannah had ever done anything sordid enough to merit being blackmailed. And if she had, she would've told me or I would've guessed. Her ability to maintain a poker face was even worse than mine.

I tried to shake off the lingering worry and focused on Kevin's interrogation.

But now Jaglom was standing up, meaning the interview was over. What had I missed while my mind was wandering?

"Thank you, Ms. Moore," Jaglom said. "If we have more questions, we'll contact you."

Damn. *Cookbook* and *blackmail* were all I got from Kevin's conversation and not much explanation of either topic.

So I came up with my own theory. I could only go by her reaction earlier tonight, when Baxter revealed the cookbook. She had appeared shaken and angry. And just now, in her interview with Jaglom, she'd said the word and seemed to feel actual physical pain as she spoke it. At least, that's what it looked and sounded like to me.

I didn't think she could have faked that visceral reaction. And to me, her unhappy reaction meant that she couldn't have stolen the book from Baxter's kitchen. If she'd stolen it, she would have tried to look calm in order to hide her smug satisfaction about getting it.

Instead, she was distraught, and I wanted to hope that it meant she hadn't stolen the book and, therefore, couldn't have killed Baxter. At least, not in the scenario I was currently imagining.

Did that make any sense at all? I would have to think about it later and talk it over with Derek.

Jaglom waved to the cop across the room, who brought Colette over to be interviewed.

Jaglom couldn't hide his admiration for the beautiful blonde as he stood and waited for her to be seated. Then he sat down and asked Colette if she'd seen anything unusual that evening.

"Nothing at all," she said, her voice chirpy despite the late hour.

I had no difficulty hearing Colette talk. She had a distinctive, high-pitched voice that carried halfway across town.

And in a heartbeat I remembered meeting the woman when I was in Paris. She had stopped by Savannah's flat, but I was the only one home. She'd stayed for a few minutes, strolling around the apartment while making small talk. I asked her if she wanted to leave her friends a note or something, but she said she would catch up with them at school the next day. I didn't see her again during my visit.

Funny that I would remember her by her perky voice and not her appearance. I was usually good with faces and hers would be hard to forget; she must've altered her hair and makeup drastically since then. But that voice was the same.

Now Colette told Jaglom the same basic story that we'd heard from Savannah. Raoul had gone back to the hotel earlier than the others. He wasn't feeling well and Colette was worried about him.

Not so worried that she hadn't stayed an extra hour to drink with her old buddies, I thought.

"Frankly, I'm glad my husband left early," Colette said, fiddling nervously with her neck and the collar of her shirt. "He wasn't himself tonight."

"Why is that?"

"Well." She seemed to weigh her next words, then decided to go for it. "It might've had something to do with Baxter."

Jaglom looked up from his notepad. "Why do you say that?"

She sighed. "Well, he sort of hated him."

"Your husband hated Baxter Cromwell?" Jaglom said.

"Oh, I don't mean he *hated* him," she quickly corrected herself. "I mean, they were old friends. Well, friendly rivals, I guess you could say. All during our time in Paris, the two of them were in competition. You know, they were both good-looking and all the women were mad for them. Even the teachers liked them. They both graduated at the top of the class."

She was really full of it, I thought. Both men might've been considered handsome and talented, but Raoul was also smart and nice, with a good sense of humor. He was so well liked and so gifted that he'd been given several classes of his own to teach.

Baxter, on the other hand, was an opportunistic bastard who'd treated my sister shabbily. In my book, that lost him plenty of points on the handsomeness scale.

And as far as graduating at the top of their class, Savannah had been up there as well. The three of them had been the only ones of their group to go all the way through to receive Le Grande Diplôme, meaning that they'd successfully completed all the classes of all three levels of cuisine as well as the three levels required to obtain the Diplôme de Patisserie. They had also received the Diplôme de Sommellerie, the Wine and Management diploma.

So who was it that Colette was trying to fool? Besides the police? And why was she trying to make Baxter sound like such a saint? Even more important, why was she throwing her cutie-pie husband under the bus?

Jaglom turned the page in his notepad and looked across the table at Colette. "Do you know if any other chefs have similar strong feelings about Mr. Cromwell?"

Colette twisted her lips as though she was hesitant to tell the truth. "Well . . . there's Savannah, of course. You know all about her, right?"

My ears perked up as Jaglom leaned closer. "What exactly should I know about Ms. Wainwright?"

Colette bit her lip, then blurted, "She dated Baxter for a while in Paris, but he dumped her. It was an ugly breakup."

"I see."

No, you don't see! I wanted to shout. Savannah was the one who had dumped Baxter. Why was Colette turning it around? Why was she making Savannah sound like a woman scorned?

She was doing exactly what I'd warned Savannah about!

Colette whispered dramatically, "I think their biggest fight involved Savannah's sister, Brooklyn. She liked Baxter, too."

"Her sister?" Jaglom said. "Are you referring to Brooklyn Wainwright?"

"Yes," Colette said with a knowing nod. "Anyway, Savannah took the breakup really hard and was upset for a long time. I'm not even sure she's over it yet."

You bald-faced liar! Where was my laser gun when I needed it? That big mouth of hers had to be silenced.

I didn't dare sit up and look in her direction; if I did, Colette would feel my lethal vibes drilling into her devious mind. So I continued pretending to be asleep while taking copious mental notes. She wouldn't get away with incriminating Savannah. Maybe she thought Savannah was too polite to strike back. But I wasn't.

Even through my thin veil of hair, I could see Colette with both her elbows propped on the table and a look of phony concern on her face. I knew she was faking it. Anyone could see she was enjoying herself as she racked up the lies. I didn't like the way Jaglom kept nodding his head and scribbling rapidly. Great. He'd scored a major bean spiller. What would she say next?

Jaglom flipped back a few pages in his notepad. "I'd like to return to the subject of your husband's animosity toward Mr. Cromwell."

"Oh, no, there's no animosity," she said, running her hand up and down her neck. It was a nervous gesture she'd done several times. "Raoul and Bax are great friends, really."

So she was backpedaling now? Colette was definitely getting on my nerves.

Jaglom stared at her hard. "But you did say that your husband still harbored some negativity toward the deceased."

"Oh, you must have misunderstood. The two of them were laughing and joking with each other all night."

Huh? Clearly, she was having problems keeping her own lies straight.

Colette continued. "I guess I was being overly sensitive about Raoul's feelings tonight because, well, Baxter and I used to have a little *thing*. Raoul's still jealous about that, but he has no right to complain after he had his affair with Margot. And I'm almost glad he did because it evens the playing field—you know what I mean? Of course, Margot had an affair with Baxter, too. But then, who didn't? Oh, well, that's all ancient history. We're all great friends now."

Friends? This was how she dished about her *friends*? To the police? Did the woman have no filter? Ah, but at least she was an equal opportunity slanderer. And yet, despite all her mean-spirited blabbing about philandering and culpability, I wasn't getting a killer vibe from Colette. All I got was a stupid, disloyal, bitchy vibe. But again, I'd been wrong before.

Now I was wishing I could listen in on the men's conversations with Inspector Lee. Maybe if I invited Lee over for a glass of wine, she would share everything the male chefs had said. Not likely to happen, so maybe I could convince Derek to try and get the scoop from her.

Let's face it—I was nosy. But why not? This was my

sister's life on the line, and I was willing to do what I had to do to protect her.

I would've loved to hear Raoul's responses to the same questions Colette was answering so blithely. But I already knew that his basic good nature wouldn't allow him to carelessly incriminate another person. Unlike his wife.

"I don't believe for one moment that you're sleeping," Derek said quietly in my ear, startling the hell out of me.

I lifted my head slowly, hoping that anyone paying attention would think he had just awakened me. Glaring up at him, I whispered, "Shh! I'm trying to listen to her."

He slipped into the booth beside me. "I can hear her clear across the room."

"You can? Is Savannah listening, too?"

"I'm afraid Savannah's sound asleep."

I leaned against him. "We should all be asleep."

He put his arm around me and I got more comfortable, laid my head on his shoulder, and closed my eyes.

"We can leave anytime you're ready," he murmured.

I thought about it. Did I really need to hear what Margot told Jaglom? Yeah, I really, really did. She was the most suspicious one of them all, as far as I was concerned. But if we stayed ... ugh. It had to be three o'clock in the morning, but I didn't have enough energy to check.

I looked up at Derek, stifling a yawn. "I would love to stay longer, but I'm beat."

"My sleepy little private investigator." He gave me an affectionate squeeze. "Let's get you home."

He was mocking me, but I was too tired to protest. "I'm just glad you heard what Colette said. You can help me convince Savannah that she's a lousy friend."

"I'm not sure Savannah will believe you. She seems to find something positive in everyone."

"And that's a losing proposition."

He whispered, "So cynical, my love."

"I hate to be," I whispered back. "But you heard Colette try to implicate her, didn't you?"

"I did." His eyes narrowed. "And I didn't like it."

"Me neither." I told him how I'd dragged Savannah into the ladies' room earlier to warn her against telling anyone what had happened tonight.

"That was smart of you," he said. "She's too naive for her own good."

"What do you expect? She's a vegetarian."

He chuckled, then sobered as Inspector Jaglom finished his interview with Colette.

I glanced up at Derek. "Will you promise to talk to him tomorrow and find out what everyone said? Especially Margot."

"You know I will," he said with a half grin.

We turned to watch Jaglom push his chair back and stand as Colette walked away. Once he thought no one was looking, Jaglom stretched and yawned hugely. I couldn't help it—I began to yawn as well. Halfway through his yawn, Jaglom glanced over and saw Derek and me responding in kind.

Jaglom cut off his yawn and chuckled. I felt punch-drunk, wanting to laugh and cry at the same time.

Derek nudged me. "Time to go."

Chapter 7

Derek and I rose late the next morning. I was just starting breakfast when Savannah tiptoed into the living room, carrying her shoes in her hands.

"Where do you think you're going?" I called from the kitchen.

Derek leaned against the breakfast bar with his arms folded across his chest. "You weren't honestly thinking you could sneak out of the house, were you?"

"You're staying for breakfast," I added. "We need to have a little powwow."

Her shoulders sagged. "Brooklyn, I don't want to talk about it, all right? I'd rather just put it out of my mind for a while and I can't do that in San Francisco."

I glanced at Derek, who nodded. "It's on the news this morning. I turned it off."

I grimaced. We always had one of the morning news programs playing in the background. "We don't have to listen to the news."

"For how long?" she wondered.

"Never mind. You still have to eat breakfast, right?" I poured her a cup of coffee. Once she'd had something to eat, she would be more interested in talking. She needed to talk about it. I'd been waiting all night for her to talk about it.

"I'm not hungry." But she took a big gulp of the coffee I offered. She wrapped both hands around her mug as if she couldn't get warm enough.

"Thanks for the coffee," she said a moment later, setting the empty mug on the bar, "but I'm not staying for breakfast. It's just a ploy to get me to talk about Baxter and in case you didn't hear me, I don't want to. Besides, I've got a restaurant to run."

I saw the vulnerability she was fighting so hard to hide, and it worried me. It took a lot to shake Savannah. Derek simply ignored her words, reached for her arm, and led her over to the dining table, where he pulled out a chair for her.

Resigned, she sat down. "There. Happy?"

"Yes, love," he said.

Savannah looked up and seemed to notice Derek for the first time. She smiled, and who could blame her? Derek's broad shoulders, strong jaw, and beautiful dark eyes gave a girl plenty to smile about.

"Sorry I'm a grump," she said. "I didn't sleep very well last night."

"How could you?" I said from the kitchen. "You were traumatized by what you'd seen at the restaurant."

Her shoulders tightened and I instantly regretted my words.

Derek sat down across from her. "None of us slept much, but it would be worse for you. I'm sorry."

"Here. Eat." I plunked a plate of pancakes in front of her and Derek passed her the warm syrup-and-butter mixture I'd made. Comfort food. She stared at it for half a minute, then began to eat as though it had been a week since she'd last bothered. Which could be true. She was, after all, the sister who tended to skip meals.

"I had a nightmare," she said, once the pancakes were gone and she came up for air. "I dreamed that Baxter was still alive in the kitchen when I walked in and pulled the knife out. He looked into my eyes and said, 'You killed me.'"

Derek reached across the table and grabbed her hand. "Listen to me carefully. You did not kill Baxter Cromwell."

"That's right, damn it." I shook my finger at her. "You are innocent and we are going to prove it. We'll find the person who did it and they will pay."

"We?" Derek repeated softly, but I ignored him.

"I know you don't want to talk right now," I said. "But once you get home, if you remember something else about last night, any little detail at all, please call me or Derek."

"I will." She rubbed her face with both hands and the weariness in her voice tugged at my heart. "I'm so tired. And I still can't believe that someone I know might've killed him."

I leaned closer. "Sweetie, why don't you go back to bed for a while? You can leave in another hour or so."

"No, no. I've got to get home."

"Let me call you a driver, then," Derek said. "We were all up much too late last night."

She smiled as she pushed away from the table and picked up her plate. "Thank you, but it's not necessary. I'll be fine. Thanks so much for breakfast. And the pep talk. I appreciate both."

"I don't want you to worry," I said, following her into the kitchen.

"Once I'm back at work, I'll be fine."

I didn't believe that for a minute. After all, Baxter had been killed in his restaurant kitchen. If anything, her going back to work at her own restaurant could freak her out even worse. But I wasn't about to plant that thought in her head, so I kept quiet.

Because Savannah was still a little wobbly, Derek rode down in the freight elevator with her and walked her to her car. Then he took off for work and I was left alone in my studio.

I'd made Savannah promise to phone me when she got home. But knowing she might forget or, more likely, deliberately avoid talking to me, I called out the big guns: Mom and Dad.

"Hi, sweetie," Mom said cheerily. "Your father just left for the winery."

"That's okay. I called to ask if you'd keep an eye on Savannah for the next few days. Maybe stop by the restaurant later this afternoon and see how she's doing."

"Why? What's going on?" She was instantly on red alert.

Too late, I realized my strategic error. Knowing that she would find out eventually, I went ahead and filled her in on what had happened to Baxter last night. The conversation went downhill quickly.

"No!" Mom cried. "Oh, sweetie, I'm so worried about you. Are you okay?"

"Me?" I held the phone out and stared at it. Was she not listening? "Mom, Savannah's the one who found Baxter. She's the one who pulled a bloody knife out of his stomach. She's the one having nightmares. Not me. I'm fine."

"No, you're not," she insisted. "How can you be? You were there! You found your sister with a dead body. Good grief, what are you up to now? Ten bodies? Twelve?"

"But who's counting?" I mumbled. "Mom, this isn't about me."

"Of course it is."

"No, it's—"

"Let's get real here." Mom lowered her voice as though she was about to share a deep, dark secret with me. "We both know Savannah can pump ice water through her veins when she needs to. And I'm saying that with love. She might be a little flipped out right now, but she'll be fine in a few days."

"I guess so, but—"

"It's all to your credit that you're so concerned about her. But, Brooklyn, you're the one who's on the edge of gory here. I don't want to see you fall into the abyss."

"I think it's the edge of *glory*, Mom."

"See? You don't even know what edge you're on. That's not good. Why don't you drive up here for a few days? I can work one of my spells on you. I've got a new one that's a real crackerjack."

I almost groaned out loud. "No way."

"Fine, if that's how you feel. But you should still come up here. You can get a massage at the spa. Drink wine, relax. Your father would love to see you."

"I'd love to see both of you, but I—"

"Oh, I forgot to tell you!" she said, forging ahead. "I'm taking a workshop on exorcism. I think you're going to love the results."

Oh, sweet Jesus, I thought. *What next?* At least she hadn't suggested I try an espresso enema this time. I loved my New Age mother, but she was the original wackadoodle flower child. I took a deep breath. "Mom, I just called because Savannah needs—"

"Brooklyn, sweetie, don't worry," Mom said, sounding reasonable again. "I'll look after Savannah."

"Thanks, Mom. Honestly, I've never seen her so sad and helpless. It was hard to watch. She's usually strong and snarky."

"Yes, she is." Mom sighed. "Poor thing. I'll drive over to the restaurant to see how she's holding up."

"Thank you," I said, since I knew she was trying to placate me. "She'll appreciate it and so will I."

"I'm still more concerned about you. I know this must be troubling for you."

"Mom, please."

"Brooklyn, honey," she said, her voice softer now. "We've talked about this. The last time it happened, I had to give you a chakra adjustment over the phone. And the time before that, you were so upset that you even spoke about it to Robson. I know it took a lot of courage for you to open up to him and I admire you for it. And it's lovely that you're expressing your concern for Savannah instead of yourself, but I'm your mother and I know what hurts you."

What could I say? Except for the fact that she had succeeded in driving me to tears, I appreciated her concern.

"I love you, Mom."

She sniffed a few times and I realized I'd driven her to tears, too. Could I feel any more guilty?

"I love you more," she whispered.

I smiled. "I love you most."

She giggled, then sniffled once again before changing the subject. "Now, when will we see you and Derek?"

"I thought we might come up this weekend."

"Well, that's wonderful! Why didn't you say so?"

"I was getting around to it." Actually, I had only just decided after hearing her tear-soaked voice. But now that I'd brought it up, I knew it would be a good idea to get away to the wine country. I just hoped Derek would agree.

Mom and I finished our conversation and I gave Derek a quick call. He was happy with the plan to drive up to Dharma for a few days and thought he might like to work in the vineyards with my brother Austin. Now that our plans were firm, I was excited at the thought of seeing my friend Robin, who lived with Austin.

Before I hung up the phone, I asked Derek if he'd spoken to Inspector Jaglom about the chef interviews yet. He assured me he had left a message for the detective and would let me know if he heard back from him.

I filled my coffee cup, headed into my office, and found the copied pages of the old cookbook on my desk. I couldn't resist reading a passage or two before I settled down to work.

16 April 1774. I spend my mornings in the galley
with Cletus, the ship's cook. Cletus lost his scullion
in the storm that took Mrs. Branford so in exchange
for cooking lessons, I am content to do scullery work,
cleaning up, peeling potatoes, and gutting fish.

"Gutting fish." I gulped. Instantly, the image of a fish
knife and Baxter's lifeless, blood-covered body in the
restaurant kitchen lurched to the forefront of my mind.

"Okay, enough reading." I rubbed my stomach, then
set the pages aside and spent the next three hours at my
desk taking care of the business end of things. I tackled
my calendar first, since I had recently accepted a three-
week summer gig in Lyon, France, where I would be
teaching bookbinding at l'Institut d'histoire du livre. I'd
taught at the institute twice before and loved it there.

For many die-hard European book lovers, Lyon was
considered ground zero for the book arts. The institute
specialized in the history and practical application of
book design, conservation, and restoration. The city also
boasted a printing museum, and the municipal library
had its own superb book collection with fabulous dis-
plays of textiles and papers.

Besides being a slice of heaven for book wonks, Lyon
was also a beautiful old city built on a picturesque river.
There were other fine art and historical museums around
town, including a fascinating puppet museum. And since
it was France, there would be food. Lots of fabulous
food.

My old friend Ariel Hodges lived in Lyon with her
adorable French husband, Pascal. Ariel had moved to
Dharma years ago to work with my bookbinding mentor, Abraham, on several projects for the Sonoma Art
Institute. While in Dharma, Ariel and Robin and I had
become fast friends.

Now as I read over the Lyon offer and the brochure
they'd included, I was reminded that I hadn't heard from

Ariel and Pascal in a while, so I dashed off an e-mail message to them.

I signed the contract and made a copy, then stuck it in an envelope to mail. Now that I was committed, I wrote out a tentative schedule for the next six months, centered around the Lyon job. I thought how nice it would be if Derek could come along or meet me afterward for a little vacation time in Paris.

After a few minutes of happy daydreaming, I settled down to the task of paying all the bills related to my bookbinding business and balancing my checkbook.

I worked for another forty minutes updating my Web site with pictures of my latest projects and some nice new client endorsements.

As I went through the images I'd taken of the book box and pouch I'd fashioned for Baxter, I remembered my conversation with Inspector Lee the night before. So I attached the photos to an e-mail, wrote a quick note telling her what was included, and hit *Send*.

Feeling virtuous for having completed all the mundane tasks that kept my business alive and thriving, I gave myself the rest of the day to play. That is, to work. On books. Tearing them apart and putting them back together again. Fun stuff.

I rose from my desk chair and stretched my back before moving to my worktable. I'd already started on the first of six antiquarian books I'd been asked to restore for the Covington Library. My friend Ian had come up with an idea for a new exhibit of works by British women, featuring beautifully bound books by Jane Austen, the Brontë sisters, George Eliot, Beatrix Potter, Mary Wollstonecraft, and her daughter Mary Wollstonecraft Shelley, Ann Radcliffe, Georgette Heyer, the Mitford sisters, and many others.

Ian's plan had evolved from my bringing him several tall stacks of old paperback mysteries that belonged to my neighbor's aunt Grace Crawford. The books themselves were yellowed and falling apart, but the covers were fabulous. Screaming redheads, busty blondes, bulging eyeballs, and tantalizing silhouettes of women, all intent on luring men to their deaths.

Ian had created a small but eye-catching display of three dozen of these lurid noir book covers from the forties and fifties. He'd titled the exhibit "Pulp Fiction," and it was attracting lots of new visitors to the library every week.

Grace's collection had also included several Agatha Christie mysteries, and that's where Ian had come up with the idea to feature female English writers in his next exhibit.

Ian had obtained many of the English authors' books from the library collection itself and from a number of outside book collectors and benefactors. For the most part, the volumes were in beautiful condition, but Ian had given me six books that were in desperate need of my help. That was my job, after all: bookbinder extraordinaire, or so I liked to think.

All six of them were laid out on my worktable, waiting for me to attend to their needs.

I was almost finished with the first book, a small, charming edition of Mary Shelley's *Frankenstein*, published in 1818.

This was the easiest restoration job of the six. The smooth black morocco calfskin leather cover and endpapers were in exquisite condition, and the gilded title on the red embossed spine was still shiny. On a number of pages I found foxing, those patchy reddish-brown spots that looked like dirt but were thought to be caused by chemical reactions from microorganisms or oxidation. There were also two minor tears that Ian wanted me to fix. The back cover hinge had become loose, a simple problem that was easily remedied in five minutes.

I always liked to start with the easiest book first. That way, I could finish it up quickly and feel positive and upbeat about myself instead of feeling like a deadbeat loser incapable of accomplishing anything.

A neurotic approach, but it worked for me.

The book in the worst shape was a delicate first edition of Charlotte Brontë's *Jane Eyre*, published in 1847.

I often fancied myself a surgeon as I took unhealthy books apart and put them together again. But once in a while, I turned into a pathologist as I tried to unlock the mystery of why a particular book had fallen into such a sad state of disrepair. Occasionally it was simple. The owner had packed the book away in a rat-infested attic, or dropped it in a puddle, or left it on a sunny shelf to be baked half to death.

Poor *Jane Eyre* had required extensive examination before I was able to reach a diagnosis: bad bookbinding. Yes, there were sloppy bookbinders out there, and this pitiful creature had suffered because of it. To begin with, the boards were crooked, having been unevenly fitted to the spine. Also, the book was wider at the fore edge than it was at the spine. This meant that over the years, as the book was opened and closed, the text block and the boards worked against each other, ultimately resulting in the hinge popping loose.

I supposed it was unfair to blame this uneven structure problem entirely on the bookbinder. A century or two ago when the book was made, this type of design had been considered visually pleasing. Nowadays, though, it was one of the top five reasons a book was rushed to me for restorative surgery.

Along with all the skeletal problems *Jane Eyre* had suffered, it had dermatological issues as well. Its forest green, three-quarter morocco binding was peeling and rotted out. Part of it had turned to leather dust. The book would require a brand-new cover, obviously. It hurt my heart to see all the damage that had been done to the book, but knowing I could make it look beautiful again was a point of pride.

I decided to save this book for later and turned to the others that needed work. These last four were a matched set of Ann Radcliffe's formidable series, *The Mysteries of*

Udolpho, published in 1794. The four books were extremely rare and antiquarian, and I was honored to be working on them. Ian had insisted that they were in good condition, given their age. I suppose "good" was a matter of interpretation, since all four brown leather spines were rubbed bare of any gilding. Two covers were severed from their texts and the inner hinges on all four books were tender.

It was remarkable that despite the damage, there were no loose signatures. But the corners of each book were worn through to the boards. The pages were untrimmed and browned and there was foxing throughout.

The books had been rebound once before, so my strict book conservationist self felt free to construct new bindings. Although I would stick with historical accuracy, I planned to make them shine, adding new endpapers and retooling the spines with fresh gilding and raised bands.

In the box of books he had sent me, Ian had included a lengthy write-up for each volume. I enjoyed reading his comments and often gleaned some good historical perspective to guide me in my work.

This was one of the best things about the Covington Library exhibits—besides the books themselves. Ian and his team of curators took great care to give visitors a detailed picture of each book on display and the history behind it. They always included background information on the physical book: Who published it? When and where? Who was the bookbinder? What school of bookbinding did he follow? Why was a particular gilding tool or design popular at the time? What about the stitching? Was it unique to a school or a time in history? What was the provenance of the book? Who first commissioned it? Who had owned it subsequently?

Alongside that information were details about the story itself and the author's life: What genre did the book represent? What themes ran through the plotline? Who were the author's influences? What was happening in history during the time she wrote the book? Whom did she inspire?

I scanned the page Ian had sent on *The Mysteries of Udolpho*. Some of the descriptive information had to have come from the bookseller or auctioneer, such as the condition of the leather and vellum. But there was information about the author, too. I had never read *Udolpho*, so I was fascinated to discover that Radcliffe was credited with establishing the Gothic genre of fiction and had directly influenced Jane Austen's *Northanger Abbey* and Charles Dickens's *Little Dorrit*, among many others.

My skills would be tested on these four volumes, mainly because they all had to match exactly. But that would come later.

I picked up the first one and began with the simple task of brushing each page until the book was completely free of dust, dirt, and the occasional tiny bug carcass. Some bookbinders preferred a soft brush, but I liked to use a slightly stiff, short-bristled brush to get at every tiny grain that tended to gather in the center folds.

As I worked, I munched on my favorite snack, caramel chocolate kisses. I had become adept at unwrapping the little treats and popping the candy into my mouth without actually touching the chocolate, so I was able to keep my hands clean.

This is an advanced skill. I wouldn't recommend it to amateurs.

It was almost four o'clock before I realized I was starving for real food and more than ready to make dinner. I covered the books with a white cloth, hopped off my high work chair, and walked back to the kitchen.

I checked the fridge to see what I could make and found leftover chicken and tortillas. There was still time to run to the market to buy the rest of the ingredients for tacos. Yes, I was actually capable of making tacos. I could shred the chicken and chop veggies and grate cheese. It was just cooking and baking that required more skill than I possessed.

Making a mental list, I grabbed my purse and keys and left the house, carefully locking the door behind me.

At the market, I picked up all the necessities for tacos. Then, on a lark, I wandered down a few more aisles to gather the ingredients to make another syllabub. I couldn't screw it up any worse than I'd already done. It was essentially a pudding, for God's sake. My mom used to make pudding all the time when I was a kid. Although, to be honest, it came in a box and she just added water. But still, I knew I could do this. And if I succeeded this time, Derek wouldn't look so squeamish the next time I mentioned I was cooking dinner.

The syllabub was a disaster. Again.

How was it possible to make something that was lumpy in some spots and runny in others? It was a puzzle. But at least it didn't curdle like it had the last time. That was nasty.

And luckily for me, Derek spent the hour before dinner on the phone with one of his brothers, Dylan, who was on his way to Singapore for some sort of international man of mystery conference. That's what I imagined, anyway, since Derek and his brothers had all held exalted positions in the military or government service in the past, and some of them currently.

So while Derek was preoccupied with his phone call, I'd prepared the taco ingredients, putting each in its own bowl. After whipping up a batch of margaritas, I'd experimented with dessert.

I was stuffing the lumpy, runny, pudding-y mess down the garbage disposal, swearing and muttering under my breath, when Derek came into the kitchen.

"Perfect timing," I said, pasting a bright smile on my face. "Dinner's ready."

"Everything looks delicious," he said. Brushing my hair off my cheek, he kissed my temple and my ear, sending zings and shivers through my system.

"Can't miss with tacos," I said lightly.

"I'm sorry I wasn't more help," he said, then helped immensely by pouring me my first margarita.

*   *   *

The next day, over coffee, I read more of Obedience Green's diary. These pages were so much easier to read than her recipes, which I didn't seem to be able to fathom at all.

> *27 August 1774. I have hired a butcher. Our barnyard is filled with plump pigs which are thriving whilst my master is starving for their meat. Quandary: I have never killed an animal for its meat and I don't believe myself capable of doing so. Truth be told, I've eaten meat but once. At Budding House, our meals consisted of grains in watered milk and an occasional potato.*

> *28 August 1774. I took to my bed last evening with an apoplectic pain in the head. Henceforth, I shall limit my menu to potatoes rather than subject myself to another pitched battle in the barnyard between butcher and livestock.*

> *31 August 1774. Mr. Grunwald, being the butcher, arrived with a wheelbarrow filled with pig meat he'd prepared for roasting and stewing. To dissuade me from my vow to eschew animal flesh, for which he blamed himself, he offered a morsel of bacon he had smoked himself. Unwilling to further shame Mr. Grunwald or myself, I agreed to taste the tidbit and nearly swooned from its goodness. Now verily, my mouth waters at the thought of dining on such delicacies.*

Who didn't like bacon? I thought with a happy sigh.

I put the diary pages aside and headed for my workshop, where I spent the rest of the morning cleaning up the four *Mysteries of Udolpho* volumes. I was so tempted to stop working and start reading the story, but the work came first. Plus, if I finished these books, I could start tearing apart the *Jane Eyre*. That was where the real fun happened.

I yawned. I hadn't slept well, and while tossing and turning, I decided I wanted to re-create the book box I'd made for Baxter. I'd slipped out of bed and spent an hour in my studio, searching through swatches of leather hide, trying to decide if I had enough of the exact color I'd used before. Derek finally woke up and dragged me back to bed.

So now I was a little obsessed with making a new book box. Before I could do that, though, I would have to finish these books for Ian. But since I needed to wait for the glue to dry on one of the volumes, I took a quick break to study my leather pieces again to see if I had the perfect piece for a new box. Only a true book lover could relate to the excitement I felt at that moment. I could be such a geek sometimes.

I headed back to the kitchen to pour myself another cup of coffee and was returning to the studio when the phone rang. It was Inspector Lee.

"Hey," she began, "I wanted to thank you for sending those photos of the book."

"You're welcome. I thought about delivering them in person, then realized e-mail would be faster."

"Gotta love modern technology."

"So I don't suppose you've found the missing book yet," I said.

"Give me a break with the damn book, will ya? I'd like to find the killer first."

"Find the book and you'll find the killer," I said in my best Obi-Wan voice.

"It doesn't always happen that way, Grasshopper."

"I know," I muttered. Inspector Lee was being way too polite, even as she disagreed with me.

"So, listen, I need some more info," she said, finally getting to the reason she'd called.

I'd figured she wasn't just calling because we were new best friends. "Sure, what is it?"

"I need to know how big that book box thing was," she said. "I couldn't tell from the pictures you sent."

"I should've given you the dimensions in the e-mail. Sorry about that. The box is twelve and a half inches long, nine and three quarters inches wide, and three and a half inches deep."

"Just happened to have those measurements on you, huh?"

"Sure did." They were fresh in my mind because I'd been measuring leather scraps for the new book box. If I wanted to cover it in black leather, I had enough in stock. But if I wanted to repeat the dramatic dark red I'd used for Baxter's gift, I would have to order more.

"Okay, thanks, Wainwright," Lee said. "Talk to you later."

"Wait," I said. "What's happening with the investigation? Did you talk to the other chefs yet? Do they all have alibis? Have you arrested anyone?"

There was a pause, and then she asked, "Did you graduate from the police academy and forget to tell me?"

"No," I said, drawing the word out. "But my sister's involved, so I'm curious. Besides, I thought we were friends."

She snorted a laugh. "Good one. I'll keep you posted."

"Promise?"

She was still laughing as she hung up.

Chapter 8

To test the freshness of an egg, hold the great end to your tongue. If it be warm, it is new; if cold, it is rotten.
—The Cookbook of Obedience Green

The next day Savannah called me. "I've invited the chefs to Arugula for dinner next Monday night. You're coming, too."

I was puzzled but pleased by the invitation. "Are you having some kind of a wake for Baxter?"

"We'll do something more official later in the week. But this dinner is just a chance for us to get together for old times' sake."

Who was I to turn down dinner at Arugula? Savannah did the most amazing things with veggies, even for a die-hard red-meat fan like me. "I'd love to, but I'll have to check with Derek first. Can I call you back?"

"Derek already knows," she said.

Well, that was weird. "You already talked to him?"

"Yes."

Now I was just plain puzzled. "What's going on?"

She huffed. "You know how that detective told me not to leave town and then Derek told him I live up here in Dharma and I own a restaurant so everyone knows who I am and where I can be found most of the time?"

"Yes." I remembered all too well what Jaglom had said.

"Okay. So I thought it would be nice to invite everyone up here to see my place and have dinner. I called Kevin first and found out that the cops told her and the others the same thing. Like, don't leave town. So nobody is allowed to leave San Francisco, which is a complete drag. So I called Derek."

She called Derek before calling me? I guess I couldn't blame her. I would've called him first thing, too. It was sort of like having a doctor in the family. If you were having sharp pains in your side, you called your brother-in-law the doctor, right? So if somebody in my family was having trouble with the cops, who else would they call but Derek? It made perfect sense.

"So what happened?" I asked.

"Well, Derek calls the detective and next thing I know, Kevin calls me back and says the cop called her to say they can all come for dinner, as long as Derek is here as our chaperon."

"Interesting," I said, wondering what Derek thought about babysitting a roomful of murder suspects. Knowing him, it would probably strike him as just another day at the office. "I'll call you right back."

A minute later, Derek confirmed the story. "That's right, I spoke to Jaglom for quite a while. He's allowing the dinner to go forward as a favor to me."

"So you're playing chaperon."

"I prefer that term to babysitter." I could hear the smile in his voice. "But it's not a bad assignment, all things considered. Your sister is an excellent chef."

"Good point," I said. "And you don't mind staying over in Dharma Monday night?"

"If Savannah is cooking, I absolutely insist. But I'll probably have to spend half the day on the phone with my office."

"I don't mind if you don't," I said, then changed the subject. "Did Jaglom give you any hints about the chefs?"

He knew what I was asking. "As a matter of fact, he wanted to give me a heads-up on who to watch out for."

"That's right, you'll be in charge of the whole gang. So what did he say?"

Derek hesitated, then said, "Margot says she heard Kevin threaten Baxter."

I scowled. "I don't believe it."

"I didn't think you would, but that was her statement. She claims that she followed Kevin back to the kitchen after Baxter opened Savannah's gift. And she overheard Kevin say to Baxter, 'I'm going to kill you for that.'"

I pondered the statement, then sighed. "Oh, hell. Kevin really did look angry enough to kill him."

"Yes, she did."

"Did Jaglom say anything about that?"

"He thinks Kevin's hiding something from the police. She mentioned that Baxter was given an old cookbook and she thought maybe someone wanted it. But she wouldn't go into detail about it."

I nodded. "I heard her say the word *cookbook* to Jaglom, but I couldn't hear what she said about it. And she also used the word *blackmail*. Did Jaglom mention that?"

"No. But perhaps Jaglom is keeping something back from me."

"Darn him," I said. "What else did Margot say?"

"She told Jaglom that Baxter was a rat bastard and she's glad he's dead. But she didn't kill him."

"Of course she'd say that," I murmured. "But it's interesting to know what she really thought of him."

"No one liked the man," Derek surmised. "Each of the chefs who came to our table had negative feelings for him. They all hated him."

"Except Savannah."

"True," he said. "And yet your sister had the best reason to hate him."

"But she didn't kill him," I said quickly. "Colette

claimed that Margot slept with Baxter. Maybe he dumped her. But then he invited her to cook at his new restaurant, so she must have gotten over it. Unless . . . never mind. I'm going in circles."

"And I've got a client arriving in a few minutes."

We hung up a moment later and I called Savannah back to officially accept her dinner offer. I loved her cooking, of course, but I was even more excited by the prospect of having dinner with all those suspects . . . er, chefs.

I wondered if one of them would already be in jail by Monday's dinner. I hoped so. I was already antsy to get to the bottom of Baxter's murder investigation. Derek thought Inspector Jaglom might be holding back information, and if that was true, it wasn't fair. They'd put Derek in charge of the suspects, so he should've gotten every last detail the police had. I was tempted to call Inspector Lee myself, but I knew that would not turn out well.

Of course, I could always turn on any TV station and hear wild-eyed speculation about each of the chefs involved. The crime news networks featured round-the-clock coverage of Baxter's murder, with segments called "Bad Boy Bump-Off," "Cuisine de Carnage," and "Kitchen Crimes." Hungry newshounds were turning over every rock in the city, looking for dirt on anyone remotely involved in the case. Finally, Derek and I stopped watching television altogether, which was probably a good thing on any number of levels.

To distract myself, I headed for the bedroom to start packing for our weekend in Dharma. As I scoped out my wardrobe for the big Monday night dinner, I found myself hoping that one of the chefs would share some tips on how to avoid lumps in my syllabubs.

I had to wonder what it said about my life that I was more interested in obtaining dessert tips than in the fact that I would be dining with a murderer.

Saturday morning, Derek and I got an early start for Dharma, trying to avoid the usual weekend wine country traffic. As we breezed across the Golden Gate Bridge in Derek's ridiculously elegant black Bentley, we held hands and chatted about the latest plans for our apartment expansion.

It was early spring and the morning sun shining through the moonroof warmed my shoulders. The choppy surface of the bay glittered like a thousand diamonds. Everything seemed clean and new and crisp today. Or maybe it was just me and my happy mood.

Listening to Derek's ideas and plans for our future was like being in a dream. Sounded sappy, but really? He was perfect for me. Everything I'd always wanted in a man, but never really expected to have. No wonder it was so hard to keep the smile off my face. Every minute or so, he would squeeze or kiss my hand as he spoke about things he hoped we would do together. Design our new living space. Visit his parents in England. Sneak away for a long weekend in Chicago or New York. Sweet.

Oh, I still had moments when I doubted that Derek could really love me. I chalked it up to a quirk of human nature that made most people insecure when it came to trust and love and all those matters of the heart. But in my case, I had no idea why. I'd been raised by two wonderful people who had shown their immense love for each other and their children every day of my life. Why wouldn't I automatically expect to experience the same joy and fulfillment in my own life?

I sighed. It was another mystery for the ages. But for now I refused to dwell on doubts and instead vowed to enjoy every minute of our time together. Just in case, I offered up a little prayer to any gods who were listening, to please make us always happy to be with each other.

"Brooklyn, love, did you hear me?"

I was jolted out of my reverie. "What? Sorry, I was thinking about . . . never mind. What did you say?"

"Have you decided if you'll speak with Robson while we're in Dharma?"

"Oh, you mean about the ... Yeah, that." I'd told Derek about my mother's reaction to Baxter's murder and how she was more worried about me than about Savannah. Derek agreed with Mom's reasoning. He also agreed that having another conversation with Guru Bob might be helpful.

"I'm not sure it'll do any good, practically speaking," I said. "I mean, it's not like he can put an end to murder."

"True."

"But talking to him always makes me feel more at peace with myself."

Derek nodded. "Things do seem calmer when he's around."

Guru Bob, otherwise known as Avatar Robson Benedict, was my parents' spiritual advisor and leader of their commune, the Fellowship for Spiritual Enlightenment and Higher Artistic Consciousness. He had established the group more than twenty-five years ago when he and a few hundred followers had moved to Sonoma County and purchased a thousand acres of prime wine country farmland.

My parents believed that Guru Bob was a man of divine higher consciousness, whatever that meant. He was certainly compassionate and a good listener. And he was smart. He saw the big picture, not just in spiritual matters but in everything. He also recognized a good investment when he saw one and had enjoyed watching his family — as he called all eighteen hundred of us — prosper over the years. With our thriving winery, thousands of acres of primo grapevines, and a small town center filled with charming stores and upscale restaurants, the commune had grown rich and the members eventually made the decision to incorporate the town. The group had voted to name our little corner of the world Dharma.

Strictly speaking, the word *dharma* meant *law*, but in a broader sense it meant "to live in harmony with the law." Or as Guru Bob chose to interpret the word, "to follow the Path of Righteousness." This was the basis of his teaching, and his followers thought it was the most appropriate name for the home they had found with him.

Derek cracked open the moonroof and let the outside air filter through the car.

"The cool air feels good," I said, then glanced at him. "I guess I'll make up my mind when we get there. See if an opportunity presents itself to talk to Guru Bob."

"Sounds sensible."

"Oh, and I almost forgot to tell you," I said, changing topics. "My mother has announced that she's taking a workshop on exorcism."

"That's a bit disturbing," he said, as a small furrow of concern appeared on his brow.

And who could blame him? My mother was a wonderful woman and I loved her, but her experiments in the realm of otherworldliness could, and often did, get out of hand.

"I thought she was going to be a witch," he said.

"She's that, too," I said. "I'm trying to keep an open mind. She's threatened to perform a protection ritual for me and I'm a little worried that she'll try to work in some devil extraction chant."

"I wouldn't be surprised," he muttered, then chuckled. "Your mother is certainly one of a kind."

"Isn't she?"

"And on the positive side, you can always use the extra protection."

I smiled, grateful that Derek appreciated my mother's quirks as much as I did. The two of them were great friends, having once conspired with each other to save my life, using a pizza and not much else. It had brought them a closeness I almost envied sometimes.

Derek and I didn't talk much as he skirted the flat, wide marsh and wildlife area along San Pablo Bay before turning onto Highway 121 and heading north toward Sonoma wine country.

Finally I turned to him. "I don't suppose Inspector Jaglom ever called you back."

He smiled. "He did call back."

"Well, don't just sit there driving," I said. "Tell me everything."

Sadly, there wasn't much to tell, despite the fact that Inspector Jaglom had always been deferential to Derek.

"Nathan phoned me back to reiterate his earlier warning that I call him if anything untoward occurs during the dinner."

"That's it? He didn't give you any more meat?"

"No meat."

"But you're in charge of these characters for the night." I frowned. "He should've gone over all their alibis with you. Their quirks. Turn-ons. Pet peeves."

His mouth twisted in a smile. "He did give me a number of overall impressions. For instance, Montgomery was seriously overwrought."

"Like we needed a cop to tell us that," I muttered. "And it's not really fair. I know Monty calls *himself* a drama queen, but he isn't. Well, once in a while maybe. But that's true for everyone." Except Derek, I added silently.

Derek paused to check his rearview mirror, then continued. "Nathan also told me that Peter appeared suspicious and nervous. And that Raoul charmed Inspector Lee to such an extent that Nathan finally had to tell her to stop talking about him."

"Good to know she can be charmed," I said. I could relate to Lee's reaction. Raoul was irresistible to most women. Except maybe his own wife. "What did he say about Colette?"

Derek glanced at me. "He thought she was lying."

"Really? I thought so, too. And it annoyed me that she tried to make everyone sound culpable, especially Savannah. And her own husband! Did Jaglom give you his opinion about her?"

"He thought she came across as insecure and shallow," Derek said, frowning. "She talked too much, and that made him wonder what she might really be hiding."

"Wow," I said. "Way to make a good impression."

But as soon as I said it, I felt a tug of sympathy for Colette. I immediately gave myself a stern internal lecture. Feeling pity for Colette was stupid and contrary to my own best interests, considering how she'd practically slandered my own sister.

There. I felt better. "What did he say about Margot?"

"He liked her," Derek said. "She made him laugh. She also offered to cook for him, which is apparently the way to touch his heart."

"Mine, too." I shifted in my seat to get a better look at Derek. "Did he say anything about Savannah?"

Derek reached for my hand and I took that as a really bad sign.

"Something's wrong," I said. "What did Jaglom say?"

He squeezed my hand. "He said he liked Savannah very much and hoped she wasn't guilty."

"Oh, great." I made a grouchy face. "That means he's not sure yet." I refused to dwell on that detail. I knew Savannah was innocent and it was only a matter of time before the police realized it, too. "Did he say anything else? Any dark secrets? Did he tell you who his chief suspect is?"

"Give me a minute," he said, checking the rearview mirror again. The car ahead of us was moving too slowly, so Derek waited a few more seconds until he got a clear view of the road ahead, then revved the engine and passed the car. Once we were back in our own lane, he said, "Except for Colette, Jaglom didn't single out anyone else in a negative way."

"Okay, did he give you any positive impressions of anyone?"

"Yes. Raoul is madly in love with his wife. Kevin is obsessed with an old cookbook."

"He still didn't mention anything about blackmail, did he?"

"No, nothing," Derek said, as his eyes narrowed in deliberation. "And that's interesting. You heard her say the word, yet Jaglom said nothing. It makes me think the subject of blackmail might be a hot topic for the police. We'll have to keep our eyes and ears open for any hints."

"Yes, we will." I settled back in my seat and spent the next few minutes lost in thought, absorbing the news. Before I knew it, we had reached the small town of Glen Ellen, where live oak trees sheltered the highway like a tunnel. I loved these old trees with their dark, gnarly branches that twisted and turned and dipped before spreading up to the sky.

For me, the crooked old oaks typified Sonoma County and its rustic, rugged terrain. Our wine country was not the manicured green hills and refined tourist mecca that Napa was famous for. No, we were still the Wild West compared to our more civilized neighbors over the hill. And that worked for us.

Another mile farther and we turned onto Montana Ridge Road and headed toward Dharma.

Things had improved around here since the first time my family had traveled up Montana Ridge to our new home. Back then, this had been a pitted one-lane gravel road lined with flat-roofed farmhouses whose front yards featured rusted-out appliances and automobiles on cinder blocks.

At the time, we kids were not impressed. Where in the world were our parents taking us?

Nowadays, though, Montana Ridge Road was two—count 'em, two!—lanes wide and freshly paved. We'd come a long way, baby. Stately oak trees lined the winding road at intervals, and those boxy old farmhouses had either been spruced up or torn down to make way for more vineyards. The fact that Dharma was now a popular wine country destination spot had helped spur the beautification effort.

More twisted, knotted live oaks shaded our way as we drove down Shakespeare Lane—Dharma's main street, known far and wide as "the Lane." We passed through the charming center of town and began the climb up Vivaldi Way to my parents' home, situated at the crest of the hill.

As soon as we parked, I heard the screen door slam and watched Mom and Dad come rushing down the front porch steps.

"You made it!" Mom cried as she dashed for the car. Today her blond hair was pulled back in a ponytail. She was dressed sedately in a homemade tie-dyed sage green skirt that swirled down to her calves, a pale yellow sweater, and a snug, deep green vest that I knew she'd knitted herself. Rugged brown boots completed the outfit. And yes, for my mother, that was considered sedate.

Dad wore his usual plaid flannel shirt with worn blue jeans and work boots. As soon as I opened my car door, he had my small weekender suitcase in his clutches.

"Hey, kiddo," he said fondly, dropping the suitcase to pull me into his arms for a tight hug. "Missed you."

"Missed you, too, Dad." I breathed in the familiar hints of wood smoke, peppermint, and Old Spice, and knew I was home.

Mom had gone around the car to greet Derek with a hug, but was back to grab me as soon as Dad let me go.

"There's my girl," she whispered as she held on to me. Finally, she reached out and stroked my hair a few times. "You look so pretty today. So happy."

"I am happy, Mom," I assured her quickly. "Promise."

She pressed her fingers to the middle of my forehead and chanted softly, "*Om shanti . . . shanti . . . shanti.*"

It was the Sanskrit word for *peace*, and touching the middle of my forehead was like connecting to my center of consciousness, my third eye. I closed my eyes and felt my shoulders relax. When repeated three times, *Shanti* was said to safeguard the receiver from the three stresses or disturbances brought on by nature, by the modern world, and by one's own negativity.

I opened my eyes and met her worried gaze. "I swear I'm okay."

She sniffled once, then nodded. No tears, thank goodness. I had sympathetic tear ducts and nobody got away with crying alone when I was around.

"It's wonderful to be here, Rebecca," Derek said as he clicked his key to lock the car doors. "Thank you for inviting us."

Derek was the only person besides Guru Bob who called my mother by her formal name. She usually corrected people and told them, "Call me Becky," but when Derek did it, she would go all giggly. It might've had something to do with that accent of his.

"It's our pleasure," Mom said, patting his arm as we all strolled up the walkway to the front porch. "We're just thrilled you're willing to spend time here with the old folks."

I snorted at that line. My parents looked and acted younger than anyone I knew. My siblings and I had been teasing them about their youthful exuberance for years now.

"It's such a beautiful day, isn't it?" Mom said cheerfully. "I hope you're hungry because I've made way too much food for lunch."

Derek tried to be casual, but I could swear I saw his ears perk up. "Did you happen to make your Crazy Delicious Apple Crisp?"

Derek was a junkie for Mom's apple crisp. She made it with apples picked fresh from her small orchard growing on the side of the hill below the back terrace. The spicy, lightly sweetened apples were topped with crunchy, crumbly, crispy layers of deliciousness, and she served it with a hard caramel sauce that made grown men moan.

"Of course I did," Mom said. "I made it just for you."

"I don't suppose you'd consider running away with me, would you?"

Mom beamed like a schoolgirl. "Silly man."

"Don't tease me, Rebecca," Derek said, touching his hand to his heart. "When it comes to your apple crisp, I'm deadly serious."

Dad slapped Derek's back jovially. "Don't blame you, dude. But I'm afraid I can't let her go."

Derek shook his head in mock defeat. "You're a lucky man, Jim."

"And a hungry one," he said, chuckling.

Mom rewarded Derek with a sweet smile as she tucked her hand into Dad's.

I loved that Derek was able to joke with my parents. For a big, bad, dangerous international spy guy, he had a great dry sense of humor. It was one of the qualities that had first attracted me to him. Well, that, and the fact that he was handsome and strong and sexy and willing to catch me whenever I fainted.

"You're pretty lucky yourself," Dad said to Derek.

"Don't I know it," Derek said, his lips curving in a private smile for me.

Mom led the way down the wide hall toward the guest room. "I hope it's okay that I've invited the whole town for lunch."

"The whole town," Dad repeated emphatically.

Mom waved her hand lightly. "Well, at least fifteen people, anyway."

"Sounds like a party," I said.

At the end of the hall, Mom pushed the door open to the guest room, then left us to settle in and unpack before everyone else arrived at noon. The room had formerly been the childhood bedroom I'd shared with my younger sister, China, and often with my friend Robin. Mom had redecorated it in warm brown and taupe shades to accommodate more grown-up visitors. Namely, Derek. Thank goodness, because the shocking-pink Hello Kitty bedspreads and matching lampshades would have been met with his howling laughter.

In my defense, the Hello Kitty motif had been China's idea. I'd wanted a Nirvana bedspread, but Mom claimed she couldn't find one.

Twenty minutes later, Derek went off to track down

my dad in hopes of doing a little wine-barrel tasting while I headed into the kitchen to help Mom.

She was stirring something in a pot on the stove, but turned when I walked in. "The weather's so nice, I cleaned off both picnic tables on the terrace."

"Okay, I'll set the . . . Whoa." I gazed around the kitchen. "You weren't kidding, Mom. You cooked way too much food."

"It won't go to waste," she said easily.

"No way." I arranged glasses on a tray to take outside. "They don't call us the thundering hordes for nothing, right?"

Growing up, it had been my father's pet name for his six rowdy kids. Especially when Mom would call us in for dinner.

"Is that chili?" I asked, getting close enough to take a whiff of the zesty mixture. "Smells spicy."

"Tastes good, too. I think it's my best batch yet. And let's see, we've also got hot dogs and turkey dogs, hamburgers and veggie burgers, green salad, potato salad, Savannah's special coleslaw, tabouli. Robin baked a cake and I've got apple crisp and ice cream. And berries." She glanced around, frowning. "Oh, and I threw together a pan of lasagna and a shepherd's pie, just in case."

"Just in case of what? The Apocalypse?"

"Oh, you know." She shrugged good-naturedly. "In case we run out of food. It could happen."

Right. "Guess I don't need to make my guacamole," I said, frowning at the small shopping bag that held all the ingredients I'd brought with me.

"Of course you should," Mom said. "We love your surprises."

"Thanks, I think." My family was used to my bad cooking and odd recipes, but this one wasn't my fault. A few years ago, I called Savannah to get a good recipe for guacamole, but our connection was scratchy and I misunderstood what she said. Instead of "grated garlic," I heard her say "grapes and garlic." The resulting Guaca-mole Surprise became a family favorite.

I chuckled as I pulled knives and forks out of the drawer to set the tables.

"And, Brooklyn?" she added. "After lunch I'll per-form my protection spell for you."

That wiped the smile off my face. "Mom, no. It's not necessary. I'm fine. And I'm not in danger."

"But your psyche might be." She held up her hand to stop me from protesting further. "Please, just humor me."

When she put it like that, how could I say no? Besides, I could see her lip quivering and any minute now she'd start crying. Damn it. Just like that, tears of my own sprang to life and I surrendered. "Okay, Mom. Sounds good. Thank you."

"That's a good girl," she said, her tone indicating she knew all along I would capitulate. "And as a reward, later I'll show you the new goat gland facial I discovered. It's guaranteed to obliterate the ravages of time."

"What ravages of time?" Slightly panicky, I touched my face. "I don't have ravages."

"Of course not," she said pleasantly. "Oh, don't forget the napkins. It's going to get messy out there."

Chapter 9

It is my humble wish to please both the eyes and the appetites of my guests without stooping to pernicious ways for the sake of false beauty. To say it simply, I shall never fluff my flounder.

—The Cookbook of Obedience Green

As I was setting the outdoor tables, China arrived with her husband, Beau, and their adorable baby daughter, Hannah. I gave them all hugs and kisses, and China handed me the baking dish she was carrying.

"I brought a taco casserole," she said.

I laughed. "Thank God, more food."

"I figured it was probably overkill," China said, "but we can always take home leftovers."

"Good point." I took the casserole and placed it on the side table.

China owned Warped, a beautiful knitting and weaving shop on the Lane. Beau worked in production for the winery and often gave tours and tastings because he was both knowledgeable and a charming speaker. He and China had fallen for each other the minute he showed up in Dharma six years ago.

Beau passed baby Hannah over to China and headed for the industrial-sized cooler to grab a beer.

"She wants to play," China said, and put Hannah down in the play yard Mom had constructed next to the terrace. We all watched the little girl hesitate before she took a step, then start walking on the padded surface. Happy with her accomplishment, she tried to run, but stumbled and fell on her butt. Instead of bursting into tears, she giggled and pushed herself back up.

I could hear China's sigh of relief.

"What a little trouper," I said. "She's moving faster every day."

China nodded. "And life will never be the same again."

Last year, Mom had transformed a portion of her vegetable garden into this dream play yard for her grandbabies. It was completely fenced in, of course, and the ground was covered in a hard rubber material so none of the kids would be hurt if they fell. The fence consisted of bright babyproof plastic panels linked together, and each panel featured something fun: a ball spinner, a steering wheel with a horn, colorful twirling shapes, and other goodies for the babies to grab and squeeze.

Toys were strewn across the play yard, along with a bouncy chair and a baby swing. When the kids got older, Mom planned to add a swing set and a wading pool. I was horribly jealous of all the fun kid stuff, especially that bouncy chair, but I managed to hide my bitterness.

The huge oak tree that shaded my parents' terraced patio was just beginning to sprout new green leaves. There was still a touch of chill in the air, but the sun made it warm enough to sit outside if you wore a light sweater.

I helped Mom set the rest of the casserole dishes and salad bowls on the side table while Dad revved up the grill.

The rest of the guests arrived in quick succession. Savannah first; then my sister London, her husband, Trevor, and their twins, Chloe and Connor. Robin and Austin showed up a few minutes later, and Mom declared it was time to eat.

Even though I was close to my three sisters and happy to see them and their families, I sat with Robin. As usual, in two nanoseconds we were laughing and finishing each other's sentences, just as we'd been doing since we were eight years old. And as soon as we thought we'd caught up on everything that had been going on in our lives since we'd last seen each other, one of us would remember something vitally important that we had to share. And we'd be laughing again.

She told me how Austin had finished building her sculpture studio and invited us to come by during the weekend to see some of her new pieces. I was so happy for her, but there was a tiny part of me that was sad. Her news put to rest any thought that she would ever move back to the city.

We had both moved to San Francisco around the same time and had lived near each other until a few months ago when her friend Alex was murdered in her Noe Valley flat. Robin hadn't felt safe there anymore and wondered if she should move back to Dharma. And then my brother Austin finally stepped up and admitted he'd been in love with her for years. The feeling was mutual, of course. Robin had been crushing on him since third grade. Now they lived together in Austin's home, a mountaintop cabin overlooking all of Dharma and beyond. I missed her living close by me in the city, but I was honestly thrilled that they were happy together.

I looked around for Derek and saw him chatting with Dad at the grill. They were soon joined by Austin, Trevor, and Beau, who gathered around to watch the meat cook, as men were inclined to do. I was happy my family had welcomed Derek into our world. He seemed comfortable with them, too, as if he'd always been around.

We ate like starving refugees and drank several bottles of reserve Pinot Noir and Sauvignon Blanc from the commune's own winery. I found myself growing sleepy in the sun. "I'm ready for a nap."

"But you've only had three hot dogs and two helpings of potato salad," Robin said wryly. "You can't quit yet."

I rubbed my stomach. "I'm saving room for dessert."

"Brooklyn, sweetie," Mom called from the sliding door, "can you help me with dessert?"

Robin snickered.

"Sure, Mom," I said, smirking at Robin. "Be right there."

Minutes later, I came back outside with a tray loaded down with a large baking dish of apple crisp, a gallon tub of vanilla ice cream, plus bowls and spoons, and headed for the side table.

"Hello, Brooklyn, dear."

"Oh!" I gasped and bobbled the heavy tray as the soft voice came from behind me. Turning, I smiled. "Hi, Robson."

Robson Benedict, aka Guru Bob, reached out to steady the tray. "I surprised you, gracious. I am sorry."

"You sure did, but it's my own fault. I should've been paying better attention."

His smile was compassionate as he took the tray from me. "Let me help you with this."

"Thank you." Was it obvious how discombobulated I was? Guru Bob usually had that effect on me. I think it was because he just always seemed to know what was going on inside my head. I wouldn't go so far as to admit that he was clairvoyant, but he definitely saw things that other people didn't.

"Shall I put it down over here?" he said, walking to the side table.

"Yes, please." I took the serving dish of apple crisp and the ice cream off the tray and arranged them on the table. The bowls and spoons were stacked in front for people to grab easily.

Mom came running over, but skidded to a stop when she saw Guru Bob standing next to me. "Oh, Robson.

Hello. I'm so glad you could make it. Would you like a hot dog or some salad? I can fix you a plate."

"Thank you, Rebecca. I might have something later. Right now, I am helping Brooklyn serve dessert."

"You—you are?"

"Yes, gracious, I am."

Mom's mouth fell open and she spluttered, "Well, of course you're welcome to help, but, but . . ." Her face was turning pink. Glad to know I wasn't the only one discombobulated by Guru Bob.

Here was the thing about Guru Bob. He called us all "gracious" because he held the stubbornly optimistic belief that people were naturally filled with grace and goodwill.

And another thing. I always called him Robson, not Guru Bob. The Guru nickname was something we kids came up with when we were insolent teenagers, but a nickname was just wrong for someone as centered and truly good as Robson.

"Thank you for your concern, Rebecca," he said. "It is an honor to be of service to your guests."

"You're my guest as well, Robson." She looked calmer now. "So whenever you're ready, there's still plenty of food left to enjoy."

"That is lovely of you, Rebecca. Thank you."

Mom leaned closer to me and whispered, "You help him." Then she walked back into the kitchen.

Guru Bob laughed out loud. "She has no confidence whatsoever in my abilities."

"She's just more comfortable taking care of her guests than putting them to work." I began to cut into the apple crisp. "Of course, that attitude doesn't extend to her kids."

Guru Bob chuckled. We worked together in companionable silence, filling dessert bowls with apple crisp and topping them with scoops of ice cream. The apple crisp went quickly, as always, and Robin's dark chocolate cake with strawberries and buttercream filling was decimated as well. Mom finished it off by snagging the last two slices. She covered them with a napkin and hid them somewhere in the kitchen for her and Dad to enjoy later.

We stuffed ourselves, all the while asking how anyone could eat dessert after that huge meal. It was a tough job, but we managed.

Derek stacked his empty apple crisp bowl on the tray with the others. "That was her best effort yet."

"I thought so, too," I said, rubbing my bursting stomach. "I should take a long walk to work off some of this food."

Guru Bob touched my arm. "I will walk with you, gracious."

"Excellent idea, Robson," Derek said. "I'll go help Rebecca with the dishes."

"She'll be in heaven," I said. "We'll be back in a few minutes."

Guru Bob led the way along the side of the house and out to the front. From there it was a short hike to the top of the hill where the road leveled out. We followed the tree line, walking in silence while I tried to figure out how to bring up the subject of murder to Guru Bob again. But he saved me the trouble.

"I understand that you and your sister were confronted with another violent death recently."

"Yes, we were," I said. We stopped walking and I stared out at the rolling, grapevine-studded hills across the wide gully that ran behind my parents' property. The ground was still brown from winter and the grapevines had not yet begun to grow their leaves back. Come summer, there would be grass on the hills and the plants would be gloriously full of green leaves and plump grapes.

Overhead, the breeze flitted through the quaking aspens, causing the pretty green leaves to flutter and spin and whistle their soft rustling sound. Billowy clouds darted past the branches. Somewhere down in the gully, a dog barked at the rushing water that babbled over the rocks.

It was a perfect moment, except for the frisson of tension grabbing hold of my shoulders.

I glanced at Guru Bob. "You probably heard it was Baxter Cromwell who was killed."

"I did."

"Savannah found him. It was awful. They're old friends and she was really upset. You probably know the whole story."

"I do," he said. "And I spoke with Savannah. I think she will be fine. I am more concerned about you."

"You're not the only one."

"Your mother worries."

"I'm fine," I lied. I mean, I *was* fine, physically. But I had to admit that it had been bothering me for a while, this whole murder-magnet thing. Why was I the one who had to stumble onto bodies?

We started walking again, headed for the copse of trees that marked the end of the narrow road.

"Last year," he said, clasping his hands behind his back as he walked, "after you shared your concerns with me, we did not speak of it again. Recently, though, I found out you have since had two more similar experiences. And now this latest event."

"That's right." I raised my shoulders in resignation and tried to smile. "Guess you were right about that whole *Nemesis* thing."

A few months ago, during a particularly upsetting murder investigation, Guru Bob had suggested that, like Miss Marple in the Agatha Christie story *Nemesis*, I might've been chosen to speak for the dead. It was crazy, of course, but what else could explain my odd tendency of finding dead bodies wherever I went?

Robson frowned. It was so unusual to see that expression on his face, I felt a little guilty for causing him any trouble.

"It brings me no comfort to be right," he said. "I would prefer to be of help."

"Oh, but you are," I said immediately. "You have

been. Just talking to you last time made me feel better. And as awful as it's been whenever it's happened since then, I've remembered your words and they've helped me. Really."

He sighed deeply. "That is heartening, although I would rather you never had to suffer this way again."

"You and me both," I muttered, then realized how unhappy I sounded. That wasn't my style. At least I was alive and healthy, not lying in some morgue. I mentally smacked myself out of my pity party.

Stopping on the dirt trail, I turned and faced him. "I'm sorry for complaining, Robson. I'm not the one who's hurting. It's the victims and those who loved them. I think about the people who've suffered so much at the hands of some vicious killer. It's horrifying. And their poor families and friends will suffer forever. They'll never see their loved ones again, but they'll relive those painful moments over and over. That makes me angry. That's what hurts most. That's what I can't reconcile. It's so unfair."

"Exactly," he said with a solemn nod.

Okay, I guess I was more upset than I thought. It wasn't like me to rant in front of Guru Bob. "Sorry to go off like that."

"There is no need to be sorry." His eyes were warm, his features set into familiar, comforting lines. "This is what is real in you. We spoke of it the last time. You clearly feel their pain so deeply. You first felt it for Abraham. I know you still hold his loss close to your heart. He was the catalyst that continues to push you to do the right thing for the others. Who better could these victims have on their side than you, Brooklyn?"

"It started with Abraham," I whispered.

"Yes, of course. It fell upon you to unravel the mystery of his death."

I frowned. *"Nemesis."*

He tilted his head, studying me. "If you will."

"I'm not pleased about this."

He took my arm and wove it through his as we turned

and headed back to my parents' home. "You have other things, wonderful things, with which to be pleased."

"True enough," I admitted.

He stopped abruptly, turned and met my gaze. "This calling does not require your happiness, Brooklyn. Only your strength, your perseverance, and your innate sense of justice."

This *calling*? Good grief, I didn't want to be *called*. I swallowed. "I'm not really all that strong."

"You kid yourself."

I laughed weakly.

Arm in arm, we walked the rest of the way back in silence. There was nothing left to say and far too much to think about.

Chapter 10

Mind if the soup is very thick, the juice of a cod's head will thin it.

—The Cookbook of Obedience Green

If I had thought I might escape Mom's protection ritual by slipping off to talk to Guru Bob, I was totally wrong. And if I'd thought she would wait until everyone left before she started the whole bizarre performance, I was wrong again.

As soon as I stepped onto the terrace, my family members perked up like little puppies waiting for their bacon treats. The anticipation was palpable. They were hankering for a chance to poke fun at me—and I couldn't blame them. I would be doing the same thing if one of them was about to become the center of attention in one of Mom's weird and wacky freak shows.

I should've been happy that everyone considered Mom's ceremonies a good entertainment value. But the scary little secret was, her spells were alarmingly effective as well.

Was it a good thing or a bad thing that my mother was gaining a reputation as a successful witch? Probably a little of both.

Mom pounced the minute she spotted me. "There you are! I've got everything ready for the ceremony."

"Shouldn't we say good-bye to our guests first?" I said loudly. *Hint, hint.*

"We're not going anywhere," China assured me. She was all tucked up and cuddly with Beau on one of the outdoor love seats on the far side of the terrace. Baby Hannah lay sleeping in Beau's arms while the grown-ups waited patiently for the show to begin.

I shot Guru Bob a look of alarm, but he just smiled back at me with that virtuous expression of his. And with an encouraging pat on my shoulder, he left me and went over to sit in the chair next to my father. No doubt it was his way of saying, "You're on your own, buckaroo."

I scanned the crowd, caught sight of Robin's smirk and knew she was recalling a similar scene from last year. After being hurt badly by a psychopathic undercover agent, Robin had been treated to one of Mom's healing rituals. It had been a big success. Not only did Robin heal quickly, but my brother Austin was there for the show and afterward, he'd seemed positively bewitched. Within minutes of the ceremony, he had swept Robin up in his arms and carried her off to his lair. It was a truly romantic sight, a real knight-in-shining-armor moment. Mom had taken all the credit for cosmically kicking Austin's butt into gear.

"Brooklyn, I've a chair for you here." Derek waved me over to the well-padded patio chair next to him. His eyes twinkled with something like ... anticipation. Or mischief?

That's when I noticed that all the patio furniture had been arranged in a semicircle so that everyone had a good view of me.

My glares had no effect on him.

"It's all in good fun," he said.

"Easy for you to say," I grumbled. "Just wait till it's your turn."

His eyes widened but he said nothing, merely held up his crossed fingers as if to ward off my evil threat.

Ah, well. So everyone would enjoy a good laugh at my expense. I had managed to live through these moments before and would do so again.

As soon as I sat down, Mom came toddling over with a sturdy wooden tray and set it on the coffee table in front of me. Anyone still standing quickly took seats on the couches and chairs. I still couldn't believe Guru Bob was staying for the show.

Dazed, I stared at the tray filled with Mom's usual arsenal of witchy tools and props. There was the ubiquitous bundle of white sage, tightly wrapped, to be burned and waved in my vicinity to cleanse away negativity; a miniature bucket filled with sand used for extinguishing the smoking sage; a bowl of blue glitter that left me curious since I'd never seen Mom use blue glitter in a ritual before; three small dishes filled with different herbs for summoning helpful spirits or banishing malicious vibes; a slender, foot-long oak branch that Mom used as a magic wand in ceremonies that called for a strong, protective wood influence; and three small, colorful candles.

I could tell that the candles had been glossed up with Mom's special blend of magic oil. She infused the oil with a light scent of orange blossom that was said to bring both harmony and power to the fore.

A witch always "dressed" or oiled her candles before she burned them in order to establish a psychic link between herself and the candles. By rubbing on the oil herself, Mom charged the candles with her touch, sending unique vibrations into the wax. The candles became an extension of her life force.

Candle colors were significant, too. Mom had chosen green for good luck and harmony; blue for protection, wisdom, and devotion; and white for peace and spirituality, always best when trying to establish contact with the goddess.

Mom slid the tray over and sat in front of me on the solid coffee table. She clasped both of my hands in hers and said, "Take a moment to ground yourself, Brooklyn."

"Okay." I snuggled in my chair and rubbed my shoes against the wood surface of the terrace.

"Visualize your root chakra shooting a light beam through the soles of your feet and into the earth, connecting you to the soil and centering your spirit. The beam runs both ways as you feel Mother Earth's energy spiral up through your body, opening and cleansing every chakra and creating a harmonious balance within."

I straightened my spine and felt the oddest tingling sensation. I breathed in and out slowly and allowed my mother's words to wash over me.

She reached for the bowl of blue glitter. "Sparkling indigo," she explained, "found in the crystalline mines outside of Marrakech and ground to a fine, shimmering powder. Indigo corresponds with the sixth chakra, your third eye. It speaks to the fearlessness within you, that part of you that seeks the truth no matter what the consequences."

I'm not fearless, I thought. More like the opposite. I felt like a phony until I saw Derek watching me intently. Could he know what I was thinking? Was he worried for me? I was worried for myself!

"Now visualize a triple circle of blue light surrounding you, holding you within its strength and power," Mom said, standing. "And repeat with me:

'Goddess, protect us with your might,
Grant us strength both day and night.' "

We repeated the chant three times as Mom circled my chair, sprinkling three thin lines of indigo crystals on the ground around me.

She came to a stop behind me, placed her hands on my head, and chanted,

"Goddess, we seek your attention,
With open heart and true affection,
Give us strength where we are weak,

Bring the answers that we seek,
Shield my girl from evil's curse,
This I plead through song and verse.
Goddess, thanks and blessed be,
As I speak, so mote it be."

There was a moment of silence, then Mom picked up the first dish of crushed herbs. "Hold out your hands, sweetie," she said, and sprinkled the contents onto my palms. "Dried bergamot leaves to protect you from harm."

"I'll take all you've got," I murmured.

Mom pressed my hands together and chanted,

"Crush the herb and bind thy powers,
Let it multiply by hours."

I rubbed my hands together until the dried leaves turned to a gritty dust. Then Mom lifted my hands above my head and opened them, allowing the wind to carry the dust away.

Next came sweet heliotrope petals to vitalize energy, mixed with sandalwood to heal, protect, and calm the mind. Mom repeated the same verse, asked me to crush the mixture, and let the powdery bits blow into the wind.

Picking up the third small bowl, she said, "The last dish contains bits of dried lemon peel to evoke protective spirits, grains of myrrh to guard against evil, and crushed apple seeds to bring peace of mind, love, and wisdom."

"Bring it on," I muttered, holding my hands out.

She repeated the words,

"Crush the herb and bind thy powers,
Let it multiply by hours."

When the last of the herbs were crushed and gone, Mom bowed in front of me, her hands pressed prayerfully together in the classic pose. After a long moment, she raised her head and smiled at me.

I was surprised the ritual was over. "That was pretty sedate, Mom, but I enjoyed it. Thanks."

"Oh, we're not finished."

Uh-oh. I watched her nervously. "What else is there?"

At this point, I expected her to throw her arms up and wail some crazy singsong chant about Krishna's belly button or something equally nonsensical. That's usually how her rituals ended. In happy dancing chaos.

Instead, she closed her eyes and began to sway back and forth in front of me. With each deep breath she took, she raised her arms to the sky, then lowered them over me. Her hands skimmed down and framed my face as she whispered some sort of prayer I couldn't quite make out. Something about gods and power and protection. She repeated the actions and words three times, summoning the power of all the gods in all the heavens to watch over me.

I snuck a glance at Dad, who wore a serious frown. China was sitting forward in her chair as though she might leap up and rush to my rescue. Did I need rescuing? What was up with Mom being so serious all of a sudden?

Derek reached over and held my hand. Good heavens, was everyone so concerned about me? Where was my happy, frolicking mother? Why wasn't she whooping and laughing and spin-dancing like the carefree Deadhead hippie she'd always been? What kind of crazy ritual was this?

After another minute or two of silent swaying, Mom uttered one gentle moan and stopped moving.

Now what? I wondered.

She opened her eyes and stared into mine with so much intensity, I knew she could see straight through to my soul. After a long moment, it was too much and I had to blink and sever our connection. She smiled then and picked up the bundle of smudged sage. Holding it over my head, she tapped at the loose singed bits.

Sage ashes whirled around me like a mini-tornado. I closed my eyes and absorbed the odd moment. And felt more calm, alive, and happy than I had in days.

*   *   *

Two nights later, Derek and I walked into Arugula, ready for dinner and our chaperon assignment with the chefs. The restaurant was closed on Mondays, so the eight of us were the only guests.

The main dining room looked beautiful tonight. There were clusters of small candles on every table. Subtle ceiling lights cast a warm glow on the walls and the blond wood floors. Down the center of the main dining table were small glass vases from which all sorts of pretty pink and blue flowers rose gracefully. In between the vases, thin willow branches and strands of ivy were entwined around tiny white blossoms. It all resembled a still-life painting.

I was so proud of my sister. She had spent years trying to figure out what to do with her life. She'd taken a few cuisine classes at the Sonoma Institute of Art, then bummed around for a while. Finally, at a friend's suggestion, she had enrolled in Le Cordon Bleu in Paris.

After graduating, she spent a year in the Loire Valley at the famous Maison Troisgros near Roanne, where she was hired as an apprentice chef. She came home and worked in a number of Bay Area restaurants, then moved to Point Reyes, in the wilds of Marin County. There she planted an acre of her favorite greens, mostly arugula, which she distributed to restaurants all over Northern California. Finally, she came home to Dharma and opened Arugula, and the rest was history.

Glancing around, I noticed that the other chefs had dressed up for the occasion, so I was glad I'd decided to wear one of my more elegant outfits: black silk pants and matching jacket, a burgundy satin blouse, and sparkly diamond hoop earrings. Derek looked ridiculously handsome in his navy Armani suit, crisp white shirt, and burgundy tie. Did we look like proper, serious chaperons? I hoped not! But I thought we looked good.

Tonight I was excited and a little antsy after two days of relaxing since Mom's protection ritual. I'd been taking naps and going on long walks through the vineyards. The urge to delve into Baxter's murder investigation had subsided. But now it was back with a vengeance.

It was as if I'd been on a tropical vacation too long and was desperate to get back to reality. Except in this case, I had no idea what *reality* I wanted to return to. I just knew I wanted something to happen. I wanted action.

And what better way to be where the action was than to have dinner with a murderer? Not that I expected Baxter's killer to reveal himself—or herself—tonight. And not that I wanted to share a meal with a killer, particularly. But if I had been looking for a thrill ride, I'd found it. I was going to watch every move these people made.

As Derek helped me off with my jacket, I spotted Kevin across the room. One of my self-assigned tasks this evening was to find out why she'd had such a bizarre reaction when Savannah gave Baxter the old cookbook. There was a story there. I just hoped the story didn't end with Kevin being carted off to prison.

"What is going on in that devious mind of yours?" Derek murmured in my ear.

I shivered as his warm breath met my skin. Was I that transparent? Of course I was. I couldn't tell a lie to save my life. I turned and whispered, "Stop trying to distract me from my devious thoughts."

"Darling, I'd like nothing better than to distract you." He kissed my neck. "But I must behave myself. I am, after all, the chaperon this evening."

"That doesn't mean I have to behave, does it?"

"No, but I'd like you to be careful."

I gazed up at him. "Nothing bad will happen as long as you're here with me."

He tugged me closer. "I have no intention of leaving your side."

After a quick kiss, we joined the others in the bar. Derek handed me a flute of champagne and for the next half hour, we moved from group to group, making small talk. It irritated me to see that the chefs would wait until Derek and I walked away before beginning to whisper among themselves. I could only catch snippets of their conversations and was tempted to yell at them all to speak up.

"We can't be their only suspects," someone murmured.

"Have they arrested anyone?" another asked.

"It's not fair. We all loved Baxter."

Who said that? I wondered, and whipped around to see if I could pick out the delusional chef who'd uttered the words. Four of the chefs stood talking together in a tight circle and I didn't have a clue which one had said what.

It didn't matter, because as soon as I turned away, Colette said slyly, "Some of us loved him more than others."

Good thing I could pick her voice out among all of them. Still, I found the snippets depressing, so I looked around for someone else to talk to. Kevin walked out of the kitchen just then and I pounced on her.

"Kevin, how are you?"

She set her empty glass on the bar and gave me a halfhearted hug. "I'm fine, I suppose. It's just all so depressing, really."

"You mean the murder? Or the investigation?"

"Both, really," she said, then lowered her voice. "And knowing one of your friends is a cold-blooded killer. That can put you off your tea, right?"

"Yes, it can." I leaned closer. "Can I ask you something?"

"Sure."

"I saw your face when Baxter opened Savannah's gift. You looked so distressed, I was worried about you."

She stiffened until she was almost shaking. "I don't know what you're talking about."

"Kevin, is there something about the cookbook that upset you?"

"Let it go, Brooklyn," she said wearily.

"I will, but I just need to know one thing. Are you mad at Savannah?"

"Savannah?" She looked puzzled. "Why would I be mad at her?"

"Well, Baxter did give her the book." I shrugged, uncertain how to explain myself. "I was thinking maybe he promised it to you, but then gave it to Savannah instead."

"Oh, please." She laughed without humor. "He *promised* me? Look, Brooklyn, Baxter Cromwell was a stone-cold bastard. Everything he ever had, he lied, cheated, and stole to get. *Promise* me? No, he never promised me a damn thing. But you can bet your ass I promised to see him in hell before he ever took anything from me again."

With that, she turned on her heel and dashed back into the kitchen.

"Okay," I said under my breath. "Maybe we'll talk later." I grabbed a glass of champagne and took a swift gulp. What had I expected? One of the casualties of murder was that you could no longer trust anyone in your circle of friends.

"Where did she run off to?"

I spun around. "Oh, Peter." I gave him a quick hug and then we both glanced at the swinging kitchen door. "She's helping Savannah in the kitchen."

"Savannah's in the kitchen? I'm disappointed. I was rather expecting her to pass the work off to an assistant and join us out here."

"I'm sure she'll dine with us."

"I hope so." Peter leaned against the bar and sipped his cocktail. He was dressed casually yet elegantly in a thin black cashmere sweater and black trousers. "So, did you get a good grilling the other night like the rest of us?"

"You mean with the police? Yes. How about you?"

"Oh, yes. We all did. I was the last to be interviewed. Practically fell asleep at the table."

"Were you too sleepy to provide a good alibi for yourself?" I teased.

"Never," he said stoutly. "I'm a good scout. Always prepared, especially with an alibi."

I smiled. "And were you able to tell them anything useful?"

He edged closer. "You mean, did I confess to killing the bastard? Hell, no. Would I have liked to? Hell, yes. And does it bother me that he's dead?" He frowned. "Hell, no."

I took a quick look around. "I have a feeling your sentiments are shared by a few of the others." More like *all* of them, I added silently. I didn't think any of the chefs missed Baxter.

"Don't I know it." Peter steered me over to the bar, where he held up two fingers and the bartender went to work. Less than a minute later, Peter had a fresh cocktail and, for a refreshing change, I ordered a glass of water. I wanted to be relatively sober and aware tonight, in case a killer revealed himself—or herself.

"Thanks," I said.

"Cheers." We clinked glasses and he took a sip, then frowned again. "Now, Brooklyn, do they honestly believe one of us killed Baxter? I don't mean because we didn't like him, because let's face it, most of us barely tolerated the man. But, well, who does that? I mean, who goes and kills someone? Certainly no one of my acquaintance."

I knew what he was saying, but unfortunately, he was wrong. It was highly likely that somebody in this room had picked up that hideous fish knife and killed Baxter.

"And another thing," Peter continued. "How could any of us get away with it? We were all there in the kitchen minutes before, laughing, chatting, saying good night. And suddenly, he's dead? Murdered? Within minutes?"

"The timing does seem pretty tight."

"Yes." He leaned closer. "Did you see anything? Do you know how he died?"

"Not really," I lied. "Did the police tell you much?"

He glanced to his left and his right, then whispered,

"They asked me what I know about fish. I thought it was an odd question. I'm a chef, so of course I know something about fish. But what do you suppose they meant?"

I shook my head, feigning cluelessness. "Maybe Baxter died from poisoned fish."

Peter froze and his face turned a pale gray. "Why would you say that?"

"I—It was just a guess. A bad one, obviously. I'm sorry. I didn't mean anything by it."

"No, of course not." But he couldn't hide the fact that he was trembling. From fear? Or was it guilt? Maybe he was bluffing about the fish knife. Maybe he knew exactly how Baxter had been killed.

He set his drink on the bar. "Excuse me, will you? I need to, er, check on something."

"Are you all right?"

"Yes, of course. Just . . . excuse me, please. I'll be back."

"Okay." I watched him rush off toward the rear of the restaurant. The restrooms were back that way, as well as the door to the parking lot. Maybe he needed some fresh air.

I sighed before taking another sip of water. He was acting strange tonight. Almost as strange as Kevin. I wondered why. I hated to think either of them might be guilty of murder because I liked them so much. We had always been friends. And I needed all the friends I could get.

Chapter 11

Always boil your pigs' ears and pat dry before frying in beer batter.

—*The Cookbook of Obedience Green*

"Ah, Brooklyn," a seriously sexy Latin voice murmured near my ear. "It has been too long."

That intoxicating male tone brought an instant smile to my face, and I turned to face Raoul. What woman wouldn't smile at the sound of his voice? And seeing him up close in the flesh was pretty awesome, too. I gave him a big hug, then held him at arm's length. He wore a beige linen suit with a black T-shirt and high-top Converse sneakers. Raoul Luna was impossibly cool.

"Raoul. It's wonderful to see you." I'd met him only two times in Paris, but we had clicked. Of course, he'd probably clicked with every woman he'd ever met. One evening he came over to Savannah's apartment for dinner. A few nights later, he invited all of us to his small flat for the most incredible Spanish feast I'd ever experienced. He was generous, funny, and sweet. And did I mention gorgeous?

"And you, *mi querida.*" His gaze traveled slowly up

and down my body—to which I took absolutely no offense. "How beautiful you look this evening. I regret we did not have the chance to talk much the other night."

"I'm sorry, too." I gave the room a quick scan in case Derek was nearby, hoping I could introduce the two men. I didn't see him anywhere, so I turned back to Raoul. "But here we are now. I trust your interview with the police wasn't too grueling."

He grimaced. "Even the most innocent can come away feeling guilty after an hour spent with those detectives. But I am hopeful that we'll all be cleared soon and the police will look elsewhere for their killer."

"You're awfully optimistic," I said.

"True." He shrugged philosophically. "My lovely wife often accuses me of being too naive for my own good."

Did he know his "lovely" wife, Colette, had spilled her guts to the cops the other night? Did he know she had incriminated him as well as Savannah and almost everyone else here this evening? I wasn't about to bring up the subject, just tried to keep the conversation light. "I don't suppose she means it as a compliment."

He threw back his head and laughed. The sound sent at least one pleasurable little shiver down my spine.

"No, she most certainly does not," he said. "But I can't help being an optimist, as you say. I believe in the basic goodness of people, most especially my friends."

"So," I said, always willing to plunge back into dangerous territory, "do you have a theory of who might've killed Baxter?"

His lips pursed as he gave it serious thought. "I am convinced it was a random attempt at robbery. The thief entered through the kitchen door and tried to rob Baxter. When he put up a fight, the villain lashed out."

"That makes sense." I could hardly fault his theory, since I had come up with the same one myself the other night. But I didn't agree with him when it came to trusting the motives of so-called friends. I had been fooled one too many times in the past. I no longer completely trusted my instincts after being betrayed by people I'd allowed into my inner circle.

Besides, he might've been an optimist, but I knew Raoul was no more fond of Baxter than any of the rest of us had been.

"Let's hope you're right," I said finally. I honestly did hope it was a random act of violence. Better that than the other possibility.

"But of course I'm right," he said, and winked at me.

"Yes, of course you are," I said with an indulgent smile, then changed the subject. "I understand you're a pastry chef these days. How exciting for you."

He raised an eyebrow. "Exciting, you say? Some of my fellow chefs aren't quite as impressed, but I enjoy the work. And to be fair, Colette is a specialist in haute cuisine, while I tend to dabble in everything. So now I play with the desserts and everyone is happy."

He was hardly a dabbler, but I appreciated that he was underplaying his skills for his wife's benefit. Both Savannah and Peter had told me that Raoul had achieved the highest level possible for a Cordon Bleu attendee, completing the entire curriculum of the three main disciplines offered: cuisine, pastry, and wine. Colette, meanwhile, had obtained only the cuisine certificate. Not that any Cordon Bleu certificate was anything to sneeze at.

But, knowing Colette, I realized that wouldn't ring any happy chimes with her. So who could blame Raoul for trying to keep the peace? And he truly did seem happy with his decision to take a backseat in the kitchen, so to speak.

"I happen to think desserts are a critical part of every meal," I assured him. "So I'm completely thrilled that you're specializing in them now."

He casually swirled his glass of dark red wine. "Then I must find the time to bake you something sweet while I'm here."

"Sounds fabulous. Especially if chocolate is involved."

His eyes twinkled. "For you, my sweet friend, always there will be chocolate involved."

We smiled at each other until his attention was diverted by something behind me. With a sigh, he said, "Ah, Colette is signaling me. I'd better see what she needs. Perhaps we'll have a chance to talk some more later this evening."

"I hope so."

He bowed briefly, then gifted me with one of his patented sexy smiles before walking away. I turned and noticed Colette standing at the far end of the bar. She gave me a wiggly finger wave, to mollify me, I supposed. But it didn't work, especially since her smile was pinched and clearly disingenuous. I was miffed that she hadn't even bothered to come say hello before imperiously summoning her husband from afar.

And I was still irritated with her for trying to implicate Savannah the other night while talking to the police. So now I imagined her capable of all sorts of shoddy behavior. I wouldn't put it past her to have limited the amount of time Raoul was allowed to speak to each of the other women in the room. She probably had a stopwatch in her bag.

I sipped my drink and tried to brush aside my resentment. Raoul was such a sweetie, I hated not liking his wife. I decided I would make an effort to talk to her at some point and see if we could be friendly. If it didn't work, at least I could say I gave it a try. I didn't enjoy feeling so bitter toward anyone.

A young waiter walked into the bar and announced, "Dinner is served." We followed him into the main dining room, where one long table was elegantly set to seat all nine of us.

Savannah asked Derek to sit at the head of the table and she sat on the opposite end, closest to the kitchen. Montgomery sat next to her on my side of the table. I was happy to be seated between Derek and Peter, and Kevin was next to Peter. I was even happier to see Colette seated farthest from me, on the other side of the table next to Savannah.

"Where did you disappear to?" I murmured to Derek as wine was being poured.

He faced me and said discreetly, "Someone wanted to discuss my role as chaperon privately."

"Who?"

He casually scanned the guests at the table. I followed his gaze until it settled on one person.

I turned and whispered, "Montgomery?"

He nodded, but said nothing else, and we both made an effort to join in the conversations around us. But I made a big mental note to get more information out of Derek the first chance I had.

What did Monty want to know? Maybe the others had chosen him to try and get information out of Derek. It was only natural that the chefs would want to know who this stranger Derek was. After all, who was to say he wouldn't report to the police every morsel of gossip and innuendo he heard tonight? But it appeared that Derek had alleviated Monty's worries, because the jovial chef seemed completely at ease. Still, I wanted to know what the two men had actually said to each other. Just call me inquisitive.

Happily, with all the cocktails and now wine, the chefs' tongues were loosening up a little. Enough for them to confront Derek more directly now.

"So you're our babysitter," Kevin said, her tone defiant.

I jumped in before Derek could speak. "Having Derek here was the only way the police would let you all leave the city limits."

Montgomery's eyes flashed in Derek's direction. "I'm not complaining. He can babysit me anytime he wants."

I almost laughed as Derek scooted another inch closer to me.

"But it doesn't make sense," Colette said. "Why would they ask you to do it? You're dating Savannah's sister. Doesn't that make you prejudiced?"

I bristled. The woman was getting on my last nerve. "Derek served with British intelligence for years before starting his own security firm," I told her. "The police trust him implicitly. He's completely incapable of being compromised."

"Thank you, darling," he said, patting my thigh under the table before firmly resting his hand on my leg. He had to know I was itching to leap across the table and smack that buxom bitch silly.

Hmm, so much for my vow to be friendlier toward Colette. Honestly, what did Raoul see in that woman? I mean, besides her beautiful face, perfect hair, and gorgeous body? Other than that, she was thoroughly unpleasant.

I hoped the chefs' suspicions would subside and we could all enjoy our dinner, but suddenly Savannah piped up. "Brooklyn has worked with the police on other murder cases, so they trust her completely, too."

Six pairs of eyes turned and stared at me with suspicion. And I knew I wouldn't get any more answers from anyone.

But then Montgomery winked at me. "So I guess you're not a suspect."

"No, but I have been in the past."

"Tell us what happened," Kevin said eagerly. I prayed the enthusiasm in her voice meant that she had forgotten her earlier anger.

Throughout the first course, I entertained them with tales of how Derek had once suspected me of murder.

Kevin smiled. "Strangely enough, that makes me feel a bit better."

Montgomery glanced around. "But we're still suspects."

"That's right," Colette said, sounding dejected. "Any one of us could be carted off to jail at any moment."

"For no reason!" Margot cried. "None of us would ever hurt Baxter."

Silence hung in the air like a noose for several seconds after that heartfelt statement.

Raoul broke the silence with a fond pat of Margot's hand. "That is very sweet of you to say."

"And very naive," Colette said scornfully.

Margot frowned. "Why? Because I don't believe any of us would kill one of our own?"

Peter laughed. "No, because you actually considered Baxter 'one of our own.'"

"He was," Margot insisted. "And I still refuse to believe anyone in this room could've killed him."

Was she serious? Or was Margot's sweetness-and-light act just another way of manipulating the others?

"I suppose you could be right," Colette said, though her tone belied the words. "But obviously, the police don't agree with you. They're looking for someone to pin Baxter's murder on, and they'll take whichever one of us has the weakest alibi."

With a calculated gleam, Colette's gaze moved slowly around the table. It was a little creepy. Was she analyzing her fellow chefs' vulnerabilities? Comparing them to her own?

"In that case," Montgomery said, standing and hoisting his wineglass, "I have only one thing to say. Eat, drink, and be merry, y'all, for tomorrow we die!"

With that, he gulped down the entire contents of his glass. Peter and Raoul joined him, standing and emptying their glasses as waiters circled the table, replenishing drinks and removing empty plates.

After that, despite my qualms, the evening turned out to be delightful. The chefs regaled us with their kitchen horror stories. Savannah had everyone in complete stitches as she recounted tales from her six months living on a pig farm in rural France. No wonder she became a vegetarian.

Montgomery kept us laughing as he described all the ridiculous cooking shows he had auditioned for. The worst one involved sampling different sorts of cuisine while riding on a Harley-Davidson motorcycle. The show had been given the unfortunate title of *Pigging Out on the Hog*. What a shock that it didn't take off.

Even Colette was giggling finally, although it took her a while—and several glasses of wine—to warm up. The champagne and fine wines were flowing, and at one point I felt so comfortable that I slipped out of my shoes and pulled my earrings off to give my aching earlobes a rest. I didn't wear earrings often enough for my ears to get used to them.

Peter and Kevin shared stories of growing up with Baxter in their small Devonshire village of Gipping-on-Plym. There was plenty of laughter as they described themselves as a once-inseparable threesome, part of a rough-and-tumble gang of kids who practically lived outdoors, playing games, running across the fields, and splashing in the slow-moving river that meandered through town. It sounded like an idyllic childhood, much like my own growing up in Dharma.

The three of them must have been awfully good friends to end up at Le Cordon Bleu together. Peter had mentioned something a while ago about Kevin and him deciding to go and Baxter tagging along. I couldn't remember his exact words, but I made another mental note to ask him or Kevin about it. *If* Kevin would talk to me at all.

Savannah served dinner family-style, with large bowls and platters placed in the middle of the table and each of us helping ourselves. There was an unbelievably tasty Belgian endive salad, chopped with shallots and fennel and dressed with a light vinaigrette, and another salad made with Napa cabbage and shaved ginger covered in some kind of amazing honey-infused Asian dressing. There were four or five side dishes and three main courses that included gorgeous stuffed mushrooms and a warm goat cheese and herb cannelloni that literally melted in my mouth.

Everything was vegetarian, but you'd never have known it by the way all of us meat eaters stuffed ourselves. When the table was cleared, the servers brought dessert, Savannah's famous chocolate soufflé with heavy whipped cream and chocolate fudge on the side.

I might have been hallucinating, but I was pretty sure I had found heaven.

Later, on the ride home, I realized I'd left my earrings on the table at the restaurant. I gave Savannah a quick call and she promised to ask her people to keep an eye out for them. Even if the earrings weren't hugely expensive, I wanted them back. They were a special gift from my parents and had sentimental value to me.

The best part about the night was that everyone seemed to have a great time. Oh, and no one died. I was happy for Savannah's success and glad I'd finally had a chance to chat easily with Kevin and Peter. It was also gratifying to see everyone get along so well with Derek.

I was secretly thrilled when the chefs invited me and Derek to attend the private service in Baxter's memory later in the week. I assumed there would be other, more public services for him later. He was, after all, a world-renowned chef and celebrity. But meanwhile, the chefs had been in a jolly mood as they discussed the arrangements for their event.

Call me morbid, but I was psyched that they had decided to throw the party—I mean, memorial service—at BAX, Baxter's restaurant in the city. They hadn't set the date yet, but would let us know as soon as the police cleared it as a crime scene. I knew it was gruesome, but I relished the notion of returning to the scene of the crime. Perhaps the killer would do something to reveal himself or herself to us that night. It could happen.

There was another reason I was excited to attend the memorial service at Baxter's. It would give me another chance to search the kitchen for Obedience Green's cookbook.

Chapter 12

For a grand entertainment, garnish your stewed carp with a sprig of myrtle.

—*The Cookbook of Obedience Green*

The next day, Derek called me from his office. The police had informed him that Baxter's restaurant was no longer a crime scene. I telephoned Savannah to let her know and she hung up to call Peter and tell him the news.

I felt as if we were playing the telephone game.

A while later, Savannah called back. "Peter says the memorial party will be Friday night."

"Great," I said. "Are we still invited?"

"Of course," she said. "By the way, Peter told me he's been contacted by Baxter's attorneys. Apparently Baxter had no living relatives, so he made Peter the executor of his will."

"Really?" That surprised me a little. I knew Baxter had grown up in the same small village as Peter, but it had always seemed as though Peter didn't like Baxter. Maybe they were closer friends than Peter had let on. "That's interesting."

"Is it?"

"I guess it depends on your point of view." Realizing that the things Savannah and I found interesting were probably worlds apart, I changed the subject. "So tell me about the memorial party. Are you cooking?"

"I'm not sure yet." She hesitated, then said, "I'm not even sure where we'll have it. The thing is, Brooklyn, Peter swung by the restaurant earlier and it's still a mess. Not only are there paparazzi lining the sidewalks outside, but there's blood everywhere in the kitchen and that icky black fingerprint powder is smeared all over the place. Peter says it's revolting, and the police aren't even responsible for cleaning it up."

"No, they're not," I murmured.

"So we're not sure we'll have our dinner there. I'm so bummed."

"Look, tell him not to change plans," I said. "I'll call a cleaning service."

"I doubt if a couple of housemaids will be able to handle it."

I smiled inwardly. "I'm talking about a specialized cleanup service that deals with crime scenes and biohazard spills and stuff like that. These guys show up in hazmat suits and when they're finished, you'll never be able to tell that anything bad happened there."

"You do know the most interesting people," she said.

I had to sigh. Really, when had my life become so complicated? "I do, don't I?"

We hung up and I put a call in to my buddy Tom, who owned the crime scene cleanup service I had used for my friend Robin's house after that man was killed in her bedroom. Tom had been recommended by Inspector Jaglom and he really knew his stuff.

What I liked about Tom was that for someone who dealt with the grisly aftermath of violent death, he was one of the friendliest guys I'd ever met. Big as a bear, he was kindhearted and deferential to his clients, who, after all, were the loved ones left behind once the body was taken away. Tom took his job very seriously, especially when blood had been spilled. His cleanup crew would wear full hazardous material suits, covering themselves from head to toe in order to work in the biohazard environment of Baxter's kitchen.

Tom and his crew were available the following morning, so I arranged for Peter to be at Baxter's place to let them in. They would spend all day wiping down and disinfecting every surface of the entire restaurant, and by the time Friday night rolled around, all evidence of bloody murder would be gone.

If only it was that easy to wipe away the memory from all of our minds. But none of this would really be over until we found out who had killed Baxter.

I finished the call to Tom and immediately felt at loose ends. I had interrupted the intricate job of fixing the *Jane Eyre* book to call the crime scene cleaners and now I didn't feel like going back to work. It was alarming to realize that despite my revulsion for murder and mayhem, the conversation with Tom had charged me up.

I thought about dashing off to visit Ian at the Covington Library, even though I'd seen him just a few weeks ago when I stopped by to show him Savannah's old cookbook. I'd known that as a fellow book geek, he would be sure to get a kick out of it—and he had.

It was always fun to see Ian. I'd known him for years and loved him like a brother. At one point in our past, we'd even been engaged to marry for a brief time. Our plans were doomed from the start, however, and Ian was now happily gay and living with his cutie-pie partner, Jake. So much for my ability to choose appropriate men. Well, until Derek came along, anyway.

Now the only thing that kept me from driving over to the Covington Library was all the work I needed to get done. Namely, the work I owed Ian on the English authors' books.

Then my gaze landed on my desk where the file I'd

made for Savannah's cookbook lay. It was filled with the photocopied pages of Obedience Green's cookbook as well as all the pictures I'd taken of the book and the book box. I opened the file folder to study everything.

As I flipped through Obedience's quirky recipes, the thought of spending the afternoon cooking began to appeal to me. I wasn't sure why since I was such a failure in the kitchen. But maybe all this time I'd spent with the chefs lately had caused some of their magic cooking powers to rub off on me.

I had tried to make the syllabub five times now, with increasingly disastrous results. So why was I tempted to try it again? Because, darn it, I wanted to succeed at this. And because I just liked the idea of making a syllabub. Maybe it was the silly name that appealed to me. It was so old-fashioned and English and fun. Much more interesting than a mere pudding.

It reminded me of another silly-sounding dessert I'd had in Scotland, Spotted Dick. I had searched the old cookbook for a recipe by that name, but couldn't find it and finally Googled the name. It turned out that Spotted Dick hadn't come into fashion until the 1840s, long after Obedience Green wrote her cookbook. That was too bad, because it would be a special treat to be renowned for my Spotted Dick.

Did I dare give the syllabub another try?

"Oh, why not?" I muttered. I made up my shopping list, grabbed my purse, and headed for the grocery store.

"This is delicious," Derek said, running his spoon around the small dessert bowl in order to scoop up every last drop of the syllabub I'd made. "Where did you buy it?"

I smiled serenely, although I was quivering with excitement inside. "I didn't buy it. I made it."

"That's very funny," he said, licking his spoon. "God, it's fantastic. Thick, creamy, not overly sweet. A touch of espresso. And highly alcoholic."

"Is it too much?"

"Are you serious?" He abandoned his spoon in favor of running his finger around the inside of the bowl. I'd never seen him do that before. "It's perfect."

"Really? Thanks." I was ridiculously pleased with his praise. "There's no espresso in there, but I did add a dash of coffee liqueur for flavor." Along with two other types of alcohol, I thought, but didn't mention it. "You can still taste the alcohol because it's not cooked. That's the difference with a syllabub. You whip it up and put it in the refrigerator to set it."

"Fine by me," he said absently, scraping up one last bit of it from the bowl. "Seriously, darling, where did you find this?"

I sighed. "Derek, I made it."

"All right, don't tell me. I just hope you bought enough for a second helping."

I pushed away from the table and walked over to the bar, where I retrieved the copied pages of the various syllabub recipes. Waving them in front of him, I said, "Look, I made it. I really, really made it. The recipe's right here."

He stared at the recipe, then gazed up at me. "You made this all by yourself?"

"I did."

He opened his mouth to speak, then closed it.

"Oh, my God," I said indignantly. "Look at yourself. You're stunned. Speechless. You don't believe I could possibly make something this good."

He paused to consider his words, then said, "I'm pleasantly surprised."

"Oh, come on. You're gobsmacked."

"I wouldn't go that far," he said, leaning back in his chair. "Dumbfounded, perhaps."

With a laugh of outrage, I smacked his arm. "Admit it. You're staggered. Stupefied. Shocked beyond all reason."

He was biting his cheeks to keep from grinning. "I'm merely taken aback. But very, very proud of you and happy as a man can be."

"Aww, sweet. Thank you." I wrapped my arms around his neck to hug him. He took the opportunity to pull me onto his lap and held on.

"My little chef," he murmured, nuzzling my neck. "What's next then? Roast beef and Yorkshire pudding?"

"Hmm . . ." The only thing that flashed through my mind was a recipe requiring that a dozen garden snails be stuffed into a flannel bag and dropped into a pan of hot bacon drippings. Obedience recommended that the resulting ointment be rubbed on aching joints. "Maybe we should take this cooking thing one day at a time."

"Probably wise," he said, with a grin that told me he'd be around long enough for me to improve my cooking skills. Good to know, since that might take, oh, *forever*.

After a minute, he took the pages from my hand and started to set them aside, but something caught his eye. He examined the top page, then flipped through the others. "Why didn't you show these to me before?"

"I did."

He stopped to think. "I suppose you did, but I should've studied them more carefully."

I turned to see what he was looking at. "Oh, you mean those little notations? They're all through the book. They look like hieroglyphics, don't they?"

"Yes," he said, frowning.

"Do you think they mean something?"

"I don't know." He turned to another page that had similar symbols drawn up and down the margins.

"I wonder if it's something that cooks have always done," I mused. "You know? Like, maybe they mean something specific in cooking terms."

"Maybe," he murmured, still staring at the pages.

"I wouldn't really know, having barely managed to concoct something that resembles pudding." I rested my head on his shoulder. "That concludes my cooking expertise."

But Derek had tuned me out to scrutinize another page. When he turned it upside down and continued staring, I sat back. "I know you. You're serious. You think those little squiggles actually mean something, don't you? Some sort of code? But how can that be? This book was written hundreds of years ago."

He blew out a breath, then pointed to the page. "This group of symbols definitely looks like some sort of classic code."

"A secret recipe, maybe."

"I doubt it."

I glanced more closely at the page. Numerous odd-looking characters were lined up neatly in the margins. They resembled the type of signs and symbols I'd seen in photographs of the walls of the pyramids. Hieroglyphics. Except here in the margins, it looked more like doodling. There were squares and triangles, astrological signs, crescent moon shapes pointed in different directions, an eyeball or two, a few infinity signs, oddly shaped stars, dots, and dashes. And numbers. Lots of numbers in random order.

Now I was frowning. "Maybe Obedience was making notes for the next edition but wanted to keep her revisions a secret."

He glanced up and stared at me almost as intently as he'd studied the book. "No honor among cooks? So she created a code to keep from having her recipes stolen? Perhaps."

"What else could it be?"

"Probably nothing."

"But you don't look convinced."

He shrugged. "No, your theory is as good as any. It's just that . . . Well, it's nothing. Yet." He resumed his study of the pages, continuing to turn them upside down and sideways. After several long minutes, he set the pages down on the table, pushed his chair back, and managed to stand with me still in his arms.

"Is it bedtime?" I asked, in the mood for romance after cuddling in his arms all this time.

"Not quite," he said.

I could tell he was distracted, especially when he tipped me until I was standing with both feet on the floor. So much for cuddling.

"Do you mind if I make a quick phone call?" Without waiting for an answer, he grabbed the rest of the cookbook pages and walked toward his office in the second bedroom.

I laughed as I stared at his back. "Oo-kay." The romance was over, apparently.

He stopped, chuckled sheepishly, and returned to plant a quick, hard kiss on my lips. "Forgive me, love. I need to call my brother Dalton."

"Oh." I felt instant guilt for teasing him. "Is he all right?"

"Yes, he's fine." He looked preoccupied and he was still clutching the cookbook pages. "But I have a few questions for him, and he's going to want to see this."

"How fun. Does he like to cook?"

"No, he likes to solve puzzles. He's a cryptographer with MI6."

"Huh. My mistake."

He chuckled again. "It'll only take a few minutes and I'll be back to help you with the dishes."

"Sounds perfect."

I finished the dishes, changed into my pajamas, washed my face, and brushed my teeth. Derek was still on the phone, so I sat down to watch some TV.

At some point, Derek woke me up. My head full of fuzz, I looked around and realized I'd fallen asleep on the couch. "Your brother. What happened?"

"I'm sorry, love. My phone call took longer than I thought it would."

"That's okay." I rubbed my eyes. "It's time for bed."

"Yes, it is." He picked me up in his arms again and carried me into the bedroom.

"That's nice," I mumbled, my mouth pressed up against his shirt. "Mm, you smell good."

He didn't reply, but I felt him smile.

As we got into bed, he said, "Do you mind a house-guest for a few days?"

"Guess not," I said, half asleep already. "Whoozit?"

"My brother Dalton."

Late the next afternoon, Dalton Stone arrived on my doorstep carrying a steel briefcase and a small duffel bag slung over his shoulder. His jacket was wrinkled, his hair was mussed, and he was in desperate need of a shave.

I hadn't met Dalton Stone before, but I knew this was him—and not just because Derek was standing there as well. No, I knew because despite his disheveled appearance, Dalton could've been Derek's twin. Both men were pure male, formidable, and simply gorgeous. I found myself struggling for breath just staring at the two of them.

Like his brother, Dalton was tall and muscular, with dark brown hair and dark blue eyes. Looking into those eyes, I could tell that, also like Derek, Dalton Stone was capable of killing a man with his bare hands if he had to. He stared back at me, piercing me with his narrowed gaze. I would have shivered in fear if I hadn't already been on the receiving end of that same look from Derek more than once. Instead, I smiled at him.

"Brooklyn, I presume?" Dalton said in that same clipped British accent I found so sexy and alluring and charming and dangerous and—

"Darling, are you all right?" Derek asked.

I blinked. "What? Yes. Fine. Good. Dalton, I'm so happy to meet you." I wrapped him in a big hug before pulling him into my house. "Come in, come in. How did you get here so fast? Do you need help with your bags? You must be starving. I thought we'd have cheeseburgers tonight. I don't know what Derek's told you about my cooking, but I do make a really good cheeseburger."

He turned and grinned at Derek. "Isn't she lovely?"

"Yes, she is," Derek said. "And her cheeseburgers are quite respectable."

I frowned at him. "Respectable?"

"Fantastic," he amended with a smile.

"That's better."

Dalton looked at me. "I'm not saying I'm famished, but if you've got a decent ale to go with that burger, I might have to marry you."

I glanced at Derek, who rolled his eyes. "Feel free to ignore him."

"Impossible," I muttered, and turned to Dalton. "It's Derek's ale, so you'll have to take up that offer with him."

Dalton snorted and the brothers insulted each other mildly as I led the way through the house to the second bedroom. Dalton even walked like Derek, I noticed. It was more of a prowl than a walk, really, as though there might be enemies lurking behind every chair.

"How did you arrive so quickly?" I asked again as Dalton plopped his duffel bag on one of the chairs in the corner of the bedroom. He unzipped it and rummaged through the jumble of clothing.

"Hitched a ride on a friend's private jet."

I nodded, impressed. "You have nice friends."

"They're useful, anyway," he said, and dragged his hand through his hair in a weary gesture. His hair was longer than Derek's and tended to flop onto his forehead. It was adorable, but I preferred Derek's cleaner, close-cropped look.

Derek leaned against the doorjamb with his arms crossed. "Darling, the *friend* he's talking about is our brother Duncan's wife."

There were five Stone brothers altogether. If the others were as irresistible as these two, I wasn't sure I'd ever be able to handle all five of them together. "Your brother's wife owns a private jet?"

"Several, actually," Dalton said, as he roamed the room, perused the closet, and hung up his jacket. "Daphne's family owns the company that makes the jets."

"That's handy, isn't it," I said.

"Indeed," Derek murmured, and pulled me close to

him. He eased his arm around my shoulder and I leaned into him as we watched Dalton pull clothes and toiletries from his bag.

"I had holiday time coming," Dalton said, "so I rearranged a few things and flew here straightaway. I can't wait to get my hands on that code."

"It can wait," Derek said. "Finish unpacking."

I was starting to detect some subtle differences between the brothers. While both men were complex and, yes, dangerous, Dalton was a few years younger and seemed a bit more tightly wound. He still had a few rough edges, while Derek had a smooth, classic style that I found infinitely more appealing.

Dalton zipped up his bag and stowed it behind the chair. Then he rubbed his hands together briskly. "That's enough tidying up. Let me see those codes."

"You're welcome to rest a while before dinner," I said.

"That's kind of you, Brooklyn, but I'd prefer to get to work."

Good. Derek had been waiting to see if Dalton agreed with his theory or not, so the sooner they started, the better.

"I'll get the pages for you," I said.

Earlier that morning, over coffee and toast, Derek had filled in a few blanks about his brother's visit. He'd already explained that Dalton worked as a cryptographer in a highly secretive section of MI6, Britain's intelligence service. Dalton dealt with espionage and terrorist cells, but he also enjoyed tracking down the latest conspiracy theories and the crackpots who believed in mayhem in the name of some obscure ideology. Dalton was brilliant at his job and had broken dozens of complicated codes over the past few years.

"Dalton was the one responsible for foiling a major bombing attempt on Buckingham Palace last month," Derek had said at breakfast, his voice revealing his pride.

I thought for a minute. "I don't remember hearing about a bombing attempt on Buckingham Palace."

"Exactly," he had said, without explaining further.

I led Dalton out to the kitchen bar, where I'd left the copied pages of the cookbook. "Here you go."

He took one look at the pages and turned to Derek. "Where's the book?"

"I told you, the book was stolen," Derek said mildly.

"You didn't tell me that."

"Of course I did," Derek told him. "I don't make mistakes like that. You simply don't remember."

"Maybe you told me," Dalton muttered as he riffled through the pages brusquely. "But damn it, how was I supposed to remember every detail of our conversation? You woke me out of a sound sleep."

"I sent you a photo as well."

"It was fuzzy."

Derek snorted. "Your brain is fuzzy, mate."

"Hell." Dalton paced a few steps back and forth. "Shit, I should've—"

"Language," I said cheerily, sounding like my mother. "Besides, the book might not be stolen."

Both of them turned to me and all that combined energy caused my throat to dry up. I swallowed carefully. "It might still be somewhere in Baxter's restaurant. We never got the chance to search the kitchen thoroughly, so I thought I might do it when we go there for dinner tomorrow night. Can you work off the copies until then?"

"I'm going with you," Dalton said immediately.

I'd lost the train of thought somehow. "Going . . . where?"

"To dinner. Tomorrow night. I'll help you search."

"Um, okay," I said slowly. "I'll call my sister and let her know."

"In other words, you're not invited," Derek said, glowering at his brother. "But behave yourself and we might finagle an extra invitation."

Dalton replied with a grumble, "I'll behave as long as we can find that damn book." With that, he sat down at the bar and pored over the copies of the cookbook pages.

I turned to Derek. "I'd better give Tom a call to see if

he or one of his crew saw the book while they were cleaning up."

"Good idea, love." Derek squeezed my shoulder before giving his brother a sharp look. Then he walked into the bedroom office to finish some work.

I headed for my studio to make the call to Tom, hoping it wasn't too late in the day. I caught him just as he was leaving.

"Nope, didn't see anything like you're describing," he said after I explained what I wanted.

"Did you clean the entire restaurant or just the kitchen?" I asked.

"We concentrated on the kitchen, of course," he said. "But I always have my guys go over every inch of floor space in the place because you never know if some material got tracked out by the cops' shoes. So let's see, we got the restaurant itself, plus the bathrooms, the private dining room, and that little office near the kitchen."

"Good to know." I was glad all over again that Tom was in charge of this kind of stuff. I hadn't been aware of the little office, either, so I was doubly glad I'd called him. Had Baxter hidden the book in a desk drawer in his office? Had the cops searched that room the other night?

After thanking Tom, I hung up the phone and tried to concentrate on my work. Surveying the mess I'd made earlier of the *Jane Eyre*, I frowned at the dusty, peeling strips of leather that lay like wounded soldiers around the ragged, stringy text block. I'd been in the midst of pulling out the loose threads when Dalton arrived, so I continued the job for another hour before stopping. I still needed to clean the individual signatures and resew the pages together, but that would have to wait until tomorrow morning. I was too excited about Dalton's visit to work any more today. I laid a clean white cloth over everything and turned off the lights.

Back in the kitchen, I retrieved three wineglasses from the cupboard and Derek went to the hall storage closet to pick out an extranice bottle of wine.

Dalton looked up as I was wiping spots off the glasses. His lips curved in a smile of apology. "I was a clod earlier. Forgive me. Jet lag is hideous, and when I get focused on something, I tend to lose my ability to interact in polite society."

"Don't worry about it. Derek told me about your work as a cryptographer. It sounds intriguing." What could be more fun than spending one's days solving puzzles? I often did the same thing with the books I worked on. I liked puzzles.

"It can be interesting," Dalton said amiably, glancing back at me. "But Derek never should've mentioned my job to you. No one outside my family knows my true occupation. You seem like a lovely girl, but I have no choice but to kill you now."

I laughed, but his expression remained impassive, unnerving me. "You're good at that."

"Am I?"

"I'm sure you're kidding, but—"

"Am I?"

I suppressed a groan as I shook my head. Brothers were the same everywhere on the planet. "Fine. On the off chance that you're serious about killing me, I'll just mention that I was about to pour us all some really good wine and start dinner."

His eyes twinkled. "In that case, the killing can wait."

Two hours later, over cheeseburgers, I asked him more questions. "What exactly are you looking for in the cookbook?"

He swallowed the sip of wine he'd taken. "I'm always on the lookout for a new code to break. And from what I can tell, many of the symbols in that book are exactly the same as those used by a number of secret societies in existence during the American Revolutionary War."

"That's why I called him," Derek said to me. "I knew he wouldn't be able to resist once he saw the point within the circle."

"The point within the circle?"

Dalton explained, "It's a small item, but it always raises a red flag."

"But what is it?"

Dalton illustrated it on a piece of paper. It was literally a circle with a dot in the middle.

"And that's the big deal that got you to travel all the way here?" I asked, laughing. "It's nothing."

"It is rudimentary," Dalton agreed with a smile. "Yet it's one of the primary symbols used by members of the Illuminati back in the eighteenth century. They used it in their correspondence and in any secret documents that were passed around. They identified each other by that symbol, among others."

"What's the Illuminati?"

"A super-secret cult of prominent men who may or may not have been trying to overthrow the governments of every important nation in the world."

I blinked. "For real?"

"Maybe."

"You're yanking my chain."

"I can't seem to help myself," he said, grinning. "But yes, the members of the Illuminati were real, even though they've long since died. However, there are crackpots all over the world who refuse to let them fade away. To this day, whenever a juicy conspiracy theory erupts somewhere on the planet, the Illuminati are dragged out and accused of everything from devil worship to anarchy."

"And you think one of the members of this secret society wrote these symbols in Obedience Green's cookbook?"

"We'll see," Dalton said obliquely.

I frowned. "Well, I hope you find something of interest to make your trip worthwhile."

"Oh, it's already worthwhile," he said. "I was curious to come and see why my brother left London and relocated halfway around the world. And here you are."

"Me?"

Dalton grinned. "You must realize I'm expected to return home with a full report on you."

I glanced from Derek to Dalton. "You're going to report everything about me to your family?"

Dalton grinned. "Every last detail."

"That should make for a fascinating visit."

"Immensely."

I folded my arms across my chest. "I think you only came to see the book."

"If that were the case, I would've had Derek fax me the rest of the pages." He leaned back casually. "No, I wanted to come in person to make sure you're good enough for my big brother. Turns out you are. Now the question is, is he good enough for you?"

"Of course he is," I said immediately.

"Of course I am," Derek said with a smirk.

Dalton tilted his head to study me as if I were some visitor from another planet. "I like you."

Smiling, I said, "I like you, too."

"But I don't want you hanging over me while I work."

I rolled my eyes. "I'll try to resist."

"Good." He scowled. "Nothing worse than a cipher groupie."

I looked at Derek. "He's kidding, right?"

"He's an idiot," Derek said mildly.

I turned back to Dalton. "What has Derek told you about the murder investigation?"

"Murder?" Dalton frowned.

Derek swirled the liquid in his wineglass. "I've told you more than once."

"Oh, right. Sorry. Jet lag's a bitch." Dalton took a quick sip of his wine. "You said the cookbook was stolen at the same time Baxter Cromwell was killed. And that's why we're going to the restaurant tomorrow night. To hunt down the cookbook."

"That's right," I said. "But here's the deal. My sister is a prime suspect in Baxter's murder and I want to clear her name. If there's anything in the cookbook that might provide a motive or a clue or something, I'd like to know as soon as possible."

"You can't be serious," Dalton said. "You expect a cookbook written back in the days of King George to provide the motive for a contemporary murder?" He paused to consider. "Unless the book is worth a lot of money. That's often motive enough."

"It's extremely valuable," I assured him. "It's also historically significant, obviously, and should be in a museum. But I was thinking more in terms of something important that actually might be written in the book. Specifically, the code that you're here to decipher."

Dalton thought for a moment, then said, "That's a ridiculous theory."

"Then prove it wrong," I said, laughing.

He frowned at Derek. "Remind me again why I thought I liked her."

"Cheeseburgers, mate," he said.

"Ah." Dalton smiled. "Cheeseburgers."

Chapter 13

The French are best at curing the bite of a mad dog.
—The Cookbook of Obedience Green

On Friday night, we fought our way through the throng of photographers to the entrance of Baxter's restaurant. Derek pushed the door open and the three of us rushed inside. The door closed behind us, shutting out the noise and clamor.

"Hooray! You survived the onslaught," Kevin said. She appeared to be the official greeter and hugged me as though she hadn't seen me in months.

"Barely," I muttered, rubbing my upper arm where some stupid photographer had slammed his camera into it. "Those guys are horrible."

"We've called the police to complain, so I'm hopeful that they'll back off."

"Good." I slipped my jacket off. "It's great to see you."

Derek took her hand in his. "Thank you for inviting us."

"You're an integral part of our little gang now," she said with a smile, and stretched to plant a kiss on his cheek. She looked gorgeous in a black lace top with her hair pulled into a soft, sexy updo.

Her gaze sharpened as it slid toward Dalton. She gave

him a quick up-and-down look (and who could blame her?) and asked, "Another member of our gang?"

"Ah," Derek said. "Kevin, my brother Dalton."

"Wow. Okay. Nice to meet you." She gave me a wink as if to say, *Great gene pool in the Stone family!*

I nodded in silent agreement.

With a wave of her hand, Kevin said, "I'm waiting for a few more arrivals, so go and join the others at the bar."

"Excellent plan," Derek said.

As we walked away, Dalton whispered, "She has a boy's name."

"She does," I said, "but she's a girl."

"Indeed she is," he murmured, gazing back at Kevin.

"Her name is Kevin Moore," I said, pulling him back to the conversation. "She was named after the Dublin street where her parents fell in love."

"Isn't that charming?"

We crossed the elegant room and I was happy to see that the amazing wall-length waterfall was running again. Once we got to the bar, Derek took care of introducing Dalton to the small group while I went off to look for Savannah. I found her in the hallway outside the kitchen. She was wearing her white chef's coat.

"There you are," I said. "Are you cooking tonight?"

"Not exactly," Savannah said. "We all decided to cook one dish in Baxter's honor, so I made a simple salad. Other than that, it's mainly a carnivorous menu."

"Yippee!" I raised my fist in the air.

"You flesh-eating heathen."

"That's me," I said, grinning. "And proud of it. So, can you sit with us after the salad is served? I want you to meet Derek's brother."

We both smiled, recalling my phone call to her yesterday. When I'd told her that Dalton was in town and asked if he could come to dinner tonight, she'd replied, "Derek has a brother? Wow, God is great." When I mentioned that he had three more back home, she was close to hyperventilating.

"I'm looking forward to meeting him, too," Savannah said. "As soon as I finish plating the salads, I'll get rid of these chef duds and come join you."

"Good. By the way, did you ever find my earrings?"

"No, I'm sorry," she said, as she turned to go back to the kitchen. "I asked everyone to check around, but we couldn't find them."

"That's okay. Thanks for looking." But I was bummed. My parents had given me those diamond-studded hoops for my twenty-first birthday. I had numerous pairs of earrings, but those were my only sparkly ones. I'd worn them to every dressy occasion for the past twelve years or so, which sounded a little pathetic, I guess. It was way past time I bought another pair or two to replace them. But still, that original pair was important to me. A milestone in my life and a sentimental touchstone as well.

"There you are," Derek said. "Champagne?" He handed me the glass without waiting for an answer. As if I would ever turn down a glass of good champagne!

"Thank you," I said, smiling up at him. Savannah wouldn't be out for a few minutes, so I settled in to enjoy my drink.

"I don't see why we have to wait around all night before starting the search," Dalton grumbled.

"Shut up and drink your champagne," Derek said genially. "We'll have the run of the kitchen and back rooms once they've served dinner."

"Fine. But pretending to be here solely for a dinner party seems ridiculous, doesn't it?" Dalton took a reluctant sip of the very expensive champagne.

I couldn't quite believe my ears. "You do realize these are some of the top chefs in the world, right? This might be the best dinner of your life."

He winked at me. "I'm looking forward to it. I just like to give my brother a hard time."

"I can appreciate that," I said, relieved to hear him say it. I'd hate to think this wonderful food would be consumed by someone who didn't appreciate it. Besides, there was plenty of time for cloak-and-dagger activities. Food came first in my book.

"Do we know who's cooking tonight?" Derek asked.

"Everyone's contributing something to the meal, but there's probably one person in charge. Savannah said she's doing a salad, but other than that, it's a carnivore's paradise."

"Good to hear," Derek said under his breath.

I tiptoed over to the kitchen door and peeked through the porthole window. The scene was one of organized chaos, with Peter doing most of the pointing and gesturing.

"Looks like Peter might be top dog tonight," I said.

Dalton joined me and took a quick look through the window. "Let's hope he hurries things along."

I elbowed him as I would any of my own siblings if they were starting to whine. "You need more champagne."

Derek gave me an approving nod. "Yes, let's return to the party."

Back at the bar, Margot greeted me with an air kiss and a shrewd smile. The redhead was dressed in black from the top of her head, where a beaded black tiara held back her wild-tigress hair, to the tips of her black patent leather spiked heels. Her one splash of color—other than her hair—came from a see-through, filmy black shawl studded with purple and yellow sequined butterflies.

"How are you holding up?" I asked, trying to be friendly. I knew Baxter had arranged for the chefs to stay in a fabulous luxury hotel in Union Square. But still, they were away from home and living out of suitcases.

And now I had to wonder if they would be stuck with the bill.

"I'm positively thriving in this weather," she said. "It's been pouring rain in Seattle, but it's gorgeous here. Cold, but sunny and clear every day."

"I'm glad we could provide you with good weather," I said solemnly, as if I had personally arranged it. "But you must miss your home."

"I do," she said, then shrugged. "But we had all planned to be here for two weeks working with Baxter, so I'm not expected home for a while."

"You're from Seattle?"

"Not originally, but I've made it my home. I have two restaurants there and I love it. Except for all that rain."

"I'll have to get up there sometime," I said, trying to sound sincere. I liked Seattle, but I wasn't so sure about Margot.

"You're always welcome."

Monty walked up. "Did you tell her about our contest?"

"Not yet," Margot said coolly.

"Margot and I have decided that since none of us can leave the city anyway, we're going to have a cooking competition. And you and your hunky man are invited, of course."

"Do I have to cook?" I asked. "Because that would be a big mistake."

Monty laughed. "No, no. We'll do all the cooking."

"What are you competing for?"

"Oh, you know, most inventive appetizer. Spiciest sauce. Tastiest entrée. Prettiest dessert. We'll have score-cards and give away blue ribbons as prizes."

"It'll be very silly," Margot said, "but it'll keep us occupied until the police decide to let us leave."

"Margot's cooking first," Monty said. "Two nights from now. And I'll assist her. I hope you and your two handsome men can come."

Selfishly, I loved the sound of the impromptu contest, but I almost hesitated to accept the invitation. How long could I keep consuming all this rich food? On the other hand, how could I refuse? It was amazing food, after all, and someone else was cooking it. I'd worry about diets and poundage when things got back to normal. "We would love to come. Thank you."

"Wonderful," Monty cried. "Won't we have fun?"

A minute later he and Margot wandered off and I smiled at the thought of more yummy dinners.

"Hi, Brooklyn."

I whipped around. "Oh—hi, Colette. How are you?"

My surprise must have shown on my face because she giggled. "I'm doing a lot better now than I was the other night at Savannah's, thanks."

I wasn't sure what she was talking about. "Were you sick?"

"You couldn't tell? I was in such a foul mood, I'm surprised anyone's still speaking to me."

"I honestly had no idea." That was a lie. She'd been awful the other night, snapping her fingers at Raoul while he was talking to me. But I'd thought it was her natural state.

"Well, that's something, I guess." She touched her neck self-consciously and I remembered her doing the same thing the night Inspector Jaglom interviewed her. It seemed to be a nervous gesture. Was I making her uneasy? I guess the feeling was mutual, because I didn't trust her at all and it felt weird to make small talk with her.

"I had a horrible migraine that day," she continued, "and stayed in bed for hours. Raoul would've been perfectly happy to stay at the hotel with me, but I rallied later on and insisted on going to Savannah's with him."

"I'm sorry to hear it. I have a friend who suffers from migraines and they sound just awful."

"They make me wish I was dead. And if the headache alone weren't bad enough," Colette said with a grimace, "the medication I take just drains me of all energy."

"How miserable for you."

She laughed. "I don't mean to be such a downer. I'm feeling great now, so I just wanted to say hello, and see how you're doing and assure you I'm not usually such a bitch. I haven't talked to you at all since we've been in San Francisco, but we actually met briefly in Paris. Do you remember?"

"Yes, of course I remember." Now I wondered if she'd come to Savannah's Paris flat that day looking for Baxter. Had she and Baxter been cheating on Savannah and Raoul?

And if Colette had been cheating on Raoul, she had to be the dumbest woman in the Northern Hemisphere.

"Are you still working with books?" she asked cheerily.

"Yes," I said, glad that she couldn't read my mind. "That's how I make my living. I restore old books, give them a new lease on life, so to speak. I love it."

"That's so fascinating." Colette looked as though she actually meant it. Most people's eyes began to glaze over when I told them what I did. "Savannah said you made that gift she gave Baxter. That book box thing? I saw it up close later in the evening and I was so impressed. It was beautiful and intricate." She shook her head. "You're so talented. I'm not sure how I would ever begin to make something like that."

"You saw the book box?" I said, pouncing on her words. "Where? Who had it? Do you remember the last place you saw it?"

"Um." She took a step backward and I couldn't blame her. I was like a rabid dog when it came to that book box.

"I'm sorry," I said quickly. "It's just that I spent so much time on it and now the police can't find it. Do you know where it might be?"

"Not at all. Baxter set it down on one of the counters while we were talking, then I took off. That's about all I remember. But as I was saying, it's really beautiful. I suppose I wouldn't blame someone for taking it."

"Thanks." She probably didn't realize that whoever took it was most likely Baxter's killer.

"Did you have to take a lot of classes to learn how to do that?"

"It's definitely an acquired skill," I said. "Like your cooking ability. I wouldn't know how to begin to make a chicken potpie, so I guess we're even."

She laughed and then continued to compliment me until I couldn't quite remember why I had disliked her so much before. Oh, yeah, that's right—Colette was the one who had gone out of her way to make my sister appear suspicious to the police. So what was her excuse for doing that? Another migraine? I doubted it.

I listened to her fawn over my talents and continued to smile and chuckle with her. I realized I was enjoying our conversation, probably because it was all about me, but I still refused to trust a single word she said. As my father would say, it was fine to forgive, but don't ever forget.

We talked until Raoul approached and draped his arm around Colette's shoulder. "And what are two such beautiful women talking about that they look so chummy?"

Colette gave his stomach a friendly pat. "Oh, honey, I don't think that's a word."

"But you know what I mean," he said, and grinned at me. "How are you, Brooklyn?"

"It's great to see you, Raoul," I said, thinking that *chummy* sounded like a perfectly good word to me. "Are you both cooking tonight?"

He smiled down at Colette. "Yes, we have each devised something special for our contribution to tonight's dinner."

"Raoul is making the most sinful dessert," Colette said, beaming with pleasure. "My dish is not quite as dynamic, but I think everyone will like it. It's an appetizer of spicy wild boar sausage served on a bed of soft polenta."

Two things I really loved talking about. Books and food.

"Oh, my God," I said. "My taste buds are trembling with excitement. That sounds wonderful."

"Colette grinds and stuffs the sausage herself and it will melt in your mouth, Brooklyn." Raoul brought his fingers to his lips and kissed them dramatically. *"Fantástico."*

Colette blushed pink and smiled up at her husband. "He's slightly prejudiced."

"Maybe just a little," I said, smiling from one to the other. "But it really does sound unusual. I can't wait."

"I hope you like it."

"I know I will." I took a quick sip of champagne, then leaned in closer. "Can you give me a little hint about the dessert?"

"I can give you a one-word clue," Raoul said in a confidential tone. "*Chocolate*."

I fanned myself and whispered, "Thank you."

Colette and Raoul laughed. Just then Margot waved at them from the kitchen hallway. They excused themselves and walked over to speak with her.

"I'm beginning to think your sister doesn't exist," Dalton said right behind me.

I turned. "She does, I promise. She must've gotten delayed by some kitchen emergency, but she'll be out here soon."

"Good. I've met every chef in the known universe tonight except for the great and powerful Savannah."

Derek joined us and took my hand in a gesture I found sweet and comforting. "Now, what sort of rubbish has my brother been spouting?"

"He's behaving himself so far." I glanced up at Dalton, expecting a funny retort from him, but his eyes seemed to have glazed over and his mouth was hanging open.

"We, um, we were just talking about Savannah," I explained, and frowned at Dalton for tuning us out.

Derek took notice of Dalton's expression, too, but continued our conversation. "I take it she's still in the kitchen?"

"Yes," I said, then gave up. "Dalton, what's wrong?"

His full attention was drawn to something over my shoulder, so Derek and I both turned. "Oh, Savannah. Thank goodness. Have you finally been untethered from the stove?"

"Yes, for now." She had removed her chef's jacket and was adjusting the sleeves of her scoop-neck black sweater. "I plated the salads and we'll be eating as soon as . . ."

"As soon as what?"

She didn't answer me.

"Savannah?" I frowned at her. "Hello?" She was frozen in place and didn't seem to hear me.

"Earth to Savannah," I said, and was about to snap my fingers at her. "What's wrong with you . . . oh."

She was staring up at Dalton.

He was staring back.

Both of them seemed to have been struck deaf and dumb. This couldn't be a good thing.

Dalton recovered first. "My God, woman. You're completely bald."

Savannah struggled to take a breath. "Y-yes, I am. Some people have a problem with that."

"Are you kidding?" He almost growled. "It's the sexiest damn thing I've ever seen in my entire life. I . . . I have to touch it. May I?"

She reached up and glided her hand across her shiny pate, then nodded slowly. "Yes."

Savannah was beautiful, petite, and wacky. A few months ago she had shaved her head on a whim, and from the very beginning I thought the look suited her. She usually wore a perky red beret, but tonight her head was gloriously bare. Not that it mattered; she was adorable, hair or not. Dalton seemed to agree. He looked ready to swallow her whole.

I stared at Derek in alarm and then noticed that his hand had turned into a fist. Was he going to punch his brother out? I appreciated the thought, but I grabbed his arm just in case. We didn't need to make this scene any more bizarre than it already was.

Dalton ignored us both and stepped closer to Savannah. After a moment of hesitation, he reached up and touched her shiny bald head. "Smooth. Soft."

"Mm, yes," she said.

"And you smell like heaven."

"That's tarragon," she murmured, batting her eyelashes at him. "It's an aphrodisiac."

Oh, come on. Savannah had never batted her eye-

lashes in her life. And since when was tarragon an aphrodisiac? Although, come to think of it, I did tend to go
a little crazy over a well-made béarnaise sauce.

Savannah had her hand on Dalton's chest now and he
was still touching her head. I'm sorry, but this was
strange. I had never seen my sister act like this before.
And as for Dalton ... what had happened to Mr. Cool
Calm Secret Agent Man? Derek's brother was staring at
my sister as if she'd just dropped down from heaven.

This was weird. I whirled around and glared at Derek.
"Make them stop!"

"Stop what?" He looked as mystified as I felt. He
knew exactly what I was talking about, though, because
his next question was, "How?"

I looked around. "Somebody get a hose."

He laughed, and the sound of Derek's laughter sort of
settled me down. "That won't do."

"Dinner is served," a waiter cried.

"Oh, hell," I muttered. "Don't let them sit together."

"It's too late," Derek said.

I watched helplessly as Dalton led Savannah over to
the long, elaborately set table and took his place beside
her. They continued to stare rapturously at each other as
Dalton discovered new and exciting places on Savannah's bald head to touch or pat or rub or stroke. Good
grief.

It was like watching my great-uncle Roddy the one
and only time he ever took us to the racetrack. Everything was fine until Roddy suddenly spotted a little person in the crowd. He ran over and rubbed the small man's
head for good luck until the little guy finally kicked him
in the shins. "This ain't the Wonderful Land of Oz," he
said with a snarl. And that was the end of Uncle Roddy's
good-luck streak.

But even Uncle Roddy hadn't had the stupefied look
on his face that Dalton did.

"You're enjoying this," I accused Derek.

"I'm enjoying you," he said, and leaned in and kissed me.

"Well, okay, that was enjoyable," I mumbled. "But if you weren't freaked-out, why did you have your fists ready when they first started their staring and drooling contest?"

A little wryly, Derek smiled. "Instinct. Frankly, I've never seen Dalton behave this way—"

"Savannah's never done anything like this before either. For heaven's sake, she's still letting him pet her head!"

Derek laughed and squeezed my hand. "Let's sit down."

"I'm concerned," I whispered as we walked to our places at the table. I chose to sit directly across from my sister and Dalton to keep an eye on them. But now that I was stuck watching them coo and giggle at each other, I realized that it wasn't my best idea ever. How had this happened?

My sister was practically purring with every stroke of Dalton's fingertips along her shaved head.

"It's just a passing fancy, darling," Derek said quietly, and I wasn't sure if he was trying to convince me or himself. "Dalton will only be here a few days."

"But Savannah is vulnerable."

"Everyone is vulnerable, love," he countered.

"Everyone isn't my sister."

"I do understand," Derek whispered, leaning in close to my ear. "I'm fairly protective of your family myself. But this is my brother, not some stranger off the street. Let's just take a wait-and-see attitude, shall we?"

Not like we had much choice, so I nodded and squeezed his hand back.

I tried to mope, but it wasn't a comfortable state for me. So I drank a little wine and tried to get my sister's attention, to no avail. Savannah was still too enraptured by Dalton to notice a little thing like her own flesh and blood. Then I suddenly wondered if I had had the same blurry look the first time I saw Derek. Well, wouldn't that be humiliating to discover?

I nibbled on a few grilled artichoke leaves and tried to zing Dalton with threatening glares, but he didn't notice.

When Savannah lifted some delectable bits of Colette's sausage and polenta onto her fork and held it up to Dalton's lips for him to taste, I reached the limit of my endurance and had to look away. My sister was on her own for now.

We would talk later.

I forced myself to smile and listen and react to other conversations. Gradually I joined the party. As dish after dish was served and the meal progressed and the wine flowed, I shook off most of my tension and managed to enjoy myself—as long as I ignored the flirting and cooing across from me. The food was spectacular, after all. Impossibly, each dish was more phenomenal than its predecessor. And as each one was presented, the chef who was responsible for it received our grateful applause as he or she explained the concept, the ingredients, and the reason why he or she was dedicating it to Baxter.

Derek and I carried on a lively exchange with those seated closest to us, mainly Kevin, Margot, Montgomery, and Peter. Dalton and Savannah occasionally added a word to the conversation, but those moments were few and far between. It was as if they'd been bewitched. I considered asking my mother to work up a magic spell to bring them both back to earth.

Kevin and the others regaled us with more funny kitchen stories. One involved a famous cooking show chef who specialized in Italian cuisine. His wife was allergic to everything and could eat only egg noodles with a dash of bland vegetable oil. Kevin said that everyone on the staff knew when the chef was cheating on his wife because he would whip up two orders of extra-spicy pasta *puttanesca* before taking off for his illicit dates.

As Kevin spoke, Peter cast so many surreptitious glances her way that I started to wonder if he might still be in love with her. I hoped so. They had been such a sweet couple back in Paris. I still didn't understand why they'd ever broken up.

After Raoul's dessert—a breathtaking chocolate cake alternately layered with almond meringue, praline buttercream, and chocolate ganache, served with homemade vanilla bean ice cream and hot fudge sauce—we relaxed with after-dinner drinks and coffee.

Without any planned agenda, the chefs began, one at a time, to stand and give a toast to honor Baxter. Most of their words were much kinder than Baxter deserved, but I suppose they were all keeping in mind the axiom that it was bad luck to speak ill of the dead. Some shared their memories of Paris and tales of horrific kitchen disasters. We laughed, we cried, but mostly we laughed.

Their words were so gracious and heartfelt. And yet . . . more than once during the speeches, I gazed at their faces and wondered which one of them had killed Baxter Cromwell.

I hoped and prayed that someone else entirely had done it.

Besides, Baxter had to know plenty of other people in San Francisco. Maybe he'd had a falling-out with one of his local business partners and that person had had him killed. Or maybe another rival chef did him in. Baxter seemed to thrive on making enemies and ridiculing people on his show. Could he have driven someone past the brink of sanity, causing him or her to lash out at him?

And there was still the random-robbery theory. While the Mission District was gentrifying rapidly, there were plenty of unsavory elements in the area. And that back kitchen door made a convenient entrance and exit for the killer. It was an unlikely scenario, but that didn't mean it was impossible.

Realistically, however, the likeliest suspect was here among the chefs in Baxter's immediate circle, the people sitting around this table. And if one of them did it, what was the motivation? Baxter could be a real bastard, of course, but bastards were seldom murdered. There had to be some stronger emotion driving the killer. Revenge? Greed? Something more personal, like jealousy?

I remembered the look I'd seen in Kevin's eyes when she saw Baxter open Savannah's gift. Her expression had turned to open hatred or, at the very least, contempt for Baxter. Or maybe Savannah. She had dodged my question when I asked her about it the other night, so I was still clueless about her connection, if any, to the book.

And speaking of the book, was it the motive for murder? It was close to priceless, but besides its obvious value, was there something contained within it that was worth stealing?

Were those strange symbols important to someone? I'd seen for myself how Derek had reacted to them. And Dalton had come all the way from England just to get a good look at them. What did they mean? The sooner Dalton figured out those symbols, the sooner we might have an answer. Another long shot, but I was willing to consider anything at this point.

But how could some strange code in a two-hundred-and-thirty-year-old book be a motive for murder?

And if the cookbook wasn't the motive, then where had it disappeared to? Had the killer stolen it? If not, where was it hiding and how could we get our hands on it? I wanted Dalton to solve the puzzle of the odd symbols right now.

The speeches and toasts had grown more and more bawdy as more cognac and port were passed around. Amid the laughter, Montgomery stood to make yet another speech. His bow tie was askew and his mild Southern accent had thickened to a syrupy bayou drawl. He lifted his glass theatrically and said, "All y'all raise your glasses again because I wanna give a toast to that fancyass cappuccino machine over yonder on the bar."

He gestured dramatically, sloshing his drink. Everyone at the table turned to get a look at the glistening copper extravaganza perched at the service end of the bar.

"Why are we toasting a machine, Monty?" Kevin asked, laughing.

"Well, sugar," Monty said, slurring his words, "I gotta figure that's where all the money went."

More alert now, Peter said, "What money are you talking about?"

Monty gazed blearily at Peter. "Hell, man. The money Baxter was blackmailing from me."

Chapter 14

If your soup isn't brown enough, add a spoonful of brown mixture.

—*The Cookbook of Obedience Green*

"Blackmail?" Savannah whispered. She glanced at me and I knew our stunned expressions were identical.

Of course I'd known Baxter was a creep. But blackmail?

I remembered hearing Kevin mention blackmail to Inspector Jaglom. Had she been blackmailed as well?

Everyone in the room stared in shocked silence at Montgomery. Their faces showed varying degrees of disbelief, from mild skepticism to sheer astonishment, like mine, but there were a few shifty gazes avoiding contact, and my suspicious nature made me wonder if there might be more than one case—or even two—of blackmail going around this crowd.

Amazingly enough, I noted, it had taken the revelation of blackmail to wrestle Savannah's attention away from Dalton.

"Montgomery." Derek said his name carefully. "You're saying that Baxter was blackmailing you?"

It was such a serious accusation, Derek probably wanted to make sure Monty wasn't tossing words around flippantly in his drunken state.

"S'what I'm sayin'," Monty muttered, and gulped down another sip of his expensive port.

"Oh, Monty," Margot said. "Why didn't you tell us? We could've done something to help."

Monty waved off her question. "I didn't need y'all thinking I was a bigger ding-a-ling than you already believe I am."

"Nobody thinks you're a ding-a-ling!" Savannah cried. "We love you, Monty."

Margot ignored Savannah's outburst. "I guess most people wouldn't want to admit they were being blackmailed."

"You think?" Peter said it sarcastically, but he looked miserable. That couldn't be good.

"Well." Margot glanced around, then chuckled a little too cheerfully. "Monty, you should know that you're not alone. I'd like to think my money went toward some of these nice new chairs. Comfortable, aren't they?" She bounced back against the chair's plush upholstery.

"What?" Peter shouted. "You were being blackmailed, too? But why?"

Margot gave him a patient look. "For the same reason anyone is blackmailed. Because I have a secret in my past that I want to stay there. Baxter knew all about it and threatened to see that secret splashed across the morning newspapers. So I paid him."

Savannah reached over and squeezed Margot's hand. "But you're a wonderful person, Margot. What could you have ever done that was so bad?"

She laughed harshly and shook her head. "You're cute, Savannah, but do you really think I'm going to tell you what it is? It was a secret, for God's sake. And I had to pay to keep it that way because somehow Baxter found out."

Peter scowled. "I'd like to know how."

"You and me both, pal," Margot muttered and reached for her wine.

"He had a gift," Monty said dryly.

"But when you don't talk about it, the blackmailer gets away with it," Kevin insisted. She looked around the table. "Anyone else? Might as well jump into the confession booth while you can."

There was a long moment of silence, then Peter cleared his throat.

"Oh, no, Peter!" Kevin cried. "Not you, too?"

He shrugged, obviously embarrassed. "He had me right where he wanted me. You all knew Baxter. Remember how he was always in need of quick cash?"

"This is the truth," Raoul said calmly. "I can't tell you how many times he forgot his wallet and I had to pay for his dinner."

"That was one of his favorite tricks," Colette agreed.

Savannah's lips twisted. "He pulled that one on me a few times, too."

"Right-o." Peter nodded. "The story he gave me was that because of the economy, he was having trouble rounding up investors for this place. When I told him I couldn't help him, he suggested that I might not want a certain bit of information to become public. So I was forced to become a *silent partner*, as he put it. I gave him the start-up money for BAX."

"Ah, so it wasn't *blackmail*," Kevin said, her voice dripping with sarcasm. "It was an investment."

"Exactly," Peter said, unable to meet her blunt gaze. "Pretty stupid to let him do that to me, I know. But at the time, I couldn't think of another way out."

"Join the club," Margot said, then added bitterly, "That was our Baxter. Manipulator extraordinaire."

"I prefer the term *royal ass hat*," Peter grumbled.

So much for all that love they'd been spewing forth all evening. What did it say about me that I was more comfortable with them now that they'd dropped the pretense? I'd known all along that Baxter didn't have friends—just people he hadn't used yet. But I'd been willing to go along with the respectful, if less than honest, tone of the group. Guess that was over.

"Well, I'm shocked," Colette said righteously. "I can't believe so many of you could allow yourselves to be used and abused like that."

Monty snorted. "Oh, shut up."

"Come on, Colette," Peter said. "You know how Baxter was. When I told him I didn't appreciate being black-mailed, he laughed. Laughed! He'd justified in his mind that it was simply a case of friends supporting friends."

"It's a wonder no one's killed him before this," Dalton muttered darkly.

"True enough," Derek finished, giving a brief nod to his brother. "So, Peter, you, Margot, and Montgomery were being blackmailed. Is that it?"

No one else spoke up. I looked around the table, studying the faces of people I'd thought I knew. Any of them could still be guarding their secrets. Protecting themselves. Or that could be the end of it. Peter, Margot, and Monty, and no one else. Who knew with this crowd?

In the silence, Margot stood, took in a deep, cleansing breath, and spread her arms in earth mother style, her filmy butterfly shawl flowing around her. "I've accepted my fate and I refuse to be negative anymore. The money's gone and Baxter is, too. I choose to believe that my money allowed him to see his dream become a reality. He opened this beautiful space and invited us all to be a part of it."

"That's lovely," Savannah said, and I almost shook my head at my sister's genuine goodness and naïveté. If Savannah had been on the *Titanic* and someone had tossed her a deck chair as she floundered in the icy sea, my sister would have been charmed by the lovely grain of the wood.

Always looking on the upside, that was Savannah.

"That's bullshit," Colette said.

I leaned toward Colette's opinion. I took one look at

Derek's expression and knew we were both thinking the same thing. There was nothing lovely about blackmail.

But we did have a lovely new motive for murder.

Derek, Dalton, and I left the chefs to their drunken commiserations and went to the kitchen. Despite knowing the place had been searched by the police and then scrubbed clean by Tom and his crew, Dalton was determined to do one final hunt for the cookbook. I thought it seemed pointless, but I still wanted to check out Baxter's office, so I headed there first.

The room was no bigger than a glorified broom closet, but Baxter had managed to outfit it with a small but elegant desk, two utilitarian chairs, and a bookcase overloaded with cookbooks and a stack of cooking magazines.

It took almost no time to search the desk where I found various bills, papers, handwritten menus, and a few office supplies, but no Revolutionary War–era cookbook. I faced the bookshelves. Could Baxter have hidden Obedience's cookbook behind these books? It was possible, so I spent another fifteen minutes searching behind every single book on the shelf, but found nothing.

Disappointed, I returned to the kitchen, where Dalton was on his hands and knees, pushing aside every sponge and spray bottle of cleanser under the spacious industrial sink. With a grunt of disgust, he stood and brushed off his trousers.

"Nothing?" I asked.

"No," Dalton grumbled. "And I'm sweating like a stevedore." He pushed the back door open and stepped outside for some cool air. Derek and I joined him out in the passageway, ready to admit defeat.

Dalton wasn't quite willing to give up yet and began to examine the restaurant's brick facade, looking for a cubbyhole big enough to hide a book.

Exhausted, Derek and I leaned against each other for support. Something furry rubbed up against my ankle and I let out a shriek.

"What is it?" Derek demanded.

I was shuddering and squealing like a little girl while I practically crawled up Derek's body. "Is it a rat? Get it away!"

"Stop yowling, woman," Dalton said, grinning. "It's just a cat."

"A cat?" I summoned my courage and glanced down. It was the pretty white cat we'd first seen the night of Baxter's death. "Okay, I'm not proud, but it scared the hell out of me."

"Yes, well, and I can see why. Terrifying creature, to be sure." Dalton laughed as he poked fun at me. He squatted down to check out the animal. "It looks awfully well fed for a stray."

"Someone may be feeding it," Derek assured him. "We've seen it before."

"It's a very friendly cat." I bent down to greet the animal. "Hello, Bootsie."

Dalton looked askance. "Bootsie? You've named a stray cat Bootsie?"

"It's a perfectly good name." I pointed at the cat. "Look at her. She's got four black boots."

Dalton stared at the cat, then gave me a stern look. "She's plainly mortified by the name."

"She is not," I said, laughing.

"And she's not a stray," Derek said. "She's clean and well behaved. I believe she's roaming the neighborhood, hunting for a safe place to have her kittens."

"Oh, she's pregnant," Dalton said. "My God, how did I miss that? Her stomach is huge."

"What's going on out here?" Savannah asked, as she stood in the doorway.

"That little white cat is back," I told her while the animal in question purred under Dalton's fingers. Then I took a harder look at my sister's features. Her normally cheerful expression was tight, as if strained to the breaking point. A hard night could defeat even Savannah's easy nature. "Are you okay?"

"Not really," Savannah admitted, folding her arms across her chest. "Everyone's leaving. It's time to go home."

We left Bootsie to her nocturnal hunting and returned to the dining room to say good night to our dinner mates. While we chatted with the chefs and made plans for Margot's dinner two nights later, Dalton took the opportunity to check behind the bar for the cookbook. He searched every conceivable hiding place but had no luck back there, either.

The cookbook was nowhere to be found.

We arrived home at one o'clock in the morning. There was no way Savannah could drive back to Sonoma tonight, so she helped me fix up the couch for her to sleep on. It might have been a futile exercise, judging by the temperature of the looks she and Dalton were giving each other. Odds were, she'd spend the night in his bed. But we carried out the task of making up a place to sleep anyway.

And why did I suddenly feel like somebody's mother, chatting inanely while pretending all was safe and sunny? A few minutes later, Derek and I went off to our room and left the youngsters on their own.

"I feel so old," I said as I climbed into bed.

Derek chuckled. "Me, too. We're like the grown-ups chaperoning the children on their first date."

I groaned. "Then we're doing a crappy job as chaperons. Their first date is going to be a lot hotter than ours was, I think."

"Come here, then," he said, pulling me closer to him. "I'll just make that up to you, shall I?"

I laughed. "That's such a great idea. I love it."

"And I love you."

I kissed him. "Love you, too. But please don't ever call me a grown-up again."

The next morning I stumbled out of bed and ran into Savannah at the coffee machine.

"Praise Buddha for automatic coffeemakers," I mumbled, reaching for the pot.

"Hallelujah." She held out her cup.

I filled her cup, then mine, then gave her the once-over. She wore a simple turquoise sleeveless crop top and a pair of pajama bottoms that didn't match. Not the world's hottest outfit for a night of wild jungle sex with a gorgeous stranger. That left me wondering whether she'd slept on the couch all night or not. "You sort of look like you could use another eight hours of sleep."

"Thank you, sis. You look pretty, too."

I chuckled, then sobered. "Look, Savannah, if you don't feel like talking about it, I understand, but I'd really like to know if—"

She held up her hand to stop me. "I'm not discussing where I spent the night, so don't bother asking."

I pulled the half-and-half out of the fridge and added some to my coffee. "I don't care where you spent the night." Liar, liar.

"Then what're you talking about?"

We both sipped our coffee until I couldn't hold back any longer. "Was Baxter blackmailing you?"

She bobbled her coffee mug. "W-what?"

"You heard me. You don't have to tell me what he was blackmailing you for specifically. But if he was doing it, if you were paying him money, I want to know."

"Why in the world would he blackmail me?"

"He was blackmailing every other chef you went to school with. Why not you, too?"

Her shoulders drooped a little and she shook her head. "No, he wasn't blackmailing me."

I studied her expression, looking for the tiniest sign that she might be lying to me. Finally I sighed. "Okay, I believe you."

"Great." She sniffed. "And if you'd thought about it for more than a split second, you would've realized I have nothing in my past that's worth being blackmailed over."

"That's not a bad thing, Bugs."

"Yeah, yeah. I'm boring. The always cheerful, do-the-right-thing good girl. Lucky me." She gulped down the rest of her coffee, rinsed out her cup, and placed it in the dishwasher. Then she opened the refrigerator to forage for food. "Listen, do you mind if I stay here with you for a few days?"

"Not at all, but what about your restaurant?"

"I called Steve and asked if he could fill in for a while."

Steve Farelli owned Umbria, the Italian restaurant down the Lane from Arugula. He was a member of the commune and our family had known his for years. He had three grown sons who also cooked, so among the four of them, they could cover both restaurants.

"Aren't you afraid he'll slip some pasta Bolognese onto the menu?"

She smiled. "He promised to keep things clean." She pulled a small dessert dish from the fridge. "What's this?"

"It's a syllabub. It's like a pudding."

"I know what a syllabub is. But where'd you get it?"

"I made it."

"No way." She turned it this way and that, examining it clinically. "It's so pretty."

"It tastes good, too." I grabbed a spoon from the drawer and gave it to her. "Try it."

She hesitated, but then managed to take a small bite. "Wow. It's delicious."

I wanted to squeal with glee since this was supreme praise from my sister the chef, but I managed to maintain some dignity. "Thank you."

"You really made it?" She took another bigger bite. "It's so good. Mm. How'd you get it so smooth?"

"Okay, now you're just teasing me."

"No, I'm serious. This is excellent." She stuffed another spoonful into her mouth. "You should make this for one of our dinners."

"Do you mean it?" Coming from my sister, that was a huge compliment. "I could do that."

"Good. I'll tell Margot." She gobbled up the last spoonful. "Is there any more left?"

"There's one more, but I should save it for Derek."

She pouted and used her spoon to scrape the sides of the bowl. "Okay, but you have to make it again."

"I will." Wow, this was great. My first real cooking success! Almost enough to take my mind off of murder and blackmail. Almost.

I took her dish to the sink and rinsed it. "So, listen, do you need to borrow some of my clothes while you're here or . . ."

"No, Dalton and I are going to drive out to Dharma to pick up some of my things, then we'll be back later this afternoon. You sure you're okay with me staying here?"

"Of course I'm okay with it." I gritted my teeth and added, "I just don't want you to . . ."

She planted her fist on her hip. "Don't want me to what? Have sex in your guest bedroom?"

"No, smart-ass." I lowered my voice. "I don't want you to get hurt."

She was taken aback at first, but recovered and grabbed me in a fierce hug. "I love you. You're my favorite sister."

"Of course I am." I rubbed her back. "I love you, too."

"Believe me, I don't intend to get hurt," she whispered. "Dalton's awesome and everything, but I've got my eyes wide-open." She stepped back, grabbed her already-rinsed mug and refilled it. "Now butt out, please."

I laughed softly. "Okay, okay. Not that I can blame you. My God, he's so cute."

"I know!" She did a dramatic sigh. "It's like I've got my very own Derek doll."

I snorted. "Please don't let him hear you say that."

"Hear you say what?" Derek said.

We both jumped and I laid my hand against my heart. "You scared me silly."

"He should wear a bell," Savannah muttered, then glared at him. "How long were you listening in?"

"I just got here," Derek said, as he wiped his forehead with his gym towel. "And I brought bagels." He pointed to a brown bag on the bar.

"My hero." Fresh bagels from Hello Deli, a favorite spot over by South Park, were a rare treat. "Thanks."

"Cream cheese is in the bag." Derek nudged his way into our compact kitchen area. "Is there any coffee left?"

I moved out of the way to give him access to the cof-feepot. He wore gym shorts and a faded Oxford T-shirt with the sleeves torn off. His tanned skin glistened with sweat from his morning run. My poor little heart was getting quite the aerobic workout.

Savannah eased past me and left the kitchen. "Oh, hi."

"Hello there," Dalton said, his voice low and seductive.

I glanced through the bar opening and saw him kissing her. He was dripping in sweat, too, but she didn't seem to notice or care.

Oh, yeah, no danger there.

My sister didn't stand a chance.

I hadn't seen Dalton standing on the other side of the bar and I wondered again how much of our conversation the two men had overheard. I mentally replayed our words and decided it didn't matter all that much, except for my sister's slightly twisted "Derek doll" comment.

Savannah's cell phone rang and she pulled it out of her pocket. "Hello?" There was a long pause as she listened and then she said, "What?"

She sounded so distressed that I hurried into the dining area to find out who was calling her. Derek joined me and we watched her eyes widening more and more at the news she was hearing. A minute later, she hung up, looking shell-shocked.

"What's wrong, Bugs?" I demanded. "Who was that?"

"It was Kevin. She's freaking out. The police have taken Peter in for questioning. She thinks he's going to be arrested for Baxter's murder."

Chapter 15

A fat neck of mutton eats well if soaked in red wine twenty-four hours.

—*The Cookbook of Obedience Green*

"They must've found out about the blackmail. Why else would they arrest him?" Too frantic to sit down, Kevin zigzagged back and forth across the living room of her plush hotel suite. Wearing trim jeans, a simple T-shirt, and flip-flops, she looked like she'd be more at home playing catch on the Marina Green.

"They haven't arrested him, Kevin," Derek pointed out. "They're just asking him some questions." Derek had called Inspector Jaglom on the way over to Kevin's hotel. He was in the middle of the interrogation, but had briefly told Derek they weren't planning to arrest Peter. Not yet, anyway.

"Kevin, you should sit down," I said. "You'll make yourself sick if you get too worked up over this." I watched her from the elegant club chair I'd chosen. Two matching chairs had been arranged on either side of a delicate tea table in front of the large window that overlooked Union Square.

The view was fabulous and the room was beyond deluxe. I had been impressed with Baxter's generosity when I heard that he'd paid for these Campton Place suites for his chef friends. But now, after hearing all the blackmail accusations, I had to wonder who had really picked up the tab.

"But who told the police about the blackmail?" Kevin demanded of no one in particular as she ignored my pleas and kept up her frantic pacing. "I mean, it was just us there. And if someone told about Peter, why not Monty and Margot, too? Why Peter in particular?"

"We don't know that it is only Peter being investigated," Derek said in that oh so calm British manner of his.

I blinked at him. Hadn't considered that. Just because we hadn't heard about anyone else being called in didn't mean others hadn't been.

"That's true," Kevin said, and she seemed to take a calming breath.

"Besides," I continued, "the police might be questioning Peter about something completely different."

"What could that possibly be?" Kevin's eyes widened.

"All I meant was," I said quickly, "maybe they're just trying to clear up some loose ends."

She flashed me a look of hope that faded quickly. She wasn't totally buying my words and I couldn't blame her.

"But . . ." Savannah frowned in confusion. "Kevin's question still stands. How did the police find out about the blackmail?"

Dalton sat on the arm of the suede love seat next to her. "It does seem a bit of a coincidence that they picked Peter up less than twelve hours after several of you confessed to being blackmailed."

In silence, the five of us exchanged glances with each other, trying to figure out what that might mean. Savannah finally broke the silence. "It had to be one of us. Some big-mouth chef squealed to the cops."

Squealed? I almost laughed. "You channeling Edward G. Robinson or what?"

She scowled at me. "Maybe I am. I'm so pissed off. It wasn't a coincidence. Somebody called the cops on Peter. That's so mean."

"You're right," I said. "It was mean and nasty and a complete betrayal of the friendships you've all maintained for years. But which of you did it?"

Tiny lines of worry appeared on her forehead and I knew what she was thinking. She could accept that someone had betrayed Peter, but she didn't want it to be someone she knew and liked. She could accept that there were harsh realities in the world, but she didn't want to see them up close and personal.

This was my sister in a nutshell.

"Maybe it was one of the waitstaff," she said weakly. "They were there all evening, listening to us talk."

"You think one of the waiters called the cops?"

"No." She groaned and waved her hands in frustration. "I don't know, but I'd rather believe it was a stranger than one of our friends."

"I know you would," I said sympathetically.

"But why just Peter?" Kevin's voice cut through it all. "I mean, as far as we know, he's the only one being questioned, but Monty and Margot both confessed to being victims, too."

"We won't know anything for sure until the police have finished," Derek told her, keeping that smooth tone in his voice. "Then I'll call Inspector Jaglom again and try to get more information."

"Good. That's good." Kevin nodded desperately and wrung her hands as if looking for a lifeline to cling to.

Savannah's nerves didn't seem to be doing much better, so Dalton knelt before her and took her hands in his. "Peter's not in any trouble. He's just being questioned. They won't arrest him."

I willed his words to be true. Then I looked at Derek. "Did Inspector Jaglom tell you how they found out about the blackmail?"

"No." He thought it over. "I'm not going to wait to

phone him. I'll call right now and leave a message for him to call me when they're finished."

"Would you?" Kevin said, rubbing her arms nervously. "I'd like to know that Peter's all right."

Savannah caught my gaze and raised an eyebrow quizzically. I gave her a quick nod. We were reading the signs and Kevin's feelings for Peter definitely seemed to be growing stronger. I would love to see them get back together—if the man Kevin loved didn't end up rotting in a jail cell.

But even as that thought crossed my mind, I pushed it aside. I just could not imagine Peter as a killer.

As Derek stepped into the small foyer to make his telephone call, Kevin continued with the pacing.

"Can I get you a drink or something?" I asked.

"What?" She glanced at me as if she had just realized I was there. "Oh. No, thanks. I'm just nervous."

"I understand."

She brushed her thick, dark hair back from her face and massaged her neck. "Oh, God. I'm just afraid his reason for being blackmailed might be so much worse than the others. Which means his motive for murder is stronger. At least, that's how the police will see it. Won't they? I assume that's why they brought him in."

"So you know the reason why Peter was being blackmailed?"

She flopped down in the chair across from me, leaned over, and held her head in her hands. "Yes."

"You don't have to tell us," Savannah said quickly.

I flashed her a look of disbelief along with my telepathic message: *Are you crazy? Let's hear it!*

"You're right, I don't have to tell you," Kevin said, "and I wouldn't if Peter hadn't already confessed to everyone about the blackmail. Now, though, I want you to know. Maybe if the people in his life know what he's been through, he'll finally be able to let it go."

"It might help," I said encouragingly. Okay, I felt a

tiny, tiny twinge of guilt. Yes, I wanted to help Peter and Kevin. Of course! But my inherent inquisitiveness was clamoring for information, too.

Kevin shook her head in weary confusion. "I'm still upset that he actually paid Baxter money to keep it a secret."

Derek stepped back into the living room area. "I left the inspector a message."

Savannah smiled at him. "Thank you, Derek."

"Come and sit down," I said. "Kevin is about to tell us why Peter was being blackmailed."

"Yes, very juicy stuff," she said, and I was glad to see her humor was returning, despite the unhappy revelation she was about to make.

"I can see we're all ears," Derek said, his lips twisting sardonically as he looked straight at me. Was there anything better than having a man in your life who knew all your foibles and loved you anyway? He pulled a chair away from the dining table and sat.

The confession was juicy indeed. Kevin revealed that when Peter first opened his restaurant in London, he worked with a partner who tried to cut corners everywhere possible. Peter was too busy keeping the kitchen running at the highest possible level to pay attention to his partner's bad habits. That is, until the day the knucklehead went out and purchased a large order of fish that wasn't quite fresh. When a number of Peter's customers came down with food poisoning, the restaurant was almost closed down by the health department.

Peter disbanded the partnership and cleaned up his act immediately. He took control of his business and reestablished relationships with all the vendors the partner had alienated.

"Baxter must have found out somehow," Kevin said, "and was able to use that information to extort money from him."

I suddenly remembered my conversation with Peter the other night when I happened to mention poisoned fish. No wonder he had turned so pale. He must have thought I was either psychic or just plain evil.

Savannah sighed. "The last thing a chef wants is a reputation for making people sick."

"But it wasn't even his fault," I said. As a blackmailable (if that was a word) secret, it was pretty slim. I don't know what I'd been expecting, but it wasn't this. There had to be hundreds of chefs around the world who'd had the misfortune of buying tainted fish at least once in their careers.

"It was his restaurant, his responsibility," Kevin said morosely. Then she began to chew her lower lip nervously. "But there's more."

"More? Good grief," Savannah said.

"Now, I doubt this had anything to do with why Baxter was blackmailing him," Kevin admitted. "But I might as well spill the entire jar of beans. I'm sick to death of all the secrets."

"Spill away," I said, trying not to sound too eager. I was curious, I admit it. And seriously? I needed there to be more to Peter's deep, dark, secret past than a bad partner who bought old fish.

"All right," she said. "It's just that Peter used to be a bit of a . . . well, a kleptomaniac."

"What?"

Savannah glared at me. So maybe I'd shrieked the word, but honestly? A kleptomaniac? It was positively Dickensian. In other words, *oddball weird.*

"I know it's quite odd," Kevin admitted. "But Peter grew up in a wretchedly poor family. He never had much of anything nice. I've always had a feeling that was the reason he was attracted to shiny things. When he was very young, he would find little bits of glass and pretty shells and keep them in a cigar box. He showed them to me once. But as he grew older, he started to take things that belonged to other people. Small things, like a brightly colored pen or a Christmas ornament."

"Doesn't sound too awful, I suppose," Savannah murmured aloud, although she looked at me as if to say, *She has got to be kidding.*

Good to know my sister and I were on the same mental pathway. I mean, come on. Peter? A kleptomaniac?

"I don't even know if he considered it stealing," Kevin said. "And if a friend mentioned that something had gone missing, Peter would return it, simple as that. It usually happened around a special occasion when he wanted a memento to remember it by. Or when he was under quite a bit of stress."

"Does he still do it?" Dalton asked, and I noticed he didn't sound as amused as Savannah and I did.

"He finally went to therapy to overcome the problem. But to be honest," Kevin said on a sigh, "I'm afraid he might still do it once in a while. Not often, but again, stress plays a big part."

"I'm not sure he would want us to know this," Derek said softly.

"Oh, the entire village knew about it," Kevin said matter-of-factly. But she was biting her lip again, so I wondered if Derek's comment had upset her. "If anything went missing, the townspeople always checked with Peter first. He was quite casual and open about it. And honestly, it was harmless for the most part. He never took anything significant or expensive."

Derek's smile was reassuring. "In that case, I don't believe you've betrayed any confidences."

Savannah said, "Maybe this was why Baxter was blackmailing him. He might not have known about the rotten fish."

"It's possible," Kevin said. "But if this was Baxter's reason for threatening him, Peter couldn't have taken it seriously. Honestly, there were a hundred different people back home who already knew about it."

"And when you think about it," I added, "since he was a world-class chef, even if his secret got out, it would simply make him appear, you know, eccentric."

"Right," Kevin said. "So if he did give Baxter any

money over it, Peter might've considered it simply a way to help out an old friend."

"Then it wasn't truly blackmail," Dalton reasoned.

But Derek shook his head. "I can't agree. I think this was the reason he was being blackmailed. Perhaps a few folks back home knew the truth, but if Baxter was threatening to tell the whole world of his kleptomania, Peter would have felt he had no choice but to pay him off. I can't imagine you'd want the clientele of your five-star restaurant to know that the chef might be pilfering their pocketbooks while they were dining."

"Oh. Well. I suppose, since you put it that way. No chef would want that," Kevin mused.

"Kevin," I said, "do you think Peter and Margot and Montgomery were the only ones being blackmailed?"

"I have no idea. He wasn't blackmailing me, I can tell you that much. I would've kicked him in the . . . well, you know."

"Yes, we know where you'd have kicked him," I said, swallowing a laugh.

She bared her teeth in a grim smile. "And I'd have handed him his bollocks stewed in sauce."

There was a moment of bemused silence.

"You always were a creative chef," Savannah said finally, as Dalton squirmed uneasily in his chair.

Later that afternoon, Derek and I were lounging in the living room when Inspector Jaglom called back to let us know that the police had just sent Peter home. Jaglom confirmed that they had received a call about Baxter blackmailing a number of chefs. He assured Derek that the cops would be questioning the other two chefs who'd admitted to being extorted.

As soon as they ended the call, Derek related the rest of the conversation to me.

"Did he tell you who called in the tip?" I asked.

"It was anonymous."

"Damn." I jumped up and paced back and forth along the couch. "Did you ask if it was a man or a woman?"

"Yes, love," he said. "They think it was a woman."

"They *think*?"

"That's about the same tone I took with Nathan," Derek said, his lips quirking up.

"Well, what did he say?"

"He said they'll analyze the tape if it becomes an issue."

I was pretty sure my eyeballs were rolling like whirlybirds. "If it *becomes* an issue? It's an issue!"

"Yes, love," he said, chuckling at my righteous ire, and reached out and grabbed me, pulling me down on the couch next to him. "I convinced him of that."

"Good." I leaned against him and rested my head on his strong shoulder. My poor brain was racing with too many questions and not enough answers. "Thank you. I should get up and call Kevin to let her know, but I'm too comfortable to move."

"Then stay here." He wrapped his arm around me. "And Peter's probably called her already."

"Oh, good thought." I sighed and cuddled up to him. "Do you like them?"

"I presume you're referring to Kevin and Peter. I do like them."

"I do, too." I glanced up at him. "I always have. And I hate seeing them so worried. I was thinking maybe we could invite them over for dinner sometime this week. Of course, she's a chef, so I wouldn't dream of actually cooking for her. But we could order in Thai food or something."

"Something." Derek grinned.

"Kevin was really nice to me in Paris. I just hope she and Peter get back together."

"Kevin is charming," he agreed.

I frowned at him. "I'm hearing a 'but' in there somewhere."

"You've got good ears." He turned and faced me. "*But* I'm frankly worried that someone you consider a friend might be unmasked as a murderer."

My mouth dropped open. "You think Kevin killed Baxter?"

"No, I honestly don't," he insisted, though his thoughtful scowl told me there was more coming. "But we've been wrong before about such things, haven't we?"

Frowning, I stared at my hands. We had been wrong before, damn it, and I really didn't want to be wrong this time. I really needed a manicure, I thought absently. Working with paper made my nails so darn dry.

"Darling?"

"I'm thinking," I replied grumpily. I knew what Derek was talking about. Last year, I'd met a really nice woman while on a job, and we became fast friends. I invited her into my home and introduced her to my family, only to find out much later that I was being used as a pawn in a clever killer's game. It wasn't a good feeling and I never wanted to go through anything like that again.

"But this is a different situation," I claimed, determined to let the past go as we worked toward a solution to the present problems. "I've known Kevin for years. She's one of Savannah's dearest friends and she was very good to me when I was in Paris. And there's Peter, too. We've known him a long time."

"I see." He nodded soberly. "So in a way, you're saying they've been vetted."

I smiled. "Exactly."

"All right, I'll go along with that. The fact is, I like them both, too. So we'll hope for the best and proceed apace."

Proceed apace? How could I not love it when he talked like that?

"Aye, Captain," I said, giving him a smart salute. Because, truly, he sounded like the commander of Starfleet. And, yes, I wasn't just a book nerd, I loved *Star Trek*, too. But was that really the issue? "I'm going to call and invite her over for dinner. Peter, too. I'll make it Wednesday night. And I'm hoping Savannah and Dalton will be here, too."

"Sounds like we're having a party," he said, and squeezed my shoulders gently. "But you might want to prepare yourself."

"For what?"

His jaw tightened. "For the moment when one of the chefs you've grown so close to is arrested for murder."

Chapter 16

As for all fish, scale them, gut them, cut off their heads.
—*The Cookbook of Obedience Green*

Early Monday morning, Derek left for the office and a while later Savannah and Dalton went out to explore the city. The two of them planned to swing by BAX sometime in the afternoon to check in with the other chefs already prepping for the competition dinner tomorrow night.

Another dinner. I could already feel my hips expanding at the thought of all that rich gourmet food I'd be consuming. So in a lame attempt at a preemptive strike, I did fifty sit-ups and then decided to race up and down the stairs three times. I went a little crazy. There were six floors in my building, so by my second trip up the stairs, I was dragging and moaning with each step. It wasn't pretty. I was thankful none of my neighbors or housemates were out there to ridicule me.

On the upside, I'd worked off at least, oh, a half serving of ravioli, maybe? That was just sad.

I took a quick shower, dried my hair, and dressed for work in jeans, sweater, socks, and Birkenstocks. I was sort of happy the house was empty because I found myself easily distracted lately. On the other hand, I wished Dalton had stayed home to work on Obedience's cookbook.

I needed him to put all the pieces together because it was possible that something in the book would clear Savannah's name. But what? Did the squiggles and noodlings in the book mean anything? Were they part of a secret code that some desperate person might kill for? Or were they simply the doodles of a bored housekeeper? Did the book have anything to do with Baxter's death? Or was the connection merely coincidental?

With a sigh, I realized I couldn't exactly force Dalton to work on the book because, essentially, he was on vacation. And I didn't begrudge him spending time with Savannah because she was so happy and they were obviously having a good time together. But the fact was that as long as the murder remained unsolved, Savannah was still a suspect.

Not that Dalton was to blame for that. But still, I was anxious for him to figure out what those symbols and figures meant. Who knew if the answers would lead us to the killer, but at this point it was as good a theory as any.

I filled my coffee cup and left the kitchen. At the end of the bar were the scattered, dog-eared copy pages of the cookbook, right where Dalton had left them.

I picked a page at random, as I'd been doing lately, and read the first entry.

> 2 October 1775. I was counseled at an early age to depend upon my good character alone to recommend me to society. Miss Ashford at Budding House advised that, as an orphan, I was to adhere to those rules and maxims that best established the female character: Virtue, modesty, good sense, good will. These, together with a pleasant countenance, would go a long way toward separating the governess from the chimney sweep.

"Poor Obedience!" I wanted to cry for the girl. I knew she was brave and honorable and smart, but she had always had to fight for her place in society, simply because of an accident of birth.

I dropped the pages onto the bar and walked down the hall to my studio. And there was poor *Jane Eyre*, lying battered and bruised on my table. I was surrounded by plucky heroines! I could hear *Jane* calling my name, begging me to fix her up. Or maybe it was Ian's voice I heard, yelling at me to finish the damn book. So I did.

At my worktable, I removed the white cloth protecting the chunks of heavy board stock, peeling, rotted leather, and stiff paper. The mere smell of the book pulled me right back into the concentration zone. How could I not want to be here? *Jane* so clearly needed my help. I scooted my high chair closer to the surface as an interesting cover design concept began to take shape in my mind.

Ian had given me carte blanche on this book restoration, which meant I was free to choose any cover style, color, and endpaper design I wanted. The reason he wasn't concerned was because the book's historical significance was minor and the cover had already been replaced once before, in 1923.

Ian had known me long enough to know that I would never be tempted to veer too far from the guidelines of the American Institute for Conservation. In other words, the antiquarian book world would frown on a shocking pink-and-tangerine-striped *Jane Eyre*. So I played by the rules and always tried to be mindful of a book's historical integrity. The materials I chose would be close to identical to those found in any bookbinding studio back in 1847 when the book was first created.

That same philosophy went into the method of stitching the pages back together and affixing the new cover to the text block. I would try to be as true to the original materials and style as possible, minus the mistakes that had caused the structural problems in the first place.

Days ago I had cleaned and brushed the pages free of the musty bits of dirt and dust that seemed to collect in old books despite the care owners took to keep them safe.

Now *Jane* was ready for her final deconstruction.

After popping two malted milk balls into my mouth for energy, I picked up my trusty surgical scalpel and began to cut the strands of old binding thread from the middle page of each signature. I separated the assembled pages one by one, pulling more threads away as I went. The loose pages were stacked neatly on a new pile.

Once the entire text block was free of the gnarly old threads and bits of hardened glue left from the original binding, I lined up the pages exactly even and placed them as a block into a press, sewn side up. I measured exactly where I wanted the eight new sewing holes to go, and then I measured again. And then I did it again.

I was still paranoid about getting these measurements right because I'd done them wrong once, many years ago. My teacher had given me so much grief that I never forgot the lesson. *Measure twice, cut once,* as my father always advised. In my case, it was measure *three* times, cut once.

I pulled out my handheld razor saw and lined the blade up with the pencil marks I'd made. I sawed through the thick paper block precisely one-sixteenth of an inch in the eight marked spots.

In case it isn't instantly obvious: I can be a little anal when it comes to this stuff.

My sewing frame was already set up, and now I took three lengths of linen tape and secured each of them around the top rung of the frame. I slipped a weight on the ends so each would hang down straight and even. Once the text block was lined up next to the linen tapes, I tightened the frame enough that the tapes became taut.

Then came my thread. I cut off a lengthy piece of thick white bookbinding thread and ran it through a chunk of beeswax to coat it. That would keep it from tangling and spinning. Then I threaded a serious-looking, three-and-a-half-inch bookbinder's needle.

I grabbed a few more malted milk balls to help me concentrate, because threading the needle sounded simple, but it wasn't. You had to dent the thread in one spot and actually pierce the thread in another.... Well, I couldn't begin to describe the intricate way a bookbinder threaded her needle. That is, I could, but I might put you to sleep. Besides, it was something you had to see for yourself, like the Grand Canyon or Old Faithful.

I got lost in my work, sewing signature after signature, securing the entire block to the linen tapes with tiny stitches that would hold everything together.

When Dalton and Savannah walked into the house, I raised my head and only then noticed the time. Almost five o'clock. Wow, I really could focus when I wanted to.

I greeted them, then confessed, "I was going to order dinner, but I got a little carried away with my work."

"We brought food home," said my darling, wonderful, thoughtful sister, holding up several grocery bags. "I'll cook."

I tried to contain my yelps of joy. While Savannah carried everything into the kitchen, Dalton stayed and stared at the odd-looking contraption on my worktable, trying to figure out what I used it for.

Then he made a guess. "Ah, it's a frame."

"That's right."

He continued to circle it, studying it as though he were Sherlock Holmes trying to solve an irksome mystery. He finally declared, "It's ingenious in its simplicity."

I pointed out the features, explained the wooden screws, the linen tabs, and the kettle stitch. His eyes were still clear, not blurry, so I considered my mini-lecture a success.

"Fascinating." He wandered around the workshop, pulling open the map drawers where I stored the materials I used for covers and endpapers, and then examining the Peg-Board that held fifty different colors and gauges of thread.

"What's the hot plate for?" he asked.

"I use it to heat my tools for gilding."

"Brilliant."

"Are you going out again tomorrow?" I asked.

He abandoned his tour and joined me at the worktable. "Alas, no. Today was a lark and your sister's a charming companion. But tomorrow I've vowed to work on the cookbook code."

"Thank you."

"Now I can't promise to clear your sister's name, but I do pledge to crack the code."

I was glad to hear it. The whole idea of finding a secret code in a cookbook was intriguing enough to have my natural nosiness kicked into high gear. Of course, it would probably turn out to be some meaningless recipe tips, but the fact that Dalton was intrigued enough to give it a try made me happy.

"I'll be working in here," I said, glancing around my workshop. "But it's fine with me if you'd like to use this desk. It's a little roomier than Derek's desk in the bedroom. But the bedroom will be quieter, if that's what you'd prefer."

"Thanks." He pushed away from the table and gave me a wink. "I'll see how I feel in the morning after a short run. By the way, did you know you live a mere six blocks from a Major League Baseball stadium?"

"Yes," I replied with a laugh. "That was a major selling point for this place as far as my father was concerned."

"I agree completely. I'd love to catch a ball game there sometime," he added wistfully. "I'll bet you can see the Bay from the seats."

"You can, and you're welcome to come back for a ball game anytime," I said, smiling up at him.

"We'll see about that. Now I'm off to get a cooking lesson."

I just had a thought. "You're not a vegetarian, are you?"

"Lord, no. I was just joking about getting a lesson. My real job title tonight is apprentice sous chef."

"Lucky you," I said, as I cleared away the last of the tools from my worktable.

"I think so. Can't wait to try Savannah's cooking."

A wry voice in my mind whispered that her cooking was the only thing he hadn't sampled yet. "You won't be disappointed."

"Absolutely not." His lips twitched. "I'm pathetically grateful to anyone who's willing to cook me dinner."

Ah, something we had in common. Dalton really was charming.

"I know what you mean," I said with a short laugh.

"I'll admit to you, it's not just the food I'm grateful for. It's the chef." He shrugged a little and his smile turned tender. "'Tis Savannah, after all. I won't be disappointed."

The next morning I walked Derek out to the front door. "You'll swing by and pick me up tonight?"

He leaned in for a slow kiss that gave me a bigger jolt than my first cup of coffee. "I'll call you as I'm leaving the office, but I expect to be here by seven. I'm looking forward to another gastronomic feast."

"Me, too." I patted my stomach. "But you'll be sorry. I'll need a new wardrobe by the time the chefs leave town."

He snaked his arm around my waist and yanked me up against him. "I'm mad about the way you look. Never worry about that. Every part of you is perfect."

I smiled, delighted. "And I love you. Have I told you lately?"

"Not enough," he said, his blue eyes twinkling with laughter. "But I've scheduled a full week next month to give you time to have your way with me."

"Only a week? It won't be nearly enough time."

"We'll make do with what we have."

I reached up and cupped his face in my palms. Honestly, what had I ever done to deserve this amazing man being in love with me? "Why wait? Kiss me, please? And I'll tell you now."

He did, several times, and grinned as he left. From my doorway, I watched him walk down the hall to the elevator, where his cell phone began to ring. He answered the call and almost instantly his smiling features went hard and flat. A twist of nerves flared in the pit of my stomach. I continued to watch as his body grew more tense. When he looked back at me and scowled, I ran down the hall to him. He slipped his free arm around me and held tight. What in the world was going on?

Finally, he said, "We'll be right there."

"Who was that?" I demanded immediately when he hung up. "What's wrong? What happened?"

His lips compressed in frustration and anger. "It was Peter." His arm tightened around me and I knew it would be bad. Still, when he spoke again, I couldn't believe it.

"He and Kevin arrived at Baxter's restaurant early to help prepare for dinner and they found Montgomery. He's dead."

Savannah was inconsolable and I couldn't blame her. I shed plenty of tears myself, and I had barely gotten to know Monty over the past week. But he was such a lovely, giant panda bear of a man, so funny, sweet, and mischievous in all the best ways. How could anyone who'd ever met him help but love him?

As it turned out, though, there was someone who hadn't loved Montgomery at all. And I had no doubt that it was the same person who had killed Baxter. Perhaps Monty had figured out who the killer was and confronted him or her. If he had, there was no way the killer could have allowed Monty to live.

What other reason could there possibly be? Baxter had had tons of enemies. But Monty . . .

Savannah cried quietly in Dalton's arms in the backseat of Derek's Bentley, all the way to BAX. I admit I had to wonder if Dalton might be coming to regret being mixed up in her life, but he seemed wrapped up in her completely. And for that I could've kissed him.

Not that I didn't think any man on the planet wouldn't be damned lucky to be involved with my sister, but there were a lot of emotions flying around these days. Some guys didn't handle emotions well. I'm just saying . . .

By the time we arrived at BAX, police cars and emergency vehicles surrounded the place. We had to wait at the door until a uniformed officer could find one of the detective inspectors to allow us inside. Even then, we were shuffled off to a few corner tables to wait with the other chefs and restaurant staff.

As soon as Colette and Kevin saw Savannah, the three women ran to each other and held on. There were sobs and sniffles and teary-eyed questions asking why this had to happen to Monty, of all people.

That was the real question, after all. And I couldn't help but think that anyone in this room might have the answer to that question. What had happened to Monty pretty much put the ol' kibosh on the random mugger theory. The killer was definitely one of the chefs.

But which one?

I glanced around. Raoul and Peter were talking quietly in the corner. Raoul was weeping openly and it made me like him even more than I already did. There was something so honest and real about a strong man showing such naked emotion.

"Oh, Brooklyn, isn't it awful?"

I turned and saw Kevin, who grabbed me in a teary hug.

"I'm so sorry," I whispered, meaning every word.

"It was so horrible," she said, her voice trembling.

"What happened? Can you tell me?"

She nodded, then sniffed a few times to catch her breath. "Peter drove me and Margot over here and we walked in talking and joking, acting like we owned the place. Peter and I were teasing Margot about the menu."

"What about the menu?" I asked.

Kevin giggled, right on the edge of hysteria. "She'd forgotten the hoisin sauce recipe for her spareribs. She was mortified! But when she called her sous chef up in Seattle to get it, he reminded her that she had threatened him with death if he ever gave away that recipe. So she's yelling that it's her recipe, but he's adamant. 'How do I know this is really you?' he says."

Kevin was laughing and crying now and had to stop and take a few deep breaths to calm down. "Anyway, we were the first ones to arrive. We waited out here for Monty, chatting and such while Margot made cappuccinos at the bar. But after ten minutes or so, Monty still hadn't arrived, so Margot finally decided to get started. She turned the corner into the kitchen hallway and screamed." A shudder wracked Kevin's entire body. "I've never heard anyone scream so loudly. It was awful. I'll never forget that sound."

I completely understood, having both heard that sound and been the one making it in times past. "Did you see what she was screaming about?"

"Yes." She gulped a few times, then said, "Monty was on the floor in the hallway. It was a gruesome sight. His back was arched up and stiff, you know? Like he was lying on a big exercise ball or something. Peter got close enough to check for a pulse, just in case. I stayed back, but I could still see Monty's eyes." She shuddered again and wrapped both arms around her middle as if trying to soothe herself, but it wasn't working. "They were wide-open and . . . and there was some vile dried substance around his mouth and . . ." She gulped loudly. "Oh, God."

Suddenly she cupped her hand over her mouth and ran out the front door. I assumed she was losing her breakfast, and I was feeling a little queasy myself now.

But my mind was too busy to indulge my uneasy stomach at the moment. Monty's back was arched? A substance dried on his mouth? Eyes wide-open? What in the world could have caused him to die so horrifically? I was hardly an expert, but it sounded like some kind of poisoning to me.

And, that traitorous voice inside whispered, who knows better how to poison someone than a chef?

"Darling."

I turned and saw Derek hovering inches away. Absurdly relieved, I pushed all thoughts out of my mind, walked into his arms and grabbed hold of him. "Did you hear what she said?"

"Yes," he murmured. "It sounds like poison. Possibly strychnine."

"I was thinking poison also." I tipped my head back to look up at him. "But other than that, I don't have a clue."

"Strychnine poisoning is a terrible way to die," Derek murmured, his tone grave. "Severe muscular contractions cause the victim to asphyxiate. It's extremely painful but short-lived. Death comes quickly."

My turn to shudder now. "Okay, too much information."

He hugged me a little tighter. "Sorry, darling. I'm used to you wanting more information, not less."

"I'm rethinking my position on that." I appreciated that he was trying to keep me in the crime scene loop, but Kevin's description had creeped me out thoroughly. No wonder she went tearing out of here.

Strangely enough, I'd recently been involved in another murder by poisoning. If things kept going like this, I was going to need a follow-up therapy session with Guru Bob.

Thinking of Guru Bob reminded me of something else. While I might've been grossed out by the thought of Monty dying in such a horrible way, this wasn't about me. No, this was all about poor Monty, big, brawny, fun-loving Monty, who didn't have an enemy in the world until last night. Somebody had killed him brutally, painfully, willfully. And I vowed to go to any lengths necessary to bring that cold-blooded killer to justice.

I also had to find a way to wrap this up quickly. With two chefs murdered now, I was more worried than ever about Savannah. What if she had inadvertently seen something? Or heard something? She might be oblivious to whatever it was, but if a killer thought she was a threat, he'd stop her as Monty had been stopped.

Oh, God.

Just the thought of how Monty had died turned my stomach, but I had to stay strong. Not just for him, but for my sister and the other chefs who were my friends.

"I'm going back to the kitchen to talk to the police," Derek said, snapping me out of my short mind trip. "Will you be all right out here with your sister?"

It was official. Derek thought I was a wimp. Damn. I was *not* a wimp. Okay, I never did too well around blood. And I hated this "gift" of finding dead bodies. But I wouldn't run and hide. Never had, never would. (Despite how much the craven part of me might want to!)

After a few head-clearing breaths, I said, "I'll stay here, but only because they won't tell you anything if I'm with you. But I'm going to want to know what happened, okay? I was just a little woozy there for a minute after Kevin and I talked. I'm fine now."

He lifted my chin, studied my eyes, and then nodded. "You are absolutely more than fine, my love. I promise to tell you everything, even if it's not pleasant."

"Thank you." And it wouldn't be pleasant, I thought, as I watched him cross the room and disappear down the hall.

Chapter 17

Rub all things with butter.
        —The Cookbook of Obedience Green

I noted at least one glaring difference between the aftermath of Baxter's death and that of Montgomery's: the amount of tears that people shed. With Baxter, there were a few sad moments when the chefs first heard the news. But with Monty, everyone was overwhelmed with grief and it didn't seem to be subsiding.

Oh, there was plenty of laughter when someone recalled a funny line of his or some melodramatic rant he'd taken off on. But then people would stop and remember and dissolve into tears all over again.

I didn't think I could take much more of it, mainly because I was a sympathetic weeper. Within minutes of arriving, my eyes were drenched and it was a pretty good bet they would stay that way for as long as I remained with the other mourners. Of course, there was no way I could leave, not while Derek was still back there talking to the police. And I wasn't about to go without Savannah. She was a mess. I was pleased to see that Dalton had remained at her side. I could've hugged him for that.

So I stayed where I was and occupied my time by watching everyone else. Looking for a clue. Any clue. Because a stone-cold murderer might not stop at just two deaths.

I thought I had gotten to know these people, but I didn't know them so well, after all. If one of them was wearing a mask, it was going to be difficult to see past it.

Colette and Margot huddled together in a quiet corner, and every few minutes one of them would hiccup or sniffle or melt into another round of tears.

Margot had already contacted Monty's boyfriend, who agreed to call his restaurant manager and his parents. That was a thankless task and I was glad I didn't have to do it.

I was worried what would happen when the press and the paparazzi got wind that another chef had been killed. But I refused to dwell on those ugly details right then.

Kevin sat at the bar, talking softly to Peter, who stood close by. She was leaning into him and he was comforting her, and the love they felt for each other was downright palpable. To me, at least. I thought it was too bad they'd found each other again under such painful circumstances. If they made it through these next few days together, their relationship would be that much stronger for it.

Raoul stood alone, leaning against the large plate-glass window and staring out at the street. Was he gazing at the park across the street, wishing he was out there flying a kite instead of here in Baxter's restaurant where murder was becoming the special of the day? Mission Dolores Park provided such a beautiful view with its green grass climbing up that massive steep hill and the chunky, iconic palm trees that lined Dolores Street's median. Who wouldn't rather be out there than in here?

He looked so lonely gazing out the window that I almost walked over to console him. But I didn't want to intrude on his private grief, so I stayed where I was and continued to play the casual observer. It was a good thing, because a moment later, Raoul turned and I saw something in his soulful brown eyes that I'd never seen there before. Burning anger mixed with raw hatred.

Who was he looking at?

Suddenly it was hard to breathe. His expression so unnerved me that I stood up and dashed to the ladies' room to escape the corrosive quality of his vibe. Staring at myself in the bathroom mirror, I felt a little silly for getting so worked up. I splashed some water in my face and told myself to snap out of it. Whatever "it" was. Fear? Shock? Sadness? Maybe a little of all three. Make that a *lot*, especially fear. That look in Raoul's eyes had freaked me out. He was normally such a sweet, easygoing man. What had happened to make him so bitterly angry? To fill him with so much of the hate I'd read in his eyes? Or had I glimpsed the *real* Raoul in that expression while the man I thought I knew was only the mask?

I'd always imagined Raoul was too kind ever to hurt another living creature. Now I wondered if he'd been fooling us all for years. Had the anger inside him turned him into a killer?

I kept replaying that moment in my mind, when he turned away from the window and focused that laser beam of anger on . . . who? I pictured the room in my mind, the small groups of people sitting together in different parts of the restaurant. Peter and Kevin. Colette and Margot. Dalton and Savannah. Me. The uniformed officer standing guard at the hall entrance.

"Are you all right?"

I glanced at the door and saw Savannah peeking in. "Come in. I'm fine. I just got a little light-headed out there for a minute."

She walked in and closed and locked the door behind her. "I know how you feel. I'm so emotionally unbalanced right now, I wouldn't be surprised to find myself crawling on the ceiling."

I gave her a sympathetic smile. "It's scary, but you'll get through this. We all will, eventually."

"But two murders in just a few days? It's too much."

She shook her head, at a loss as to how to take it all in. "I don't know how you do it, Brooklyn, but you're obviously built to handle these things better than I am."

Et tu, Bugs? I thought. I was getting that a lot lately. Why did everyone assume I was attracted to this kind of stuff? I frowned at her reflection through the mirror. "You know I don't do it on purpose, right?"

"I know, sweetie." She sat on the small couch behind me. "But you know what I mean. It's different for you. You have this natural but weird sort of thought process you go through. It's completely unlike mine. I'm not sure why—maybe it's from working on all those books. They're like puzzles. You take them apart and then have to figure out how to put them back together in a whole new way. And when you have a problem to solve, you look at it from all these different angles, and then you fix it. It's a lot like solving mysteries, isn't it?"

I turned and smiled at her, inordinately pleased that she actually understood me. "That's exactly what it is." Leaning closer, I added, "But I'd still rather not deal with so many dead bodies."

"I don't blame you there." She shivered. "Gross."

"Totally." I turned back to the sink and splashed one more handful of water into my puffy, tear-soaked eyes, then dried my face and hands and fixed a smile on my face. Checking the mirror, I could see I looked a little grim, but it would have to do. "Let's go."

The police were well into the interview process when we returned to the main room. I didn't see Derek anywhere, so I figured he was still somewhere in the back with the cops. I avoided looking at Raoul. I wanted to talk to Derek about what I'd seen, but that would have to wait.

"Ms. Wainwright?" Inspector Lee had just led Kevin out from the private room where she was conducting interviews.

"Yes?" Savannah and I answered at the same time.

"Not you, Wainwright," Inspector Lee said, her lips twisting in a wry grin. "Your sister. Let's go."

Savannah looked at me. "Is she talking to you or me?"

"She's talking to me," I explained, "but she wants to talk to you."

Perplexed, Savannah shook her head, but followed Inspector Lee, who got a few feet away, then whipped around and pointed her finger at me like it was a gun. She made a clicking sound as if she'd shot me. Then she laughed and walked on with Savannah.

"Funny lady," I muttered.

"You seem to know her pretty well," Kevin said, joining me.

We sat down at the nearest table. "Yeah, I know her. She's kind of gung ho, but usually fair."

"I hope so." She gazed around the room. "It's hard to believe this is all happening, you know? Do you remember that first night we were here? I thought this room was one of the most beautiful I'd ever seen."

"I remember, and I thought the same thing."

"Once this investigation is over, Brooklyn, I hope I never have to see it again."

"You won't," I assured her. "But for now we're sort of stuck."

She sighed. "Seems we are."

"How was your interview?"

"Oh, just dandy." She rolled her eyes. "It only took a few minutes. Basically just a follow-up, since they already interviewed us earlier."

"Earlier?" I couldn't remember seeing the inspectors interviewing anyone. "When was that?"

"You weren't here yet." Her eyes widened. "Oh, and I didn't have a chance to finish telling you. I was halfway through my story when I got so wretchedly sick to my stomach."

"That's right." It was only a few minutes ago, so I was surprised I'd forgotten already. Although, considering everything else that was going on . . . "You look like you're feeling better."

"Yes, I'm fine." She shook her head like a wet dog, as

though she was trying to shake the memory out of her brain. "I absolutely hate getting sick like that. And in public, for all my lovely new street friends to see. I'm such a class act."

"You couldn't help it," I said. "But tell me the rest of the story. What happened?"

"Right." She leaned forward with her elbow on the table and spoke in a low voice. "We'd only just found poor Monty when those two homicide inspectors walked in."

"They got here that fast? Did one of you call them?"

"No," she whispered. "They claimed that Monty called them."

"Wait. What?" I sat up in my chair. "Monty? But . . . when? How?"

"Frankly, Brooklyn, I don't believe they meant to tell us as much as they did. I think they were so blown away at the sight of him lying there, dead, that they just blurted it out."

I thought about it, tried to picture Inspector Lee walking in on that scene. "She's usually tight-lipped as a clam, so it must've been a shock for her. What all did they say to you?"

"Just that Monty called them late last night and told them he knew who the killer was. But he couldn't talk on the phone long. Apparently he asked them to meet him here at ten o'clock this morning and said he would tell them what he knew."

"What he knew? But why didn't he just tell them the name of the killer?" It was like a bad plotline from a B movie. "It doesn't make sense."

She shifted in her seat and her voice dropped even lower. "Margot thinks he wanted an audience for his big reveal. You know how he's such a drama queen, right?"

"Well, yes, but the police don't know that." This didn't make sense. Why would Monty put himself in the crosshairs, so to speak? If he had known the name of the killer, why not go to the police immediately and keep himself safe? And what about the police? "If they had someone calling in, claiming to have information critical to their investigation, why didn't they just go to his hotel and question him?"

"If they'd done that, he'd be alive." She contemplated that for a moment, then shook her head in disgust. "They probably thought he was a raving lunatic and didn't want to encourage him."

"That's possible." But knowing Inspector Lee as well as I did, I couldn't believe it. She was a fanatic when it came to finding the truth. *But wait a minute*, I thought. Lee had brushed me off more than once when I'd pushed my theories on her. I hated to admit it, but she could be a little arrogant about civilian involvement in police matters.

Was that why she hadn't moved on Monty's information? Could she have assumed that because I was involved my friends would be irritants, too?

I wasn't trying to blame myself, but if that was the reason why Inspector Lee didn't follow up on Monty's story, it was just sad. Monty might still be alive if they'd checked up on him. Even though, sorry to say, he probably had sounded like a drama queen.

On the other hand, we didn't have all the facts. Maybe Monty hadn't actually spoken with the homicide inspectors. Maybe he'd left a message with a dispatcher who wasn't able to reach the people in charge of the case in time. It would be rushing to judgment to blame the police before I knew what had really happened.

Yet more answers I desperately needed.

"Kevin's story is essentially true," Derek said as we drove home an hour later. "Montgomery did call in. Unfortunately, though, he never got the chance to speak to either of the inspectors. The dispatcher's message didn't show up on either of their phones until early this morning."

"That's downright tragic," Savannah said.

"Yes, it is," he said, clearly disgusted. "Obviously

there's a breakdown in their system somewhere. They're investigating that side issue, as well."

I turned in my seat to face him. "Do they think the killer overheard Montgomery's phone call?"

"That seems the only plausible scenario," Derek admitted.

So the police would be tracking down which of the chefs had been at the restaurant at the same time that Monty made his fateful phone call. I wondered if we could find out that information as well.

We were mostly silent the rest of the way back to my place. Derek pulled up in front of our building and after a quick discussion about alternative dinner plans, Savannah, Dalton, and I climbed out of the car and Derek took off for his office.

Two hours later he returned home unexpectedly.

"This is a nice surprise," I said, greeting him with a kiss.

"I'm afraid it's not as pleasant a reason to come home as we'd like it to be."

"What's wrong?"

His expression was grim. "The police are right behind me."

My two favorite detectives showed up ten minutes later. They'd come to talk to Savannah, who, in case we'd all forgotten, was still the prime suspect in the murder of Baxter Cromwell.

Derek, Dalton, and I lurked in the kitchen as Savannah was being interviewed in my studio.

"Why couldn't they do this at the restaurant?" I grumbled, although I was just as glad to be home rather than still sitting in Baxter's gloomy dining room. Still, I was scared to death that my sister might be led out of my house in handcuffs any minute now.

"They might not want the other chefs to know they're talking to Savannah," Derek said.

"I'm going to take that to mean that they're trying to protect her from anyone who might try to hurt her."

"Yes," Derek said, reaching for my hand. "That's exactly how I meant you to take it."

"I'm not sure if I should be more worried or less."

"Go sit at the table," Dalton said. "I'm making tea."

I stared at him in surprise as Derek led me over to the dining room table. We sat next to each other at the far end and he took my hand. "Savannah will be fine," he said.

A few minutes later, Dalton walked over with a tray on which he'd placed the teapot, four mugs, and a plate of cookies.

"That's so sweet of you," I said, giving him a grateful smile.

"Sometimes one simply needs a cup of tea," Dalton said.

He was right. We sipped our tea, and after a while the two cops and Savannah walked into the room.

"Would you care for a cup of tea?" Dalton asked.

Inspector Lee stared at him, then looked at Derek. "Whoa. There's two of you?"

"Didn't you meet Derek's brother at the restaurant earlier?" I asked.

Lee frowned at me. "I must've thought he was Derek."

"Understandable." I introduced her to Dalton and we all talked for another few minutes. The inspectors refused the offer of tea and finally took off. Derek walked them to the door.

Savannah sat at the table and Dalton poured her a cup of tea.

"How are you doing?" I asked her.

"Fine. She's so nice and pretty."

"Who are you talking about?"

"Inspector Lee."

"Oh. Yeah, she is. Pretty, I mean. Nice? Not always."

"She was nice to me," Savannah said.

"Figures," I muttered. "So what did they ask you?"

"They went over some of the stuff I told them last time and then they asked me about Margot."

I frowned. "Margot?"

"I couldn't believe it, either," Savannah said. "I assured them she wouldn't hurt a fly."

I wasn't so sure about that. "What did you tell them?"

"Well, they knew I used to be involved with Baxter, so they—"

"Where'd they hear that?" I interrupted, even though I knew it was that big-mouth Colette, who'd told Jaglom a bunch of lies that first night.

"They heard it from me," Savannah said. "I told them all about our relationship when they first interviewed me."

"You did?"

"Well, sure. Don't you remember? I told them everything. That's what you're supposed to do, right? Tell the truth."

I smiled. "I love you, sis."

"I . . . love you, too?" she said warily.

With a laugh, I gestured for her to continue.

"So they'd heard a rumor that Margot had carried on affairs with both Raoul and Baxter and they wanted to ask me about all three of them. Can you imagine? I assured them they were way off base."

"Off base about whom?" I said cautiously.

"About all of them!" Savannah cried. "None of them would ever hurt anyone, especially not Monty."

"But what about the affairs?"

She waved her hand. "Oh, who cares about that? We were all kids back in Paris. Everyone was sleeping with everyone else. Doesn't mean anyone's a killer."

She didn't have much more to add and I didn't press her. But I wasn't about to kick Margot off the suspect list. She came across as friendly and flirty, but she really wasn't. She was always watching, judging, gauging . . . something. Why? Was she just insecure? You'd never know it by the way she dressed. Flamboyant and sexy, which would have been fine if only it matched her real personality. But it didn't.

A while later, Derek caught up with me in our bedroom. "I have some news, and it isn't pleasant."

"What is it?"

"It's about Montgomery. He was injected with a massive amount of rat poison. Its main ingredient is strychnine, as we surmised."

I sank down onto the love seat. My heart ached for poor Montgomery. He'd suffered an agonizing death and he hadn't deserved it. In fact, no one deserved that. "That's horrifying. But how was he injected? And when?"

"Apparently, it was very late last night," Derek said. "The killer used a meat injector."

"A meat . . . ew." I shivered at the thought. But it made an awful kind of sense. Most chefs probably carried their own with them wherever they traveled. Now that I thought about it, I realized that even my father owned one. He used it to marinate the Thanksgiving turkey, among other things. It was sold as part of a kit along with several needles of different sizes.

Needles. Ugh. And there went my stomach.

"That's just unbelievable. Terrible." I rubbed my queasy belly. "Do they have any idea who did it?"

"Not yet, but they plan to conduct a much more thorough search of everyone's kitchen tools."

I gasped and jumped up from the couch as a thought suddenly struck me. "It can't be Savannah!"

Derek leaned his hip against the bureau. "No, of course not. But why do you say that?"

"Because she's a vegetarian!" I laughed. I knew it was tasteless to be happy at the moment, but there was nothing more I could do for Montgomery, while Savannah needed all the help she could get. "She doesn't even own a meat injector."

He chuckled. "Good point, darling. I'll mention that to the inspector."

"Wait—it can't be Raoul, either. He's a pastry chef."

"Yes, love," Derek said softly. "But he's married to someone who specializes in meats."

I frowned. "Well, whatever." It was a shabby come-back, but I couldn't help it; I was in shock or something. The thought of someone using a meat injector to kill a sweetie like Montgomery made me feel sick and de-pressed.

I went in search of some ginger ale to calm my stom-ach and felt better after a few minutes. Derek was needed back at the office, so he took off after promising to return home by six o'clock.

By mutual, silent agreement, the rest of us all wan-dered off to do our own thing. I walked into my studio, where, true to his vow, Dalton had settled in at the desk and was poring over the cookbook pages. He had his laptop open and a spreadsheet in front of him.

I took a peek at the spreadsheet and saw a long col-umn of the same hieroglyphic symbols I'd seen in the cookbook. He had transferred each symbol onto the sheet and was testing different letters of the alphabet as well as short phrases that might correspond to each of the squiggles.

Dalton had a tendency to swear under his breath ev-ery so often. I couldn't blame him. If I was looking at that never-ending line of squiggles and numbers, I'd be cursing, too.

Savannah, meanwhile, had piled some of her cook-books and several issues of *Cook's* magazine at the op-posite end of my worktable and pulled a high chair over to get some work done. She was compiling new menu selections, a job that was more difficult than it sounded, since it involved a lot of research, then experimenting and cooking and sampling and figuring out wine pair-ings.

Okay, that didn't sound difficult in the least. In fact, it sounded like a dream job to me.

Savannah, though, worked night and day to maintain the level of quality that kept her at the top of the list of great chefs in the country. So I guess I could cut her some slack.

I got back to my own work and finished sewing the *Jane Eyre* signatures to the linen tapes, then cut the text block loose. I trimmed the tapes and then put my sewing frame back in its cupboard. After that, I prepared a batch of polyvinyl acetate. PVA was strong and water soluble and it stayed flexible for a long time. Plus, it didn't yellow or crack, so that made it the glue of choice for discerning bookbinders everywhere.

I slipped the text block, spine side up, into a wood block press and tightened it carefully. Then I picked out a fat, round wooden glue brush and began to slather glue onto the spine edge of the signature block, saturating the linen tapes and threads and making sure the mixture got into every seam.

The glue would take a while to dry, so I washed out the brush and straightened up my work space.

At that moment, Dalton waved the clutch of cookbook papers at me. "What do we know about Obedience Green?"

"Just what I've read in her journal. You've got the pages right there."

"I've only seen the pages with the encryptions."

I took the pages, flipped through them, and handed him the journal section. "This is her life, right here. She traveled to America, where she worked for an English army general who was unmarried. She met all sorts of Americans here and I think she was influenced by some of them. After six years, she returned to England and continued to run the general's household until . . . she died? I'm not sure. It just sort of ends with her trip back to England."

"Did you ever Google her?" he asked.

"No." I frowned and asked myself why I'd neglected to do that. "I have no good excuse. I'll do it right now."

"Let me know what you find," he said. "I have some ideas, but your results will give me some perspective."

I moved my laptop over to the worktable and powered it up. Once online I looked up every source I could find on Obedience Green. Unfortunately, those two words combined brought up a million different odd links, such as *dog obedience training in Green Valley, Montana*.

I added the word *cookbook* to the search and after combing through every last link, I found something enlightening—and chilling.

Police Call Off Search for Stolen Cookbook. No leads in museum theft.

The short article posted from the *Gipping Gazette* told of a theft of several articles from the local historical society museum, including a cookbook written by Obedience Green, a resident of the village from 1788 until her death in 1836.

The article was sixteen years old.

I printed out the news clipping and handed it to Dalton. He skimmed it and stared at me. "That shines a rather different light on the subject, doesn't it?"

"You bet it does."

"It doesn't do squat for my encrypting work, but it certainly could affect your murder investigation."

"I've got to call the police." I took a breath. "No. I want to talk to Kevin. I'm going to call her." I started for the phone, then stopped. "No, I'll call Peter. Or maybe I should . . . oh, hell. I don't know what to do."

Dalton grabbed my arm. "Call Derek. He'll come home and we can plan our next move."

"Right. Absolutely." I rubbed my forehead, where a headache was forming. "You know, before I do anything else, I'm going to go to the market to buy stuff for dinner."

I needed to get outside, let the wind blow through my hair and maybe, just maybe, blow all of my random thoughts into some kind of order. But that wasn't the only reason I needed to get out of my apartment.

"Savannah," I said, "come with me."

She glanced up. I could see she was about to decline

my request, but then she read my expression and said, "Yeah. Okay."

I patted Dalton's shoulder. "Will you be all right on your own for a while?"

"Of course," he mumbled, already wrapped up in his squiggly cryptographic world.

"What was that all about?" Savannah asked as I rushed her to the elevator.

I gave her a shortened version of what I'd found out online.

When I was finished, she nodded and said, "We need to talk to Kevin and Peter. They'll know what happened."

I valet-parked at the Campton Place Hotel and we hurried inside and found the elevators. On the tenth floor, we tried Kevin's room first, but there was no answer.

"Let's try Peter's," I said.

His room was two doors down. I started to knock on the door, but then realized it wasn't closed all the way. An icy chill slithered across my shoulders, causing me to tremble. A door ajar was never a good sign.

I knocked first, then nudged it open a few inches. "Hello? Peter? It's Savannah and Brooklyn."

I hesitated, waiting for a response, but Savannah waved her hand anxiously. "What're you standing here for? Just go in."

"Okay, okay." I shoved the door open all the way and walked into the sitting room of Peter's elegant suite. It was identical to Kevin's suite, except Peter's was a chaotic mess. Sofa cushions were tossed on the floor. The entertainment hutch was open and DVDs were scattered across the carpet. Several chairs around the dining table had been tipped over.

It looked like a very messy burglar had been at work. My nerves screamed at me to back out of the suite and call the police, but I ignored my instincts and stood my ground. What if Peter was in trouble? Needed help?

"What happened here?" Savannah's voice quivered. "Where's Peter?"

"We'll find him." I moved cautiously into the bedroom, where the first thing I noticed was another door leading out to the hallway. An escape route?

There was a big black suitcase lying on the bed. A backpack was splayed open next to the suitcase and many of Peter's cooking tools were scattered across the bed. A few had been tossed onto the floor.

I wasn't surprised to see all these utensils in a chef's room because I knew Savannah traveled with many of her own, too. But I doubted that Peter had thrown them every which way like they were now.

"Men can be so messy." Savannah bent down to straighten up a pile of wooden spoons. My sister, the good little housekeeper. Obviously she hadn't considered the violent-intruder theory yet.

"Savannah, honestly," I whispered impatiently. "Do you really think Peter made all this mess?"

"Well, who else would—" She blinked. "Oh, crap!" She dropped the spoons as if they were on fire. "Somebody else was in here tearing this place apart."

"That's right." I checked the suitcase zipper. It wasn't locked.

"So let's call the police and leave."

"Not yet," I said, unzipping the small front pocket of the suitcase.

"What are you doing?"

I felt inside, but nothing was there. "Look, someone was here searching for something. They probably made a run for it when they heard us come in, so maybe they didn't get a chance to finish their search. I just want to take a look around for a minute or two. Then we'll call the police."

"Do you know what you're looking for?"

There she went, getting all logical again. "Not really."

She looked around anxiously, as if half expecting some masked marauder to leap at her from the closet. I shivered. It could happen.

She whispered, "You're crazy, you know that?"

"You might've mentioned it a time or two." I unzipped the larger section of Peter's suitcase and flipped it open. And lying there on top of Peter's neatly folded clothes was my burgundy leather book box. "Oh, sweet Mary Jo."

"Hey, that's my cookbook," Savannah said.

"Yes, it is." Although in my own mind it was *my* cookbook. I reached for it slowly, reverently, and finally held it in my hands. In my imagination, the "Hallelujah Chorus" rose in the background.

I could tell by the weight of the box that Obedience Green's cookbook was still inside. But just to be sure, I lifted the panel and checked. There it was, neat and snug, tucked on top of its matching suede pouch and resting in its perfectly carved-out cubbyhole.

"I did a really good job on this," I murmured, gliding my hand across the smooth dark morocco leather.

"Oh, for God's sake," Savannah groused. "Let's get the hell out of here."

"I want to call Derek first," I said, pulling out my cell phone. "If Peter stole the cookbook, he's probably the one who killed Baxter."

"No," she moaned. "Not Peter. He didn't do it."

"I'm sorry, honey," I said. It hurt me, too, to think that Peter was a coldhearted killer, but the evidence was damning. I pressed Derek's number and seconds later I heard his phone begin to ring.

"Darling," he said. "I was just thinking about you."

"Aw, that's so nice."

"Oh, my God, you're flirting?" Savannah said in disgust. "Just tell him what's going on and let's get out of here."

"Is that your sister?" he asked.

"Yes. She's in a mood." Funny, but now that I had the cookbook in my hands, my nerves were quiet. We could still be in danger, and yet somehow I felt as if everything was turning our way.

"What does she want you to tell me?"

I gave Savannah a dirty look, then said to Derek, "Okay, the thing is, we're here in Peter's hotel suite, and we just found the missing cookbook. So I'm afraid Peter might've had something to do with Baxter's death."

"Oh, just say it," Savannah hissed. "You think Peter killed him."

"I heard her," Derek said, and let loose a string of expletives that shocked me. "I'm calling the police and I want you out of there right now. Go downstairs and wait in the lobby. I'll be there soon."

"Okay, okay," I said, walking away from Savannah to the other side of the room. Derek rarely swore, so it caught me by surprise. Without thinking much about it, I pushed the door to the bathroom open.

"Hey, look what I found," Savannah said.

I didn't get a chance to see what she'd found because I had found something much worse. My scream echoed against the tile walls and I moved out of the bathroom and slammed the door behind me.

"What is it?" Savannah cried. "Brooklyn, stop it!" She grabbed me by the arms and shook me, looking even more terrified than I felt.

"Peter," I mumbled, dropping the phone. "Blood . . . ugh . . ." That's as far as I got before I slithered from her arms and crumpled to the floor in a dead faint.

Chapter 18

I have come to understand this much: to serve food is to beckon judgment from any and all.
—The Cookbook of Obedience Green

"Wake up! Damn you, wake up!"

It was sort of like déjà vu, only instead of a rich, deep, sexy British accent urging me awake, it was my sister's shrill voice bitching at me. And she was slapping me!

"All right, all right," I muttered, and struggled to sit up while at the same time pushing her hand away from my face. "I'm fine. Stop beating me."

"Oh, thank God." She grabbed me in a hug so tight it cut off my air supply. I was about ready to pass out again, but I managed to smack her arm hard enough to break the contact.

"Don't you ever do that again!" she cried, as she stood up. "Do you have any idea what it's like to watch your eyes roll back and then see you keel over? You scared the hell out of me! I almost fainted myself."

"All right, calm down," I said, pushing myself up off the floor until I was standing again. The effort cost me. I slid onto a side chair and took some gulps of fresh air. "What happened to Derek?"

"Derek?"

"The phone." I sighed, bent over, and covered my face with my hands. Oh, man. I just passed out while talking to Derek. "He's going to kill me."

"I might help him with that," she grumbled as she reached for something on the floor.

"Hey, I have a little problem with blood. Sorry."

Savannah handed my phone to me. "Here's your damn phone. He hung up."

I groaned. I could just imagine what Derek was thinking. He probably guessed that I was out cold, which meant he was on his way over here, which meant that I was going to hear all about this for days. "Okay, give me a break here. At least we found the book. And Peter."

"Yes, and I think you owe him an apology."

"Who? Peter? Savannah, he's dead."

"Which means he's *not* Baxter's killer."

"You're right, and I'm sorry." The fact was, Peter still could've killed Baxter, but in the interest of sisterly agreeableness and the fact that Peter lay bloodied and dead in the bathroom, I conceded. For now.

"Oh, wait," I said, suddenly realizing something. "I'd better check to make sure he's not still alive."

"What did you say?"

I grimaced. "He looked dead, but I didn't check. He could be alive."

"What?" she shrieked. Oh, dear God, that really was horrifying. "What are you talking about? Are you crazy? You said he was dead in the bathroom!"

"Shhhhh," I said, grabbing my head. Her voice had reached an octave only dogs could usually hear. "The whole place will hear you."

"I don't care!" She stood before the closed bathroom door, hesitating. "Come on. You're coming in with me. We should check, but I'm not doing it alone. And you'd better not faint again, because I'm not going to catch you."

"Okay, okay." But my throat was suddenly dry as sand. I snatched a fresh bottle of water off the console in the living room, popped the top open, and started gulping it.

"Those aren't free, you know."

"Not important right now." I grabbed her hand. "Let's do this."

We walked steadily into the bathroom. Peter lay on the floor at an odd angle, as though he had fallen backward after being attacked. Streams of blood had dried on his cheek and temple from the wound on his head. He'd been bludgeoned severely.

In the corner of the bathroom floor was a heavy-duty steel mallet, the kind used for tenderizing meat. It could be one of Peter's own cooking tools. I crept closer and noticed there was dried blood caked on its surface. It had to be the weapon someone had used to hurt Peter.

I swallowed hard and took a deep breath. No way was I going to faint again. Using every last ounce of courage I possessed, I knelt and pressed my fingers to Peter's neck. My hand was shaking, so I had to try again. After a few long seconds of concentration, I thought I felt something. Then I felt it again. A pulse. "He's still alive! Barely. Call nine-one-one for an ambulance."

Savannah let out a cry and ran to the bedroom phone to dial the emergency number.

I stayed with Peter. I didn't want to shake him or move him, so I just touched him and hoped he could hear me. "Peter, we'll get you taken care of. Don't die, do you hear me? No dying. That's an order."

He moaned. It was the faintest sound, but I heard it and rejoiced.

"That's right, mister," I said. "You're going to be all right. Just stay with us." Tears sprang to my eyes and I brushed them away. There was no time for that now. "Stay with us."

Oddly enough, now that I knew Peter was still alive, I didn't even notice all the blood caked on his skin. All I could see was his handsome face. All I could concentrate on was the thready beat beneath my fingers.

"They'll be here in just a minute," Savannah said when she rushed back into the bathroom. "Union Square has its own emergency services."

"Good." I could see the minute movement of Peter's chest rising and falling now. Silently, I focused on that slight motion, willing it to continue. "That's good."

"We can't leave now, can we?" Savannah said, sounding resigned.

"No, we'll stay until the police arrive." Any hope of slipping out of Peter's hotel suite with the cookbook intact was gone. "The cookbook!"

In all the worry over Peter I'd almost forgotten about what we'd found. I scrambled up off the bathroom floor, ran into the bedroom, and picked up the leather book box from the jumble on the bed.

"We're in so much trouble," Savannah muttered.

"We're not in any trouble," I insisted, heading back to the bathroom to check on Peter. "Derek knows we're here. The door was open when we arrived, so all we did was enter the suite to check on our friend."

"Right."

"But here's the thing," I said, walking back to the bedroom. "I'm not letting the police take the cookbook. It won't fit in my purse, so can you stick it in your tote bag?"

She shook her head in disbelief. "Is that the only thing you can think about?"

"Not the only thing, but it's important, Savannah." I held it out to her. "Please. Dalton needs it."

Oh, that was so cheap, but it worked. Her expression softened and her attitude changed. "All right, give it to me. I'll hide it in my bag."

The closet door slid open with a bang. "No! You're not keeping it. It's mine!"

We both turned and stared as Kevin pushed her way

out of the mirrored closet, brandishing a wicked-looking chef's knife.

"Kevin?" Savannah said, truly mystified. "What're you doing here?"

"That book is mine!" she shouted. "First Baxter steals it, then Peter, and now you? Give it to me or I'll—"

I held the book in front of me like a shield. "Did you do that to Peter?"

"No!" She was wild-eyed and not acting real coherent. "I was trying to help him, but I heard someone coming, so I hid in the closet."

"You were hiding in there all this time?" Savannah asked, astonished. "Why didn't you come out when you heard us talking?"

Not the point right now, I thought.

"Put the knife down, Kevin," I said. "Let's talk about this."

She waved the sharp knife at me. "Not until you give me the book."

"No," I said, and held on to the cookbook a little more tightly. "This is ridiculous. Put down that stupid knife before the police get here."

"As soon as you give me the cookbook," she repeated through clenched teeth.

"Oh, for God's sake," Savannah shouted. "Enough with that damn book! People are dying, Peter's nearly dead, and you're acting like a complete wacko!" Before I could stop her, she grabbed something from Peter's untidy heap of tools and lunged at Kevin.

I screamed. "Savannah, no!"

Kevin shrieked, dropped the knife, and cowered, shaking wildly. "Don't hit me!"

Good grief. What kind of a killer was she? I took advantage of the moment and grabbed Kevin around her waist, trapping her arms. Then I pushed her onto the bed and jumped on top of her, straddling her to hold her down.

"Let me go!" Kevin cried as she twisted back and forth, trying to free herself. "I didn't do anything."

I bounced hard on her just because she was making me so mad. "You could've killed either one of us with that knife."

"I wasn't going to kill anyone." She began to cry. "I just wanted the book."

"Right," I said derisively. "Tell that to Peter. He's barely alive after you attacked him. I just hope he lives to tell about it."

And all of a sudden, reality hit me hard. Kevin Moore, this woman I had thought was my friend, the one I'd invited to my house for dinner, the one I'd hoped would find love again with darling Peter, was the cold-blooded murderer of at least two chefs. How could I have been so completely wrong about a person? My personal judgment wasn't worth a damn, I thought sadly. It made my stomach hurt and I had to sit back on my ankles and take in a few breaths.

"What's wrong?" Savannah said. "Are you okay?"

I gulped again and deliberately steadied my stomach. "Fine. Just . . . I'm bummed." I cast a glance at Kevin. "I thought you were my friend."

"Me, too." Savannah's eyes glistened with tears. But then she snapped out of it. She stomped over to the bed and glared at Kevin. "Did you kill Baxter? Did you kill Montgomery? Did you try to kill Peter?"

"I didn't kill anyone!" She writhed in protest. "I just wanted the book."

I glanced at Savannah, then did a double take when I noticed what she was clenching in one fist. *This* is what she had grabbed to defend us both from a mad-dog killer? "What is wrong with you?"

"Me? Why are you yelling at me?"

"Because you could've gotten yourself killed. An egg whisk is not a weapon."

She glanced at the whisk in her hand, then gave me a cool look. "It was the right tool for the job."

The paramedics were able to stabilize Peter and he was rushed off to the hospital. Unfortunately, he remained in a coma, but I was hopeful that as soon as he recovered, he would be able to name his attacker.

One question remained, though. What had his attacker been searching for? Kevin had insisted that Peter was already knocked out when she arrived. If she wasn't lying—and that was a big "if"—then someone else had been in the room looking for something. Was it the cookbook? Who else wanted to get their hands on it?

As the police hauled Kevin off for questioning, she continued to maintain that she hadn't hurt anyone. She only wanted the cookbook, insisting that it belonged to her. She claimed that Peter had stolen it for her, which seemed wildly improbable.

The uniformed officer at the scene looked at me quizzically. "Do you know what cookbook she's yelling about?"

"I have no idea," I said with an innocent shrug.

Part of me lived in fear that once Kevin was sitting in interrogation, facing Inspectors Jaglom and Lee, she would break down and tell them that I'd taken the cookbook. But since she hadn't specifically pointed the finger at me yet, I wondered if she, like me, would rather keep the fragile old book out of police hands.

I would have to wait and see.

An hour later, Derek was clutching the wheel of the Bentley so tightly that his knuckles were turning white.

"I'm sorry," I said again. "But when I found out that Obedience Green's cookbook had been stolen from the Gipping-on-Plym village museum sixteen years ago, I had to find Kevin and Peter and ask them about it."

His jaw worked as if a hot torrent of words was fighting to get out and he was only barely managing to keep them back. Finally, he ground out, "And you didn't once consider that you might be facing a killer with nothing to lose and no fear of multiple fatalities?"

I thought about his words for a moment. Okay, maybe he had a point. And the way he put it really made me cringe. Hmm. "No. I honestly never thought that either Kevin or Peter was capable of doing what was done to Baxter and Monty. I just thought they might know more about the cookbook than they were letting on."

He sent me a quick look that was filled with so many emotions, it was hard to read them all. I did pick up on the love and the fear and the frustration, though. "You know you scared the living daylights out of me—and that's not an easy thing to admit."

"I know. I'm sorry, Derek." I really did feel terrible. The downside to being in a loving relationship was the fact that you could make each other crazy with worry. Of course, as far as I could see, that was the *only* downside. "I wasn't thinking, really. And I so didn't expect to walk into another crime scene." Tears sprang to my eyes. Sadly, I'd done this to him before and been gut-wrenched by his reaction.

He blew out a breath. "Do you know what it's like to race across town, all the while wondering if you're still alive or if I'll find you in a bloody heap?"

"I—"

"I bloody well hate it." He cut me off, which told me just how upset he was, because Derek usually was the absolute soul of politeness. "Besides the actual worry, it's . . . lowering, damn it." He pounded the steering wheel. "To . . . feel . . . so much, and be able to do so little. It's intolerable."

"I know." I sniffled and brushed away my tears. Damn stupid tears. "I can only say I'm sorry over and over again. I know what it feels like to worry, and I regret having put you through it. I didn't mean to do it, Derek. I wouldn't deliberately worry you and I hope you know that."

"I appreciate your pretty apology." But he didn't sound particularly appreciative and I had a feeling this conversation was far from over.

In that case, I took another stab at trying to defend myself. After all, I really did feel bad about worrying him, but I had worried *about* him, too. And it wasn't as if I was a ten-year-old. I was an adult and I couldn't make every decision in my life by first thinking, *Would Derek be angry?*

"I thought we were going to talk to friends about an old cookbook that was stolen from their childhood village," I reminded him, keeping my voice steady and reasonable. "I didn't expect to find a bloodied body close to death and a crazed woman wielding a freaking butcher's knife."

"When you put it like that," he said, his tone sardonic, "what else can I do but forgive you?"

I laughed, but not in a happy way. "Oh, yeah, I can tell you've forgiven me."

He reached for my hand, brought it to his lips, and then held it tightly as he drove. I guessed that was a good sign. Most likely, we would keep butting heads over situations like this. But honestly, I ask you, what could I have done differently?

As we came to a stoplight, Savannah coughed discreetly from the backseat. "I hate to interrupt you two, but I found something you might want to see."

She sat forward and dangled a gold chain with a delicate silver-and-glass locket between Derek and me. The two of us stared at the locket, then at each other. His intensity almost fried me, but it wasn't anger I felt from him. It was love. It filled my heart and I had to press my hand to my chest to contain it.

He shook his head and rolled his eyes at me and I felt a bit like an incorrigible mutt. But I knew he'd forgiven me. At least, I hoped so.

I forced myself to focus on the locket. "Whose is that?"

"It's Colette's," Savannah confirmed. "She's worn it for years. Never takes it off."

Derek raised an eyebrow. "Where did you find it?"

"In Peter's backpack," Savannah explained. "I found it while you were in the bathroom."

"How did Peter get hold of it?" I wondered.

"I don't know," Savannah said, then added, "but I also found these." She reached over the seat and dropped something onto my lap.

I looked down and gaped. "My earrings?" I turned in my seat. "You found these in Peter's bag, too?"

She nodded. "He must've picked them up off the table the night you had dinner at Arugula."

"They're shiny," I murmured, holding the pair up to catch the light.

"Yes," she said. "Peter likes shiny things, remember?"

"So he must have taken your earrings," Derek surmised. "Then later the locket."

"I think the locket went missing first," Savannah said. "I've been trying to remember the last time I saw it and I think she lost it the night of Baxter's death."

I thought back to that night and tried to picture Colette talking to Inspector Jaglom. I remembered her rubbing or stroking her neck a number of times in a nervous gesture. Now I knew why. She was used to playing with the necklace she wore.

"So how did Peter get it from Colette?" I wondered aloud.

Savannah shook her head. "She never would've given it to him voluntarily. It's a family heirloom from Raoul."

"Did she ever mention to you that she lost it?"

"No."

"Maybe she took it off in the ladies' room that night."

"Oh, right," Savannah said. "When she went in to wash her neck."

I chuckled. "Okay, that was stupid."

"We have to give it back to her," Savannah said.

Derek shook his head. "No, it's evidence. We have to give it to the police."

"Do we have to tell them where we found it?" I asked.

There was silence in the car while we contemplated the consequences of informing the police that Peter was a kleptomaniac. It didn't seem to have any bearing on the deaths of Baxter and Montgomery. Or did it?

"I'll call Inspector Jaglom and tell him we have it," Derek said. He brought the car to a stop in front of our building and waited for the traffic to break before turning into the garage below.

"What'll we tell Colette?" Savannah wondered.

"Let's not tell her anything until we think this through," Derek said. "I'd like to find out how Peter got it from her, but that won't happen until he regains consciousness."

I frowned at him. "Do you think Colette . . ."

"I don't know what to think," he said as he backed his car into his reserved parking space. "Let's talk this through upstairs."

Dalton got an earful from Derek, who blamed his younger brother for letting the womenfolk out of his sight. Okay, Derek didn't actually say that, but that's how I was reading it.

Dalton fought back like any brother would. "It's not my fault. They said they were going off to the market. Why would I suspect them of lying? Look at the two of them. They're the epitome of innocence."

"Oh, hell, yes," Derek said, casting another heated glance at me. "The innocent one whose hobby is murder. And her sister, who could have told you that she was flying to the moon for lunch and you would've bloody believed her."

"I wasn't lying," Savannah insisted.

My hobby was *not* murder. And apparently, I told myself, Derek and I were not finished with our conversation.

"Leave them both out of it," I said to Derek. He looked directly at me, and I met him stare for stare. I really do love Derek very much, but I'm not going to be treated like an idiot child. "I get that you're angry, but don't direct it at Savannah or Dalton. I already told you I'm to blame for everything. I dragged them both into it and I'm sorry. I suck. But enough already."

I'd reached the point where I was about to cry again,

and that was so not going to happen. So instead of humiliating myself, I stomped off to my bedroom to wallow alone for a while.

I curled up on the love seat and recalled the good times when Derek and I had worked together so closely on other murder cases. We'd had such fun. Well, except for those awful times when I'd stumbled upon dead bodies and those other bad times when I was confronted by cold-blooded killers.

Was I maybe romanticizing the past a little too much? It didn't matter because it seemed that those days were over. And that was sad. And since I was sad and wallowing anyway, I wondered if maybe Derek was over me and our relationship, too. For a few minutes in the car, it had felt like we were okay again. Now, I wasn't so sure. And that hurt a lot.

Suddenly I was irritated at myself. Why in heaven's name was I sitting alone in my room, brooding? I hadn't done anything wrong, and oh, by the way, I'd probably saved Peter's life because I had shown up there.

If Mr. Tall, Dark, and Dangerous wanted to give me more grief, I would be ready for him. I walked into the bathroom and splashed water on my puffy eyes, something I'd been doing a lot of lately.

I patted my face dry, slapped on some moisturizer and lipstick, and walked back into the bedroom just as the door opened and Derek stalked in. He came straight at me, wrapping his arms around me and holding on.

Okay, this was nice. If this was a prelude to round two of our fight, it was a good one. We stood like that for a long time. He stroked my hair and kissed my neck.

"I was so bloody afraid," he murmured. "I heard you scream. And then Savannah screamed and then . . . nothing. I shouted your name, but you never came back on the line."

"I'm sorry," I whispered, feeling my eyes well up again. Damn it, I really did suck. I should have called him back. "Oh, God, I'm so sorry."

"Going forward from here," he said, pointing his finger at me, "the first person you call is me."

"But I did call you," I said.

He held me at arm's length and gazed at me. "I don't mean from the hotel room. You call me before you go off to follow an impulse. Please. Even if you think nothing will happen."

"I really didn't think anything would happen."

He actually grinned. "Of course not. You were in the moment and on the move."

"Exactly."

His smile faded. "But, darling, we've both had our suspicions over the past few weeks that Kevin or Peter might've taken the cookbook. And then when you found out it had been stolen from their village—"

"Oh, hell." I grimaced, realizing I hadn't connected the dots. Again. No wonder I stumbled across bodies. I rarely stopped to figure out all the connections in whatever case we were wrapped up in. As Derek said, I tended to follow my impulses. "You're right. I wasn't thinking. And then I went and dragged Savannah into it."

"Yes," he said mildly. "Although I'm grateful you weren't alone in that room. And I must say, she appears to have weathered it well enough."

"She was awesome," I said, smiling. "She actually fought Kevin off with an egg whisk."

He laughed. "Only a chef would think of that."

"Only Savannah."

He pulled me back into his arms. "But in future, instead of dragging your sister or anyone else into the thick of it, I would prefer that you drag me instead."

So we still have a future, I thought, and smiled. "I promise I'll drag you into everything from now on."

Dalton, who was thankful to finally have the real Obedience Green cookbook in his hands, returned the favor by making margaritas while Savannah prepared a delicious dinner of black-bean-and-veggie tacos, cheese enchiladas, and guacamole. While we dined, Derek and I concocted a deliciously devious plan that counted on several different theories coming together at once.

Savannah and Dalton contributed to and improved on it, and I couldn't have been prouder. We were a real family of investigators! After dinner, I cleaned up while Savannah made a few phone calls and arranged everything for the following evening. It was becoming clear that my good-hearted, clean-living sister had a natural ability for scheming and conniving that warmed me right down to my bones.

Or maybe it was the margaritas.

Chapter 19

*In preparing hare soup, if you disapprove of the red
herring you may leave it out.*
                            —*The Cookbook of Obedience Green*

Derek worked from home the following day. In between
conference calls, he would wander into the dining room
to monitor Dalton's progress as his brother tried to unlock the secrets of the cookbook code. Even though Dalton insisted it was a one-man job, he seemed to enjoy
sparring and trading theories with Derek.

Dalton had taken over the dining room table and papers were spread everywhere. Savannah was there, too.
They were all having such a good time and the subject
matter was so intriguing, I was tempted to give up on my
bookbinding work and join them.

It was a dilemma for me. I should have begun the process of dampening the leather for the cover of *Jane Eyre*,
but once I started that job, I would be forced to see it all
the way through. Knowing our big plans for the evening,
I decided that today was not the day to begin anything
too complicated.

Instead, I took an hour and completed the rest of the

work on *Jane Eyre*, everything but the leather cover. For the endpapers, I picked out a sheet of mottled navy and burgundy I'd made a few months ago. The blend of colors would suit the navy leather I'd chosen for the cover. Then I glued the boards and spine to the text block and slipped *Jane* into the book press for the rest of the day.

I tidied up my workshop, then dashed into the dining room to join the others. It was all too fascinating, but I was stumped from the get-go. "How on earth do you figure out the code when there are such random symbols and numbers and squiggles like this?"

Savannah agreed. "There's no rhyme or reason to it. Is it just trial and error or are there certain patterns you follow?"

Dalton was happy to explain to his rapt audience. "These days, we depend on computers to help establish algorithmic codes. It makes decryption faster, though not necessarily easier. Believe me, none of it is a walk in the park."

Savannah shook her head. "I can't imagine anything more difficult. You're basically starting with nothing."

Dalton smiled at her. "I suppose digging ditches is a more difficult way to earn a living, but this does tax my mind a bit." He pointed to one of the cookbook pages. "The problem with these old codes is that they required the different parties to work together. Each of them needed access to the code pattern as well as a decoder book of some sort."

"Oh, I get it," I said. "You need the super-secret decoder ring."

His lips curved. "Yes, like the ones that used to come in our breakfast cereal."

Savannah stared at the page in front of her. "So without the secret passbook, how do you decode this?"

"There's always a method and a pattern to it, whether it's obvious or not." Dalton sat back in his chair and crossed his arms. "Whoever was sending these coded messages back and forth through this cookbook had to have a decryption chart or booklet. So there is a pattern. And I believe I'm close to breaking it."

"Really?" I said, hoping he didn't hear the doubt in my voice. "How exciting."

Dalton frowned. "Yes. What threw me off at first was the fact that some of these symbols equal a letter of the alphabet, while the same symbol sometimes refers to a whole word or phrase. For instance, I believe this pinwheel design here is a *W*, so it's used with other symbols or numbers to spell out a word. But it also refers to Washington, the general, as well as, occasionally, his headquarters or his camp or his next maneuver. Does that make sense?"

"Yes, it does," I said, allowing myself to feel a smidgen of excitement. "So a coded sentence might actually spell out the word *water* using all the letters, *w-a-t-e-r*. But if it was something related to General Washington's next move, the pinwheel alone would be sufficient to indicate the entire word."

"Exactly."

"I can see how that would make things very complicated and confusing for you," Savannah said, gazing at Dalton with even more adoration than usual.

"It can be complicated," Dalton said, with a humble nod of his head. "Luckily, though, I'm very good at what I do."

"And modest," Derek muttered.

"So true," Dalton said with a self-effacing shrug. Then he grinned. "Now, regardless of whether I break the code completely or not, my gut feeling is that this gentlewoman, Obedience Green, was recruited by the Yanks to spy on her employer, the British Army general Blakeslee."

"But why would a woman in that position agree to do something that would endanger her very livelihood?" Savannah wondered.

"And quite possibly her life," Derek added.

I walked over to the kitchen to start a new pot of coffee. "Maybe she was being blackmailed," I said. Because blackmail seemed to be an ongoing theme, I thought, as I poured water into the coffeemaker.

"It's possible the Yanks were using her," Derek said. "Tricked her, played on her emotions. Perhaps convinced her that one of their men was in love with her and coerced the information out of her that way."

"And she would've had plenty to reveal," I said. "She must've heard Blakeslee telling his men all sorts of things during meals or after dinner with his fellow officers gathered around. They would be talking about troop movements and stuff like that all the time, right?"

"And poor Obedience would report it all to her lover," Savannah said. She had clearly taken the cook's side in this dastardly plot.

"Through coded messages in her cookbook," I said, returning to the table. "Brilliant. But how would they pass the information back and forth?"

"That's easy." Dalton tapped the cookbook lightly with his knuckles. "She would write out the message in code on a predetermined page. Then she would take the cookbook to the marketplace with her. At some appointed spot, she would leave it or pass it on to a contact. A few days later, the book would be returned the same way."

"Poor Obedience," Savannah said again, with a sigh. "Betrayed by love."

"Isn't it possible that Obedience was the one doing the betraying?" Derek suggested. "She and the general were in cahoots. He was deliberately feeding her false information and she was passing it on to her friends in the revolutionary army."

"Oh, that's good." Savannah clapped her hands. "I like that Obedience might've had a little more gumption than just being a fool for love."

"It's feasible," I said. I knew it was all conjecture at this point, but it was fun to hypothesize. "She was very loyal to the general. He could've dumped her when he found out she didn't know how to cook, but he allowed her to stay and learn on the job. Obedience was grateful for that."

Dalton nodded. "I read one small passage where she spoke of being scared to death of the American savages. So she would be extremely grateful to have a job and a home."

"Savages," Savannah said, frowning. "That's probably what the British people considered us upstart Americans back then."

"We still do," Dalton said, and grinned when Savannah smacked his arm. "But to my point, perhaps the general and Obedience worked out a plan for her to catch the attentions of a gullible Yank. The British, after all, were far superior in the art of deception, having been at it for centuries already."

"Hey, we Yanks got pretty good at it, too," I said stoutly. "Wasn't Benjamin Franklin considered some kind of master spy?"

"Indeed he was," Dalton said, beaming at me as though I were a brilliant second grader. "The war for American independence spawned a world of covert societies and secret codes. Franklin was said to have an extensive network of agents and couriers and often sent out false information to catch the moles and traitors within his own circle."

"And don't forget, he was a Freemason," Derek said.

"They're everywhere," I murmured.

"Yes," Dalton said. "The paranoid conspiracy theorists would have a field day with this diary."

"I still don't know how you can decipher this thing." I grabbed one of the loose copy pages. "Some of those symbols look like something you'd see in an ancient cave drawing."

"Interesting you should say that," Dalton said, turning the page sideways and pointing to the margin. "You see these wavy lines here and this curlicue pattern?"

I leaned over for a closer look. "Yes."

"According to my best guess, it's—"

"Don't let him fool you," Derek interrupted. "He never guesses."

"True," Dalton admitted. "I know for a fact that these symbols were derived from a different alphabet than the rest. It was used by certain tribes of indigenous Americans living in Massachusetts during the sixteenth and seventeenth centuries. Possibly Wampanoag or Mohican."

"Wow," I said softly. "Kind of makes you wonder how all those disparate groups wound up in a recipe book written by a British cook."

"Someone clever and learned devised this code," Derek said. "Obedience just followed the rule book."

"Exactly, but there's more to see here." Dalton scanned the scattered copy pages, then picked up the one he'd been looking for. "Some of the symbols can be traced to an old Jesuit manuscript. And some belong to the Freemasons, as was clear from the beginning."

"To you, maybe," I muttered.

"This General Blakeslee was almost certainly a Freemason," he continued. "Most of the high-ranking British army personnel were. But so were Washington and Franklin and many of the most prominent American politicians of the time."

"So you really think there was a conspiracy between the British and the Americans through their affiliation with the Freemasons?"

"No," Dalton said, grinning. "But any conspiracy theorist worth his salt would think so."

I was almost afraid to ask the next question. "Does any of this have to do with our murder investigation?"

"No," Dalton said easily.

"Then why are you so happy?" Savannah asked.

"Because it's all so fascinating, isn't it?" He scooted forward in his chair, his enthusiasm palpable. "It was these Illuminati symbols that caught Derek's attention first."

"And those Masonic figures," Derek added. "I knew it would grab his interest. I didn't want to explain too much to you until Dalton could verify the code."

"You told me some of it," I said. "I just didn't know it would be so detailed."

"Nor did I," Dalton admitted. "American and British branches of the Freemasons. A possible Illuminati connection. Jesuits. Aboriginal groups. It's a fantastic find."

"And it's all in an old cookbook," Savannah marveled.

"I told you it was important," I murmured. I picked up the book and ran my hand across the smooth, worn leather.

"Were you able to translate any of the codes?" Savannah asked.

"Yes," Dalton said. "Would you like to hear some of it?"

"Heck, yes," I said. "Why didn't you say so?"

Dalton grinned. "I doubt there's anything here that will help you, but it's interesting." He reached for his notes and skimmed the pages until he found the one he was looking for, then handed it to me. "Here's what the coded message looks like."

I stared at the page with its curlicues, stick figures, numbers, and odd squiggles. "Okay."

"And here's the translation. 'Smith's army to cross Tanner Bridge eastward midnight three days hence.'"

"Cool," I said, and pointed at one of the symbols. "Do these arrows indicate the direction?"

"Yes," Dalton said. "I proceeded on the assumption that the arrows conveyed the same directions as those on a map, with north pointing to the top of the page and south to the bottom."

I nodded.

"And I also looked up Tanner Bridge," he said with a clever grin.

"That was so smart," Savannah said.

I laughed. "Read some more."

"All right." He handed me the corresponding pages as he read the decoded messages.

"Gunpowder shipment arriving from Britain fortnight Portsmouth harbor."

"Commander Howell being held at field camp outside Wooster."

"Soldiers planning to burn Worthington residence."

"That's terrible," Savannah said. "I'm glad Obedience was spying for our side."

"How many more pages were you able to complete?" I asked.

"Another five or six," Dalton said, "but I plan to take the pages back with me to work on. I'm hoping that Obedience reveals the name of her contact eventually. I imagine it's a highly placed American officer with connections to the Freemasons."

"Or it could be a fellow cook in that American officer's home."

"Indeed," Dalton said, his eyes twinkling. "Although a cook might not have access to such a code. It's all a puzzle."

I sighed. "I'm bummed that there's no real motive that could incriminate Baxter's and Monty's killer, but I still believe there has to be a connection somewhere."

Derek leaned over and squeezed my shoulder. "We'll find out tonight."

As if on cue, his cell phone rang. We all watched as he listened to the caller for two full minutes while voicing the occasional "Hmm," or "I see."

Meanwhile, Dalton, Savannah, and I waited impatiently.

"Thanks, Nathan," Derek said finally, and ended the call.

"Was that your office?" Savannah asked.

"No, it was the police." He glanced at Savannah. "They've released Kevin."

"Oh, thank goodness," she said.

"Jeez, Savannah," I said. "Remember how she attacked us with a knife?"

"That was totally lame," Savannah said, waving my statement away. "I beat her back with an egg whisk."

"I specifically remember a big-ass chef's knife pointed right at me," I insisted.

"Apparently, the police agree with Savannah," Derek said.

"I'm so glad," Savannah said. "I'm going to go call her now."

I might've rolled my eyes a teensy bit as she skipped out of the room. Turning to Derek, I said, "Tell me everything they told you."

"Kevin insisted she was only after the cookbook. She found Peter in the bath and thought he was dead. But before she could do anything, you and your sister arrived. So she hid in the closet, thinking Peter's killer had returned."

"That's weak."

"I thought so, too. But the police also found a partial thumbprint on the bloody handle of the meat pounder used to bludgeon Peter."

It was gruesome but exciting. "Did they say who it belongs to?"

Derek scowled. "The print was too smeared with blood to be of any real use except to eliminate Kevin as a suspect in Peter's assault. The thumbprint was too large. It belonged to a man."

"Or a woman with large hands," Dalton mused.

"Kevin has small hands," I muttered. I was happy that Kevin was absolved of attacking Peter, but it left us with a bunch of other questions. Staring at the copied pages of the cookbook scattered before me, I asked, "Did Kevin say anything else about the cookbook? Why does she want it so badly?"

Derek sipped his coffee for a moment. "It's what we already knew. The book belongs to her village museum and she wants to get it back to them. She also claims there's some relation between the book and the fact that her father is being knighted for service to the queen. I'll admit that Jaglom sort of lost me there."

"Google it," Dalton suggested.

"Good idea," I said, and sat down at the computer.

"This is absolutely the last time I'm coming to this place," Kevin said by way of greeting me at Baxter's restaurant that night.

I glanced around, no longer charmed by the exotic decor or the amazing waterfall. "Me, too. But you know how Savannah is. She's so worried about everyone and wanted to organize one last dinner in Monty's honor. She's determined to make sure you all remain friends. Even though . . ."

Kevin breathed deeply. "Even though one of us is a murderer."

"I'm sorry," I said lamely, although everything was going perfectly well, according to the plan Derek and I had dreamed up the night before with Dalton and Savannah's help.

"I'm the one who's sorry, Brooklyn," Kevin said. "I'm so ashamed of myself for frightening you. I was beside myself, honestly didn't know what I was doing. I was shut inside that stupid closet, worrying about Peter and wondering if you were his killer. Then I heard you take the cookbook and it was too much. I hope you'll forgive me someday."

"How about today?" I said, spreading my arms and taking a step closer to her.

She let out a tiny whimper, then wrapped her arms around me in a tight hug. "Thank you," she whispered.

When we finally broke apart, she smiled with teary relief. But I wasn't about to let her off too easily. I wanted some answers, especially after doing a little research on her father earlier that afternoon.

I wound my arm through hers and ambled over to the bar, where flutes of champagne were waiting. I took a sip, then said, "Tell me about the cookbook. And your father."

Her mouth opened, then closed quickly. Disconcerted, she grabbed a glass of champagne and took a healthy gulp. "I suppose I owe you that much."

"I'd say so." I hopped up on a barstool and said to her, "Have a seat."

She sat, took another few sips of champagne — liquid courage? — and finally began. "Obedience Green grew up in Gipping-on-Plym. That was two or three hundred years ago, of course, but in England, it's like yesterday. So we all loved her and claimed her as one of our own, a fellow Gippinger."

"Did she return to the village after the war?"

"Yes, indeed. With her Yankee husband in tow."

"No way," I said, downing my champagne and reaching for another glass. Hey, my throat was dry.

"Oh, yes," Kevin said. "Quite the defiant one, was our Obedience."

"But wouldn't he be considered an enemy of the British?"

"That part's a bit murky. Nobody seems to know whether he was working for or against our side."

"What about Obedience's job with the general? She had to quit working for him, didn't she?"

"She did," Kevin said. "But they remained friends and she trained his cooks to prepare all his favorite dishes. He especially loved her syllabub."

"Did the king strip the general of his rank?"

"Heavens, no." She looked at me as though I'd lost my mind. "Despite his humiliating failure to crush the Americans and losing the king's confidence as a result, General Blakeslee returned a true war hero. After all," she added with a smirk, "he'd managed to survive among all those Yankee barbarians. Gippingers were overjoyed by his return and held a festival in his honor. It continues to this day. And Blakeslee House is still standing, as a matter of fact."

"What happened to Obedience's Yankee lover, now husband? I can't believe he wasn't run out of town by an angry mob."

"He arrived with too much money to be turned away."

"What was his name?"

"Jeremiah Spencer." Kevin sighed happily. "He'd become quite wealthy in America, trading with the Indians. He spoke several languages, and when he arrived, he quickly bought the nearest country house. He and General Blakeslee became lifelong friends."

I frowned at her. "But Jeremiah was passing secret

information behind Blakeslee's back. Don't you think Jeremiah was the one who convinced Obedience to betray Blakeslee?"

"Actually, it was the conclusion of the local scholars that General Blakeslee used Jeremiah. But in the end, it didn't really matter. You see, Blakeslee was a rabid partridge hunter and Jeremiah had the best hunting hounds in the region."

I choked out a laugh. "Seriously? It only took a few hounds to win him over? Are you kidding?"

She peered at me. "Have you ever been to England?"

"I've been to London and Oxford and Scotland," I said.

"Ah, well," she said with a chuckle, "come to Devon and you'll see how the real English live."

I was glad Obedience had found true love. It probably caught her by surprise, too, because she'd written something early on that indicated she might just eschew the marriage thing.

> 6 December 1775. If ever I marry, it will not be to a man who professes to fight for the rights of all men to be free while insisting on maintaining absolute power over his wife. I would just as soon sleep with the dog.

Derek was watching me from across the room, so I waved at him to come and listen to the rest of Kevin's story.

"How lovely, you've brought champagne," Kevin said, taking the fresh glass from Derek. She took a sip, then looked at me. "Where was I?"

"I was about to ask you to fast-forward to when the cookbook was stolen."

"Right." Her shoulders sagged a little, but she recovered, straightened up, and shook her hair back. Glancing around, she noticed more of us listening in, so in a clear voice she said, "And thus begins our true tale of treachery and murder."

She could have been an actress, because those words

caused me to shiver with dread. Savannah and Dalton closed in to hear the story.

"The villagers were heartbroken when the cookbook was stolen. The first rumor to circulate implicated Peter, but he had never taken anything so valuable before. He allowed his rooms to be searched, but the book wasn't found and the villagers became resigned to living without it." Kevin took a sip of champagne, then continued. "Several months later, my father received a generous contribution to build an irrigation system for the African town where he'd built his missionary school. The benefactor was anonymous, and word began to circulate among our townspeople that it was all a bit too coincidental."

I felt instant guilt for having the same thought pop into my head.

Kevin sighed. "You see, Daddy was always soliciting money. It's just the way charities have to operate. So when the cookbook was stolen, some people wondered aloud if Daddy had taken it and sold it for the money to keep the school running. It was a huge scandal, as you might expect. The local constable looked into it, but found nothing to pin the crime on Daddy."

"Baxter stole it," Savannah murmured. "And later gave it to me to hide his crime."

Kevin turned in her chair. "Yes, that's what it looks like. I don't blame you, Savannah. How could you have known?"

"I'm sorry, anyway." Savannah shook her head. "Baxter managed to use me while destroying your father's reputation."

"Yes," I said. "I wouldn't be surprised to find out he started the rumor about your father."

Kevin blinked. "I never thought of that. But of course it was him. He had to throw the guilt elsewhere so it wouldn't land on him."

"He was just slimy enough to do it," I said. "And he probably spread the rumor that Peter took it, as well."

Savannah scowled. "He really was a horrible person."

"Yes, he was."

This talk of Baxter reminded me of another question I had. "Why did all three of you go to Le Cordon Bleu together? Peter said it was because Baxter couldn't think of anything better to do, so he tagged along. But that can't be the real reason."

"It's not," Kevin said, chewing her lip as she considered her next words. Then she said, "I've never told anyone this, but when I was thirteen, Baxter wanted to be my boyfriend. He was always trying to kiss me and I was constantly pushing him away. Finally I'd had it with his nonsense and began to ridicule him in front of our friends. I admit it was awful of me."

"You were just a kid," I said.

"Yes, but Baxter was furious. I can hardly blame him, because our friends were relentless with their teasing. Baxter told me I'd regret it, said he'd follow me forever and make sure I always knew he was watching me. He said he'd ruin my life in ways I couldn't understand, but one day I'd figure it out and look back and regret snubbing him."

I shivered. "That was creepy."

"Poor Kevin," Savannah said.

Kevin's laugh was gruff. "Yes, poor me."

Savannah's eyes were focused on her friend. "You really think that's why he went to cooking school with you?"

"Absolutely," she said. "But when he got there, he discovered he was really good at it. It was the first time in his life he'd received so much positive feedback and good attention. I was happy for him, honestly, but it was also a relief to finally get him off my back. Until recently, that is."

"What happened recently?" I asked.

Kevin pinched her lips together. "He tried to blackmail me."

Savannah reached out to grab Kevin's arm. "How?"

"He thought he could extort money from me to keep

my father's so-called crime a secret. You see, Daddy's on a short list of people being considered for knighthood. If the story got out that he'd stolen the book . . ."

"So Baxter was going to blackmail you to cover up the crime that he committed himself." I shouldn't have been shocked, but I was. "That's diabolical."

"The man had balls," Dalton murmured.

"And not in a good way," Savannah added. "But, Kevin, you said you weren't being blackmailed."

"I wasn't," Kevin said. "I told him to take his blackmail scheme and shove it up his arse."

"Good girl," I said.

"But when I saw him open your gift," she said, her eyes narrowing as she wagged her finger at Savannah, "I knew in an instant that he'd stolen the book, and yet he'd been trying to blackmail me at the same time. And I wanted to kill him right then and there."

Chapter 20

If your tongue is a dry one, soak it in water all night.
—The Cookbook of Obedience Green

Margot gasped. She had just joined the conversation and heard only the last few words.

"You killed Baxter?" she whispered.

"I didn't get the chance," Kevin grumbled. "But I'll be glad to thank whoever did it. The man was a plague on the earth."

I wouldn't go so far as to thank a cold-blooded killer, but I understood Kevin's feelings. "It's no wonder you wanted that book so badly."

She nodded. "I need to restore my father's good reputation and return the book to the village museum, where it belongs. I want him to get his knighthood. There's not a better man in the world than my father."

By now all the chefs were gathered on both sides of the bar, listening to the end of Kevin's story. I just wished I knew which one of them had killed two people and injured a third.

I touched Kevin's knee. "Thank you for telling us what happened. I'll return the cookbook to you tomorrow."

"Thank you, Brooklyn."

We both stood and after another brief hug, I glanced at my watch. It was time to set our plan into action. Looking at Savannah, I said, "I guess we should start the syllabub."

She whirled around, gushing to everyone, "I'm so excited for you all to taste Brooklyn's crowning achievement."

Her tone was a little manic. I knew she was jumpy about what we were planning to do, so I gave her an encouraging smile. "It's just pudding," I said to the others. "Nobody's in danger of me taking over their job, but I think you'll like it."

Savannah's phone calls the previous evening had been specifically designed to coax Colette into cooking tonight. Margot had agreed to assist. It made sense because except for a side dish or two, they were the only two chefs who hadn't gotten the chance to show off their talents.

I hated accusing anyone of the two murders, but it had to be done. Maybe Colette was innocent, but her locket in Peter's backpack was too big a clue to go unquestioned.

We had argued for hours the night before about the explanation for Peter having the locket. And about where Monty fit into the scheme.

Had Colette killed Baxter? Had Peter witnessed her doing it? Doubtful. But I was still voting that Colette had argued with Baxter and then stabbed him with the knife. Maybe during the struggle, Baxter had ripped her necklace off and flung it somewhere. Somehow, Montgomery found the blood-encrusted locket and threatened to tell the police, so Colette had killed him.

Derek wasn't certain. He didn't think a woman would have the strength to shove that big knife into Baxter's stomach. But Savannah had disagreed. Female chefs had to be strong, she'd argued, pointing out that both Colette and Margot were tall, well-built women.

I continued to try and plot out how Peter had obtained the necklace. Since he was the first to discover

Monty's body, perhaps he'd found the locket clutched in Monty's fist. The locket was shiny and Peter was under a lot of stress, so his kleptomania kicked in and he took it.

Somehow Colette, who was looking more and more guilty in my eyes, had figured out that Peter had the locket and she went looking for it. When he tried to stop her from taking it, she coshed him with the first weapon she'd grabbed from his pile of tools.

Like I said, it was a loose theory. But how else could we explain how Peter had obtained Colette's necklace?

Colette was the sturdiest of the four women chefs, so I agreed with Savannah that Colette had enough strength to jam that big fish knife into Baxter's gut. And as far as injecting Montgomery with that rat poisoning, she'd only had to sneak up behind him to do it.

Was she being blackmailed by Monty or Peter? Was she a cold-blooded killer? Or was I just overly annoyed with her and willing to peg her with the crime? We would soon find out.

Standing in Baxter's kitchen, I glanced at the other chefs. "I'm just going to take over this little corner to put my syllabub together." Luckily Savannah had already claimed the spot for me and had laid out everything I would need, including ten glass dessert bowls.

Raoul flashed one of his sexy grins at me. "Can I help you with dessert? I am somewhat of an expert."

I smiled at him. "I think I have everything under control. I'm sorry I'm invading your bailiwick tonight."

"It is my pleasure," he said, and pointed to a plastic storage container on the counter. "I took the liberty of making miniature biscotti to accompany your treat."

"That's so nice," I said. "Thank you, Raoul. Biscotti sounds perfect."

"Raoul!" Colette yelled. "I need you over here."

He winked at me before rushing off to her side. I figured that famous migraine of hers was back, because she sounded like a cranky bear.

I peeked at Colette whenever I could and noticed her

acting peevish, as usual, but she had more of an edge this evening. She continually touched her neck, obviously reaching for the locket that wasn't there.

A half hour later, I placed the beautifully filled dessert bowls on a large cookie sheet and carefully slid it onto a shelf in the walk-in refrigerator. My cooking was done and now I was ready to make trouble.

Colette had made it easy by banishing Raoul from the kitchen until she was finished preparing the meal. And since Derek's plan included him keeping an eye on Raoul, he was gone as well. I didn't expect him to walk into the kitchen anytime soon, either. Colette and I were alone at last.

"Can I help you with anything, Colette?" I asked.

She clutched her neck for the umpteenth time, then squeezed her empty hand in frustration. "No, I doubt you can do anything for me. You should go have a drink until we're ready to serve."

"Oh, I just noticed you're not wearing that pretty locket you always wear," I said innocently.

"So what?" She took off her chef's hat and pushed her hair back from her forehead.

"What happened to it?"

She let out an exasperated breath. "If I knew what happened to it, I'd be wearing it."

"I guess you would." I leaned against the counter and folded my arms. "So it's a good thing we found it."

"You found . . ." Her eyes widened. "Where?"

"In Peter's room."

"Do you have it? I want it back."

"I'll bet you do. The thing is, it's evidence now." I shrugged. "Derek is giving it to the police."

"No!" She swore under her breath as she sagged against the counter opposite me, looking defeated for just a moment. But then she rallied. "Look, I really want it back. Can you tell Derek to give it to me? I—it's very special. A family heirloom. You know how it is."

"I sure do. I wonder how Peter got hold of it?"

"I don't care. I just need it back."

"Okay, I'll talk to Derek. But he's going to want to know how you lost it and how Peter found it. See, if it was me, I would just give it back to you, but Derek's a law-abiding kind of guy. He likes to know all the details."

A little too late, she tried to turn on the charm. "Derek seems like a great guy. You make a cute couple."

"Thanks."

She swallowed nervously. "But if Raoul realizes I've lost the locket he gave me, I'm going to be in so much trouble. You understand, right? Can you please get it for me?"

"I'll try. If you'll tell me how you lost it, I'll get it from Derek right away."

She seemed to be weighing the odds involved in telling me the truth, so I went for broke. "Did Baxter take it from you, Colette? Was he blackmailing you?"

Her eyes widened. "No!"

"Then how did Peter get hold of it?"

"I don't know!"

"Did you kill Baxter?"

"What? Are you crazy? No!" She seemed genuinely shocked and I began to doubt my theory that she had killed him. But she still seemed nervous. She blinked a few times and her breathing was heavier. "God, no."

"Okay, just wondering."

But her face was glowing with sweat. Something had to have occurred between her and Baxter, and I was determined to find out what. "Tell me what happened, Colette, and I'll get your necklace back."

"I don't know what you're talking about," she said, her voice wavering.

"Okay, then." I glanced around. "Look, I need to use the ladies' room so I'll—"

But she'd been thinking fast. She grabbed the nearest weapon from the counter, a knife, and pointed it at me. "Get it for me now."

Oh, crap. What was with these chefs and their damn knives? Was I willing to get myself sliced up for a stupid glass locket? No. But I wanted to hear the truth from her. *Keep her talking*, I thought.

"If you're willing to use that knife on me," I said, "I have to believe that you killed Baxter."

"I didn't!" she said, practically hissing at me.

"And Montgomery," I added.

"No!" she insisted. "Why would you think I could kill anyone?"

"Because you're threatening me with a knife and because . . . Baxter was blackmailing you for money?"

"That's ridiculous," she shouted, but then she hedged. "Well, he tried to, but I told him to shove it."

"Because whatever he thought he knew wasn't true?"

"No, because I didn't have the money to pay him."

"Oh." Good point. I kept a close eye on that sharp knife in her shaky hand. "Why did he want to blackmail you?"

"Why would I tell you?"

"Because any minute now Raoul is going to walk back in here and wonder what in the world you're doing pointing that dangerous knife at me."

"Oh, God," she moaned, and dropped the knife. It fell to the counter with a loud thud.

I let go of the breath I'd been holding. "Tell me about Baxter blackmailing you."

She visibly deflated. As she pushed her hair back slowly with both hands, I could tell she was utterly exhausted. "Fine. I'll tell you, but I don't want anyone else to hear it." Her gaze darted around the kitchen and she pointed to the walk-in refrigerator. "Let's go in there."

There was no way in hell I was walking into a giant icebox with this chick. "Look, just tell me what Baxter tried to do. The police will give you the benefit of the doubt if he was blackmailing you."

"You're as bad as Baxter," she said, her tone an uncomfortable mix of anger and defeat. "Forcing me to tell you what happened to my locket. It's like blackmail all over again."

"I'm nothing like Baxter," I said irately, not bothering

to mention that she had been pointing a big, scary knife at me a minute ago. "I just want to hear the truth from you for once."

She began to pace along the service counter, then stopped suddenly and looked at me. "Baxter got me pregnant with my first child."

My mouth opened, and then closed. I had not expected that. But it was a really good reason for blackmail. "Does Raoul know?"

"Of course not," she said, sounding irritated. "That's why Baxter was trying to blackmail me."

"I see."

"There's more," she admitted.

"What is it?"

Reluctantly, she said, "He's also the father of my second child."

Wow, that was creepy. "So I guess you liked him a lot."

"No! I hated him."

"But it sounds like you'd been having a long-term affair."

"You. Don't. Understand." With every syllable, Colette pounded her hand against the counter. She definitely had anger management issues. "He threatened to tell Raoul about the boys."

"Oh." I frowned at her. "So he was blackmailing you for sex?"

Her shoulders dipped. "Yes."

"Colette, did he rape you?"

She reacted with horror. "No!"

I was relieved to hear it, but it was still strange that she had continued to sleep with Baxter. I would've rather come clean to my husband—but that was me.

She struggled to continue. "No, it was mutual."

"But why?" I knew it was none of my business, but I had to say it. "You had Raoul. I mean, he's awesome and he loves you."

Her bottom lip began to quiver. "He was having an affair with Margot."

I couldn't imagine it. True, Raoul could have any woman he wanted, but it was crystal clear that he only wanted Colette, even if she was a harpy. "How did you find out?"

"I heard it from a very good source."

"Who?" I demanded. "Margot?"

"I'm not saying."

Damn, I smelled a six-foot-tall, redheaded rat. "Did you confront Raoul?"

"Why? So he could rub my nose in it?"

That didn't sound like something Raoul would do, but what did I know about the inner workings of their marriage?

"Anyway," she continued, "I was so upset about their affair and Baxter was there for me and he was so sympathetic and so giving, we just . . . well, that's when it started. We carried it on for a few years, but when I finally tried to break it off with him, he pulled that blackmail baloney."

"Creep," I muttered. "But are you sure Raoul doesn't know the boys aren't his? I mean, he and Baxter look nothing alike."

She shrugged. "The boys look like me. There was never a question that they weren't Raoul's."

"I see. So it's no wonder you killed Baxter."

"I didn't!" She smacked her fist against the poor defenseless counter again. "But I'm glad he's dead. He was ruining our lives, turning me into a nervous wreck. The night after he died, I got my first good night of sleep in years."

"He was really awful," I said in all honesty.

"He was a son of a bitch."

"So who killed him?"

Her eyes widened and she looked away quickly. "It wasn't me. It was probably someone else he was blackmailing."

"Probably."

She pinched her lips together stubbornly. "Now I want my locket and you're going to get it for me."

"Okay." I pushed away from the counter. "I'll go tell Derek to give it to you."

"Wait." She grabbed my arm. "I don't want Raoul to know any of this."

"I won't say anything to him."

"I—I'm going with you."

"Fine." We crossed the kitchen and I shoved the door open in time to see Derek and Dalton and the rest of the chefs scramble backward.

Derek grabbed me as the chefs all began to talk at once. Raoul rushed forward and took Colette in his arms.

"Thank you for sticking close by," I whispered in Derek's ear. "Did you hear any of that?"

"Every word," he murmured.

"Why did you have that knife, Colette?" Raoul asked in a low voice.

"I put it down," Colette cried.

"Not right away," I said.

Colette wrapped her arms around Raoul. "She was going to tell everyone I lost my necklace, but I didn't, Raoul. I swear. It's missing, though. And . . . and she thought I killed Baxter. I had to try and keep her quiet."

"I wasn't going to say anything," I said heatedly, tugging away from Derek to glare at her. "Tell the truth for once."

"Yes, my love," Raoul crooned, as he held his wife and stroked her hair as if she were a little girl.

"Noooooo!" Colette howled.

He squeezed her lightly. "It is time for the truth."

"Please, Raoul, don't!" Colette cried.

"What's the truth?" Savannah wondered aloud.

Raoul met our gazes one by one. "Baxter Cromwell had to die."

Colette sagged against him. "No, no, no."

Whoa. Was that a confession? Did Colette know or had she merely suspected? I spun around and looked at Derek. He didn't appear quite as surprised as I probably did. Darn! Had he deduced before now that it was

Raoul? Why didn't he say something before I was forced to confront that knife-wielding wench?

"The honor of my family was at stake," Raoul said, with one of his unruffled shrugs. "It was as simple as that."

"Not quite that simple," I said. Derek yanked me closer to him, probably trying to keep me quiet.

"No, not quite," Raoul said, gracing me with his sexy smile, though it no longer held much charm. "But when Baxter attempted to blackmail me, I knew I had to do something about it."

Colette blinked at her husband. "He tried to blackmail you, too?"

"Yes, my love." Raoul took hold of her shoulders to explain. "He showed me a document from a laboratory service that proved his paternity."

Colette emitted a high-pitched keening sound and then collapsed against his chest. I couldn't blame her. Not only was Raoul aware of her multiple indiscretions, but worse, he would be thrown in prison, leaving her without a husband and a father for her two boys.

"Baxter had proof of paternity?" I asked Raoul.

"Yes, apparently he planned ahead." Raoul scowled. "A few months ago, I invited him to stay with us for a few days. While he was in our home, he took samples of our boys' hair follicles to be tested for DNA. He showed me the lab results the night of his restaurant opening. He ridiculed me, called me a cuckold while boasting of his own prowess."

"What an awful man," Savannah whispered.

"Yes," Raoul said, absently flicking a crumb from his chef's coat. "I could live with his disdain, but then he mentioned that he had tried to extract money from my wife and she refused. He insisted that I pay him instead and threatened to ruin Colette's reputation as well as my sons'. That was when I took it upon myself to end it. Any man would do the same."

He sounded like a Spanish nobleman from the eighteenth century, dueling for his lady's honor. Did he really believe he had the right to take Baxter's life?

Derek cast a quick glance my way, then looked at Raoul. "After you killed Baxter, did you take the lab results with you?"

Raoul's jaw clenched. "No. When he admitted it to me, he shoved them in his pocket and walked away. But later that night, after Savannah gave him that lovely gift, I saw him slip a piece of paper inside the box and I suspected strongly that it was the laboratory results."

"Inside the leather gift box?" I asked, just to clarify.

"Yes. After everything happened, I looked for the box, but I couldn't find it."

My eyes were wide as I met Derek's gaze. Dalton had been poring over the cookbook for a full day now. Had he found the lab results and tossed them aside? We needed to get home and find it, but there were still more questions to be answered.

"You could've called the police and sent Baxter to jail for all the blackmailing he'd done," Savannah said. "Why did you have to kill him?"

Raoul paused for a moment and seemed to argue with himself. But since we all knew what he'd done, it was useless to hold back information. With a sigh, he said, "The night of Baxter's first dinner, after the diners had left, I found Baxter in the private dining room arguing with Colette. I almost burst into the room, but I hesitated. The door was partially opened and I saw him snatch the locket from her neck."

With tears streaming down her cheeks, Colette touched her throat as if she was reliving that moment herself.

"For that alone," Raoul said, staring down at Colette as his hands bunched into fists, "he would have had to die. But then I heard him refer to his bastard children, heard him laugh, and saw you cry. I could barely restrain myself from ripping his heart out right then, but I knew I would have to wait. I left you all early that night, but returned later and waited at the back door until Baxter was alone. It only took a moment to kill him, but I made sure he knew why he was dying."

I exhaled slowly, only just aware that I'd been holding my breath. I was doing that a lot these days.

"And Montgomery?" Derek asked, breaking the silence.

Raoul sighed wearily. "When I heard him make that phone call to the police the other night, I confess I didn't know what to do. He told the police he knew who the killer was. I moved closer to hear his words. As he spoke, he pulled Colette's locket out of his pocket and smiled as it glittered in the light. He must have found it somewhere in the kitchen and I believe he'd made up his mind that Colette had killed Baxter."

Colette leaned against his strong chest and wept quietly.

"It wasn't Colette, of course, but at that moment I knew what he was about to unleash on my family. It was too much to bear." Raoul tightened his hold on Colette. "I felt betrayed and couldn't think, could only act on impulse. The meat injector was in the dishwasher. The poison was under the sink. I'm not proud of what I did, but I would do it again to protect what is mine."

Epilogue

Fricasseed Tripe is much esteemed by the American gentry.

—The Cookbook of Obedience Green

Like so many other mornings, I woke up in desperate need of coffee. Today was different, however. It was not going to be an easy one for so many reasons, but the sooner I got started, the faster I would get through it.

As I washed my face and brushed my teeth, I thought back on the terrible night we'd been through.

It had been painful to hear Raoul admit his guilt. He truly believed he'd done the right thing for his family. Maybe that would help lighten his sentence somehow, but I couldn't condone what he'd done. I had thought he was a good man, a good husband, but he had killed two people in cold blood. Even though Baxter was a son of a bitch, that was no justification for murder. But it was Montgomery's death that really struck home and left me feeling nothing but contempt for Raoul. And sadness, damn it. He had broken all of our hearts and I would never forgive him for that.

And what would happen to their two little boys? Colette had been arrested, too, for wielding that stupid knife at me. I figured she would be released shortly, but not Raoul. Had he even considered what his children would do without him? No, he hadn't considered anyone or anything beyond his own stupid vengeance.

Sometimes people really sucked. I had a long list of the ones who did, and Baxter was on it. Margot was on it, too, because it was obvious that she'd tried to cause trouble between Colette and her husband. But Raoul topped the list. Besides killing Monty, he had almost killed Peter. He needed to pay for that.

Last night, Derek had asked Raoul to fill in the blanks regarding Peter's attack. Raoul had rubbed his eyes, clearly exhausted. Finally he had told us what happened.

"Montgomery began reacting to the poison almost immediately," Raoul said. "It was a hideous death, but I was determined to watch and wait until it was over so I could search him for Colette's necklace. But then I heard someone coming and I ran from the building. I went back the next morning to search for it, but others had arrived before me. Margot told me that Peter was the first to find Montgomery. So I took a chance, went to Peter's hotel room to ask if he'd found the locket. By now I was crazed with worry. When he said that, yes, he had taken the necklace, I demanded it. But he began to ask questions about Colette. I let a few of them pass until he suggested that she must have killed Baxter. He wanted to call the police. I simply lost all control. I grabbed the nearest weapon and he ran. I chased after him and hit him. I regretted it immediately. I didn't plan to do it. I have no more excuses."

I wondered what Raoul would have done if he'd found the cookbook in Peter's luggage. Had he even thought to search for it—or the locket, for that matter? He hadn't found what he was looking for, thank goodness, but I wondered if he'd tried.

"Did you look for Colette's locket in Peter's room?" I asked.

"I began to," he muttered. "I turned over his backpack and his tools went everywhere. Before I could search more carefully, I heard someone open the front door of the suite. I escaped out the bedroom door and down the hall."

I glanced at Kevin, who stared wide-eyed and disbelieving at Raoul. Did she realize she was the person who had interrupted his search? Would she have been his next victim? I'd shuddered at the thought and Derek had wrapped his arm more tightly around me.

The police showed up within minutes of Raoul's confession.

Shortly after Raoul and Colette were taken away, we got word that Peter had come out of his coma. It was the happiest news we could have received after Raoul's devastating confession.

Everyone rushed to the hospital room where Peter lay sleeping. His skin was pale and he wore a massive bandage around his head. He looked beaten up. The doctors were keeping him overnight for observation.

He awoke finally and was pleased to see us gathered around him. He confessed that he had indeed found Colette's locket clasped in Montgomery's cold, dead hand. All he could think when he saw it was that it was pretty and shiny, so he grabbed it.

"I—I have a bit of a problem with taking things," he said weakly. "It happens when I'm upset. And seeing Monty that way, well, it upset me, to say the least."

"To say the least," Kevin echoed.

"Did you take the cookbook, too?" I asked, changing the subject.

He gave me a pained look. "Yes, I took it that first night. I knew the instant Baxter opened Savannah's gift that he'd been the one to steal it from the museum. So later that night, while everyone was drinking at the bar, I snuck back to his office and grabbed it and hid it in my knapsack."

"Good," Kevin said bluntly. "Among his many crimes, he was also a thief and a liar."

"Yes," Peter said. "I'm glad I took the book. However, I'm not proud of stealing the locket. To tell the truth, I didn't even connect the locket to the killer. I just saw something shiny and took it."

"Everyone here knows about the kleptomania," Kevin said. "I told them already."

"You told them?" he said, trying for as much outrage as he could manage, given that his head was wrapped in a bandage and he looked like he might pass out at any moment. "How could you?"

"I thought you were dead!" she cried. "We were trying to figure out who might've hurt you."

He reached out and took her hand in his. She sat down on the bed and squeezed his hand with both of hers.

"All right," he said with a wan smile. "You're forgiven."

"I told them about the dodgy fish, too."

His eyes widened and he gazed around the room before he stared back at Kevin. "It seems you've given away all my secrets. Anything else you want to tell me?"

"Well, at least no one can ever blackmail you again," she said, and burst into tears.

Peter pulled her close and held her. I had great hopes that the two of them would be back together soon. They were meant to be a couple.

I blinked away my own tears, relieved that at least one thing had ended happily last night. I finished brushing my hair and added a touch of lipstick. Then I slipped on jeans and a turtleneck and wandered out to the kitchen.

There on the bar was the book box I'd created for Baxter. Last night when we got home, Derek had searched the book for Raoul's lab results, but didn't find them until he opened the box itself and found the suede pouch. Inside was the folded sheet of paper Raoul had killed for. Derek planned to deliver it to the police sometime today.

Dalton would be leaving shortly to go back to London. Late last night, he had run out to an all-night copy service to make another copy of the cookbook pages; he planned to continue deciphering it once he was back home.

While Obedience Green's cookbook had turned out not to be the inspiration for a major breakthrough in the field of cryptography and spying, it was exciting and significant enough to warrant more study. Dalton intended to contact the Gipping-on-Plym museum to arrange a study schedule as soon as they received the cookbook from Kevin.

I heard the muted voices before I'd even reached the coffeemaker.

"You're really leaving me," Savannah said. "I don't know why I thought you might stay. Silly, I guess."

Oh, dear, I thought. *Poor Savannah.* Was I going to be crying again soon? It was so early in the day. I peeked around the wall to see if it was safe to walk in.

"I'll always be here," Dalton said, and pressed his hand against her heart. "And here," he added with a grin, smoothing his hand across her bald head. "I'll be back as soon as I can get away."

"You will," she said, tugging his shirt until he was pressed up against her, "or I'll hunt you down like a bloodhound."

"How did you know that's my favorite dog?"

She laughed and touched his cheek.

"Come here," he muttered, and wrapped her in his arms and kissed her slowly on the lips. It was a while before he let her go. Then he turned and almost ran into me.

"Oops," I said, pretending I'd just walked in. "Sorry. Just me, looking for a cup of coffee. Hey, you're not leaving, are you?"

"Yes, he's leaving," Savannah said calmly, though her arms were crossed tightly in front of her. "Get out of his way, Brooklyn."

He took one look at me and said, "Perhaps I can squeeze in one more cup of coffee."

I heard a noise and turned. Derek stood watching me from the hallway door. I knew what he was thinking—that I was going to take Dalton's departure worse than Savannah would. He was right. At least Savannah had prepared herself for Dalton to go. I hadn't.

I didn't know who to go to first, but Dalton was closer, so I walked straight into his arms. He hugged me tightly and said, "I'll miss you."

"I'll miss you, too."

"Are you sure you have to leave us?" I whispered foolishly.

"The man has a job and a life elsewhere," Savannah said, her tone crisp and practical.

I wanted to tell her that Derek had had all that, too. And yet he'd left his home and traveled thousands of miles to be with me. But that would've hurt her, and really, who knew how Dalton truly felt about my sister? He seemed to like her a lot, but they hadn't had enough time to really get to know each other. Perhaps they would meet again sometime soon. I hoped so.

I felt Savannah's hand on my back. It was meant to comfort me, and didn't that just say it all? As predicted, I wasn't handling Dalton's departure half as well as Savannah was. And she wasn't just losing Dalton. I thought of the close friends she'd lost over the past few weeks and wondered how she could be so strong.

Time to activate that stiff upper lip, I thought, and eased away from Dalton. Giving his arm a light punch, I smiled brightly. "Well, that's it, then. Don't be a stranger. Travel safe. Off you go now."

"Jeez, Brooklyn, easy on the clichés." Savannah rolled her eyes at me. "You forgot to tell him not to let the door hit his ass on the way out."

"Did I?"

Dalton laughed. "I won't." He turned to Derek and gave a quick nod. "Do you have it?"

"Yes, right here." Derek disappeared from the doorway, but emerged a few seconds later carrying a cardboard box. He crossed the room and handed it to me. "We thought this might ease the pain of Dalton's departure."

Mystified, I stared into the box—and gasped. "It's a ... Oh." Wrapped up in an old towel was a tiny white kitten.

I set the box on the bar and reached for the little creature.

"What is it?" Savannah said. Then, "Oh, it's a kitty."

I cupped it in my hands and examined it. Its fur was long and silky and it was snowy white from head to toes. I held it to my chest and rubbed my chin along its fragile backbone. Its fur tickled my skin and its mews sounded like the tinkling of a delicate glass bell.

"How did you ... when did you ..."

Derek smiled self-consciously. "I'd mentioned to Dalton a few nights ago that I wanted to try and get one of Bootsie's kittens for you."

"So we drove over there at the crack of flipping dawn this morning to find the cat," Dalton said. "Wasn't easy. She'd managed to squeeze herself into the tightest crawl space in that alleyway."

"How did you find her?" Savannah asked as she ran her finger around the kitten's tiny ears.

"We heard the mewing," Derek said. "Ten kittens and one big cat make a lot of noise."

"Ten. But ... you just took this one away? Will it be okay?"

"We ran into Bootsie's owner as she was emptying her trash," Derek explained as he moved closer to pet the kitten. "Her name is Eileen and it's fine with her if we keep this little one. But she did suggest that after you've had this visit with the kitten, we bring it back to stay with the mother for a few more weeks."

"That's a good idea." Although I hated to let her go. I was already in love with her. The kitten caught a strand of my hair in its eensy claw and became entangled instantly. I laughed softly. "You ding-a-ling."

Savannah said, "Awww."

I looked up at Derek. "Thank you. I love her. It's the sweetest thing you ever could've given me." And then I burst into tears.

Savannah sniffled, too. Naturally.

Dalton elbowed Derek. "Time to go."

Derek laughed and grabbed me in a warm hug. I watched him stroke the kitten's soft fur, and then he took it from me and placed it back in its box. "I'll return the cat to Eileen on the way back from the airport. I've got her number, so we'll keep tabs on the little one's progress and have her back in a few weeks."

I nodded, unable to speak.

Dalton grabbed his duffel bag, and Savannah and I walked them both to the front door. Dalton and my sister shared one more passionate embrace and then he hugged me once more. Derek kissed me again, and the Stone brothers walked off, leaving my sister and me standing in the hall, waving until the elevator doors closed on them.

Savannah stared at those doors for a full minute, then blinked a few times and snapped out of it. "Well. That was fun, but now I'm famished. I'm going to make a pizza from scratch."

I perked up. "Can you teach me how to do it?"

"I'm a chef, Brooklyn. Not a miracle worker."

I wrapped my arm around her and the two of us walked back into my place to drown our sorrows in pizza for breakfast.

RECIPES

Brooklyn's Syllabub—
The Modern Version

Makes 4 servings

This quintessential English dessert appeals to Brooklyn because of its quirky name and the fact that it's so simple to make and requires no baking. (The alcohol content has absolutely nothing to do with its appeal!) This modern version of a syllabub calls for a sweet liqueur. Brooklyn decided to use a coffee-flavored liqueur, but it can be made with almond or orange liqueur, sweet vermouth, white wine, or even cognac. Portions and garnishes can be adjusted to suit your own taste.

⅓ cup coffee liqueur
2 tablespoons sugar
1 cup heavy cream
5 cinnamon sugar cookies, crumbled
4 dark chocolate-covered espresso beans

Pour the liqueur into a bowl with the sugar and whisk to mix. Whisk in the heavy cream and whip this mixture until it has thickened but is still soft and billowy (less than five minutes with a hand mixer).

Crumble one cookie into each of four small dessert bowls. Spoon the syllabub mixture over the crumbled cookies. Sprinkle remaining crumbles on top and garnish with a chocolate-covered espresso bean.

Refrigerate for one to two hours before serving.

Two Vintage Syllabub Recipes
from The Cookbook of Obedience Green

A Rich Syllabub

Take a quart of cream, half a pound of sugar, a pint of white wine, the juice of two or three lemons plus the peel of one lemon, grated. Mix all of these together and put them in an earthen pot. Grasp the pot firmly and shake it up as fast as you can until the mixture is thick; then pour it into fine glasses, and let them stand for five or six hours.

A Fine Syllabub from the Cow

Blend a pint of hard cider with a bottle of strong beer in a punch bowl. Sweeten with half a pound of sugar. Grate a small amount of nutmeg into the liquid, then place the bowl under the cow and add as much milk as will make a strong broth. Let it stand an hour and it will be fit for service.

Brooklyn's Mom's Crazy Delicious Apple Crisp

Makes 4 to 6 servings

This is one of the most awesome desserts ever created and the addition of Cheddar cheese in the topping is just one reason why. Derek would like to think that this recipe serves ONE, but you can stretch it out to serve 4 to 6.

Topping:
  ¼ cup plus 2 tablespoons all-purpose flour
  ¼ cup light brown sugar
  ¼ cup sugar
  ¼ teaspoon cinnamon
  ⅛ teaspoon nutmeg
  ¼ cup cold salted butter
  1 ounce extra-sharp Cheddar cheese, finely shredded
  ½ cup chopped pecans

Filling:
  6 assorted apples, peeled and cut into ½-inch chunks
  2 tablespoons apple liqueur, apple brandy, or apple cider
  ½ teaspoon lemon zest
  ¼ cup sugar

Caramel Sauce:
  1 cup brown sugar
  1 tablespoon cornstarch
  1 cup heavy cream
  2 tablespoons apple liqueur, apple brandy, or apple cider
  1 tablespoon butter

continued ...

Prepare the topping at least a couple of hours before you plan to bake the dessert. Mix together the dry ingredients. Cut in the cold butter until the mixture resembles wet sand. (You can use a food processor and pulse it a few times for one second at a time.) Add the cheese and nuts and mix well. Form a ball of dough, wrap it in plastic wrap, and let it chill in the refrigerator for at least two hours.

Preheat the oven to 375 degrees. Mix together the filling ingredients in a large bowl and pour into a round or square pan with deep sides. I use an eight-inch-square pan. Break apart the topping and spread it evenly on top of the filling. Bake until the filling is bubbly and the top is nicely browned, about 40 minutes.

While the crisp is baking, make the caramel sauce. Mix together all ingredients in a heavy-bottom pan and place over low heat. Stir frequently as it thickens to a rich golden brown. Remove from heat and serve warm.

Brooklyn's mom serves the crisp in a bowl with a scoop of vanilla ice cream and pours caramel sauce over the whole luscious concoction.

Savannah's Gourmet Coleslaw

Makes 4 servings

Napa cabbage makes this coleslaw so pretty, and the recipe is simple enough that even Brooklyn can make it.

1 tablespoon sesame seeds
5 tablespoons slivered almonds
4 cups Napa cabbage, thinly sliced or shredded
⅓ cup cilantro, coarsely chopped
½ cup green onions, thinly sliced
3 tablespoons sweet rice wine vinegar
1 tablespoon sesame oil
¼ cup peanut oil
¼ cup fresh ginger, peeled and minced

Stir sesame seeds in a small dry skillet over medium heat until light golden, about 3 to 4 minutes. Set aside. Stir slivered almonds in the same skillet over medium heat until light golden, about 5 minutes. Set aside.

Combine cabbage, cilantro, and green onions in large bowl. Add vinegar, sesame and peanut oil, ginger, and almonds. Toss to blend. If desired, season to taste with salt and pepper. Can be prepared 2 hours ahead. Cover and refrigerate. Just before serving, toss again and sprinkle with sesame seeds.

Brooklyn's Guacamole Surprise

Savannah gave Brooklyn this recipe over a scratchy cell phone, so it's not poor Brooklyn's fault that she screwed up the ingredients. (But seriously, she thought it was okay to put fruit in guacamole? She really can't cook!) Her parents were surprised how yummy her mistake turned out to be, and this recipe has become a Wainwright family favorite.

2 avocados
12 to 15 seedless green grapes, chopped
2 cloves garlic, grated or minced
2 tablespoons finely chopped jalapeño pepper
¼ cup chopped onions
¼ cup chopped tomatoes
2 to 3 tablespoons lime juice
Salt and pepper to taste
Tortilla chips

Mash the avocados with a fork. Stir in remaining ingredients. Serve immediately with tortilla chips.

Brooklyn's Triumph—
Pasta with Italian Sausage

Makes 4 servings

Finally, a pasta recipe even Brooklyn can follow! Once her sister helped her figure out how to cook pasta, the rest was easy (if you don't count Brooklyn's first three disastrous attempts and that one call to the fire department).

> 4 hot or mild Italian sausages, removed from casings and crumbled in a frying pan
> 3 cloves garlic, minced
> 5 tablespoons olive oil
> penne or fusilli pasta
> 10 basil leaves, chopped
> 1 large ripe tomato, chopped
> Parmigiano-Reggiano cheese

Fry sausage in pan with garlic and 3 tablespoons olive oil. Boil pasta according to package directions, drain, and toss with 2 tablespoons olive oil.

Add basil and tomato to cooked sausage mixture and cook briefly over low heat 1 to 2 minutes, or long enough to warm but not overcook. Add pasta and toss. Garnish with a generous grating of a rich Parmigiano-Reggiano cheese and serve immediately with a good red wine.

Brooklyn becomes a book expert
on the *This Old Attic* TV show
in the next Bibliophile Mystery,

The Book Stops Here

Available from Obsidian in print and e-book
In June 2014.
Read on for a brief excerpt. . . .

My mother always warned me to be careful what I wished for, but did I listen to her? Of course not. I love my mom, really, but this was the same woman who liked to recommend espresso enemas to perk me up. The same woman who performed magic spells and exorcisms on a regular basis and astral traveled around the universe with her trusted spirit guide, Ramlar X.

Believe me, I'm very careful about taking advice from my mother.

Besides, the thing I was wishing for was *more work*. Why would that be a problem?

I'd been in between bookbinding jobs last month and was telling my friend Ian McCullough, chief curator of the Covington Library, that I *wished* I could find some new and interesting bookbinding work. That's when Ian revealed that he had submitted my name to the television show *This Old Attic* to be their expert book appraiser. I was beside myself with excitement and immediately contacted the show's producer for an interview. And I got it! I got what I wished for. A job. With books.

That was a good thing, right?

Of course, I didn't dare tell my mother that I considered her advice a bunch of malarkey. After all, some of those magic spells she'd spun had turned out to be alarmingly effective. I would hate to incur her wrath and wake up wearing a donkey's head—or worse.

"Yo, Brooklyn," Angie, the show's stage manager said. "You look right into this camera and start talking. Got it?"

"Got it," I lied, pressing my hands against my knees to keep them from shaking uncontrollably. "Absolutely."

"Good," the stage manager said. "No dead air. Got it?"

"Dead air. Right. Got it."

She nodded once, then shouted to the studio in general, "Five minutes, everyone!"

I felt my stomach drop, but it didn't matter. I was in show business!

This Old Attic traveled around the country and featured regular people who wanted their precious family treasures and heirlooms appraised by various local experts. The production was taping in San Francisco for three whole weeks, and I was giggly with pleasure to be a part of it.

And terrified, too. But the nerves were sure to pass as soon as I started talking about my favorite topic, books. I hoped so, anyway.

Today was the initial day of taping and my segment was up first. My little staging area was decorated to look like a cozy antiques-strewn hideaway in the corner of a charming, dust-free attic. There were Oriental carpets on the floor. A Tiffany lamp hung from the light grid, which was suspended high above the set. Old-fashioned wooden dressers, curio cabinets, and armoires stood side by side, creating the three walls of my area. I sat in the middle of it all in a comfy blue tufted chair at a round table covered with a cloth of rich burgundy velvet.

Seated across from me was the owner of the book we would be discussing. She was a pretty, middle-aged woman with an impressive bosom and thick black hair styled in the biggest bouffant hairdo I'd ever seen. She wore a clingy zebra-print dress with a shiny black belt that cinched in her waist and emphasized her shapely hourglass figure.

She had excellent posture, though. I'd give her that much. My mother would be impressed.

Between us on the table was a wooden bookstand with her book in place, ready to be appraised.

"Are you Vera?" I whispered. I'd already seen her name on the segment rundown but wanted to be friendly.

She smiled weakly. "Yes. I'm Vera Stoddard."

I smiled at the sound of her high-pitched little-girl voice. "I'm Brooklyn. It's good to—"

"Settle down, people!" Angie shouted, and everyone in the television studio instantly stopped talking. Angie listened to something being said over her headset and then added loudly, "First on-camera today is the book expert. It's segment eight-six-nineteen on the rundown, people! Stand by!"

"I'm so nervous," Vera whispered.

"Don't worry. We'll have a good time." I could hear my voice shaking but I smiled cheerfully, hoping she wouldn't notice. It wasn't like me to be this anxious. All I had to do was talk about books, something I was born to do. It was a piece of cake. Unless I thought about the millions of people who would be watching. It didn't help that several zillion watts of lighting were aimed down at me, and the stage makeup I wore, while it made me look glamorous, was beginning to feel like an iron mask.

"So stop thinking about it," I muttered, and plastered a determined smile on my face.

Angie caught my eye and pointed again at the television camera to her right. "Don't forget, this camera here is your friend. This is Camera One. When you see the red light go on, it means you're on the screen." She turned and pointed to another camera a few feet behind her on the left. "Camera Two will get close-ups of the book and the owner's reactions."

"Got it," I said, nodding firmly. "I'm ready."

"Good." Angie glanced around, then bellowed, "Here

we go! Quiet, please! We're live in . . . Five! Four! Three! Two!" She mimed the word "One!" and waved her finger emphatically at me.

I took a deep breath and tried to smile at the friendly camera. "Hello. I'm Brooklyn Wainwright, a bookbinder specializing in rare book restoration and conservation. Today I'm talking with Vera, who's brought us a charming first edition of the beloved children's classic *The Secret Garden*, written by Frances Hodgson Burnett."

I smiled at the older woman and noticed her lips were trembling badly and her eyes were two big circles of fear. Not a good sign, so instead of engaging her in conversation, I gestured toward the colorful book on the bookstand.

"This version of *The Secret Garden* was printed as a special limited edition in nineteen eleven."

I touched the book's cover. "The first thing you'll notice about the book is this stunning illustration on the front cover. The iconic picture of a blond-haired girl in her red coat and beret, leaning over to insert a key into the moss-covered door that leads to the secret garden, is famous in its own right. There are some wonderful details, such as this whimsical frame around the picture, painted in various shades of green with thick vines of pink roses."

"I didn't even notice that," Vera muttered in her odd sexy-baby voice.

"It's subtle," I said. "The artist was Maria Kirk, known professionally as M. L. Kirk. She was never as famous as her illustrations were, but she did beautiful work. Isn't this lovely?"

"I think so," Vera said softly.

I picked up the book and stood it on the table near me, keeping the cover turned toward the camera. "What makes this even more outstanding is that this illustration is actually an original painting on canvas."

"It is?"

"Yes," I said. "You can see that it's been signed by the artist here in the lower-left corner."

Vera blinked in surprise and leaned closer. "Oh. And look, there's a robin in the tree."

I grinned at her, happy that she was getting into the spirit of things. The show's director had urged us to keep the owner in the conversation, so I hoped Vera would play along. "Yes, that robin has a role in the story."

"I like birds," she said with a sigh.

Uh-oh. I shot a quick look at her. Was Vera going spacey on me? My smile stayed firmly in place as I spoke to the camera. "Another unusual feature is that the painting has actually been inlaid into the leather cover. You can see how the edges of the leather have been beveled so nicely." For the camera, I ran my fingers along the edge of the beveling and gave silent thanks to my friend Robin, who had insisted that I get a manicure before the show.

"I've never seen anything like that before," Vera said, her spacey moment apparently past.

"It's really quite rare," I agreed. "The bookbinder was clearly an artist, too, in the way he chose a rich forest green leather to blend with the painter's softer green frame. And the intricate floral gilding on the leather is patterned after the vines and roses on the painting." I glanced at Vera. "Do you have any idea what the book might be worth?"

"I don't have a clue," she said, shaking her head. "It cost three dollars at a garage sale last Saturday."

I choked out a laugh. "Wow. I don't think I'm giving too much away if I tell you it's worth a little more than that."

"Oh, good." She pressed her hands to her remarkable chest, obviously relieved by the news. Maybe now she would be able to carry on a normal conversation. Her voice was high yet sultry, but it seemed to suit her personality. I wasn't sure why I thought that. I'd never met her before this moment.

I opened the book and showed the frontispiece illustration to the camera. "There are eight color plates throughout the book, all in excellent condition and each with tissue guards intact."

I angled the book toward Vera. "They're charming illustrations, aren't they?"

She nodded politely. "They're very nice."

Nice? I thought. Was she kidding? They were *spectacular*. The entire book was fantastic. I couldn't believe it had been allowed to molder away in someone's garage. But I wasn't about to criticize Vera's lackluster response aloud.

I should've been used to that sort of attitude by now. Nobody gushed about books as much as bookbinders did. I would've loved to have mentioned how rare it was that a children's book printed in 1911 was this beautifully preserved. Children were not generally known for their ability to treat books gently.

I sighed inwardly and changed the subject. "Now, obviously not every copy of this book could be printed with original artwork attached to its cover. So let me explain briefly about this particular edition. Back in nineteen eleven, when this book was printed, a publisher would occasionally release two versions of the same book. A regular edition and a limited, more expensive edition. This version is obviously one of the limited-edition copies."

"How limited?" Vera asked, her gaze focusing in on the book.

"Very." I turned to the next page. It was almost blank except for two lines of print in the middle. "This is called the limitation page. It states here that only fifty copies of this numbered edition were printed. And the number six is handwritten on the next line. So this particular book is number six out of fifty copies made. It's beyond rare."

Vera gulped. "And . . . and that's good, right?"

"Yes, that's very good. And, of course, you will have noticed that on the same page we see that it's been authenticated with the date and original signature of the author, Frances Hodgson Burnett."

"I did notice that." She bit her lip, still nervous, though this time I figured it was from excitement, not fear.

Now that she was finally showing some emotion, it was time to bum her out. Earlier at rehearsal, Jane Dorsey, the show's director, had advised us to balance things out by mentioning a few negatives. So I flipped to a page in the middle. "I should point out a few flaws."

Vera's expression darkened. "No, you shouldn't."

I chuckled. "I'm sorry, but the book isn't without its imperfections." I faced the page toward the camera and pointed at some little brown spots. "There's foxing on a number of pages. These patches of brownish discoloration are fairly common in old books."

"Eww." She drew the word out as she leaned in to get a good look. "Are those bugs?"

"No. They're microscopic spores, but that's not important. Sometimes foxing can be lightened or bleached, but you should always hire a professional bookbinder to do the work."

Turning to the inside front cover, I said, "There's also an additional signature on the endpaper, right here." I made sure the camera could see what I was referring to, and then I took a closer look at it myself. "It doesn't look like a child's handwriting. It was probably a parent signing for the child. I can't quite make out the name, but I assume it's the signature of one of the book's first owners. They used a fountain pen, and it's faded a bit."

"And that's a bad thing?"

"Writing one's name in a book can diminish its value, but that's another topic altogether."

"But—"

"Let's not dwell on the negatives," I hurried to add, "because other than those items and a few faded spots on the leather, it's in excellent condition and—"

"And what?" Vera demanded, interrupting what was about to be my rapturous summary of the book's qualities.

I pursed my lips, thinking quickly. I had been given six

minutes to talk about the book, but the director had warned me that as soon as I revealed my appraisal amount, my segment would be over, even if I had minutes to spare.

I wasn't ready to stop talking about the book, big surprise. But Vera was finished listening, and it was time to put her out of her misery. More important, I noticed Angie hovering. And Randolph Rayburn, the handsome host of the show, stood next to her, looking ready to pounce into the camera shot and cut me off.

"And for a book of this rarity," I continued hastily, "in such fine condition and with the author's original signature included, it's my expert opinion that an antiquarian book dealer would pay anywhere from twenty to twenty-five thousand dollars for this book."

"Wha—?" Vera's eyes bugged out of their sockets. "Twenty . . . Say that again?"

"Twenty to twenty-five thousand dollars," I repeated, happy I'd finally gotten a reaction out of her. The producers were going to love that look on her face.

I turned the book over again to examine the rubbed spots on the back cover. "Frankly, Vera, it would only take a few hundred dollars to have the book fully restored to its original luster. Once you did that, you could probably add another three to five thousand dollars onto the value."

"Another five thou . . . Holy mother-of-pearl!" Vera slapped her bountiful chest a few times as if to jump-start her heart. "Oh, my God. Are you serious?"

"Yes."

"But that's freaking—"

Angie shoved Randolph forward, and he rushed to stand in front of our table.

"Indeed, it is!" he said nonsensically to the camera, grinning as he blathered cheerfully about some of the items coming up later in the show. He finished with, "We'll be right back."

"And . . . we're clear!" Angie shouted.

Vera looked shell-shocked. Everyone in the studio started talking again, moving here and there between the sets, carrying on normal conversations.

I had watched the program a bunch of times, so I knew that when they went in to edit the shows, they would plaster across the TV screen a green graphic banner announcing the amount of money I had quoted, accompanied by the sound of a cash register making a sale. *Cha-ching!*

Angie approached me, but suddenly stopped and cupped her hand over her ear to hear what was being said over the headset. Her arm shot up in the air. "Quiet, people!"

Everyone in the vicinity froze. *What awesome power she has,* I thought. It was all in the headset. I wanted one.

"Randolph, don't move," she warned, as though she suspected he would disappear if given half a chance. Then she announced to the group in general, "Okay, we're gonna need Camera One to remain here. Jane wants to tape a short chat between Randolph and the book expert. For everyone else, we're moving on to the Civil War segment."

Most of the crew stirred themselves into action at the mention of Jane the director's name. They pushed the cameras and the heavy microphone boom to the opposite side of the large studio where another cozy antiques-furnished set similar to mine had been designated the War Room.

I had met Jane Dorsey, the show's director, earlier that day, during my orientation with the two executive producers, Tom Darby and Walter Williams. Jane was almost six feet tall and stick thin, with white blond hair pulled back in a severe pony tail. Today she wore knee-high black boots over her jeans and a black sweater. A long white scarf was tied around her neck and fluttered in her wake as she walked.

Apparently the long scarf was something she wore every day. Tom explained that they kept the air really cold in the director's booth so the equipment wouldn't overheat, but I figured she also enjoyed the dramatic ef-

fect. Not that she needed it. People paid instant attention
to her when she walked into a room.

Camera One remained in place, still pointed in my
direction, along with its operator and a couple of crew
members who assisted with microphones and cables.

Angie looked around anxiously. "Where did Randolph wander off to?"

"I'm here," he said from halfway across the stage
floor. "I'm here. I'm here. Don't pay the ransom."

A few of the crew guys chuckled, and Angie's lips
twisted sarcastically. "Can we get this show on the road?"

I wondered how he had escaped all the way across the
room in mere seconds. The guy was speedy for sure.

"Okay, let's do this," Randolph said, and flashed me a
rakish grin. "Hello, beautiful."

"You are so full of it," Angie muttered.

"But you love me anyway," he said, bumping his shoulder into her arm.

"Yeah, in the worst way," Angie said. She paused to
listen to a voice in her ear, then said to us, "They're not
quite ready upstairs, but don't anyone go anywhere."

Randolph snorted. "Famous last words. I'll be right
over here." And with that, he wandered a few feet away
to kibitz with one of the crew.

"You move and I'll kill you," she said.

He grinned and winked at me behind Angie's back.
He was the worst kind of flirt, completely adorable and
charming. I could tell Angie liked him. What woman
wouldn't? Maybe she didn't want to like him, but she
couldn't help herself. All of that was probably clear to
Randolph as well. Angie seemed pretty transparent with
her feelings.

She was beautiful, with pale skin and a halo of thick,
dark curly hair. They would make an adorable couple if
hard-as-nails Angie could ever learn to deal with Randolph, the charming jokester.

The stage manager ignored the star as she rested her
elbows on my table. "You did a good job, Brooklyn.

Once we're finished with the chitchat, you've got at least two hours to kick back before we tape another book segment." She turned to Vera. "You okay, hon?"

Vera blinked a few times. "Oh. I'm . . . I'm a little shaken up, but very happy."

Angie pulled two pieces of paper from the clipboard she carried. "Almost forgot. You both need to sign these releases."

"Another one?" I'd already signed my life away that morning, indemnifying everyone in the universe in case of any possible occurrence of anything, including Acts of God. "What are these for?"

"One of our local news stations is here, taping some footage for their nightly segment. It's sort of a 'Look What's Going on in San Francisco' kind of thing."

"So we could be on the news?" Vera said.

"They're taping a bunch of short segments, so it's not a guarantee," Angie said. "But either way, they need your approval, just in case."

"Okay," I said, taking the one-page document from her and scrawling my name on the bottom line. "No problem."

"This is so exciting," Vera gushed, and signed her copy with a flourish. She handed it back to Angie, who slid both pages back onto her clipboard.

A young production assistant jogged across the set and slowed down as she approached the host. With a nervous gulp, she said, "Randolph, you have a flower delivery. I put it in your dressing room."

"Thanks, kiddo," he said, flashing her a million-dollar grin. "Hey, Angie, be back in two minutes."

He strolled away before Angie could protest. Exasperated, she turned to me. "Stand by, will you, Brooklyn?"

"No problem," I said, not minding the wait. I was having too much fun to complain about anything.

Vera flashed me a wide-eyed look. "Can I ask you a few more questions about the book?"

Before I could answer, Angie shook her head. "Sorry

to interrupt, kids, but the second Randy returns, I've got to get that damn chat done and then clear this area. They'll start taping the next segment right after that, so maybe you two can set up a meeting later."

"Oh, sure." Vera stood and I got a look at her shoes for the first time. Patent-leather leopard-skin stiletto heels. Wow. They had to be six inches tall and the pattern should've clashed with her zebra-print dress, but somehow it all worked for her.

"Hey, dig those shoes," Angie said.

"Don't you love them?" Vera said, beaming. "They're my Christian Louboutin knockoffs."

Angie nodded. "They're freaking awesome."

Vera turned and bent her knee, lifting her foot behind her. "They've even got the signature red sole. See?"

Angie and I stared at the shiny red bottom.

"They rock," Angie said.

Vera gazed down at her sexy stilettos. "They were the first thing I bought myself after I left my no-good boyfriend."

"Best revenge, sister," Angie said stoutly.

"You know it," Vera said, and giggled.

I handed Vera the business card I'd pulled out of my pocket. "I'll be happy to talk with you about the book anytime you want. Or you can call me whenever you decide what to do."

She looked at the card. "Okay, good. The sooner, the better."

"Anytime," I said.

Looking relieved, she said, "Thanks, Brooklyn."

"And don't forget your book, hon," Angie said, extending *The Secret Garden* to her.

Vera stared blankly at Angie until she saw the book in her hand. "Oh, wow. I guess I'm still a little discombobulated. Thank you."

Angie pointed out the exit to Vera, and we watched her walk away a bit wobbly in her sky-high heels.

I sniffed, feeling sentimental. Vera was, after all, a first for me.

"She's adorable." Angie grinned. "And you made her day."

"I loved every minute of it," I said, happy that so far my day was going pretty well, too.

But the same couldn't be said for Randolph. The star of the show crossed the wide stage and headed straight for Angie and me, his face drained of color and his jaw taut. He looked as if he might have just witnessed his own death.

Kate Carlisle introduces her new sleuth,
Shannon Hammer,
an expert at home renovation and
an amateur at solving crimes!
Turn the page for a peek at the first book in
her charming seaside-set series,

A High-End Finish

A Fixer-Upper Mystery
Available from Obsidian
in paperback and e-book,
starting in November 2014.

"You could've warned me that installing drywall would be hell on my manicure."

I looked down from my perch at the top of the ladder and saw my best friend, Jane Hennessey, scowling at her hands. They were smeared with sticky joint compound. She had flakes of drywall stuck to her shirt, and there were flecks of blue paint highlighting her blond hair.

"I did warn you, remember? I told you to wear gloves." *And a hat,* I thought to myself but didn't bother to mention it aloud. I wondered, though, where in the world the blue paint in her hair had come from.

"The gloves you gave me are so big and awkward, it's hard to work in them."

"I'm sorry, princess," I said, hiding a smile. "Why don't you go rest, and I'll finish up here?"

She laughed. "And have you rubbing my nose in the fact that I'm hopeless at manual labor? No way."

"I would never do that." But I laughed, too, because of course I *would* do that, and I'd expect her to do the same to me. We have known each other since kindergarten and had become best friends when we realized that the two of us were taller than all of the boys in our class. These days, I am still tall, but Jane is two inches taller than me and as svelte as a supermodel.

Despite her delicate hands and my teasing, she has never been a stranger to hard work. This might have been her first experience hanging drywall, but there is no way she would give up before the job was finished. This place is her home as well as her business, so I knew she wanted to be involved in every aspect of the renovation.

Jane had inherited the old mansion—formerly a brothel—three years ago, after her grandmother died. The imposing structure was a glorious example of the Victorian Queen Anne style, with an elaborate round tower rising three stories at the front corner, steeply gabled rooftops, four balconies, bay windows, six fluted chimneys, and a wide-planked, spindled porch, which spanned the front and wrapped around one long side of the house.

But except for the common rooms on the ground floor and Jane's grandmother's suite on the second floor, the rest of the house had been dangerously moldy, musty, and drafty when we'd first started to work on it. During our first inspection, we'd found rodents living inside one wall, a nest of bees swarming in the attic, and termites infesting the wood on the western side of the house. The plaster in some rooms was cracked or simply gone. To put it mildly, the place was falling apart. Through much of the initial demolition work, we'd had to wear full-face respirators to protect ourselves from the mold, asbestos, and toxic dust, among other substances.

The rooms that hadn't been devastated by the ravages of time had been ruined by something almost worse: bad taste.

Jane's grandfather had had a peculiar fondness for 1970s-era wood paneling and had used it to hide much of the richly detailed Victorian-era wallpaper throughout the house. The gorgeous mahogany bay windows in the dining room had been covered over with a high-gloss pale pink paint. And in the bedroom where we were currently working, the decorative redbrick chimney had been disguised with fake yellow plastic flagstone panel-ing. Plastic!

No wonder Jane's grandmother had divorced the man.

Luckily for Jane, though, she had a best friend in the construction biz. Namely me. My name is Shannon Ham-mer, and I own Hammer Construction, a company that specializes in Victorian-home restoration and renova-tion, right here in my hometown of Lighthouse Cove. I took over the company five years ago when my father, Jack, suffered a mild heart attack and decided to retire.

I had agreed to help Jane refurbish the inn whenever my presence wasn't demanded at one of my own jobsites. I got some of my guys to help her out, too, and after three long years, we were getting close to finishing all fourteen guest suites. The extensive repair and intricate repainting of the exterior of the house had been completed last week. The day after that, Jane had met with a landscaper to start taming the wildly overgrown gardens that circled the large house. When she wasn't busy working on the property itself, she was tweaking the inn's new Web site.

In two months, she would officially open for business, and the place was already sold out. Everyone in Light-house Cove was excited for her.

"Okay," Jane said, rubbing her hands clean with a wet towel. "What's next?"

"Once the mud you're applying is dried and sanded," I said, "we'll be ready to paint this room." I climbed down from the ladder and picked up the pole sander to smooth out a section of dried mud on the opposite wall. "And before you know it, we'll be done."

"Hallelujah." There was true relief in Jane's voice, and I couldn't blame her for it. When she'd insisted on help-ing me get this last room completed, I'd warned her that while installing and finishing drywall wasn't terribly hard, it was, frankly, a big pain in the butt and seriously time-consuming. I admit I'd skimmed over the details about the damage it could do to one's nails, but I'd figured that was a given.

Many homeowners I'd worked with thought that hanging drywall was a simple matter of screwing some four-by-eight sheets of hard wallboard to some studs and *voilà*! You had a wall. If only that were true, but no. First, you had to measure and cut the drywall to fit the walls and ceiling. That wasn't easy for at least three reasons.

First, because you had to cut the boards evenly, so that involved clamps and rulers and math.

Second, because drywall boards were heavy and awkward for a person to maneuver around a room.

And third, because drywall had to be cut twice. I could explain why, but it still might not make sense.

And then you needed to figure out exactly how far apart the wood studs were and make marks on the drywall sheets accordingly. That way, you'd be sure you were screwing the sheets into the wood and not into semi-empty air. That involved more math and measuring. With newer homes, the wall studs were typically sixteen inches apart, but with old Victorians like this one, you just never knew.

I could go on and on about the joys of hanging drywall. No wonder I lived alone.

But here was the really fun part. Once the drywall sheets were screwed to the studs, you had to cover up the seams, or joints, with joint compound. Joint compound was a muddy concoction known more simply as—wait for it—"mud." You spread the mud along the seams and over the screw holes and then sanded it down to make the wall smooth and flat enough to paint.

Once you had a layer of still-wet mud over the seam, you ran a strip of special tape over it. Then you covered that tape with another thin layer of mud and left it to dry, sometimes overnight. The next day, you would apply another, wider layer of mud, smooth it out, and let it dry. After one more layer of mud was applied and dried, the sanding began.

For someone unfamiliar with the process, it probably seemed like a great big waste of time. But trust me, if you missed a step or cut corners, you could screw up the wall and be forced to start over.

It was enough to make a grown contractor cry.

I preferred to do things right the first time. And luckily, during those long, waiting-for-the-mud-to-dry periods, there was plenty of other work to do.

"This is going to look great," Jane said, stepping back and taking in the room.

I almost laughed as I glanced around the room. We were staring at four walls covered in plain old drywall with wide white swaths of dried mud running every which way. A paint-spattered tarp lay over the old hardwood floor. Our tattered work shirts were equally spattered. My heavy tool chest, miscellaneous pieces of equipment and power tools, several buckets, and a stepladder were gathered together in one corner. It looked like a typical, unfinished construction site to me, but I knew what she meant. "It'll be beautiful once the walls are painted and the ceiling is spackled and the moldings are added and the floor is finished."

An hour and a half later, Jane and I were covered in fine white dust from all the sanding we'd done, but we were finished for the day. After removing our masks and goggles and shaking the worst of the dust off outside, we washed up in Jane's laundry room sink.

"Oh, shoot, it's getting late," Jane said, drying her hands on an old dish towel. "I almost forgot you had a date tonight." She glanced at me. "I hope you plan on showering when you get home. You look like a raccoon."

"Thanks. And please don't call it a date."

"Oh, come on. You'll have a good time."

I gave her a look. "Really?"

She chuckled. "No, probably not. But at least you'll be able to enjoy a good meal. And Lizzie will be off your back for another few months."

"Promise?"

"Well, no."

I frowned. "I don't know why she's picking on me,

when you're the one who dreams of having a great romance."

"Because I've already been her guinea pig once this year," Jane said dryly. "I threatened to put spiders in her shoes if she ever tried to set me up again."

Our friend Lizzie was happily married with a darling husband and two great kids. Lately it had become an obsession of hers to arrange blind dates in the hopes of getting her friends married off and happy, whether they wanted to be happy or not. Of course I wanted to be happy, meet a nice guy, and settle down, but the very idea of going on a blind date to accomplish that goal made me shudder with dread.

Lizzie's persistence had worn me down, though, and I had finally relented. Tonight I would meet Jerry Saxton for dinner at one of my favorite seafood restaurants on Lighthouse Pier. Dinner, that's all it was. I refused to call it a blind date (even though that's exactly what it was). I'd never met Jerry, but Lizzie had insisted he was a great guy, nice looking and successful, with a good sense of humor.

As I dried my hands, I mentally shrugged off most of my concerns because, as Jane had said, at least I would enjoy a good dinner and maybe even have a few laughs.

But on the four-block drive home, I thought back to another one of Jane's comments earlier that day. She had wondered aloud why a man with all those so-called wonderful qualities needed to be set up on a blind date. It was a good question. Maybe he was wondering the same thing about me. I sighed as I pulled into my driveway, knowing it wouldn't do any good to dwell on those questions right now. In less than two hours, I would discover exactly why Jerry Saxton had agreed to go out with me.

Available in hardcover from
New York Times bestselling author

Kate Carlisle

The Book Stops Here
A Bibliophile Mystery

Brooklyn Wainwright is thrilled to appear on the hit
television show This Old Attic as a rare book expert and
appraiser. Her first subject is a valuable first edition of the
classic children's story *The Secret Garden*, owned
by a flower vendor named Vera.

But soon, Vera's ownership is contested by an angry thug,
and the show's host is threatened. And when Vera is found
dead, Brooklyn must enlist the help of her securities-
expert boyfriend and her cupcake-baking new neighbor to
find a clever killer—or her big chance in prime time may
be cancelled permanently.

Also in the series
Peril in Paperback
One Book in the Grave
Murder Under Cover
The Lies That Bind
If Books Could Kill
Homicide in Hardcover

Available wherever books are sold or
at penguin.com

facebook.com/TheCrimeSceneBooks   OM0131

From *New York Times* bestselling author

Kate Carlisle

A High-End Finish

A Fixer-Upper Mystery

In the charming Victorian resort town of Lighthouse Cove on the Mendocino, California coast, everyone knows that the best man for the job is, in fact, a woman—contractor and handywoman Shannon Hammer. But Shannon is ready for a change of pace. So, in the spirit of taking chances, she agrees to go on a blind date with real estate agent Jerry Saxton. But when her date gets a little too hands-on, Shannon ends up brandishing a pair of pink pliers and threatening to hurt him.

A couple days later, Shannon finds Jerry dead in a building foundation she's been hired to repair. And since everyone knows about her threats—she shoots to the top of the suspect list. Investigating on her own, Shannon discovers that she's not the only one in town who had beef with Jerry. Now Shannon's determined to catch the murderer and clear her name—before the real culprit puts the fix on Shannon…